Belonging to
HEAVEN

Other Books by
GALE SEARS

The *Autumn Sky* trilogy
Autumn Sky
Until the Dawn
Upon the Mountains

Christmas for a Dollar

The Route

The Silence of God

Letters in the Jade Dragon Box

The Missing Christmas Treasure

Belonging to
HEAVEN

a historical novel

GALE SEARS

DESERET BOOK

Salt Lake City, Utah

To my precious daughter, Chandler
Ua hilo 'ai i kea ho a ke aloha.
We are braided with the cords of love.

© 2013 Gale Sears

All rights reserved. No part of this book may be reproduced in any form or by any means without permission in writing from the publisher, Deseret Book Company, P.O. Box 30178, Salt Lake City, Utah 84130. This work is not an official publication of The Church of Jesus Christ of Latter-day Saints. The views expressed herein are the responsibility of the author and do not necessarily represent the position of the Church or of Deseret Book Company.

This book is a work of fiction. The characters, places, and incidents in it are the product of the author's imagination or are represented fictitiously.

DESERET BOOK is a registered trademark of Deseret Book Company.

Visit us at DeseretBook.com

Library of Congress Cataloging-in-Publication Data

Sears, Gale, author.
  Belonging to heaven / Gale Sears.
    pages cm
  Summary: Retelling of the story of Jonathan Napela, one of the first—and most influential—converts to The Church of Jesus Christ of Latter-day Saints.
    ISBN 978-1-60907-159-2 (hardbound : alk. paper)
  1. Napela, Jonathan Hawaii, 1813–1879—Fiction. 2. Cannon, George Q. (George Quayle), 1827–1901—Fiction. 3. Mormon missionaries—Hawaii—Fiction. 4. Mormons—Hawaii—Fiction. I. Title.
  PS3619.E256B45 2013
  813'.6—dc23
                                                                                   2012050169

Printed in the United States of America
Lake Book Manufacturing Inc, Melrose Park, IL

10 9 8 7 6 5 4 3 2 1

HAWAIIAN LANGUAGE PRONUNCIATION

A   as "a" in father

E   as "ey" in they

I   as "ee" in see

O   as "o" in no

U   as "oo" in too

"ae" and "ai" are frequently spoken as an "i" or "eye"

"oe" and "oi" are often pronounced as the "oy" in boy

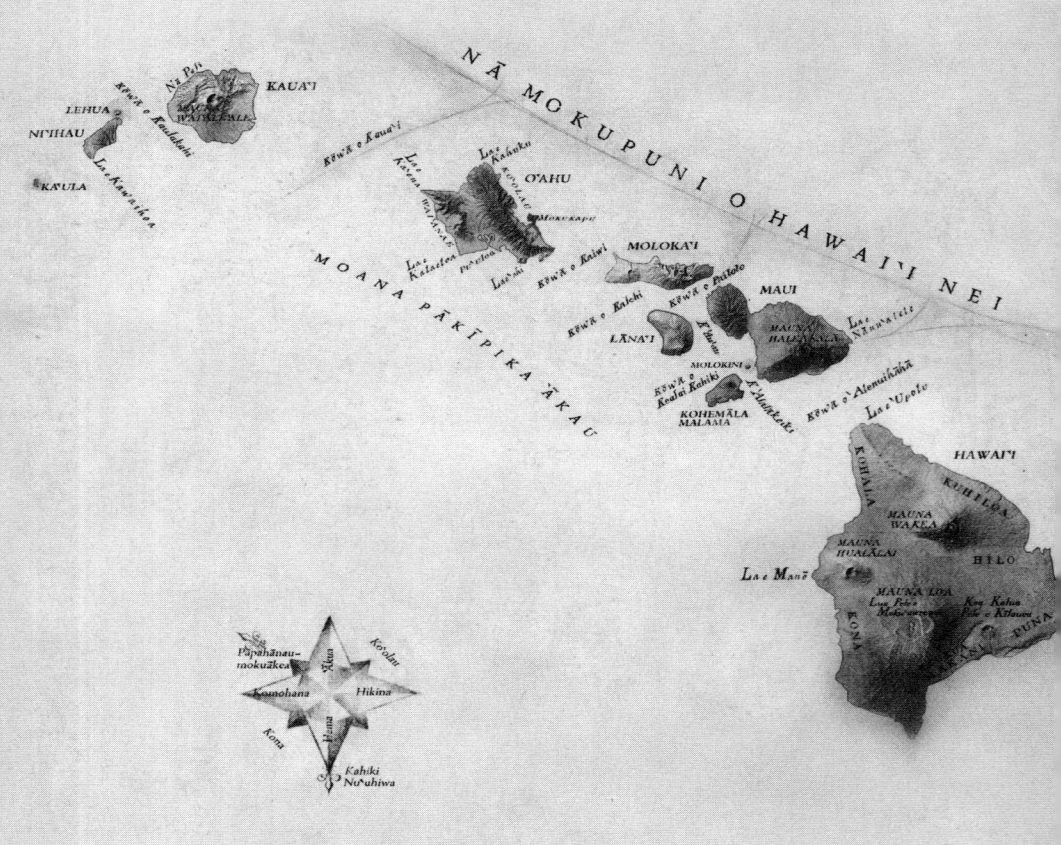

Faith
1843–1854

PROLOGUE

Oloalu, Maui

August 3, 1843

The fingertips of the rising sun reached over the barren peaks of Ukumehamo, and the fisherman felt the warmth on his back. He stood on the reef, the waves gently lapping around his knees.

"Hee mahola," he chanted. "Eia ka leho." *Here is the cowry. A red cowry to attract the octopus to his death.* "Eia ka koa, he laau." *Here is the spear, a mere stick.* "He lama noka hee mahola, no ka hee-palaha." *A spear of lama wood for the octopus that lies flat.*

The octopus twisted languidly as it extended its tentacles along the ocean floor. Golden bits of sand swirled under its spongy body. The ocean was quiet; the warm liquid from the sun poured into the water, calling the eight-legged creature from his dark hole.

"Hee mahola. Eia ka leho."

Chief Hawaii Waaole slowly let down the hook and lure. The muscles in his arms were schooled to the work. He had been taught this from his father, and his father had been taught from his father. For generations, from the great seafarers and warriors of Tahiti, the skill of the hook and the cowry—of the spear—of the knife, had passed into the sinew of his arms and the power of his dreams. The chief's movements were graceful. The strength of his legs he used in running, and fighting, and standing motionless on the reef when the wind blew strong and the waves pulled. But, today the ocean was not a warrior; today the water was calm and the wind only a piping mamo bird.

"Hee mahola. Eia ka leho."

The shiny brownish red and white cowry shell now lay on the soft sand. The fisherman pulled the line gently and the octopus shot toward the lure with amazing speed, wrapping its tentacles around the lure, and drawing it closer. Waaole gave an efficient snap to the line, and the hook embedded itself into the spongy flesh. The octopus thrashed as the fisherman pulled it from the shallows into the warm morning air. He laid the wriggling body on an outcropping of lava rock and stabbed it with his spear. The creature writhed for a few moments and then passed into death. Waaole squatted by the still form.

"Mahalo, beautiful friend. I accept your mana, and today I will pass your strength along to my son." The fisherman stood and deposited the octopus into a gourd filled with seawater. "Today my son will marry. He will marry the beautiful Catherine Keliikuaaina Richardson." Chief Waaole looked across the channel to the island of Lanai. A trading ship moved slowly northward toward the seaport of Lahaina, Maui. *Not much wind today for your many sails.* The chief smiled as he considered the good trades he made with the captains on the ships of merchandise. The whaling ships he left alone.

Waaole watched the ship slide away around the curve of the shoreline and thought of his ancient ancestors traveling the deep oceans. They came thousands of miles in their double-hulled canoes from the southern islands, thousands of miles from the Marquesas and Tahiti, with only the stars to guide them. The channel that ran past the island of Kahoolawe was called Kealaikahiki, *pathway to Tahiti*, the name passed down from generation to generation from a time before reckoning.

Chief Waaole stepped from the reef into deeper water and made his way to the shore. Much had changed in the island nation from the time his father was a young warrior for the fierce Maui chief Kahekili: British sailors under the direction of Captain James Cook had set their feet upon the lands; the islands had been united by the great Aliʻi nui, Kamehameha I; the greedy and unruly European and American seafarers had arrived, followed by the earnest Protestant missionaries who were eager to convert the heathen natives.

Chief Waaole moved out of the water onto the rocky shore and felt the breeze cool on his wet skin. He walked to the stream, drinking deeply of the clear water. He washed, shook moisture from his long hair, and tied the kapa cloth around his waist.

Wind whistled through the leaves of the kukui trees and Chief Hawaii Waaole heard the voices of his ancestors. He smiled. "Ah, yes. E pua ana kamakani." *The wind rises.* "This day one of your people will marry. My son will come with his bride, and you will leap and dance when you see her. Keliikuaaina is the daughter of a Maui chiefess and a haole man from the Scotsland. This wahine is more lovely than a sunset over Molokaʻi. My son will have many handsome keiki."

As he approached the village, the chief heard the laughter of children and the murmur of voices. It brought peace to his heart. His people, for the most part, were good and kind. Some had the akaoʻo puʻuwai, *stingy heart,* or drank too much of the English rum or American whisky. Some women had tongues that liked to run from place to place and tell unhappy stories, but mostly the people in his village were content and busy. Those who liked to be lazy soon found themselves sent up the mountainside of Haleakala to plant and dig sweet potatoes.

Today many hands were busy preparing for the arrival of the chief's son. Five fat pigs were roasting in the underground imu, along with the aku and ahi fish, breadfruit, sweet potatoes, and bananas. The kalo root had been beaten into thick poi, and later in the day wooden platters would be filled with melon, coconut, sugarcane, and mountain apples. New pandanas mats had been woven and placed around the long low eating tables. Ti leaves and ginger flowers festooned the boards and filled the air with sweetness. Lovingly crafted maile leis were ready to adorn the new couple.

Tonight the village would join in the celebration of his son's marriage, and all would sit and eat together. The old kapu of men and women eating separately had been disavowed by Kamehameha II some twenty years before. Chief Hawaii Waaole was glad for the abolishment of the kapu system. He liked to eat with his wife and to be spared from having to kill a slave whose shadow fell across his back.

Waaole walked into the village, passing thatched houses and a few small buildings made of wood and plaster like the houses of the missionaries. He stopped by the hale kuke and handed the gourd to the men making food.

"Something special for my son's dinner."

Several women who were helping peered into the gourd. "Ah," one said admiringly. "There is much mana here. Good for your son's marriage."

"He is a wise one, your son," the old woman Ipukula offered.

Chief Hawaii Waaole smiled. "Mahalo, Ipukula. You have watched him grow from a boy of mischief to a man of sense."

Ipukula's head bobbed, but her eyes and her smile held a secret. "Oh yes, 'oni kalalea ke ku a ka la 'au loa." *A tall tree stands above the others.* "The man who speaks some of the English and writes the letters. The man who looks ahead."

She stepped out of the cooking house and moved into the yard. "My heart is full of joy today. My feet and fingers wish to talk of this joy." Slowly she began to sway, her feet moving smoothly over the packed ground, and her gnarled fingers floating through the air, painting pictures with each movement. "I will tell the story—na wai 'eha. The four waters of Maui."

She began to chant:

> *Fed by the tears of heaven and the hidden pools of*
> * the mountains*
> *Oh, life-giving waters*
> *You flow down to the children of the land.*

A deep, mellow voice joined the soft piping of the old woman as Chiefess Wiwiokalani joined the dance. All the villagers stopped their activities and gathered to watch, each heart filled with reverence and wonder. Their beloved chiefess was as tall as most of their men and weighed as much as a man and his son. The brown skin of her face was smooth, and her eyes spoke of wisdom and kindness. Because her father, Kihakaulia, and her mother, Koleamoku II, were cousins, her mana was strong.

The two women danced and chanted. They were opposite in look, but united in celebration.

> *Oh, life-giving waters,*
> *Our kalo reaches out to you,*

And the lehua blossoms float in your arms.
Our voices chant for you, Wailuku.
Our bodies sway for you, Waiehu.
Our faces smile for you, Waihe'e.
Our hands strike the hallow gourd for you,
   Waikapu.
Oh, life-giving waters,
You flow down to the children of the land.

The dance ended on a shared breath, and the villagers' voices rang out in approval. Chief Hawaii Waaole went grinning to his wife and put his forehead on hers.

"Aloha nui." He breathed deeply. "You honor our son today." She smiled and he stepped back. He addressed his people. "And though Ipukula is a wonderful dancer, I must give the prize to my wife."

Ipukula smiled broadly, showing several spaces where teeth should be. "Of course he must say that to keep the peace on his son's wedding day."

The villagers laughed.

Ipukula lifted her arms to the sky. "May the gods Lono, Kane, Kanaloa, and Ku, watch over Jonathan Hawaii Napela and Catherine Keliikuaaina Richardson on their day of joining. As well as the forty, and the four thousand."

"Mahalo, Ipukula," Chiefess Wiwiokalani said grinning. "You have asked for many gods to watch over us."

The old woman grinned. "One cannot be too careful, especially on such an important day."

Wiwiokalani turned to her husband. "And you must ready yourself for the wedding."

The villagers went back to their tasks as their chief and chiefess moved toward their kauhale.

Wiwiokalani's walk was slow, and Waaole matched her pace.

"You are happy for this day," the wise chiefess stated.

They passed the celebration pavilion, and Waaole took a deep breath of the ginger-scented air. "I am. Our son is marrying a woman of great beauty."

"And wisdom."

"And beauty."

Wiwiokalani stopped walking. "And wisdom."

Waaole laughed. "Yes, and wisdom. Jonathan will need such a wife. Ipukula called him a man who looks ahead."

"And so he is. As a young man he brought the Christian faith into his heart."

"And he was one of the first graduates of the missionary school at Lahainaluna."

"And he has become a district judge in Wailuku."

The pair began to chuckle.

Chiefess Wiwiokalani clapped her hands. "He moʻopuna na Palau o Hamohamo!"

Chief Waaole laughed. "Yes, yes! Look at us, the two old braggarts."

"But, today perhaps we can be forgiven for mouths that speak too many big words."

Waaole nodded. "I am sure the Lord Jesus will be forgiving of our boastful tongues today."

The two continued on in silence, and Chief Waaole smiled as he thought about the Jesus of the many miracles and the kind ways. He, his wife, and son had been taught of the man of Jerusalem and the wise words of the Bible by the good

Protestant missionaries who had given the people of Hawaii the alphabet and the written word. With these magic letters, their language, history, and genealogies could be written down. For a thousand years, the life of the Hawaiian people had been kept in the memories and chants of the kahunas. The beauty of the culture, the model of behavior, and the important ali'i family ties were passed down from one holy man to the next. Waaole was proud that he and his wife's royal lines could be chanted twenty generations.

While Waaole and his wife felt a tie with many of the Calvinist missionary families, some of the pastors who had come to the Sandwich Islands treated his people like outcasts and heathens. There were many of the old ways that these pious men of God condemned: the kapu system, the killing of malformed children, the chanting and the hula, brothers and sisters marrying, and the keeping of slaves. Chief Waaole had once pointed out to Reverend Andrews that America still had slaves, for which he had received a tongue-lashing about the evils of slavery and how America would pay a dear price for allowing such an abomination. Waaole admired the man. Less than a year after their talk, Reverend Andrews left the mission when he found out that some of the funds for his missionary work came from slave states.

Chief Waaole agreed with the faithful of Jesus that many of the ancient ways should be condemned, but there was one judgment he did not understand—the banning of the mele and the hula. Singing and dancing were the air and water of his people's lives, and it was a weight on his heart that they could not practice these joys openly. They sang the songs of the church, and that brought him some happiness, but not to be able to sing openly of the land, and the heavens, and the people made him sad. Hawaii Waaole shook his head. There were far worse things practiced by the rowdy seafarers in the town of Lahaina. Lahaina—the name meant the land of the harsh sun—and it was a fitting name now, not only for the heat that withered crops, but also for the bars and brothels that withered men's souls. The church-going sailors of New England often left their moral restraints behind when their ships passed the Cape Horn and sailed into the warm waters of the Pacific.

Waaole thought of the school the missionaries had established at Lahainaluna. The wood, adobe, and plaster buildings sat high on the hillside overlooking the harbor. Did the holy men hope to separate themselves from the corruption of the town? One only had to look down and see the harbor chocked with ships to know that disease and darkness set anchor there. Hawaii Waaole's heart ached at the memory of sickness. Against the diseases of smallpox, measles, cholera, and pneumonia transported to the islands from exotic foreign ports, the Hawaiian people had been like children eaten by wild boars.

Wiwiokalani stopped to catch her breath. "You look like you have eaten a bitter root, my husband."

Waaole changed his expression and told an untruth. "I was thinking of the heavy clothes I must wear to our son's wedding."

"No complaining. It is for respect."

"I know, but it is a long ride to Wailuku."

"And a long ride back." The chiefess steadied herself and began her slow journey forward. "At least you are going."

Waaole gently took her arm. "I know. I will go and be happy."

"Good."

"But, I will be more happy when I am back with you."

"Only because you can change your clothes."

They came to the lava rock wall that surrounded their kauhale, and a worker came to open the gate for them. One of the missionary wives had once shown Wiwiokalani a picture of a New England cottage with a white picket fence and a gate. As soon as she'd seen it, the chiefess insisted on having a gate made for her rock wall.

The aliʻi couple moved into the compound where the many thatched houses stood in prescribed order: the halemua or the men's house, the cooking house, the halekuku, and the halenoa where the family slept together. The thatch was clean, and newly woven pandanas mats covered the floor. Stacks of pandanas mats in the houses served as sitting areas and beds.

Since the abolishment of the kapu system, Hawaii Waaole and his wife lived together in one large hale. It not only had the practical mats of his people, but an ornately patterned rug from Asia, a writing table and chair from England, and a large seaman's chest given to him by his son's soon-to-be father-in-law. The Scotsman. Waaole liked John Richardson. He was an honest man, and he told good stories of his adventures at sea and of his rugged homeland. He could sometimes be stubborn and prideful, but Waaole figured it was part of the heritage passed down from his ancestors. He aliʻi no ka malu kukui. He chuckled. *Indeed, everyone has something shady from his ancestors that he wants to keep hidden.*

Chief Waaole went to the chest, opened the lid, and drew out cotton underclothes, a white high-collared shirt, black breeches, vest, and coat. He sighed, took off his malo, and began dressing.

Chiefess Wiwiokalani reclined on her pandanas mat bed watching her husband's struggles with bemused interest. "Ke

Belonging to HEAVEN

'ehu 'ehu nein a 'ale." *The billows show signs of a rough sea.* She chuckled and fanned herself with a big woven fan.

"I am not getting angry. My fingers are too big to do the buttons."

Wiwiokalani called out through the open doorway. "Is there a keiki in the yard who could help the mighty warrior chief with his English buttons?"

Suddenly two children appeared on the threshold—a boy and a girl each trying to push the other forward.

"You, Malama," the chiefess ordered. "You have the small fingers. Go. Go help."

The girl approached her chief with some trembling. Even though the kapu system was no longer in place, the mana of the ali'i was still highly honored.

Wiwiokalani smiled at her. "Go on. Do not worry. He has hidden his power in his feather cape, so you cannot step on it."

"These buttons," Waaole grunted. "Do you know how to work them?"

"Of course, my chief," Malama said brightly. "I have a blouse from the English."

The chief looked at his wife. "Ah, she has a blouse from the English."

With effort, the young girl controlled the shaking of her hands and buttoned the buttons on the chief's shirt.

Waaole admired the job. "Well done. Well done. Mahalo."

Malama stepped back and curtsied.

"Look at that. So very English."

"I am learning my letters too," she said.

"I am too," the boy in the doorway added.

"So smart," Chiefess Wiwiokalani said, her rich voice so full of admiration that the children blushed. "Now you two run to the main cooking house, and tell Ipukula what you have done. Tell her that she is to give you each a bowl of kulolo, sweet poi."

The children's eyes widened.

"But, I didn't do anything," the boy said.

"Did you not come running to help when called?" Wiwiokalani asked. The boy nodded. "Then you get poi for your offering. Now run! And tell Pukani on your way to come and open the windows. Now go! Go!"

The two squealed with delight and ran for the cooking house.

"Soon you and I, and the old kahuna, will be the only ones in the village not able to write the letters," Waaole said, moving to the doorway to watch the children run, and to catch whatever slight breeze might be blowing.

Pukani answered the command quickly, and soon the panels of thatching all around the hale were lifted. The air began to move through, and Chief Hawaii Waaole took a deep breath.

"Do I smell the roasting pig?"

Wiwiokalani chuckled. "Not for hours yet." She shifted her weight on the mats, and when she spoke, her tone was exaggerated and full of mock pity. "Poor Waaole. You must go all the way to Wailuku, you must go into the church and watch your son married, and then you must come all the way back before those stubborn pigs will be cooked."

"It is not that far by carriage," Waaole murmured, attempting to console himself.

Wiwiokalani laughed. "Yes, so be glad our son is coming to get you in a fine carriage with wheels that turn fast."

As if their words had summoned their son to them, they heard the clop of horse hooves on the wagon track and the shouts of greeting from the villagers. Beyond a stand of coconut palms, the horses and the handsome, six-person carriage could be seen in flashes. Black fringe on the canopy fluttered in the breeze, while the red spokes on the wheels blurred in the turning. The horses moved as one, and Waaole thrilled at their grace and sleekness. He loved horses—those wondrous creatures introduced to the islands from foreign lands during the time of Kamehameha I and II. Waaole remembered as a boy in Honakawai seeing a horse and rider for the first time. The chestnut stallion was the largest land creature he had ever seen, and it caused him to scream in terror. The horse reared, the rider fell, and he had run away in panic. Since that first encounter Waaole had learned that horses were mostly gentle and extremely useful in getting from place to place. And they were beautiful.

He moved quickly to the edge of the compound and secured several handfuls of long grass to offer the animals. When he returned, his son Jonathan was tying the lines around a branch of the ohi'a tree and turning to help his soon-to-be wife from the carriage.

Chief Hawaii Waaole, warrior and son of a warrior, stood staring. His hands fell limp at his sides and words of greeting were trapped in his throat. Catherine Keliikuaaina Richardson walked beside his son in regal splendor. Her brown hair hung in waves down to her knees. She wore a white holoku in the style that was part missionary and part Hawaiian. Long sleeves covered her arms and a high collar came up to cover her neck. The soft fabric hung loosely from a square yoke that was edged with white ruffles. On her head she wore a wreath of bright yellow 'ilima flowers woven with ferns and the golden tail feathers of the o-o bird. Her golden brown skin glowed in the morning light and the sight of her drove reason from Waaole's head.

Slowly, sound penetrated his ear and he heard Wiwiokalani

chanting words of welcome, and their son chanting for permission to enter the compound. He looked at his son, and his heart swelled with pride. Here was a good man—a man who accepted the new ways, but embraced and respected the old. He wore the suit of the English and the smile of his people. A sturdy man with brown curly hair and eyes of intelligence. Tears of joy and welcome ran down the chief's face.

The gate opened, and Catherine came to him and laid her forehead on his. "Aloha, trusted father. Ua hilo 'ai i kea ho a ke aloha." *We are braided with the cords of love.*

Waaole nodded and wiped his tears on the cuff of his white shirt. "I . . . I have grass for the horses."

"They will be most grateful."

Jonathan came to his father, placing his hands on his shoulders and looking steadfastly into his still weeping eyes. "Aloha, my chief. Are you well?"

"I am well."

"Is this not a good day?"

"It is a good day."

"Is the food roasting in the imu?"

Chief Waaole's stomach rumbled, and the threesome laughed.

"I wish that the food was inside *my* imu!" he said gleefully.

Chiefess Wiwiokalani joined them. Jonathan and Catherine hugged her as Waaole's stomach growled again. They all laughed.

"Ah, your stomach has much to say today," Wiwiokalani scolded. "Go to the cooking house for sweet poi. It will not do for it to speak such words at church."

Waaole smiled broadly. "What wise counsel. I will go this moment, and I will feed the horses on my way." He headed off eagerly toward the beasts and then stopped. "Do not leave without me."

Wiwiokalani turned back to the house, motioning to the couple. "Come, there are words I wish to share with you."

The two walked on either side of her. As they helped her the few steps up into the hale, Pukani came with sweet water for them to drink.

Jonathan loved the wrinkled face of the old man. "Thank you, old father."

The man's head bobbed. "I would give you more on your wedding day, but water is all I have."

"Water is life."

The man bowed his head and left.

They moved inside the hale, and when his mother was comfortably settled on her mats, Jonathan brought the chair for his bride and then sat cross-legged on the floor.

The respected chiefess studied their faces for a long while. He at thirty and she at twenty-three were in the strongest flowering of their lives. "You are beautiful people. Children of Wakea and Papa. Children of the ancient voyagers," she smiled at Catherine, "and recent voyagers. You have found each other in a time of great change. We are now in the time of the Christians, and we can walk that way, but do not look back on the past with scorn and criticism—look back with understanding and gratitude." She shifted her weight on the mats. "Though my body cannot make the trip to the stone church in Wailuku, my spirit will ride with you over the gorge at Kamanawai, past the bay at Maalaea, and across the broad plain to Wailuku."

Jonathan looked at his bride and saw tears.

Chiefess Wiwiokalani smiled tenderly at her and then looked to her son. "I will sit in the lovely Christian church with you. I will see you in your feathered cloak. I will sit beside Hawaii Waaole on the hard wooden bench and listen carefully to the words of Reverend Richards. I will listen to your words of love as you promise to care for each other." She turned her gaze to her daughter-in-law. "Catherine, I will see your father, John Richardson, and your mother, Keliikuaaina. I will see the pride in their eyes, and the smiles on the faces of your brothers and sisters. Then, as everyone rides back for the feast and celebration, I will make sure all is prepared. The kahuna will chant the names of the ancestors, and my legs will dance for you, and my voice will sing. E lei kau, e lei hoʻoilo i ke aloha." *Love is worn like a wreath through the summers and the winters. Love is everlasting.*

Catherine ran weeping into Wiwiokalani's arms as Jonathan stood.

"Mahalo, dear mother. Our hearts will be tied to you." He took a handkerchief from his pocket and dried his bride's tears. "And now we will go and join our families." He knelt by his mother and she put her forehead on his.

"Today there is a clear sky. It is a good sign for your marriage." She hesitated, and her gaze became more intent. "I see important things for you to accomplish, my son. You will have a good life . . . a good life, but there will be . . ."

"What?" he questioned when she hesitated.

"There will be much work for you to do."

"I have never minded work." He smiled at her and she did not say more, although there were other words to say.

Two young men came to the doorway. They bowed low, and one stepped forward. "We are here to gather the ahu for their journey to Wailuku."

Wiwiokalani pointed to a rectangular wooden box sitting

next to the weathered sea chest. The men carefully lifted the box containing the exquisite feather capes, and took it to the waiting carriage.

Jonathan and Catherine said their good-byes and reluctantly left the house. When they exited, they found a crowd of villagers gathered near the carriage. The couple moved out into the embraces and well-wishes. Jonathan looked over and saw that his father had returned from the cooking house. He stood stroking one of the horse's necks and smiling.

"We have both eaten something, so now we are ready for the long, hot trek to Wailuku," Waaole said.

Jonathan chuckled as he helped Catherine and then his father into the carriage. He leaned over and whispered to him. "When we are out of sight of the village we will take off our suit coats." He climbed up, took the lines in his hands, and commanded the horses to walk on. As he waved to the villagers, Jonathan smiled. It was a smile that felt its way through his entire body. *Today was a good day.*

Inside the hale, Chiefess Wiwiokalani heard the creaking of the wood and leather of the carriage, heard the murmur of her people's voices retreating, heard the voices of her ancestors scolding her. There were words to be said, words that she'd kept locked behind her teeth. Words of warning. But, this was not the day for such things to be spoken. She wanted only to say the words of happiness. Her son would have a good life and would accomplish much. People of new ideas would come to him for help. The chiefess frowned and fanned herself. Her son *would* have a good life, but not a calm life. Na 'ale api 'ipi 'i o na kai 'ewalu. *The rough seas of the channels would find him.*

The scratching voices of the ancestors blew through the hale on a wind, and Wiwiokalani smiled. "Ah, do you think to torment? You come whispering to me from the wao, the spirit wilderness, but I am the one with the voice to speak, and today I will speak nothing but joy and celebration." She lay back against the small soft pillows that had been a gift from the missionary wives the day of her baptism. The cushions were embroidered with verses from the Bible, and Wiwiokalani liked their softness and their sentiment. She closed her eyes and flicked her hand in a dismissive manner. "Go away now, old ancestors. I will rest a little before the feast. During the celebration you may come back to see me dance and chant, and that will make you quiet for a long time."

Chiefess Wiwiokalani chuckled and went to sleep.

Notes

- In modern times the spelling of the village of Oloalu is Olowalu. Over decades and centuries the spellings of many of the ancient Hawaiian place names have been changed.
- The Western world became aware of the Hawaiian Islands with their discovery in 1778 by Captain James Cook, an English sea captain, who named them after the Earl of Sandwich, first lord of the Admiralty.
- The native population of Hawaii was organized into a tribal system ruled by ali‘i (chiefs and kings) and kahunas (priests).
- The kapu (tabu) system entailed the strict laws ruling almost every aspect of a villager's life, especially in regard to the ali‘i.
- When Captain Cook first arrived on the islands, it is estimated that there were 300,000 indigenous people. Because of diseases introduced to the islands, the native population had dwindled to approximately 50,000 by 1850 when LDS missionaries arrived.
- The Hawaiian alphabet is comprised of twelve letters, the vowels a, e, i, o, u, and the consonants h, k, l, m, n, p, w. Prior to 1820 when the Protestant missionaries established the alphabet, the Hawaiian people had only a spoken language—their stories, traditions, and genealogy being passed down from one generation to the next in chant and song.
- The four major Hawaiian gods are: Kane—the great maker of all things;

Belonging to **HEAVEN**

Ku—the god of war; Lono—the god of peace, agriculture, weather, and fertility; and Kanaloa—lord of the ocean. The number of minor gods and goddesses were said to be "countless."

- In ancient Hawaiian lore, Wakea and his wife, Haumea or Papa, are said to be the progenitors of the Hawaiian race.

- Feathered cloaks and capes were worn by the ali'i as symbols of their high status. Thousands of small feathers of gold, red, or black were fashioned into the capes.

- The Hawaiians had a firm belief in a hereafter, a place where the spirits of their ancestors went after death.

CHAPTER 1

Slap Jack Bar, California
September 1850

The fever for gold that infected the schoolteacher from Virginia and the farmer from Ohio did not beguile the young George Q. Cannon. He had longed to be called on a mission for The Church of Jesus Christ of Latter-day Saints, imagining that he might be sent to his home country of England, or the Eastern States, or even to the cold climes of Scandinavia. Indeed, the twenty-three-year-old Cannon had vowed to serve the Lord and build the kingdom of God wherever he was called. He had made that commitment six years earlier as he'd stood with a thousand other Saints of the Church, watching the wagons as they brought the bodies of the Prophet Joseph Smith and his faithful brother Hyrum from Carthage. The two were murdered in cold blood by a mob. His uncle, John Taylor, was severely wounded in the same atrocious act of butchery.

For a time it felt as though the fledgling church would not survive such a severe blow, but the twelve Apostles, holding priesthood power, restored order and declared that the Church would roll forth in mighty assurance.

Belonging to HEAVEN

George had vowed to be part of that great work, but he was not sure that this was the right place. Here on the muddy banks of California's American River, he neither felt the joy of service nor commitment to the work. After nearly a year of working the gold claim, he could not figure if he and the other twenty brothers called to this land of lawlessness and avarice had actually accomplished any of what the prophet Brigham had planned.

"Brother Cannon, I wish to call you on a mission to the goldfields of California."

"To where, President Young?"

"California. I am calling a contingent of able and clear-minded men to dig gold for the support of the Church."

"But, haven't you spoken against the Saints rushing off from the Salt Lake Valley to join the gold seekers?"

"Indeed! I do not want the feeble of faith to scatter like chaff to the wind of greed, but you are not of that character, are you, Brother Cannon?"

"No, President, but I thought . . ."

"Yes, son?"

"I thought my mission would be—elsewhere."

"Well, just like the calling of the Mormon Battalion, we often do not know what greater plans the Lord has in mind. So, what say you, Brother Cannon?"

"I made a promise during the hard times in Nauvoo, President, that I would go wherever the Lord called me."

"Well said, Brother Cannon! Well said!"

"Cannon! Mind your footing!"

George came out of his musing just in time to catch himself from stumbling into a sinkhole. He regained his balance, nodded thanks to Brother Henry Bigler for the warning, and continued on with his task. He hefted the large boulder he was carrying higher in his arms and moved slowly into the river. The clear water rushed down the hillside and pushed against his knees. It then swirled around his thighs and waist as he went deeper. George sucked in his breath as the cold made his legs ache. With the early rains and sleet in the foothills of the Sierra Nevada Mountains, the river was running high and cold. Just the day prior, a violent storm had pounded the western side of the mountains with rain, sending a deluge of water down the river; the force of it had undermined the streambed and washed away hundreds of miners' dams strung out along the river's edge. The Mormon claim had not been spared.

George and his companions had been shoring up their dam all morning and were tired of the work. The dam diverted the water's course into a long wooden trough whose greedy maw swallowed down buckets of dirt and always asked for more. George had lost count of the number of buckets of dirt he'd carried to the sluice—two hundred, sometimes three hundred a day. Dump the dirt in the top of the trough and let the fast-running water wash it down the course, separating the gold from the dirt and pebbles. With all the backbreaking toil expended, one would think the payoff would be substantial, but the take ended up to be only about twenty-five cents per bucket. George scoffed at his own naïve figuring when he'd first arrived at the goldfields. Fifty to seventy dollars a day sounded like a mighty sum, but when that was divided among the five men working each box, and haircuts cost five dollars, a loaf of bread ten, and a new pair of socks fifteen, there wasn't much left at the end of the month to send back to the Church. And, often the daily take was much less than fifty dollars. George grunted. He actually made more money working part-time at a branch store of the Salt Lake Trade Company. The makeshift store was set up on the bar to accommodate the miners, and it wasn't much more than a few sacks of flour, a couple tins of molasses, and some pork thrown on a pile under an arbor.

The water inched past George's waist and he gave heed to the task at hand. The stack of boulders rose a foot above the waterline, and George added his rock to the pile, wedging it in firmly. The diverted water ran true into the sluice box, strong enough to satisfy even the careful eye of Brother Bigler.

George looked over to the bank and saw Brother Bigler shaking hands with Apostle Charles Rich.

"Cannon!" Brother Bigler yelled. "That'll do! Come on out now."

George made his way gladly to shore, greeting Elder Rich heartily, but refusing to shake his hand. "I'm all mud and water, Elder Rich, please excuse me. It's very good to see you though. Truly it is."

"It's been awhile," Elder Rich said. "I've been supervising work at the other claims and preparing for my trip back to Salt Lake."

George nodded and sneezed at the same time.

"Go on to the tent now and put on dry clothes," Brother Bigler ordered. "We'll meet you at the place as soon as we've gathered the others."

"Yes, sir." George picked up his boots and coat from the shore and headed shivering to the canvas tent that served as both sleeping quarters and general living space for five men. George shook water from his hair and chuckled to himself. General living space meant just enough room to put on your boots. He pulled back the tent flap and entered, anticipating the warmth inside. He was not disappointed. The sun, though watery and weak after the autumn storm, had beat steadily on the white canvas all day, drying the fabric and heating the inside temperature to welcoming. George peeled off his wet clothing, dried himself with a grimy cloth, and put on his only other pair of pants and shirt. The pants were patched and the shirt threadbare. He pulled on a dry pair of socks and noted holes in the heels and toes. If his mother were alive, she'd have a fit. He missed his mother—and his father. The death of Joseph and Hyrum in 1844 had been sorrow enough to pain a young man's heart, but to lose his father two months later was a shattering occurrence. George grabbed a boot and shoved it on. He often dreamt of his father's cabinet shop—the smell of wood shavings and the sight of his father sanding a chair leg. He missed his sister Mary's lard biscuits and the noise created by his younger brothers and sisters. He was well aware that earthly circumstances could change in an instant, but that awareness brought him little solace.

George sat down on his cot, ran his fingers through his drying hair, and reached for his leather satchel. So much of life had to be trusted to the Lord, and at times it caused a testing of faith. He undid the leather strap that secured the satchel and threw back the flap. He rummaged inside, drawing out several letters. He found the one he wanted, and placed the others back in the bag.

Though solace sometimes eluded him, faith never did. When the testing came, George had always felt the deliverance of Divine Providence. Such had been the day of November 28, 1844, when he stood in the Taylor home and watched his Uncle John perform the marriage of his sister Mary to twenty-eight-year-old Charles Lambert. Charles was a stonecutter and builder from Yorkshire, England, who had arrived in Nauvoo only months before the assassination of Joseph and Hyrum Smith.

Charles was a hard-working young man who had caught the eye of his sixteen-year-old sister, and, though Mary was young, she'd had a dream that Charles was to be her husband. She also knew that he would be the guardian for her brothers and sisters—a father figure for Ann, David Henry, Angus, and Leonora. Divine Providence.

George looked down at his name scrawled in a rough penmanship on the outside of the envelope with the return name of Charles Lambert, Salt Lake Valley, Territory of Deseret. As there was no sound of men approaching the tent, George took the pages out of the envelope, and availed himself of the quiet moment to read.

> *My esteemed brother-in-law,*
>
> *I write to tell you of our safe arrival in the Salt Lake basin. It was discovered by us that we arrived one day after your departure for California. We were sad we missed you, but know you are on an errand for the Lord. Brother Taylor and some of his folks, your sister Annie, and others met us on the bench. It was a happy meeting. Angus, David Henry, and Leonora all came across with Mary and me and made it fine, though Mary had an accident that we thought would take her from us. We were just out of Soap Creek Hill, when Mary got out to walk. She soon fell under the front wheel and both wheels went over her.*

George shut his eyes and took a deep breath. Even though he'd read this letter many times, and knew the eventual outcome, it made his heart ache to know the pain his sweet Mary must have suffered. He looked back to the letter and found his place.

One wheel went over her hip and back. The company pronounced her dead, but a halt was called and she was lifted into the wagon and administered to. Then she spoke, and in three days was walking alone, though she said the spirit left the body. This was to all a miracle indeed. She still lives and is a blessing to her family.

We have settled on the lot you bought from John Warner. This property is suitable for a garden. I have planted corn, potatoes, cabbage, and onions. Many of the emigrants passing through here are glad to exchange for food and give us such things as we were not able to bring with us. We left our house, garden, and forty acres in Nauvoo and received not a cent for it.

I am halfway through with building a room that will keep off the cold of winter. I am using the adobe bricks you made before leaving for California. They are well made, and I hope you will see improvement when you return. Food is scarce and many times we have had not one grain of barley, but then there is a miracle and we know the Lord is mindful of us. He is mindful of you too, Brother Cannon. Be well, and know that we pray for you.

*Your brother in the Lord,
Charles Lambert*

Sounds of approaching voices pulled George from his thoughts. He folded the pages, quickly placing them back into the envelope and the satchel. He stood, put on his coat, and went out to meet the group of men assembling in the open area in front of the tent. George looked at their faces, faces he had come to know well over the last year and a half, and he saw, mixed with the marks of fatigue, a genuine mien of appreciation. The men were glad to have Charles Rich among them. George was glad too. Brother Rich seemed like a father among his sons, advising them what to do for the best.

Brother Bigler looked around at the assembled men. "Sit down, men. Elder Rich has something of consequence to discuss with us and we might as well be comfortable." He sat down and the men followed suit, sitting on rocks, stumps, or logs. The few precious stools were reserved for the eldest members of the group. George sat on a log next to his friend, William Farrer, while Brother Rich remained standing.

"How goes the mining, brethren?" Groans and a few muttered words peppered the group. "Brother Bigler, what do you say?"

George could see that Brother Bigler was choosing his words carefully. "Well, Elder, I am thankful that I am well, and that the Lord has preserved my life thus far." George heard soft echoes of amen. Brother Bigler cleared his throat and continued. "It is a harsh life. We buried Brother Flake the other day. He was thrown from his mule and broke his neck. Many of the men have been sick, having to live and work out in storms of snow and rain, and working in water up to their necks to rebuild our dams. I think we're mostly tired of the wicked ways of the mining camps and long to be at home among the Saints." Many heads nodded in agreement, George's being one of them.

Brother Rich caught George's eye. He gave him a half-smile before returning to address the group. "I have been in correspondence with President Young, and have reported these hardships, but I have also reported that you men have kept with you a good spirit and have acted as a pattern for those who have lost the spirit and strayed from the paths of righteousness. For this, the prophet thanks you." He turned back to George. "Brother Cannon, you are the youngest of the group at twenty-four, is it?"

Brother Keeler called out. "Ah, he's twenty-three, Elder Rich, and looking like he might be eighteen." The company laughed and George laughed with them. His young look had been a reason for teasing since the journey began.

"Twenty-three, it is then," Brother Rich said, looking steadfastly at him. "So, I have a question for you, Brother Cannon. What do you say of missionary work?"

George swallowed. He did not like to be singled out, and to speak his thoughts in a group was terrifying. His mind went blank until he thought of the times he had sat in his uncle's home in Nauvoo and listened to the elders relate their experiences as missionaries. He stood. "In my Uncle John's home I heard many missionaries talk of their journeys, and this made a deep impression on me. They went out in poverty, without purse and scrip, among strange people who were ignorant of our principles. They stood alone against mobs and persecution." The men sat mesmerized. Prior to this, none of them had heard a dozen words together come from George's mouth. "They traveled by faith, and the Lord was with them and worked miracles on their behalf. What I heard strengthened my faith, and it increased my desire to be a missionary." His voice faltered and his legs lost their strength, as he became aware of the faces staring at him. "I . . . I think there's no calling so noble." He sat down, and silence surrounded him. Finally Elder Rich spoke.

"Well said, Brother Cannon. Well said." He reached inside his coat pocket and drew out a leather pouch. He opened it and removed several pieces of paper. "Brother Bigler, you were here when gold was discovered and know the most about mining and the weather. What do you think the winter will bring to our mining operation?"

"If the winters are mild, the work can continue on with little break. But, most of the time, the mining shuts down for a month or two and then there's nothing but debauchery and drunkenness in the surrounding camps and boom towns." He looked over at the swollen river. "And it seems like this year the storms will shut us down for longer than two months."

Elder Rich nodded. "That is my impression also. I do not think it prudent to leave you men idle here in the midst of worldliness, using up what little resources you have on the expensive usury of California." He opened the papers. "I think your time would be better served seeking spiritual rather than temporal treasure." George felt warmth move through his body and he sat straighter. "Therefore, I am calling the following brethren to winter in the Sandwich Islands and do a bit of missionary work for the Lord. Henry Bigler, Hiram H. Blackwell, John Dixon, William Farrer—"

William jumped to his feet. "The Lord be praised!"

The company laughed and clapped.

Elder Rich smiled, but waited for William to sit down and the men to quiet before he continued. "John Berry, James Keeler, George Q. Cannon, Thomas L. Whittle, Thomas Morris, and James Hawkins. Brother Hiram Clark will serve as your mission president."

There was silence for a few seconds, and then a cheer went up sufficient to make other miners up and down the river surmise that the Mormon claim had just struck a mother lode vein. George was elated, and he and William Farrer rushed to Elder Rich and Elder Clark, giving each in turn a mighty handshake and a fervent oath of commitment.

Elder Rich stood up on a stump and motioned for the men to gather around. When they were assembled he spoke to them in an earnest voice. "Over the next few days I wish you to pray about this call and receive your own revelation concerning it. If it is not for you, come and tell me, and you may accompany me back to the Salt Lake Valley. If it is for you, you will be set apart for the work."

George watched as the man scanned the faces of the Mormon miners. Did he think to discern their faithfulness or commitment? When the leader looked at him, George hoped he saw uncompromising willingness.

Elder Rich nodded and continued. "I know that many of you have been separated from loved ones for a long time and that this call demands much. Put it to the Lord and He will guide you." He turned to look at Brother Bigler. "I know that this call does not come at an ideal time, Brother Bigler; the weather is bad and the mining season is at an end, but I wish you to carry on with the work for a time to see if you can accumulate enough money to outfit yourselves for the mission."

Brother Bigler gave him a crooked smile. "Not an undoable task, right?"

The men laughed.

Brother Bigler chuckled too. "I suppose if the Lord can send manna to the Israelites, He can find us a little gold."

Elder Rich smiled at him. "Well said, Brother Bigler. And what do the rest of you say?"

"Hurrah for Israel!" William Farrer shouted.

Soon the jubilant call, shouted by many voices, was heard by miners up and down the river. They stopped digging and turned their heads in the direction of the sound, wondering at the meaning of the strange words.

During the night, George's sleep was fitful, and a strange dream kept repeating itself. He was back in Salt Lake, building a house with the good adobe bricks he had made before leaving for California. Several of the rows were well laid and strong. Then, when he reached the third row, each time he placed a brick it would stay solid for a few seconds, and then crumble into rubble. Over and over he laid the bricks, and over and over they fell to pieces. He felt a hand on his shoulder and a shaking.

"Cannon, wake up!"

It was William Farrer's voice, but he couldn't tell where it was coming from. The shaking began again.

"Cannon."

George opened his eyes and tried to focus on the grey blur in front of him. "What? What's the matter?"

"Nothing's the matter, other than your muttering," a voice whispered.

George sat partway up. "William? Sorry. I . . . I guess I was dreaming."

"I figured that." William returned quickly to his cot, climbing gratefully into his blankets. "It is cold this morning!"

"And bound to get colder," George whispered back.

"It's not going to be cold where they're sending us," William whispered excitedly. "I hear it's warm morning, noon, and night."

"So, you've decided to go?"

"Of course, wasn't any question. You, Blackwell, and I are the youngest, and we've got no wives to get back to. It'll be quite an adventure, sailing into paradise." He hesitated. "You're not thinking of staying behind, are you?"

A wind gently shook the tent, and George lay back down and closed his eyes. "I'm going." With those words, a calmness entered into him, and he thought he understood the meaning of the dream. "I want to build something that will last."

"That's proper thinking, Brother Cannon! Won't it be grand—us two boys from England taking the gospel to the Sandwich Islands?"

"You boys won't live to see the day if you don't hush up," a voice growled.

"Sorry, Brother Bigler," William whispered. "It's just that George and I are caught up in the spirit of the work."

Brother Bigler grunted. "I'll catch you up in the spirit of the work when you're hauling buckets tomorrow."

George chuckled to himself and brought the blankets over his head. *Sailing into paradise.* He liked the sound of that.

Notes

- Henry Bigler was born August 28, 1815, and joined The Church of Jesus Christ of Latter-day Saints at the age of nineteen. After traveling to San Diego as a member of the Mormon Battalion, he made his way north to Sutter's Fort in northern California. He was working there constructing the sawmill at Sutter Creek when James Marshall discovered gold.

- Gold was discovered in March 1848 in California's American River by James Marshall.

- Expulsion from Nauvoo: After the death of Joseph Smith in 1844, continued mob violence forced the Saints to leave the city and travel west under the direction of Brigham Young.

- The call "Hurrah for Israel!" is synonymous with Brigham Young and Heber C. Kimball. When they were called by the Prophet Joseph Smith to serve a mission in England, both men were sick and destitute and so were their families. In order to cheer their loved ones upon their departure, they stood in the back of the wagon, waved their hats, and shouted, "Hurrah for Israel!"

CHAPTER 2

Wailuku, Maui

November 1850

The feeling of suffocation came again as Jonathan Napela struggled out of a nightmare. The kahuna held him by the back of the neck and forced him under the moonlit ocean waves. The rumble of the kahuna's voice swirled within the black water. "Moe malie i ke kai o ko haku." *Lie still in the sea of your lord.* "Do not struggle because you are the sacrifice—you are bound to die." The water filled Jonathan's ears, his nose, his mouth. He forced his eyes open. In the predawn gloom, he could barely make out the koa wood dresser, the high-back chair, and the lace curtains at the window. *This is my house, my dresser, my window. I breathe air. I smell ginger flowers in the garden.*

Jonathan pushed himself into a sitting position. He leaned his head back against the hard metal of the brass headboard and drew in several breaths. His lungs burned from the imagined drowning, and angry tears came freely. Jonathan dashed them away and reached over to apologize to Kitty for waking her, but his hand found only empty space. He looked to her abandoned place and worked to clear the sleep from his brain.

Many mornings his wife fled from uneasy sleep into the oblivion of movement. Jonathan thought of all that had filled their lives in the seven years since their wedding: his work and success as a district judge, the building of a large two-story home in Wailuku, their many social commitments in the community. He and Kitty had also planned for children to bless their home, but in this they found it necessary to take life as it was given. As Wiwiokalani often told them, "Wae aku i ka lani." *Let the selecting be done in heaven.* Life and death had woven themselves into the fabric of the young couple's existence, and a recent sorrow shredded their sleep with nightmares and restiveness.

Jonathan heard Kitty's footsteps in the downstairs parlor, the creak of the floorboards. He envisioned her movement as she left the parlor and padded down the hallway to the kitchen—the closing of a cupboard door—the scraping of chair legs—the thump as the chair found its new home—the opening and closing of the kitchen door—the footfalls moving back to the parlor where the whole cycle began again.

Jonathan rubbed his hands briskly across his face, threw off the coverlet, and got out of bed. He put on a pair of pants and went down the stairs to comfort his wife.

Kitty was pacing around the sofa in the parlor when Jonathan stepped to the doorway. She looked at him, but did not stop walking. She had on her white nightdress, and in the moonlit room she looked like a ghost. Her waist-length hair was bushy and snarled—her features pulled into a frown.

Jonathan did not speak to her. He did not reach out to touch her as she passed close. He watched her fingers clench and unclench and heard the soft whimpering in her throat. Kitty stopped at the parlor window. She pushed back the lace curtain and laid her forehead on the cool glass.

Jonathan stepped into the room.

Kitty pressed her hand against the windowpane. "Perhaps they are wandering together in the dark world. Perhaps the Lord Jesus will at least give them that comfort."

There was a forlorn longing in her voice that made Jonathan shut his eyes to steady his emotion. The sun had risen over the great mountain Haleakala eighty-five times since the death of their infant son, but the pain lingered in every room of the house—the rooms that held one day of his son's breathing. They had named him Kapo, and had laid his body in the graveyard beside his brother, Enocha, who had walked the rainbow two years earlier. Enocha, the stronger of the two, had breathed for three days.

Kitty looked over her shoulder at Jonathan. "I know what a person has to do. You have to walk carefully so that the gods do not see the imprint of your foot on the path, and you cannot dance in the sunlight, but must hide in the shadow of the kukui tree." She looked back to the dark window. "It is my fault."

"No. There is no fault in this."

"Perhaps Pele saw me when I raised my chin too high. Perhaps she was jealous of our fine sons."

Jonathan moved to stand beside his wife. "Keliikuaaina, we are Christian children now. We do not fear the old gods."

"Then I do not understand Jesus. Why would he take our little ones from us, and why would he make them wander about in a wilderness?"

"What do you mean?"

"Reverend Conde told me that our babies have gone to an intermediate place. A place where they will wait for the resurrection." She turned abruptly. "But how will they exist for so long a time without someone to hold them and care for them?"

Jonathan's heart held the same question, but his mind fought to formulate a reasonable answer. He shook his head. "I do not know. It is a mystery we do not understand at this time."

Kitty's next words were bitter and filled with loss. "But I want to know. I want a better answer. I want to know where they are!" She pushed past Jonathan and moved out of the house into the garden. The sky was beginning to pale at the eastern horizon, and the first notes of birdsong were sounding. "Ka hale koʻekoʻe o ka po." *The cold house of darkness.* "They have gone to the cold house where Milu is the master—Milu the uncaring god of the underworld. Will he hold my babies? Will he keep them warm?"

Jonathan heard the words of his wife as he stepped out onto the porch. The sorrowful sentiments clashed with the peaceful stillness of the morning. He tried to offer soothing words, but Kitty's grief had been awakened and would not rest.

"Perhaps there is no hope for them because they were not baptized. Perhaps we will never see their little faces again."

Jonathan took her gently by the arms. "Please, dear one, you are breaking my heart."

There was desperation in her eyes when she looked at him. "Then tell me where they have gone. I will find some peace if you can tell me. You are a learned man. You have studied under the American missionaries. Open the holy book and tell me the truths of the Christian faith. Tell me! Tell me, Jonathan! I cannot have our sons waiting in the dark!"

He gathered her into his arms. "I cannot tell you." She began weeping. "But I will pray for an answer. Every day I will pray. Every day. And I promise that an answer will come to us."

The light nod of her head was all the assurance Jonathan needed. Together they would get through this loss, and he would pray until an answer was revealed.

CHAPTER 3

Honolulu, Oahu
December 12, 1850

The wish of all the missionaries standing along the railing of the *Imaum of Muscat* was that they could get off the cursed ship and onto the shore. They did not detest the ship itself, but the memories she held of rolling waves, storms, and seasickness. Being held out of Honolulu harbor until safe passage through the dangerous channel could be accomplished had left the men anxious and restive. Like his fellow shipmates, George was trying to take in the beauty of the towering green cliffs, the sparkling blue water, and the quaint look of the town itself with its palm trees and thatched houses. It created a scene that he could not have imagined. He knew that even those who grew up in the green of England or Ireland were mystified by the lush vegetation and the soft warm air that brushed their skin.

"What did I tell you, Brother Cannon? Could you ever dream of an adventure such as this?" William Farrer asked. He took in a huge breath of air. "I think a piece of heaven has fallen from the sky and dropped into the ocean."

George nodded. "It's beautiful."

William scoffed. "Beautiful? Is that the best you can do?"

"I actually can't find the words. I just want to get onshore and walk around."

"Well, the captain has hoisted the signal for a pilot and he should be coming out soon." William took in another deep breath of air. "It's a miracle that we're here, isn't it? I mean the gold strike and everything?"

George nodded. "It is." He thought back on the days after the call from Brother Rich, as the men worked diligently for hardly any profit. The weather was cold and rainy and they were all discouraged—hundreds of buckets and they were only bringing out thirty dollars a day, and then a strike! They hit a rich vein of gold that ran on for five weeks, the prospects running out just when they'd garnered enough money for passage to the islands, their own personal needs, and even some to send back to the Church. To George it was a miracle. He smiled. He was especially grateful for the personal money to buy some new clothing as his pants and shirts were so worn that one could see his skin through the threadbare areas. He looked down at his light-colored suit and felt glad it wasn't covered with the mud of California.

A whistle blew and a voice rang out. "Stand ready for the pilot!"

The missionaries moved back as the captain and his first mate came forward to meet the pilot.

All eyes looked off the port side of the ship and saw the whale boat approach. Four men were at the oars, the pilot sitting grandly in the stern. He was a squat man with square shoulders and a heavily lined face. His look was serious, and George was glad he was not the captain.

"Are you all well?" the pilot shouted as the whale boat came alongside.

"We have no sickness here," the captain shouted back as the crew lowered the ladder.

"What be your last port of call?" the pilot called as he hoisted himself up the ropes.

George was amazed at the agility of so thickset a gentleman.

"The port of San Francisco," the captain replied.

The pilot climbed onboard. "And is it your wish to make port?"

"It is, sir."

"For what purpose?"

"To offload goods and passengers and to take on stores."

The pilot reached out his powerful hand and the captain took it. "Welcome back to Honolulu, Captain Ritches," the pilot barked, a broad smile splitting his face. "How was the crossing?"

The captain smiled back. "Rough, Mr. Carter."

"It usually is in this season."

George thought of the rolling waves and the days and nights of sickness, and figured there had to be harsher words to describe the four-week crossing.

"Some of the passengers will be staying as missionaries and need their permits," Captain Ritches said.

The pilot looked around until he found the most likely candidates. "No wives?"

The captain smiled. "These are not Protestant missionaries, Mr. Carter. They are Mormons from the Utah Territory."

The pilot's face took on a look of interest as he approached the group. "Who then is in charge of this bunch?"

Hiram Clark stepped forward and extended his hand. "I am, sir. I am Hiram Clark."

"Good to meet you, Mr. Clark. A few years back I met

another group of Mormons under the direction of a Mr. Sam Brannon. Are you familiar with the man?"

Brother Clark smiled. "Indeed we are, Mr. Carter. Our prophet, Brigham Young, sent Brannon's group out to see what might be made of the west coast of California."

Mr. Carter laughed. "Gold's what's to be made there, Mr. Clark! Gold nuggets as big as your fist!"

Brother Clark did not correct the man's perception.

"This prophet of yours is a shrewd businessman, I reckon. Gold nuggets as big as your fist, I tell you!" He shook his head. "Why, if I wasn't so attached to the sea, I'd go and make me a fortune." George and William looked at each other and thought only of buckets of dirt. "Well, Mr. Clark, we'll work hard to get you into the harbor by noon. You'll have to make it to the custom house before four of the clock if you want your permits today."

"Thank you, Mr. Carter."

The pilot turned his back on Brother Clark and got down to business. "Square the yards!" he called in a loud voice, and the crew jumped into action. There was no mistaking that the man was now in charge of preparing the vessel for its entry into the harbor and was masterful at his command. In a little over an hour he had the ship and crew ready for their attempt on the narrow passage. The pilot boat led out, and the man in the chains kept throwing the lead to measure the depth of the water.

As they neared the narrow channel the sea broke over the reef in a tremendous roar.

"Ah, George, look at that," William said, pointing at shattered pieces of wrecked ships caught on the rocks. "I hope our pilot is as capable as he is loud."

George smiled, in spite of his unease.

The pilot proved to be extremely capable, and soon the

Imaum of Muscat was safely in the port of Honolulu and dropping anchor.

William squinted his eyes at a patch of sunlight on the water. "What's that then?"

George shaded his eyes from the sun and focused where William was looking. "It's a boat . . . well, more like a canoe heading toward us."

The eyes of all the men now turned toward the approaching vessel. It was crafted from one long beautiful piece of wood and seemed to sit light in the water.

"That there's an outrigger canoe," one of the crewmen said in passing. "On account of the outrigger attached to the side."

George found the canoe and the men paddling it singular. The Hawaiian men had strong physics, smooth brown skin, and dark hair. They had some sort of stiff patterned fabric around their waists, but their chests and arms were bare. The men smiled broadly when they reached the side of the ship. The missionaries smiled back, especially when the Hawaiians held up baskets filled with bananas, oranges, coconuts, and melons.

William Farrer whistled through his teeth. "Look at that, men. No more dried meat and hard tack."

George smiled to himself as he thought about the letter he would write his sister Mary later that day. He looked again to the green cliffs and shook his head. How could he possibly describe that vista to her in a letter, or the scene opening up before him? Brother Clark bought each missionary a supply of fruit and paid the natives in coin. George watched the transaction with fascination, wishing he could understand the melodic and flowing language that passed between the Hawaiian speakers. He realized that learning their language would probably not be required as they were sent to preach to the white men who made their homes in the Sandwich Islands. Still, George felt drawn to the islanders' easygoing ways and youthful demeanor.

When the Hawaiians moved on to other passengers, Brother Clark gathered the missionaries around him. "Go down and get your satchels. We'll be in town for the afternoon, and then we'll be back on the ship."

George was disappointed that they wouldn't be spending the night onshore, but he knew Brother Clark needed time to find them accommodations, and they needed time to clear things off the ship. George looked out over the dazzling landscape and was heartened with the knowledge that soon he would leave the dark, cramped quarters of the ship for the beauty of Eden.

As he went below to gather his satchel, emotions made a jumble of his thoughts. William had called it a wondrous adventure, but George knew he was a stranger. He felt a pain in his stomach that had nothing to do with the gentle rocking of the ship. He did not know the language, customs, or prejudices of the people who lived here. He was unfamiliar with the laws of the land and what restraints or lack thereof men placed on themselves. The streets of Liverpool may have been crowded and dingy, but even as a young man George knew the mind-set of the people he passed on the street, and the rules that kept the society generally on a level footing. And, in Nauvoo, although the net of the gospel had gathered in a variety of people from around the country and the world, he and his family had easily merged into the society because of the religious fervor shared by all. George smiled. He supposed it didn't hurt to have a prophet at the helm.

George's heart ached at the thought of the prophet. Would the world ever know how Joseph translated ancient records, preached the gospel of the primitive church, planned cities, and gathered thousands to Zion from all over the world? A smile crept onto his lips. *If given the opportunity, he would tell them.*

William clapped him on the shoulder. "What you smiling for, George? Are you anxious to get off this ship?"

George grabbed his satchel. "That I am, William. What say you and I go to see about this adventure?"

The wide grin on William's face was answer enough.

They hadn't spent much time in Honolulu that day. After securing their permits at the custom house, the group of missionaries had walked a few shaded paths, admired the profusion of flowers, and marveled at the variety of garden fruits and vegetables for sale in the marketplace. They were disappointed though by the squalid huts and unorganized way the town was laid out. Coming from the order and cleanliness of Nauvoo, Honolulu was a hodgepodge. From a distance the scene was pleasing, but up close one could tell that the rapid influx of foreign visitors had overwhelmed the planning. They had been back on board before nightfall.

The next day they moved into a set of rooms secured by Brother Clark not far from the custom house, and George's spirits were high.

"It will be a bit cramped for a few days, brethren, until we figure out what the Lord wants done with the lot of you."

George could tell that Brother Clark's spirits were high too.

"Not to worry, Elder Clark," William Farrer responded. "It seems like a palace after those quarters on the ship."

Many voices heartily agreed.

Brother Clark nodded. "Stow your gear, and get your

satchels and canteens, men. We're hiking up into the mountains to have a prayer and to talk about our assignments."

A short time later, the Mormon missionaries set off along the road that ran from the custom house up into the Nuuanu Valley. George could not take in all the new sights and sounds. There were trees with long flowing leaves, vines with leaves bigger than his head, unique flowers with luscious smells, and small birds with vivid red and black feathers. His head kept roving from side to side, and several times he stumbled for lack of attention to his footing.

"Watch yourself," Brother Bigler cautioned. "You wouldn't want to start your mission with a broken foot."

Around mid-morning the company stopped, and George took a deep breath and got out his canteen. He looked over at Henry Bigler who was examining a species of plant that sported a red flower bigger than a man's hand.

"Did you ever imagine there could be a world such as this, Brother Bigler?"

The man looked around with appreciation. "Well, one thing's for sure, the Lord is quite an artist."

"He is that," George agreed.

The company started off again, and after another half an hour of hiking, the ascent steepened, and the road became a track. Brother Bigler called for a halt and suggested they take a pathway off to the right toward the sound of a waterfall. Brother Clark agreed, and within minutes the group came through the jungle onto a wondrous scene. A high sparkling waterfall cascaded into a broad pool of water, and the men watched disbelieving as several native boys jumped the thirty to forty feet into the center of the deep pond.

"Would you look at that," William said as he came to stand

beside George. "Those are the best swimmers I've ever seen." He started to undress. "Should we give it a try?"

George gave him a half grin. "Well, I'm going to bathe, but I think I'll leave the jumping to the experts."

The next hour was filled with mirth as ten grown men splashed in the cool water like schoolboys. George felt the sorrow of his parents' deaths wash from his body, and he wondered if the other men were feeling the same refreshing. Was Brother Bigler sloughing off the rigors of the march he had endured with the Mormon Battalion? Was Brother Blackwell forgetting the horrors of the burning of the Nauvoo Temple and the mob expelling the Saints from their beloved city? Were the memories of the massacre at Haun's Mill, or the deaths at Winter Quarters, being scrubbed from Brother Keeler's soul? George floated on his back and watched the dappled sunlight playing on the water of the falls. Perhaps they were all feeling a rebaptism of faith and commitment to the cause of the gospel.

After the pleasant swim, the men dressed and continued their journey up the mountainside, and, even though the temperature at this elevation was cooler than at sea level, the men were soon sweating and wiping their brows. George's thoughts wandered to the Salt Lake Valley, where he pictured sleet, snow, and desolate landscapes. He hoped his family was faring well, and he thanked heaven again for Charles Lambert. George's attention was brought to the present as Elder Clark stopped on an open flat plateau overlooking a valley below. It was of sufficient area for all the missionaries to gather. They waited patiently for their leader to instruct them.

"Sit down, brethren. Seek out a shaded spot; we may be here awhile." The men complied and Elder Clark continued. "I think we should begin with a song and then talk about the work before us." He turned to George. "Brother Cannon, you have one of the better voices, would you lead us?"

George felt the expected twinge of fear drop into his stomach, but he nodded his acceptance. "What should we sing?"

"How about Brother Pratt's hymn?" William offered. "'An Angel from on High.'"

Several heads nodded and George began to sing. The others joined, and soon the sweet feelings of the Spirit surrounded the group. After the song ended, it took Elder Clark some time to settle his emotions before he spoke.

"I now wish to hear your thoughts concerning the work, and then we will have our prayer."

Several of the brethren gave responses that centered on the preaching to be done and which islands should be visited. Others reminded the group to be diligent about the paperwork they needed to have in order to be able to preach. At one point Brother Bigler stood.

"I would also caution against confrontation with the good ministers already established here. Preach the word and let the Spirit work the conversion." He grinned. "Now we do hope that those who fight against this work will be confounded, but we don't need to go picking any fights."

William Farrer spoke up. "I just want to be preserved from the powers of the devil and from evil."

"A necessary wish for you, Brother Farrer," Brother Bigler teased.

"And I would like our lives to be spared so we can all make it home again," Brother Keeler added.

Several voices agreed with that sentiment.

George felt compelled to say something, but he was still uncomfortable speaking out in the group. He had shared a great deal of time and trials with these brethren, but that didn't ease the pounding of his heart.

Brother Clark stood. "Are there any other words to be spoken?"

George raised his hand. Uncomfortable or not, he had a vision of the work on the Sandwich Islands that needed to be shared.

"Yes, Brother Cannon?"

"I have a question, actually."

Elder Clark waited.

"What if the Spirit moves us to preach to the native population?" George watched his leader closely and could tell he was giving the question deep consideration.

"Most don't know much English, Brother Cannon. It would be difficult to preach the tenets of the faith without the words to do so."

George persisted. "But what if we were to learn a bit of their language—at least enough to tell them of the first principles, priesthood authority, and ongoing revelation?"

Elder Clark was silent for so long that George feared he had offended him in some way or gone beyond the mark. Finally, a slight smile brushed the leader's mouth. "In this church, Brother Cannon, we believe in personal revelation, correct?"

"Yes, sir."

"In this church we believe in the gift of tongues."

"We do."

"Then I believe it entirely possible that you may receive the personal revelation to preach to the native population. If that should occur, young man, I would hope you would follow the assignment from the Lord."

George lowered his head to hide the tears. "Yes, sir."

President Clark looked around at the group of missionaries. "And now, brethren, if you are agreeable, I will act as voice for the prayer."

George felt the Spirit flood his body as Elder Clark prayed that the door might be opened for the preaching of the gospel in these beautiful islands, that the missionaries might have the Spirit with them at all times, that their lives might be preserved, that the opposers to the work might be confounded, and that the honest in heart might embrace the truth when they heard it.

It was a simple prayer and not long, but with every word George felt the spirit of the work enter his heart, and he knew that he was exactly where the Lord wanted him. He looked over at William Farrer who nodded and grinned.

Elder Clark sat down and took some papers from his jacket pocket. "Now we will decide the pairs of missionaries and the islands to which they will be sent. I have written your names on these pieces of paper. I will choose four names and those brothers will choose their companions. And since I am not desirous to choose the place where you will labor, on these papers I have written the names of the islands, and we will cast lots." He paused for comments. Since none were forthcoming, he continued. "Now, if you find it agreeable, I have already chosen Brother Thomas Whittle to remain here with me on Oahu to organize and run the mission."

All the brethren heartily agreed, knowing that the combined skills and temperament of these two men would be a strength to the work.

As President Clark and Brother Whittle cast lots for the four who would lead the partnerships, George surveyed the brethren and felt calm about serving with any of them. Like himself, they had their foibles, but all had shown themselves to be hardworking and obedient to the gospel cause.

Brother Clark finished his conference with Brother Whittle and looked up. "The four leaders will be Henry Bigler, James Hawkins, John Dixon, and George Cannon."

George was stunned. He opened his mouth to speak, but no words came out. His mind was such a muddle; he might as well have tried to speak Hawaiian.

"We have also cast lots to decide the order in which you will choose your companions, and the first lot fell to you, Brother Cannon."

George still could not speak. He lowered his head. "May . . . may I have a moment to pray, President Clark?"

"Of course, Brother Cannon. That is probably a sound idea for all."

In the ensuing quiet, George attempted to still the doubts that were making him tremble. *I am the youngest. I fear to speak in front of people. I have no leadership experience. I would rather be a follower.* Tears pressed at the back of his throat, and he felt his weaknesses most acutely. Just as his emotions were about to overtake him, his panic was replaced by a feeling of calm. George took a deep breath and felt the spirit directing clearly that he should choose Brother James Keeler to be his companion. "I choose Brother James Keeler," George said, before opening his eyes. When he did look up, he saw that Brother Keeler was weeping.

Note

- The first Protestant missionaries sailed from Boston, Massachusetts, on October 23, 1819, arriving five months later on the shores of the Sandwich Islands. They were funded by the American Board of Commissioners for Foreign Missions.

CHAPTER 4

Honolulu, Oahu
December 17, 1850

Dear Mary,

    My thoughts are with you and the Saints in the Valley. I hope Charles was able to finish the room and that the bricks are holding up. I also hope that you are tolerating the winter fairly well and have enough to eat.
    Today Brother Keeler and I will sail for our assigned island, and I wish to relate the remarkable circumstance surrounding the call and the placement. As I have told you, President Clark is the mission leader and a very able man. As he did not like to pair us off, nor to say which of the islands we should go to, he with his partner Brother Whittle selected four out of the eight to preside, one on each of the islands: Moloka'i, Kauai, Maui, and Hawaii. One of the lots fell to me and I was to choose my companion. As all are older than myself, you can imagine my fears. My mind had not rested on any one as my choice for partner, and I was at a loss for a few moments whom to select. Then the spirit of the Lord plainly told

me to choose Brother James Keeler. I did so. I was both surprised and pleased at the manner in which he received my choice, for I, being so young, and he so much my senior, had thought that he would prefer a partner of more mature years and experience. He afterward told me that when the four were chosen, and he found that I was one of them, he had prayed to the Lord that I might be led to elect him to go with me. His prayer was heard and answered, and we both were gratified.

In casting lots for islands, Maui fell to us. When we were sailing past it on first arriving, my feelings were drawn toward that island, and I felt that I would like that to be my field of labor. I knew not why this should have been so, except that the Lord gave me the feeling. My joy was very great that day because of these precious manifestations of God's goodness. I felt that he was near at hand to hear and answer prayer, and to grant the righteous desires of our hearts.

Brother Bigler and Brother Morris will go to Molokaʻi; Brothers Hawkins and Blackwell to Hawaii; and Brothers Dixon and Farrer to Kauai.

As Brother Clark has asked Brother Morris to work for a time to help with mission costs, Brother Bigler has been given permission to accompany me and Brother Keeler to Maui. We leave on the afternoon tide. I will mail this letter to you before departing.

I pray for you always, dear sister, and hope that your trials are not too severe. Love to Ann, Angus, David Henry, and Leonora. I shall probably not recognize any of you when I return.

Your brother, George

"Brother Cannon! How are you faring?" Brother Bigler called below deck.

"I am wretched, Brother Bigler. The sea is my enemy."

"Well, I may have news to cheer you. We are in sight of Lahaina, Maui, and should make port in an hour."

George sat up, steadied himself, and put on his shoes. He gathered every ounce of strength and stood. For a day and a half he had been seasick. In fact, they had scarcely crossed the reef out of Honolulu harbor when the illness overtook him and he went below to lie down, refusing even the mention of food. The lack of sustenance had made him weak, and it took him time to gain his balance "I will go and do the things that the Lord commands," he said stubbornly, heading for the ladder to topside.

As they came off the channel, the motion of the boat calmed, and George's stomach began to settle. He made his way tentatively across the deck, hoping the breeze would clear his head and the sight of land would lift his spirit. Indeed, the sight of the island of Maui was a tonic. The mountains rising behind the town of Lahaina were not as towering or thickly vegetated as the cliffs on Oahu, but the stark mountains of short grass and ruddy rocks were slashed by deep precipices and covered with billowing clouds. Hills rolled down from the base of the mountains to the flat area of land that held the town of Lahaina in its arms. George squinted and searched for the buildings and houses of the town, but could only catch glimpses as they were nearly hidden by the dense foliage.

Brother Keeler, who had also been sick on the crossing, stood at the railing looking out over the placid water. It cheered

George's heart to see him. As soon as James caught sight of him, he grinned, and pointed at something in the water.

"Come look at a remarkable sight, Brother Cannon!"

George moved alongside his companions. He gasped and held tightly to the railing as several huge fish leapt from the water a stone's throw from the ship. "What type of fish are those?" he questioned, watching in amazement as three more leapt.

"Them ain't fish," a crewman chuckled. "Them are air-breathing mammals. They're called dolphins."

"Mammals?" George asked. "Air-breathing, like whales?"

"Yep. That'll be them," the crewman answered.

George forgot his sickness as he watched the agile animals. "They seem to be racing the ship."

The sailor chuckled and turned back to his business. "Yes, indeed. They do like their games. The Hawaiian people see them critters as signs of good fortune."

"I can see why," Brother Bigler said, smiling.

"Good fortune," Brother Keeler mused, lifting his eyes to the town of Lahaina and the whaling ships anchored in the harbor. "It seems like we might need a bit of that in this undertaking."

Brother Bigler thumped him on the shoulder. "We're on the Lord's errand, Brother Keeler. He'll point us in the right direction if we're not pigheaded." He turned to George. "Well, Brother Cannon, you are the lead missionary for this island, what is your first suggestion when we reach shore?"

George gawked at the man. Though Brother Bigler was certainly not old at thirty-five, he was still twelve years his senior, and George was acutely aware of the man's wealth of life experience and wisdom. He cleared his throat. "I . . . I suppose food and a place to stay."

Brother Bigler grinned. "Now there's wise counsel."

"Sit here under this big tree," Brother Bigler ordered and George obeyed. He was worn down by the effects of the seasickness, lack of food, and three hours in the hot sun looking for a place to stay. They did not have money enough to lodge at the hotel or one of the boardinghouses, but their options were dwindling. Brother Bigler stacked their belongings around George's feet. "Brother Keeler and I will continue the search," he announced, handing George a canteen. "You stay here and rest."

"But, Brother Keeler is unwell too."

"I'm feeling much better now that I have solid ground under my feet."

George nodded. "All right then, but come back within the hour if you haven't found anything, and we'll go to one of those boardinghouses. I don't care how much it costs."

Brother Keeler patted him on the shoulder, and the two men left.

There were a myriad of new sights to mystify and intrigue, but George hung his head and closed his eyes. Not the horrendous time in Nauvoo, nor crossing the plains, nor working with little food in the Salt Lake Valley had made him feel so weary or despondent. He thought it a great trial to come into a foreign nation to preach the gospel. Preach the gospel? That was as possible as him learning to fly. How was he going to share the good news with anyone? He couldn't even speak in front of a group. He missed his family. His stomach hurt. He missed William Farrer and his jokes.

George sat up and took a long drink of water. His boots and the cuffs of his pant legs were covered in a red lava dust, which clung like a bad omen. There was only one main street with a few minor ones intersecting, and George figured he and his companions had walked every one, with no success in finding a place to stay. In frustration he kicked over Brother Bigler's valise, which startled a small green bird into flight.

George hung his head again. *Lord, forgive me. I'm just worn down. I feel as though there's a weight pressing me down. I need Thy strength. I need this dark feeling to leave me.* He heard a rustling in the fallen leaves nearby and looked sideways to see the small bird again. George stared at it. He'd never seen a bird this color. Its pale green and yellow feathers looked more like fluff, and George longed to hold the soft fellow in his hand. He watched unmoving as the bird rooted around in the leaves. Periodically it would come up with a twig or bit of leaf, but these were soon discarded. Suddenly the bird struck, and when its head emerged from the debris, it held a large brown beetle in its silver beak. His friend's triumph made George smile. In a flutter of wings, it was gone.

"Brother Cannon!" Brother Bigler called. George watched the approach of the two missionaries. They were smiling. "We've found a house!"

Notes

- The dedication of the land of Hawaii for the preaching of the gospel, and the casting of lots to decide area mission leaders and island assignments was recorded by George Cannon in his journal. He also recorded his feelings of inadequacy at being chosen one of the mission leaders.
- The town of Lahaina on the island of Maui was the first capital of the Kingdom of Hawaii. In the early nineteenth century it was a great whaling port.
- Though fictional, the letters from Elder Cannon to Mary and to other missionaries contain many actual occurrences taken from his 1850–1854 journal.

CHAPTER 5

Lahaina, Maui

December 21, 1850

President Clark,

 We have secured a thatched house for $4 a week. I know it is a high price, but there was nothing else available. It is sparsely furnished, but there is a desk and a few chairs and mats for sleeping. We have evaluated the town and find that, out of the several thousand in population, there are only about fifty haoles or non-natives here and that includes sailors. There are only two white families in the town.

 We thought it best to go and see the American Consul Charles Bunker and get an introduction to Governor James Young Kanehoa, so that we might have the sanction of the authorities. We feel it important to be introduced to the highest authority we can find and to state clearly what our intention is for preaching. Consul Bunker was a gentleman, and he was pleased we called upon him. He was very interested about the Territory of Deseret and the troubles the Mormon people have had.

Later that day he introduced us to Governor Kanehoa. He is a pleasant old man. His mother was Hawaiian and his father an Englishman. He spoke English very well. He gave his sanction to preach as much as we wanted. We asked him about a public building in which we could hold our meetings and he did not know of one. He said he would think about it.

In the evening several of the natives came in and they told us the names of many things and sang for us. We are in considerable better spirits about learning the language.

A servant of the Lord,
Brother George Cannon

George made sure the ink was dry, folded the letter, and placed it in the addressed envelope. He thought back on the meeting with Consul Bunker and Governor Kanehoa and how grateful he was that Brothers Keeler and Bigler were with him. He had been happy to stand back and let them converse with the officials, watching and learning from their example.

George stood and went to the door of the hut looking out on the blue water of the sea. "Moana—ocean." He thumped his hand on the doorframe. "Hale—house. Mahalo—thank you. Aloha—" he laughed. "Hello, good-bye, I care about you."

Brother Bigler called to him from the yard, where he was doing his laundry in a tin bucket. "Brother Cannon, are you feeling all right? I'm a little worried about you standing there mumbling to yourself."

George walked down to him. "I was just trying to remember some of the Hawaiian words those fellows taught us last night."

"Well, you were a good deal better at it than me or Brother Keeler," Brother Bigler said, twisting the water out of his shirt and hanging it on the branch of a tree. "I couldn't get all those vowels straight."

Brother Keeler emerged from the hut. "Good morning. Cold sweet potatoes for breakfast, anyone?"

"Is that all we have to eat?" George asked, trying to keep the disappointment out of his voice.

"It is," Brother Keeler answered, walking down to them, "unless you have some eggs and bread you're hiding from us."

George shook his head and answered in a thick English accent. "Nor do I have scones, or orange marmalade, though I wish I did."

Brother Bigler nodded. "What I wouldn't give for some johnnycakes."

"Well, I think those would be hard to come by," George answered, "but I'm going into town this morning to post a letter to President Clark, and I'll pick up some bread when I'm there."

"And bananas if you can find a few," Brother Keeler added.

George turned to the house to fetch his suit jacket and then changed his mind and turned back. He felt again the disparity in age between him and his companions, but he had to trust in President Clark's prompting that chose him as leader. He gathered his confidence. "There's something I wish to discuss with you, brethren, if you don't mind." He looked out to the ocean. "I say we walk down to the water."

Brother Keeler brightened. "Sounds like a wonderful idea."

"Are you sure you're finished with your laundry, Brother Bigler?" George asked.

The man chuckled. "Doesn't take long to wash one shirt."

The three missionaries headed to the beach. As they neared the water's edge, the breeze picked up, and George felt the heaviness of the morning lift. He wasn't a man prone to sadness, but the past week had been a trial for him. At some point in every day he found himself fighting doubt and loneliness.

George took off his shoes and socks and set them in the shade of a broad-leafed tree. He wondered what the name of the tree was in the Hawaiian language. He rolled up his pant legs and walked into the water. Brother Bigler and Brother Keeler followed their leader's example. The three men stood for the longest time enjoying the splash of the water on their legs and looking out over the channel to the island of Lanai. Finally George spoke.

"It is a beautiful land." The other men concurred. "It is different from anything I could have imagined." The men concurred again. "I mean, I'd heard about the Sandwich Islands and seen a few scientific pictures, but this is different from what I expected." The men were silent. George knew he was rambling, but he was trying to organize his thoughts, gather his courage, and pray for the guidance of the Spirit all at the same time. "I say if we confine our preaching to the whites, our mission on this island will be very short," he said in a rush.

Brother Bigler looked at him squarely. "Is this the revelation you've received for the mission on Maui, Brother Cannon?"

George *had* received a strong feeling about how the mission should proceed, but as he looked at his companions, he was reminded of his youth and he stammered. "I . . . well, I want to get your thoughts on the matter."

"But, you are the leader. The decision rests with you."

"Yes, but you are my helpers and companions." *And older,* he thought. "I value your advice."

The two men shared a smile.

Brother Keeler picked up a smooth stone and skimmed it

across the water. "So, the question is, should we preach to the native Hawaiians?"

George nodded.

"Which means we would have to learn the language," Brother Bigler said.

"Yes, of course," George replied quickly.

"Because, if we preach only to the whites on Maui, our mission would probably be finished by the end of January," Brother Keeler added.

"Yes. I don't see much promise in it," George said.

"But, that would mean going against the commission we were given by President Clark to preach to the whites on the islands," Brother Bigler reminded.

"But, he didn't know the circumstances," George retorted. "Besides, he told me that if I were to receive revelation to preach to the native Hawaiians then I should follow that prompting and the Lord would help me . . . us."

"And is that what's happened? Have you received revelation?"

George was uncomfortable with the way Brother Bigler was scrutinizing him, but he wasn't going to back down. "I wish to preach to the whites and to the natives. I've made up my mind to master the language and warn the people of the islands. The spirit of the work is upon me. If I have to do it alone, I will. I cannot do otherwise and be free from condemnation."

Brother Bigler's eyebrows rose, and Brother Keeler stepped back, shaking his head. They looked at each other and Brother Bigler spoke.

"We had a feeling that's the way the horse was headed."

George felt rather foolish standing barefooted in the water, but he held the look of resolution on his face. "So, how do you answer?"

Brother Bigler looked out over the water. "If you must know the truth, Brother Cannon, I feel the same. No sense trying to preach only to the whites. I say the Lord loves all his children."

George fought back his boyish elation, and turned to Brother Keeler. "Brother Keeler, how do you feel about this?"

James Keeler gave him a half grin. "I have just one word to say on the matter, Brother Cannon. Mahalo."

Note

- With the unification of the islands under Kamehameha I, the ancient Hawaiian society was transformed into an independent, constitutional monarchy crafted in the tradition and manner of a European monarchy.

CHAPTER 6

Lahaina, Maui

December 29, 1850

Dear Mary,

    The year is almost at an end, and each New Year seems to find us living in a different place. I hope you are well. I have been fairly well, but the food is a little hard to get used to. We employed the man we rented the house from to cook our food, and it is mostly sweet potatoes and fish, or meat.

    I, along with Brother Bigler, and Brother Keeler have made up our minds to preach to the Hawaiian people, so have been studying the language for the past week or so. You would laugh to see three haole (white) men lying about on mats as the native speakers teach us.

    I will write a little about the thatched hut in which we live. Perhaps you and the children will find it interesting. Perhaps Charles will also be interested as it is so different from the adobe house he built in the Valley. These native houses are built by putting posts in the ground, on which a board is laid as a plate for the rafters to rest upon. Then poles, about the size of hoop-poles, are lashed horizontally, about six inches apart, on to the posts and rafters. The house is then thatched by fastening a durable grass called pili grass, which they have in this country, onto the poles. When finished, a house looks, in shape and size, like a well-built hay stack. Such houses are only suited to a warm country where they never have frost. Inside the house they have no board floors. The ground is covered with grass, on which mats are laid . . . the mats answer the purpose of beds, tables, and chairs. We sit upon them, and they form our beds. There isn't any other sort of furniture, but in consideration of our being white men, the man of whom we rented the house found us a table and three chairs.

 I know you will receive this long after the New Year, but know that my prayers are with the family and that I am doing all I can to serve the Lord according to His will. Today we are going to a meeting at the Native Chapel and then to the Seaman's Chapel. We are hoping they will ring the bell for us to preach. It is difficult because we do not have a meetinghouse in which to assemble and must rely on the benevolence of other ministers.

 I checked for mail at the Custom House to see if there were any letters, but none had arrived. I understand that post is sent from San Francisco only twice monthly, so I will not get too discouraged. Have you any word on how my friend Sister Elizabeth Hoagland is faring? If you see her, will you wish her well from me, and tell her that she could write me here, if she wished?

 I hope the winter weather is not too harsh.

    Your loving brother, George

"Brother Cannon!" Brother Bigler called. "Have you finished your letter?"

George stood quickly, grabbing his coat and heading for the door. "I have, Brother Bigler. Just." He waved the pages in the air as he emerged from the hut into the bright sunlight.

"It's time we were off to our meetings."

"Yes, I know. Sorry. I got carried away describing our thatched house to the family." He was struggling to hold the pages and get into his coat at the same time.

Brother Keeler reached out for the letter and held it while George dressed. "You're a much better letter writer than I am, Brother Cannon. I cannot spell to save my soul." He chuckled. "Maybe I'll do better in Hawaiian since there are so few letters in the alphabet."

George chuckled. "Fewer letters means that one word may have several different meanings, Brother Keeler."

Brother Bigler scowled at him. "That is not really helpful, Brother Cannon."

George took back his letter and patted the big man on the arm. "We do believe in the gift of tongues, Brother Bigler." He shared a smile with Brother Keeler.

Brother Bigler grunted. "Maybe I'm too old to get another language into my brain." He started off down the road. "Come on, we don't want to miss the Native meeting where I won't be able to make out a word of the sermon."

"It's good practice," George said, as he and Brother Keeler followed quickly behind.

All they could hear from the man in front of them was mumbling.

"Mr. Bigler, is it?" Reverend Taylor questioned as he reached out his hand. "I met you in my office a few days ago?"

"Yes, sir," Brother Bigler said, taking the handshake. "Good to see you again."

"Were you in attendance at the Native meeting?"

"We were, yes."

The man nodded. "Pity you cannot understand the language."

Brother Bigler gave a look to his companions. "Well, Reverend Taylor, we are attempting to learn."

"Really? It is not an easy task, let me tell you."

Brother Bigler changed the subject. "That was a mighty fine sermon you gave, sir. The wages of sin is death."

Reverend Taylor grinned slightly. "I find it appropriate for the sailors."

"Indeed."

"Thank you for reading out the note about our meeting at half past three," George said, stepping forward.

"And for the use of your meetinghouse," Brother Keeler added.

"It is my duty, gentlemen. I will be interested to hear your sermon." He nodded at them and moved off to speak with a few of his parishioners.

"I wonder if he'll be as interested *after* he hears our sermon," Brother Bigler said aside to his companions.

True to his word, Reverend Taylor rang the bell for the preaching of the Mormon missionaries, and a fair crowd of people assembled in the meetinghouse. George felt like a bug under a glass. Some people were staring at them with curiosity, while others looked downright suspicious, and he wondered what gossip and rumors had circulated during the afternoon hiatus. The gathering was not large, but as George glanced around at the sea of unfamiliar faces, he felt a coil of cold fear snake up his spine. Earlier that day he had tried to get out of preaching, but to no avail.

"I think, if we're given the opportunity to preach, that Brother Bigler should go first and teach the first principles of the gospel and the plan of salvation." Brother Bigler nodded. "And then, Brother Keeler should teach about the Holy Ghost."

"And what will be your topic, Brother Cannon?"

"Well, I . . . I will bear my testimony to the truthfulness of what the two of you have said and dismiss the meeting."

Brother Bigler had given him another of those scrutinizing looks and strongly suggested an alternative program. Now George would be speaking on the Holy Ghost and Brother Keeler would be testifying and dismissing the meeting. George felt hot and clammy. *Maybe I'll pass out and won't have to preach.*

Brother Bigler stood, and the congregation quieted. He welcomed them as friends and began immediately to preach the first principles of the gospel. He opened the Bible and taught the plan of salvation from the New Testament. George paid attention to the man's easygoing stance and the strength of voice. He also glanced at the members of the group and wondered if they realized that they were hearing the doctrine as taught in Christ's primitive church. George swallowed hard, wondering if the people would be as attentive to the words when they were offered by a much less able speaker. He did not have to wait long to find out.

Brother Bigler held out the Bible to him. "And now, Mr. Cannon will give you a discourse on the Holy Ghost."

A discourse? George felt the blood drain from his head. *Please, Lord, help me to stand up. Help words to come out of my mouth.* He worked hard to keep his hand from trembling as he reached out for the Bible. He held it to his chest and stood. He tried not to look at anyone directly.

"Dear friends." His breathing steadied. "I have a great message to share with you." His heart stopped pounding against his ribs. "I testify to you that if a man has the Holy Ghost to be his guide, it will lead him into *all* truth and not a part." His body filled with warmth. "If a man had this Spirit upon the Sandwich Islands it would reveal the same things to him that it would to a man upon the Continent of America." His voice gained strength. "And if the world had this Spirit, then men would not be split up the way they are. If a man had the light of the Spirit, then he would not be blown about by every wind of doctrine." Several sailors nodded in agreement, and George figured they knew a thing or two about being blown about in a strong wind. "My friends and I come to you to preach a restoration of light. Light that has been absent in the world for a long time."

A man stood and interrupted. "What additional light are you offering, preacher?" George opened his mouth, but no words were forthcoming. The man gave him a contemptuous look and continued. "I say that the different churches we know have the Spirit of the Lord, and light enough for me." George saw Reverend Taylor nod as the man continued. "What is your evidence that you have some additional light to give us?"

George tried to organize his thoughts, but all he could think about was the man's shock of silver hair and his black walking stick. *Perhaps he's a government official.* George stepped back, and suddenly Brother Bigler was beside him.

"Sir, our faith is founded in the same priesthood authority that marked the ancient church. Our additional light includes revelation to apostles and prophets, and the gifts of the Spirit as we read about in the days of the Savior." The man stood glaring as Brother Bigler continued. "If you want evidence of its truth or falsity you must do as the Savior recommended and ask the Father in the name of Jesus if what we say is true. If you ask sincerely then He will give you the necessary evidence."

"Are you talking about revelation in this day?"

"We are, sir."

"Revelation to a prophet?"

Brother Bigler's voice was calm. "That is what we preach, sir."

"I don't believe in such poppycock."

Brother Keeler stood and came forward. He looked past the man to the other congregants. "We invite you to pray and find out for yourself." Several angry murmurs punctuated the group. "I have done so, and I know what these gentlemen have been preaching is true. May the Lord help you to find out for yourself. We would be glad to answer questions after the meeting." He took a breath and dismissed the meeting.

No one stayed to ask questions.

George was weary from the long day, and discouraged by the spirit of opposition that had brought the meeting to a close. He kicked his feet in the red dirt as they trudged their way back to their hut.

"I'm sorry I let you down, brethren."

Brother Keeler gave him a questioning look. "How do you mean, Brother Cannon?"

"I couldn't find the words to defend the faith."

"The man was intimidating."

"But, I should have found the faith—like David before Goliath."

Brother Bigler patted him on the back. "Don't worry, I'm

sure there are going to be more Goliaths to face." He fanned his face with his Bible. "Your discourse on the Holy Ghost was good—short, but good."

George smiled. "At least the man saved me from making a fool of myself." His mood turned serious. "I just don't understand why people won't consider revelation and modern-day prophets. I heard the Prophet Joseph speak on many occasions. He had less education than me, but when he spoke the words of truth and revelation, they went right through to my heart."

"Amen," Brother Keeler said, and Brother Bigler nodded.

George stopped abruptly. "Brothers, today made me more convinced than ever that we are on the right course. We are to learn the language and preach to the good Hawaiian people. Their hearts are more open to the truth."

Brother Bigler started walking. "Learn the language, he says, as if that's an easy thing."

George hurried to catch up to him. "It will not be an easy thing, but that doesn't mean we shouldn't try. Ikaika mauna, Brother Bigler."

"And what does that mean?"

George grinned. "I think it means strong mountain."

Brother Keeler caught the spirit of George's words. "I will look to the mountains whence cometh my strength. If thou had faith to say unto this mountain, remove, then it would remove. Who shall ascend unto the hill of the Lord? Upon this rock I will build my church!"

By the end of Brother Keeler's vibrant preaching they were all laughing, and George felt the cold disappointment of the afternoon lift from his heart.

George went to bed that night with a myriad of scriptures about hills and mountains bumping around in his head, and in his dreams he was climbing mountains and descending into valleys. In the valleys he met beautiful brown-skinned people who gave him water from calabash bowls, and fruit from their trees. They were smiling and glad to see him. He felt peace and acceptance surround him. A dark storm cloud sat on the edge of the shoreline and he saw rain and flashes of lightning. Uwila. Was that the Hawaiian word for lightning? He was in a native congregation and he understood them, and he could speak to them. His heart swelled, and tears leaked from his eyes to water his pillow. He wanted the dream never to end.

CHAPTER 7

Lahaina, Maui

January 13, 1851

Dear President Clark,

Being that we are very low on funds and are unable to pay for our house, Brother Bigler, Brother Keeler, and myself are going out today to see if there are people who will take us in. Brother Bigler and Brother Keeler are already hunting and I will go as soon as I finish this letter. It is likely that we will have to split up because it would be difficult for a family to house all three of us. This is a great sadness, but we will do what we must in order to remain on the island to preach. Thank you for your letter of encouragement in our learning the language and in preaching to the native population. We feel prompted in this direction. If possible would you please send us two vocabularies of the Native for Brother Keeler and myself?

There was a sound at the door and George looked up from his letter writing to see Keala and his wife Pau standing in the doorway to the hale. George's face brightened and he stood. "Keala! Pau! Aloha! Come in, come in. Is it time for our lesson?" George knew he easily lost track of time when he was writing or reading.

The couple came into the hut. Keala reached out his hand, which George took. "It is not lesson time, Brother Cannon," Keala said grinning. "Little while. We come early to talk about problem."

"A problem?" George motioned for them to sit and they all sat down cross-legged on the mats. "Perhaps I can help."

Keala shook his head and looked at Pau. "It is not our problem. It is your problem."

"My problem?"

"Earlier today we saw Brother Bigler going out with a note in his hand. He looked troubled. We went to talk to him. He hands us the note. On note is written Hawaiian words and English words. It says that you are looking for a place to stay."

George felt emotion wash over him as he saw the looks of concern on his teachers' faces. He nodded. "Yes, we have no money for our hale, so we must move."

Pau sat forward. "Hoalo 'ha. Friend. I have brought my mother and sister. They wish to speak to you. May they enter your hale?"

"Of course," George said, standing.

Pau went to the door of the hale and called softly to her mother and sister. When they entered, she brought them forward. "Brother Cannon, this is my mother, Nalimanui, and my sister, Hoohuli. My sister is married to the Spaniard."

George gently took the women's hands in turn. "Yes, I know them. I have seen them. Aloha. Please sit."

Pau translated to her mother who beamed at being

recognized, and she and Hoohuli sat. "My mother wishes to speak to you."

George nodded.

Nalimanui began to speak in a soft Hawaiian voice, and Pau translated. "White men who come to the islands do not always behave themselves as they should. It is sad. We see some who act hilahi 'la maoli." She looked to her husband for the translation.

"Disgraceful."

"Yes, disgraceful." Her mother began speaking again. "They think because they are among the children of the land they can give up all goodness." Nalimanui put her finger to her eye. "But we see very well. We watch. We see that you are not like most whites. You are gentle, and you try to learn our language."

George nodded and fought to control his emotions. He was touched not only by what the gracious woman was saying, but because he understood many of the Hawaiian words she spoke.

"My daughter has told me that you and the other missionaries must leave your house. This is not good." Pau stopped translating and let her mother speak without interruption. When Nalimanui stopped speaking and smiled at George, Pau translated. "My mother wishes to give you her house. It is small and not very good, but it has a garden, and you may keep it for as long as you need."

George was stunned. "But where . . . where will she stay?"

"She will stay with my sister Hoohuli and her husband." Hoohuli nodded.

Tears ran down George's face. Never in his life had he been more grateful than for this offering of shelter from this dear woman. "We have no money, but we will give her blankets or anything else she wants. We will work in her garden. We will fish for her."

Pau translated his words to her mother, who smiled and nodded. She put her hand over her heart and spoke a few more words. "Mother says we will spend the day putting the house in order and you may move in tomorrow." Nalimanui began to stand, and her son-in-law, Keala, helped her. The others stood also, and George approached.

"Mahalo, dear mother. Mahalo nui, hoalo 'ha."

Nalimanui patted his cheek. "Keiki. Hapapa hewa ka malihini makamaka 'ole."

George looked at Pau for the meaning of the words.

"A stranger without a friend feels lost."

The tears started again, and George took Nalimanui's hands. "The Lord bless you for your goodness."

Nalimanui patted his cheek again and turned to leave.

The other family members followed her, and Keala stopped at the door and turned back smiling. "No lesson today! We will be cleaning a house."

Brother Keeler came in, bumping into Keala who had turned to go. "Oh! I'm sorry, Keala. Keala? Where are you going? Don't we have a lesson?"

"No lesson today!" Keala called back.

Brother Keeler shook his head. "What was that all about?" He came closer and noticed George wiping tears from his face. "Are you all right? What's been happening?"

George's face broke into a smile. "Pau's mother, Nalimanui, has given us her house to live in."

Brother Keeler sat down abruptly on a stack of mats. "Not just a room for us to sleep in?"

"No, a house."

"I can't wait to see the look on Brother Bigler's face. It is a miracle."

"A generous miracle," George answered.

"It might have been your birthday a few days ago, Brother Cannon, but I think you were given your birthday gift today."

George nodded. "Words of truth, Brother Keeler." He moved back to the desk to affix a final note to the end of the letter to President Clark.

President,

I heartily testify that the Lord is aware of all His children. A dear woman in the area by the name of Nalimanui has given us her house in which to live. We are humbly grateful for her kindness, and ask that you remember her in your prayers. The hearts of the Hawaiian people are full of goodness, and I am more determined than ever to learn the language so I can speak to them friend to friend.

A servant of the Lord,
Brother George Cannon

Note

- Nalimanui, whose name means "big hands," was instrumental in helping the early missionaries in Lahaina, Maui. From her hands came food and shelter, and from her heart the true meaning of aloha.

CHAPTER 8

Kula, Maui

February 12, 1851

Jonathan admired Kitty's beauty as she rode sidesaddle on her elegant black mare. In her English riding dress, Jonathan could easily imagine his wife riding in London, or down the streets of Edinburgh. Her father, the Scotsman, had often promised to take his family back to his homeland, but the years passed and the plans were never realized. Knowing John Richardson, Jonathan figured that the moors of Scotland no longer held any allure for him, and that he was content ruling his own little Polynesian kingdom, where he and his family were highly regarded.

Kitty's hair was woven into a thick braid down her back, and on her head sat a stylish straw hat festooned with maile leaves and lehua flowers. Jonathan studied her profile and saw that a healthy glow had returned to her skin. Perhaps the pall of sadness that diminished her spirit and body was slowly relinquishing its sullen grasp. Kitty turned her head to smile at him, and Jonathan felt brightness fill his heart. Suddenly the day of hard work did not seem so tedious.

They had started early from their house in Wailuku, riding to check on the newly planted potatoes at the farm in Pulehu. They would meet with Akuna Pake, the farm manager, walk the fields, and share a scant meal. They would also deliver the foodstuffs to Akuna and his wife, Honua. It was something he and Kitty did twice a month, and Jonathan knew the couple looked forward to the stores of kalo, fruit, vegetables, and fish that supplemented their diet of potatoes.

Jonathan looked around at the unique landscape of the Kula region. He had a fondness for the gentle, rolling grasslands that rose to meet the steeper heights of the great mountain Haleakala. He loved the patches of cactus and the groves of eucalyptus trees newly introduced to the islands. He loved the swirling fog that often covered the face of the great mountain. Others might dismiss the rugged land as nonproductive or belittle the drier, cooler temperatures, but Jonathan had always thought that a small house or thatched hale on the mountainside, where he could escape the world, was a worthwhile dream.

"You look content."

Jonathan gave his wife a crooked grin. "You know me."

"I do." She laughed. "And, I know that with every mile we travel up the sacred mountain, your heart feels lighter."

"I suppose I love the simple way of life here."

Kitty looked around. "I could live here."

Jonathan was shocked. "You could?"

Kitty laughed again. "For one day. Then I would miss my house and my friends."

"Ah, yes. Your influential friends."

"Do not make fun of my friends," Kitty said, good-naturedly. "They provide a lot of service to the community."

"Not to mention a lot of business to the merchants."

"Jonathan!"

"I am only teasing you." He gave her a wink. "It is good to hear you laugh."

Kitty was not inclined to let the conversation go. "Besides, as your wife I have a position to uphold."

"We are only little fish in the big Moloka'i fish ponds, my Keliikuaaina."

"Huh! *You* may be a little fish, but *I* am a shark!" She put her hand on the top of her hat and shouted her horse to a gallop.

Jonathan laughed loudly and rode fast to catch up.

Kitty reached the small farmhouse just seconds before Jonathan, and both were laughing when Honua scrambled out onto the front porch. The poor woman was flustered by the abrupt arrival of the honored couple and unsure how to handle their disorderly behavior.

"I . . . well . . . yes. Here you are."

Kitty took on a more dignified demeanor. "Yes, Honua, here we are. Sorry to have startled you."

Jonathan could tell that Honua was calmed by Kitty's soothing and elegant tone, but he could also tell that the woman was painfully aware of her casual speech and appearance that contrasted starkly with Kitty's precise articulation and impeccable look.

"Aloha, Honua!" Jonathan said, his voice warm and inclusive. "Where is that lazy husband of yours?"

Honua laughed as Jonathan slid from his horse. "Oh, that one? He is probably asleep under a rock somewhere."

Jonathan laughed with her as he helped Kitty down from her horse. "Well, I do not pay him for sleeping."

"If you did, he would be a rich man!"

"Who is lazy?" Akuna Pake asked as he came around the

side of the house. "I work from morning to night." The man was a head shorter than Jonathan, but much broader of shoulder. His face held the wrinkles of much laughter and his eyes the glint of a good storyteller. He went to Jonathan and gave a little bow. "Aloha, Napela. How is your life?"

"My live is good, Akuna Pake. How is your life?"

Pake took Jonathan's hand and shook it heartily. "My life is better now that I see my friend." He turned to Kitty, put his hat over his heart, and bowed deeply. "It is always an honor to have you at our humble home."

Kitty smiled. "You say that to me every time we visit."

Akuna Pake straightened and put his hat on his head. "That is because it is true every time."

Jonathan thumped Pake on the shoulder. "Well, I say we get these goods unloaded, and then to work!"

"Right! No good being lazy!"

The rest of the afternoon the men walked the field of fledgling potato plants as Honua attended to household chores and Kitty went over the farm accounts. They ate a simple meal together under the small kou tree. Honua was, as always, apologetic for the sparse meal and chipped plates. Jonathan and Kitty left soon after supper ended.

"Perhaps I will not come with you the next time," Kitty said as they rode home in the early evening.

"Why do you say that?"

Kitty adjusted her leather riding glove. "Well, I always seem to make Honua so nervous."

"That is just Honua's nature. She is either grumpy or nervous."

"Jonathan."

"It's true! Besides, I love the long ride home together in the twilight. You would not deny me that pleasure, would you?"

Kitty smiled. "Of course not."

They rode along in silence, listening to the evening choir of birdsong and watching the sun set into a ginger mist at the edge of the western world.

"I am glad you are here with me kuʻuipo." *Sweetheart.* "There is something I wish to share with you and now is the right time."

"What is it, Jonathan?"

"We have both been walking in sadness since our little Kapo walked the rainbow."

Kitty glanced at him and nodded.

"Remember I promised you that I would pray until an answer came to me?"

She pulled her horse to a stop and looked at him directly. "And has an answer come?"

He stopped beside her. "I have had a dream. He hoʻike na ka po." *A revelation of the night.*

"Tell me."

"I was standing at the edge of a large field. It was so large that I could not see the end of it. In all the large field there was not a bush or a tree. There was not a breath of wind, and yet I thought I heard voices whispering. I could not understand what they were saying. My mind thought of Enocha and Kapo, and I asked them to tell me where they were so we would not be so sad." Jonathan reached over and brushed a tear off Kitty's cheek. "I looked to my side, and a young man in white clothing stood next to me. He spoke to me, and he taught me many wonderful things."

"What did he teach you?"

"I don't know. In the dream I did not hear the words, but my heart knew that they were good words—true words."

Kitty sat pondering. "It is a deep dream, but it does not tell us about our babies."

"No, but the dream brought me great peace. It made me feel as though there are answers to our questions."

"But, where are we to look for these answers, Jonathan?"

He grinned. "I do not think we need to look, my dear Keliikuaaina. I think the answers will come to us."

CHAPTER 9

Lahaina, Maui

March 1, 1851

My dear sister Mary,

I know it has been several months since my last letter. We have been busy studying the language, and I have been unwell with stomach problems. When my Hawaiian teachers found out, they made me some arrowroot, or pia, as they call it. They mix it with water and it is very starchy, but I felt better after taking it. My teachers tell me not to worry so much, but I don't feel the work is progressing. I know there are good people waiting for the message of the gospel. There have also been many changes in the mission. Brothers Whittle, Dixon, Blackwell, and Farrer have decided to go home. I am surprised at this as we have only been here three months. I am as anxious to go home as anyone, but I feel that my priesthood and calling have to be magnified and that if I leave the Lord will hold me accountable for not doing my duty to this people. These brethren were all discouraged with how few whites there are on the islands to teach, and they did not think of teaching the Hawaiians. Brother Dixon said that it would take more than a year to learn the language. Perhaps he did not wish to try. My desire to learn to speak is very strong. It is present with me night and day, and I try and talk with the natives often to improve it.

 I will tell you, dear sister, of a gift I received from the Lord. I think it will be a good lesson for the children. For weeks I had tried to exercise faith to obtain the gift of understanding the language. One evening, while sitting on the mats conversing with some neighbors who had dropped in, I felt an uncommonly great desire to understand what they said. All at once I felt a peculiar sensation in my ears. I jumped to my feet, with my hands at the sides of my head, and exclaimed to Elders Bigler and Keeler who sat at the table, that I believed I had received the gift of interpretation! And it was so. From that time forward I have had but little, if any, difficulty in understanding what the people say. I might not be able to separate every word they speak from every other word in the sentence, but I can tell the general meaning of the whole. I feel this will be a great aid to me in learning to speak the language. I am very thankful for this gift from the Lord. So, my dear Ann, Angus, David Henry, and Leonora, I want you to know that you can trust in the Lord to answer your prayers.

 I convinced William Farrer not to go home and he has since been sent here to work with Brother Bigler, Brother Keeler, and myself. I am glad, because he is a good friend and we are close in age. And, besides that, he can make me laugh, which is no little thing.

A few weeks ago, our mission president told us he received the prompting to go to the Marquesas Islands and wanted us to leave our mission on Maui and go with him. A dark cloud hung over us while we were deciding what to do. I tell you, dear Mary, I did not want to go against the president's wishes, but each time I prayed, the Spirit whispered to me that there was a good work to be done on Maui. Finally, President Clark wrote from Honolulu and said that we need not attend him, but that he would go with Brother Morris and investigate the possibilities. The dark cloud left us after that.

I apologize that this letter is long, but there was much to tell; besides, the writing connects me to you, and I miss you. It will soon be planting season in the Valley. I hope that your and Charles's efforts are successful. Here we grow food all year long. Normally the weather is warm and muggy, but for the past week it has been blustery and rainy and has even seemed chilly.

I pray you and the family are well. Please give my love to Uncle John and Aunt Leonora. How is the Church faring? We are trying, here in the Sandwich Islands, to build the kingdom.

Your loving brother,
George

CHAPTER 10

Lahaina, Maui

March 2, 1851

William Farrer stood at the side of the hut, watching George weed the garden. Actually George seemed to be doing more standing and staring at the mountains, than hoeing. William had a hoe in hand and had set out to help, but when he saw George's obvious concentration, he felt odd at intruding. He jumped slightly when Brother Keeler came to stand beside him.

"He's still there, I see."

William nodded. "Yep. Still there. Still staring at the mountains. Is he praying?"

"I would imagine so, or pondering."

"One thing's for sure. He's not getting much weeding done."

Brother Keeler chuckled. "And you, Brother Farrer, how are you liking Maui?"

"I like it. There is a strong spirit of the work here."

"Indeed. And much of that spirit is because Brother Cannon spends a lot of time standing in the garden and staring at the mountains."

At that moment George turned to look in their direction. William waved sheepishly and held up his hoe. "I was coming to help!" he called.

"Well, come ahead!" George called back. "The field is white and brown, all ready to harvest. And you, Brother Keeler, would you fetch Brother Bigler? There is something I'd like to discuss with the three of you."

"Of course, Brother Cannon. We'll be right there!" In an aside to Brother Farrer, he whispered. "It seems something has come from his staring at the mountains." He turned to go into the hut, and Brother Farrer headed out to his friend.

"Aloha," George said as William approached. "It's a perfect day for garden work. The sun is out, but the rain has cooled things down. It is very pleasant."

William began hoeing. "It rained all the time on Kauai, well, a lot of the time, but it was beautiful. You've never seen such vegetation, George. So green and lush. It's dry here in comparison."

George nodded. "Well, this is the dry side of the island. I've been told over on the northeast side by the towns of Keanae and Hana, the vegetation is very dense."

"Perhaps we'll get over there someday."

George smiled. "I think we will. I think we will see much of this island."

William continued working. He hummed a hymn, and George sensed that his friend was glad he had not gone back to the Salt Lake Valley with the other Elders.

William stopped by the kalo patch. "I see you're growing kalo."

"Of course. No self-respecting Hawaiian garden would be without it."

"Do you eat it?"

George gave his friend a half grin and shook his head. "No, we give all the kalo to Nalimanui and her family. They make it into poi."

"Poi is one of the staples on Kauai too," William said. "Have you ever eaten it?"

"I have."

"What did you think of it?"

George looked around to see if the other missionaries were nearby. Not seeing them, he stepped closer to William and spoke in a low voice. "When Keala first offered me the calabash bowl that contained the poi, it smelled like a bookbinder's old, sour paste-pot." William stifled a laugh as George continued. "Then I put my fingers in and scooped up a glob of the purple paste, like I'd seen the Hawaiians do, and stuck it in my mouth."

"Oh no," William said, wide-eyed.

"Oh, yes. I put it in my mouth and gagged at it. I had to spit it out, because I knew I would have vomited if I'd swallowed it."

"I reacted the same way when I first tasted it. To us it's ghastly, but the Hawaiians love it."

"They do. And the sourer it is, the better they like it." George shook his head. "Keala has been very patient with me on learning the language and the culture, but I think that day when I spit out the poi, he was a bit disappointed." George took out his handkerchief and wiped his forehead. "I've been praying that the Lord might help me get accustomed to the taste so I don't offend them."

William stared at him. "That's a tall order, if you ask me."

Just then they heard the approaching footsteps of Brothers Bigler and Keeler, and both young men turned to greet them.

"So, Brother Cannon, you better have a very good reason

for bringing me away from my studies," Brother Bigler said in a gruff voice.

"It's on that very subject I wish to have a discussion," George answered, trying to put confidence into his voice. He motioned to the shade of a banyan tree. "Let's get out of the sun."

When they were seated under the tree, George asked for Brother Keeler to pray.

When the prayer ended, Brother Farrer piped up. "I bet this has something to do with you staring at the mountains all morning, right?"

George nodded. "It does actually. But first I want to hear from you brethren. How do you think we're doing in learning the language?" There was silence for a time, and then Brother Keeler spoke.

"It's coming slowly, but I think we're all working hard at it. I think you are the best among us, Brother Cannon. You seem to understand everything that's said."

"That has certainly been a blessing, but I still have trouble speaking. Of course, that's always been my problem, no matter what the language."

No one responded to this declaration.

Brother Bigler cleared his throat. "Here's how I look at it. We're studying, we try to communicate with the people in their language whenever we can, and we've fasted and prayed for help. I think maybe we just need to be patient and realize it's going to take some time."

George nodded. "Brother Farrer?"

"I have a long way to go to learn the language, but I do feel the spirit of the work here. I think if we continue to fast and pray—and study," he grinned, "then we will be blessed."

"Well said, Brother Farrer." George looked at each of them

and stood. "Thank you, brethren, for your dedication to the work. As you know, out of the ten missionaries first called to labor here, there are only five of us left—the four of us here on Maui, and stalwart Brother Hawkins on Hawaii. The Spirit has witnessed to me that there is a great work to be done here on Maui among these good people, but we must stay strong in spirit."

The three older missionaries watched him closely, recognizing a confidence not evident before.

George continued, unaware that he was being scrutinized. "And, we *must* master the language." He paused. "I know we are doing the best we can, but I feel I can do better." He began pacing. "I wish to get out among the people, to see how things are in other areas, and to immerse myself in the language." He stopped pacing. "So, I have made up my mind to tramp around the north and east sides of the island until I reach Wailuku."

Brother Bigler leaned forward. "Tramp around the island?"

"Yes."

"By yourself?"

"Yes. That is the essence of the prompting." The tenor of George's voice gained strength. "I feel strongly that the Lord has prepared a people to hear the message of truth."

There was silence. The other three missionaries stared at George and then looked at each other. Finally Brother Bigler spoke, his voice husky with emotion.

"Brothers, I think we have a David among us."

George stood at the edge of yard, anxious to be off. He had planned to set off the day after speaking to the other missionaries, but his prospects had been marred by a heavy rain and fierce winds. He had reluctantly agreed to wait for a less stormy day. The morning of March 4 dawned clear with only small wisps of clouds drifting lazily in a blue sky. George woke before the sun, said his prayers, and then hastily packed shirt, stockings, garment, and books in the valise Brother Bigler was letting him borrow. He then ate two bananas and slipped out into the morning stillness. He planned to be on his way without fanfare, but it seemed that Pau was acting as a lookout, and she had called to her husband. Now George was surrounded by his missionary companions, Nalimanui, Pau, Keala, Hoohuli, and Hoohuli's husband, the Spaniard. They were all talking at once with no attempt at any real communication. Finally Brother Bigler raised his arm and, in a booming voice, called for quiet.

"Now, I know we all want to send Brother Cannon off with our best wishes, but perhaps we could do it one at a time."

Keala spoke up. "We do not want to send best wishes."

Brother Bigler was surprised by this comment. "No?"

"No. It is very wet now. It will rain almost every day."

Pau joined in. "It is not a good time for traveling."

Hawaiian words came quickly from Nalimanui, and the word keiki was spoken several times.

Pau turned to Brother Cannon. "My mother says—"

George smiled. "Yes, I understood her. She says it is a difficult journey for a child to undertake. A child should listen to words of wisdom from those older." George thought about the trials he had already passed through in his young life: the loss of his parents, the loss of his home, the miles he had walked on the long and barren trek from Nauvoo to the Salt Lake Valley. He looked at the dear woman with tenderness and then he looked to Pau. "Please tell her that the Lord has asked me to go, and that He will watch over me. I must do what the Lord asks me to do."

Belonging to HEAVEN

Pau translated, and Nalimanui's eyes filled with tears. Finally she reached out and handed him some mountain apples. She nodded and tried to smile, but her face was lined with worry.

George nodded back, putting the fruit in his satchel. "Mahalo, dear mother." He looked at each member of the group. "And now I really must be on my way."

"Brother Keeler and I are going to walk with you a ways," Brother Farrer said quickly. "If that's all right with you?"

George beamed. "Yes, I'd like that!" He turned to Brother Bigler. "Try and keep these two in line while I'm gone, will you?"

"I won't give them a moment's rest." He took George's hand. "Be safe."

George felt a sudden reluctance to leave his familiar surroundings, and his contrived bravery gave way to doubt. He stoically pushed the feeling aside, and gave Brother Bigler's hand one last earnest shake. "Aloha." He turned and started off down the track, Brother Keeler and Brother Farrer by his side.

The three walked together for several miles, talking on many varied subjects: how the work was progressing on Maui, how the Saints were faring in the Salt Lake Valley, memories of the trek west, the horrific ocean crossing, and the beauty of the islands. George stopped to take a drink of water, knowing that it was time for them to part company.

"Brethren, I will be grateful for your prayers."

Brother Keeler gripped his arm. "Of course, Brother Cannon." He hesitated to get control of his emotions. "I knew you were the man with whom I was to work."

"You have been a great support to me, Brother Keeler. Mahalo."

Brother Farrer grinned at him. "Do you have your clean shirt?"

George smiled back. "Yes."

"Clean socks?"

"Yes."

"Map?"

"Yes, the one Reverend Taylor gave me."

William stuck out his hand. "Well, spit spot. Off you go then, and don't get lost."

George took his friend's hand. "It's an island, William. If I just keep walking, sooner or later, I will end up where I started."

William laughed. "Make it sooner then, will you?"

George nodded and turned toward the north. He glanced back once and found that his companions were still watching him. He waved and they waved back. He walked off down the track, swinging his borrowed valise, and feeling like a knight going off on a quest.

Notes

- In December 1900, when George Q. Cannon returned to the Hawaiian Islands for the fiftieth anniversary of the arrival of the first missionaries, one of the first things he did was to seek out the place in Lahaina, Maui, where Nalimanui offered them shelter and food. He later wrote:

  "I wanted to find the site of this house and the garden where I sought the Lord in secret prayer and where He condescended to commune with me, for I heard His voice more than once as one man speaks with another, encouraging me and showing me the work that should be done among this people if I would follow the dictates of His Spirit. Glory to God in the highest that He has permitted me to live to behold the fulfillment of His words."

- Because of prevailing winds and rainfall of the Hawaiian Island chain, the leeward or southwest side of the islands tends to be dry, while the windward or northeast side tends to be wet.

CHAPTER 11

Waihee, Maui

March 7, 1851

Dear Mary,

    For three days I have been tramping around the north and east parts of the island, and I tell you I have experienced singular things. When I went past the area of Napili, I saw a huge whale come out of the sea and crash down on its side. Sprays of white water shot up around it, perhaps twenty feet into the air. It was the largest animal I have ever seen. We have viewed images of whales in books, Mary, but to see the great beast with my own eyes was a wonder. Across the channel to the northwest I viewed the island of Moloka'i. It seemed a mysterious place with dark rainclouds covering the tops of its towering green cliffs. I find myself wondering what the ancients must have felt when they viewed these islands for the first time. I have learned the Hawaiian word for cliff. It is pali.

    There has been rain nearly every day or at least a portion of the day. This part of the island is covered by mountains and thickly forested valleys. In the valleys are a few huts. The people are very curious when they see me, and they gather around and wonder what a haole is doing out among them. They are friendly to me, especially when they find I can speak a bit of their language. They are surprised that someone so young should be attempting such a journey. They all call me keiki, which means child, and they want to take care of me. They carry my suitcase for me and haul me across streams. At night when I reach a group of houses I ask the villagers if there is a man who has a place for me. That tells them I need somewhere to stay, and I have been successful in finding a place every night. I talk with the people and try to tell them the first principles of the gospel, but I find that I will require considerable improvement before I am able to explain much doctrine to them. I had a dream a few months ago where I was out among the native Hawaiian people and we were talking together. That dream is now real for me, my dear Mary, and even though I still have trouble speaking, I understand more and more of what they say.

George put down his pen and went to the door of the hut to look out at the alluring and remarkable world. Earlier in the day the clouds had swirled down the mountains to fill the narrow valley with white mist. The trees had become shadowy outlines, and birdsong came eerily to the ear as though from a long distance away. Now, a heavy rain beat on the shrubbery with such intensity that the leaves of a nearby plant lay flat on the muddy red earth, and rivulets of water made small gorges in the ground around the hut. George closed his eyes and breathed deeply, the smell of wet soil and vegetation filling his senses. He knew that years later he would remember that smell and it would bring him back to this very time and place. He looked across the yard to another hut, blurred by the rainfall and the late afternoon gloaming, where his host, Mika, was spending the day with his brother's family. George had sat up late the night before, conversing with them in broken Hawaiian about the gospel. He had gone to bed displeased with his feeble attempts, but just before sleep took him, he'd overheard the family talking about him in a favorable manner. George smiled at the thought and closed his eyes again, listening to the drumming of the rain on the broad leaves.

Thank you, Father, for this beautiful part of your vineyard and for the privilege I have of meeting your sons and daughters on this island. I know you have prepared someone to receive the truth, and though I have never seen them in the flesh, I know that when I meet them they will not be a stranger to me. I have tried to be aware of any prompting from the Spirit, but I don't think I have found them yet. I will keep looking. He opened his eyes. *I will keep looking.*

He turned from the doorway and went back to finish his letter.

Before closing this letter, Mary, I want to tell you about a great blessing I have received from the Lord. It is something that I have been praying about for a long time. I have told you about poi and my inability to even smell it without gagging. It is a staple food in the diet of the Hawaiian people and in their generosity, whenever one eats at their table they always offer poi. Often there is little else for them to give. I have wanted to be able to eat this food so I won't offend them with refusal. The second night I was on this trek, I stopped at a house and they offered to feed me. They offered me poi and it smelled very sour when the calabash bowl came to me. I said a prayer and asked the Lord to make it sweet to me. My prayer was heard and answered. I ate a bowlful, and I positively liked it. It has been sweet to me ever since. I find it a marvel that the Lord is aware of such a small thing.

Depending on the weather, I will try to make it into Wailuku today. There is a town there, and it will seem somewhat like the end of my trek. I have learned much on this journey, but I also know there is much still to do to magnify my calling.

Love to Ann, Angus, David Henry, and Leonora. The best to Charles. I will post this when I return to Lahaina, which should be a week or two. Perhaps I will have other letters to send you at that time. Thank you for your letters, they bring me close to you.

Love,
Your brother, George

George was roused from sleep the next morning by Mika's two nephews. They stood outside the hut and threw pebbles through the open doorway at George's sleeping form. At first he thought he was dreaming of the rain coming through the thatch of the hale and pattering on his head, but then an oversized pebble grazed his nose and he sat up abruptly, shaking himself awake. His vision cleared just in time to see the youngest lad lift his hand to launch another rock.

"Kolohe pua 'a maiki!" he yelled at them playfully, and they squealed and ran away.

Mika came into the hale, chuckling. "Good morning, George Cannon."

It was difficult for him to say George's name, and George smiled at the attempt. "Good morning, Mika."

Mika was a man over six feet tall, with broad shoulders and long dark hair, which he tied back with a braided strip of kapa. He had a wide smile and very white teeth. His voice was low and rumbling like distant thunder. His character was affable, and George felt completely calm in his presence.

"You are right to call those boys naughty little pigs. They have been into trouble all morning. They are happy and full of mischief because there will be sun later today."

George thought carefully about how to say the words. "There will be sun today?"

Mika smiled at him and handed him some dried octopus and poi for breakfast. "Yes, sun. But we are not happy, because that means you will be leaving us."

"Leaving?" George tried to find the reply. He nodded. "Yes. Sun today. I will go. I will go to Wailuku."

"And I will go with you part of the way. I will carry you across the streams, and I will carry your bag."

George stood quickly to mask his emotion. He had just met the man the night before but was aware immediately of his temperate manner. He figured that Mika was in his thirties, but his spirit was that of a child. George discerned that the man's heart was filled with kindness, and his open expression spoke of acceptance and a lack of guile that George had never seen in another human being.

George headed for the doorway. "I need to go out."

Mika laughed. "Of course, it is morning. Go out and add your water to the rain."

It was late in the afternoon when the two unlikely traveling companions descended into the deep gorge and came upon the fourth stream of their journey. George sat down on a rock and took out his canteen. He looked at the bottoms of his light-colored suit pants and saw that they were permanently stained with the reddish mud of the island. He looked over at Mika. How much more sensible was his outfit: no shoes, a kapa skirt, and a shirt given to him by the Protestant missionaries.

"Mika?"

"Yes, George Cannon."

"You spoke little last night. I want to hear your story. You said you believed in Jesus?"

"Oh, yes. My mother was one of the first to join the Christian church when the missionaries came. When she was a young woman she was taken into the house of a sailor in Lahaina . . ." He looked George straight in the face. "You understand this?"

George nodded.

"When the missionaries found her, she was nearly dead with drinking and from the beatings of the man she stayed with. The missionaries taught her of Jesus, and Jesus saved her. She walked away from Lahaina. She walked and walked until she came to our village and met my father." He smiled that guileless smile. "And then she stopped walking. You understand?"

"I understand all the words."

Mika drank water from the stream. "You are very smart,

George Cannon, to know so many of our words in such a short time."

"The Lord has helped me." George stood. "But, I'm afraid my ears are smart, but my mouth is not so smart."

Mika laughed. "My ears or my mouth are not smart to speak the English."

George smiled, and watched a small black and white bird flit down to the stream for a drink. "And your mother, Mika, where is your mother now?"

"She has walked the rainbow, George Cannon. She and my father both."

George was puzzled. He thought he understood the words but not the meaning. "What does that mean, Mika?"

The man came and sat beside him. "When you leave this world, you walk the rainbow to the next—to the land of spirits."

George felt warmth flood his body as the Spirit testified of the truth inherent in that beautiful image. "I know that is true, Mika." He felt the power of testimony enter his heart. "My mother and father have also walked the rainbow." Tears fell. "This gospel of Jesus that I teach, it shows how we can be a family together when we have walked the rainbow. All of God's children. Ohana. One family."

Mika laid his hand on George's shoulder. "Those are good words. I promise to think much about what you have taught, and when you come again to see us, I will ask many questions." He stood and looked to the western mountain and the gathering of dark clouds. "Very soon the sun will hide behind the mountain and drop into the water, and the rain will come again. You must be on your way and I on mine." He took George's suitcase and hunched down to the ground. "Come, I will carry you across one more stream." George climbed onto his back, and the big Hawaiian man stepped down into the rain-swollen current.

George felt lonely at the parting. *When you come again to see us,* Mika had said. He wanted those words to be true, but wondered whether circumstance would comply. "Thank you for food and a place to stay," George said in halting utterance.

"Thank you for the words about Jesus. We find you very brave to take a dangerous journey to bring us your words."

"And I find you good."

Mika grinned. "Now go and be well, George Cannon."

George nodded. As a distant growl of thunder broke over the pali, he picked up his valise and turned down the path toward Wailuku. He knew that rain and darkness would come long before he reached his destination, but he did not fear. He heard the mellow voice of Mika chanting an oli of parting, and his heart felt strong, filled with the mana of water and sky and friendship.

NOTE

- The reference to George Q. Cannon's dislike for poi and the subsequent miracle of it being made sweet to him were actual happenings recorded in his journal.

CHAPTER 12

Wailuku, Maui

March 8, 1851

George awoke, not to the sound of rain, but the crow of a rooster. A cool breeze blew in through the open window, and he lay awake with his eyes closed, listening to the sound of palm branches clattering in the light wind and chickens clucking in the yard. He hardly remembered where he'd finally stopped for the night, knocking at the door of a house on the outskirts of the town and praying for a hospitable host. The old woman and her daughter had brought him in, given him bread, and then gone to a neighbor's to sleep. At least that's where he thought they said they were going. He'd been too exhausted to make sense of it. He barely remembered laying his head on the pillow and pulling a quilt up over his shoulders.

George ran his fingers over the hand stitching and opened his eyes to see the intricate Hawaiian pattern worked into the soft cotton fabric. For a moment he was back in Nauvoo, watching Mary place one of his mother's quilts over Ann and Leonora as they snuggled into the carved hickory bed his father had made them. Loneliness and loss caught in George's heart. *Left behind*. All of those things had been left behind: the hickory bed, the family, his mother and father. He took a deep breath to stop the tears and asked the Lord to comfort him. The pain lessened, and a feeling of calm replaced the loneliness. George rubbed his face and stretched. He winced at the soreness in his muscles and berated himself for not stopping at one of the houses in the small village of Waiehu, instead of pressing on to Wailuku. He had walked in the darkness and rain, stumbling in exhaustion over slick stones and tree roots that snarled the path.

George stood and looked down at his disheveled appearance. *What would your mother think of you now, George Cannon?* He vowed, if the sun were out, to find a hidden bathing area in a stream and give himself and his clothing a good scrub.

Since the sun had not quite risen, and no one was about, George left a coin on the table and snuck out into the still morning. He set off along the track that led into the town of Wailuku, trying to find cheer in the fact that it was not raining. But even with the promise of a clear sky and the delightful smell of flowers on the breeze, George was unable to shake off a feeling of melancholy.

"I'm just tired," he mumbled to himself. "It's been a tiring journey."

After fifteen minutes, George came to a stream, and the track ended. He sat down in the grass and retrieved the map from his valise. He looked up to the deep cleft in the high mountains, and then back to his map. His finger traced along the coastline and up into the mountain. "Iao Valley. Wailuku Stream." He put the map back into the valise and evaluated the stream. With all the rain of the past week, the Wailuku Stream looked more like the Wailuku River. "And no Mika to help me in crossing," George mumbled again. He peeled off his shoes and socks and crammed them into the valise. He held his valise in his right hand and balanced his satchel on the other side. He studied the water once more, hoping that he'd chosen the best crossing point. He stepped into the stream. The chill of the water made him catch his breath, and he momentarily lost his footing. He righted himself and pushed forward. When the water reached past his knees, the current came with greater force, and George found it nearly impossible to keep his balance. He swung his arm back and heaved Brother Bigler's valise to the opposite shore. He gave an inward cheer when the suitcase rolled and tumbled onto the grass, but his celebration was short-lived. The next moment his feet went out from under him, and he hit the water—hard. Head under, body writhing, George scrambled to get his footing and stand, but the current kept pushing him downstream. He was not a great swimmer, and he was not prepared for the coldness of the water. He struggled toward a calmer bit of water and got his feet under him. He steadied himself and pushed through to the shallow eddies, until he could grasp some tree roots and haul himself onto the shore. He lay on the grass for a long time, catching his breath, and vowing that his journey was over. He would not stop in Wailuku as planned, but head directly back to Lahaina. He was done. He was tired and sore. He wanted only to be back at his little hut with his missionary companions to cheer him. A shadow fell across his face. George jerked to a sitting position and found a grinning Hawaiian boy standing there holding his suitcase.

"I speak little bit some English. You speak English?"

"Yes. I speak English."

"Where you been?"

George didn't want to try and explain his entire journey so he just said, "Waihee."

"How come?"

"I've been walking about. I'm a missionary."

"We have plenty missionaries here!"

George stood, ringing water from the bottom of his suit coat and squeezing water from his hair. "Yes, I know. I want to meet some of them."

The boy's eyes widened as he took in George's appearance. "Like that? Why you wet? You want for to go swim?"

"No. I fell down."

The boy laughed. "You pretty bad swimmer. But you good throw bag."

"Thank you." George took off his suit coat and twisted it. "You saw that, did you?"

The boy nodded. "What name, you?"

"My name?" George asked. The boy nodded enthusiastically. "George. What's your name?"

"David Alama Curtis."

George looked at him straight on. "I have a brother named David. David Henry."

"Good name."

"Yes, a very good name."

"You hungry? You come my house for eat. My mother cooks ono. Where you go?"

"I'm going to Lahaina."

"Oh, very long walk. You eat first."

"Yes, mahalo. I would like that."

David brightened. "You speak some my talk."

"A little."

"I teach more. My mother just marry British man. He teach me talk English. I teach you talk Hawaiian." George nodded and reached for his valise, but David pulled it back. "Oh, no,

George. I carry." With that he took off for the town, pointing at things, and calling out their Hawaiian names. George followed, barefooted and smiling. He was familiar with most of the objects, but was so enchanted by his young teacher that he did not interrupt him.

It was the best breakfast George had eaten in years. There were oranges, bananas, sweet muffins, and butter. There was bacon and coconut pudding. He kept thanking her, and Mrs. Curtis kept smiling and putting food in front of him. David's mother was a lovely Hawaiian woman who had learned to cook many of her British husband's favorite foods mixed with island flavors. Mr. Curtis worked for a British trade company and was ready with a strong opinion on commerce, agriculture, and the Christian faith. He would not give pause to hear George preach of a book other than the Bible, and he kept making loud oaths about false prophets and being aware of wolves in sheep's clothing. He was so fixed in his opinion that George finally changed the subject and talked about Liverpool. The conversation went well after that, with the two men talking about memories of home. When it was time for George to leave, Mrs. Curtis put food into a cloth bag and insisted he take it.

"Mother says you are too thin," David announced, pressing the bag into his hands.

George had understood those words. He smiled and thanked her sincerely for the food. When he went to the door, David went with him.

"You go see other missionaries. You talk Bible with them."

George smiled. "They may have the same thoughts about my doctrine as your father."

David didn't quite catch the meaning of these words. "They missionaries from America. They like hear your stories." He pointed to the road leading up toward the Iao Valley. "Just up there past the church. Pretty white house."

George picked up his valise. "I will think about it. Thank you, David, for helping me." He moved down the path to the road

"You learn swim better," the boy called after him.

George chuckled. "I will." Just then David's mother called him.

"Oh, I must go work. Aloha, missionary George."

"Aloha, David." George went out to the road and hesitated. He looked up toward the mountains and said a prayer. He opened his eyes and began walking toward the Iao Valley.

I will just go see the house. If anyone is outside, then maybe I'll call to them. If they come to talk, I will just ask a few questions. If they ask me questions, I will tell them . . . what? Young as I am and in such an awful state, they'd never take me seriously.

He passed the stone church on his left and kept walking, his stomach churning against the big breakfast.

The gospel will speak for itself. The first principles and ordinances . . . priesthood authority . . . perhaps they won't want to hear about priesthood authority. I'll just spend time visiting. I'll let them tell me what they've learned about the island and the people. I can tell them how I admire the Hawaiian alphabet and their translation of the Bible into the Hawaiian language.

George was so caught up in his thoughts that he almost walked past the white house. He moved toward it, admiring the well-kept yard and the basic structure of the lovely home. It was two stories with a veranda and an upstairs balcony, all painted a gleaming white with green shutters and green vines curling along the balcony railing. George imagined upholstered chairs, hardwood tables, and china dishes inside. He put his hand on the gate and stopped. An image of his scruffy beard, unkempt hair, and rumpled clothing came into his mind, and he lost his confidence. He stepped back.

I can't go to meet the reverend now. He is probably a well-kept gentleman, and his lady will be finely dressed and mannered.

A dark feeling invaded George's thoughts, assuring him that he was nothing more than a country yokel whose grasp of doctrinal truths was infantile at best. He turned away from the house and hurried off down the road. As he walked, he passed several lovely homes on his left and saw movement in one of the yards.

George glanced over to see two Hawaiian women, dressed in fine British clothing, watching him with keen interest. He thought he heard one of them call him keiki, and the words never seemed truer. He kept walking. He reached the road that headed back toward the west and Lahaina and heaved a sigh of relief. He'd scarcely put one foot in the direction of Lahaina when the Spirit told him to stop and go back into town. He stopped, but he argued with the prompting. He did not want to go back, and he felt the ache of tears in his throat. He put forth a myriad of noble excuses: his ineptitude, his tiredness, his ragged appearance. He pointed out that the soles of his shoes were wearing thin and that his stomach hurt.

Finally, when the prompting persisted, George stopped his murmuring, squared his shoulders, turned around, and went back. He came to the crossroads and stood staring at the impressive Ka'ahumanu church. Fatigue and doubt overwhelmed him, and it took his last bit of fortitude to turn up the road and trudge toward the white house. He heard the Hawaiian women in the yard across the street calling out to someone in the house.

"E ka haole! E ka haole!" *Oh, the white man!* "Jonathan! Jonathan! E ka haole!"

George walked more quickly. He did not know why they were calling out in such a strange manner. He was sure they met whites frequently and it was nothing unusual for one such as himself to pass by. George wondered if he had offended them in some way. He put his head down and kept walking. He glanced over to see three Hawaiian men coming from the house and moving quickly to the gate. *Dear Father, help me,* George prayed silently. He looked tentatively into the face of the man in front, who was watching him with great interest. "Aloha," he said as he passed.

"Aloha," the man returned. "Where are you going, young man?"

George stopped. In broken Hawaiian he stammered out, "I . . . I am going to see the Protestant missionaries."

The man stepped forward. "Are you a missionary?"

"I am," George said quietly, trying to match the softness and warmth of the Hawaiian's tone. "I am a missionary from The Church of Jesus Christ of Latter-day Saints."

The man's face filled with wonder, and he turned to look at his companions. "E ka haole." He stepped closer to George and extended his hand. "Aloha, friend. I am Jonathan Hawaii Napela. I would like to hear your words."

George took his hand. "You . . . you would?"

Jonathan grinned. "Yes, I think I have been waiting for you."

George sat at the Napelas' kitchen table in borrowed clothes. He was bathed, and clean shaven, and mystified. He looked at the people sitting around the table: Mr. Napela; his cousin, H.K. Kaleohano; his friend, William Uaua; Napela's wife, Catherine; and her sister, Nele Richardson.

The women were the loveliest women George had ever seen. Their light brown eyes sparkled, and their dark wavy hair cascaded to their waists. They wore long skirts and white gauzy blouses with lace collars and pearl buttons. The three men also wore proper British clothing, although at the moment their coats were slung over the backs of their chairs and their collars were unbuttoned.

George looked from face to face, ending at Mr. Napela. George tried not to be intimidated by the fact that this man, who was fourteen years his senior, was also a district court judge and a son of Hawaiian royalty. The only thing that kept George from bolting for the door was the Spirit testifying that this was the man the Lord had prepared to hear the message of the gospel.

In fact, the entire company seemed eager to learn about prophets, modern-day revelation, and the first principles and ordinances of the gospel. George was amazed by their sincere questions and lack of guile as they listened patiently as he faltered to teach them in their language. It was frustrating because he could understand almost every word they said, but when it came time to speak, the words jumbled in his brain. The members of the group also spoke a little English, and they willingly tried to substitute words when George's vocabulary gave out. They seemed to him to be very intelligent, and so it did not surprise him when he discovered that all three of the men had graduated from the Lahainaluna Seminary in Lahaina.

"I know your school," George said. "It is on the hillside above where we live. Were you all planning to become ministers?"

William Uaua shook his head. "It was not theological training we received, though some of the first graduating class did join the ministry. Others became teachers, or government administrators, or judges." He grinned at Jonathan, and then turned back to George. "And you, Mr. Cannon, where did you study to become a preacher?"

George inwardly braced himself for their response to his answer. "I did not go to school to become a preacher. Like those disciples in Christ's day, we who are called on missions, study, pray, and seek for the guidance of the Spirit."

The three men who had been leaning forward, all sat back in their chairs and stared at him. Finally Jonathan spoke.

"You have received no training?"

"No."

"And you are very young."

George pushed back at the fear that was eroding his confidence. "I am young, but I have seen many things. I have experienced many things, and I have a testimony of the doctrine I've been preaching to you."

Jonathan grinned. "I know a thing or two about testimonies." George nodded, and Jonathan leaned forward again. He seemed very much the judge seeking out truth. "You have a testimony of this vision of Joseph Smith?"

"Yes."

"You have a testimony that God is again speaking from heaven?"

"Yes."

"You have a testimony that this message you bring is for us?"

George's eyes filled with tears. "Yes." He fought to steady his voice. "I was told that if I went on this journey, the Lord would prepare someone to hear the message of the gospel. I believe that someone is you."

There was complete silence in the room, and George was again afraid that he had offended them. He wanted to speak and explain, but the Spirit told him to be still and have faith. After what seemed like an eternity, Mr. Napela spoke.

"Mr. Cannon, what did you think when you heard my wife calling out when you passed by our house? E ka haole. Do you know what it means?"

George nodded. "Oh, the white man."

"Did you find that unusual?"

George looked over at Mrs. Napela. "I did, yes."

"Well, Mr. Cannon," Jonathan continued, "just as you were looking for me, I have been waiting for you."

George glanced around at the others in the room to assess their reaction to these words, but there was no indication that each person did not take Mr. Napela's words for the truth.

"Several weeks ago I had a dream where a stranger, dressed in white clothing, was sent to me to deliver an important message. The dream made such an impression that I told my wife and friends."

Catherine Napela spoke softly. "We have spoken of the dream many times, wondering about its meaning." She smiled at him. "When I saw you, the dream came to my mind."

George stood, beaming at his hosts, and wiping the tears from his cheeks with the palms of his hands. For once he felt like the child that everyone saw when they looked at him. "I do have an important message to give you, Mr. Napela—a message that will change your life."

Jonathan smiled at him. "My life has changed many times, Mr. Cannon. I am not afraid of change. But, you must teach us from the scriptures. You must teach us the words of Jesus."

"I would not want you to listen to me if I did not teach from the scriptures, Mr. Napela. We teach the doctrine of the primitive church, and we want you to pray and find out for yourself if the doctrine is true."

Jonathan stood. "As Paul said. Try all things and hold fast to that which is good. Well then, you will stay with us and we will listen, and tomorrow I will take you up to meet the Reverend Daniel Conde and his esteemed wife, Andelucia."

The euphoric feeling drained from George's spirit, and doubt returned to cast a shadow on his hopes. He did not know if he was up to speaking with a Congregationalist minister—a man much older who had gone to school for years to train for his position. George also knew that Reverend Conde would have command of the Hawaiian language, a blessing he longed for, but did not as yet possess.

"Are you all right, Mr. Cannon? The color has drained from your face. Here, sit down," Jonathan ordered and George sat. "Would you rather not stay with us for a time?"

"No . . . no, it's not that," George stammered. "That is a very generous offer. I would be honored." He managed a smile. "I just have one question: will you stay with me when we visit Reverend and Mrs. Conde?"

Jonathan smiled. "Of course, Mr. Cannon. I will keep you in the canoe if you feel there are sharks in the water."

George thought Mr. Napela quite clever for coming up with that image. "Oh, one more thing: I would like it if you called me George instead of Mr. Cannon, if that's all right?"

"Of course, I will call you Brother George and you can call me Brother Jonathan."

George liked the man. He did not know what the future would bring, but for now he was grateful for the guidance of the Spirit that had led him to this home in Wailuku.

Notes

- The incidents of falling in the water and of the meeting of Jonathan Hawaii Napela are recorded in George Q. Cannon's journal.

- Lahainaluna Seminary was a school established by Protestant missionaries with the American Board of Commissioners for Foreign Missions in Lahaina in 1831. It was the first school founded in Hawaii, and many young men from high-ranking Hawaiian families were educated there, including David Malo and Jonathan Napela. Lahainaluna School continues to operate as a coed boarding school. It is the oldest high school on American soil west of the Mississippi.

- Haole meains a fair-skinned person or a foreigner.

CHAPTER 13

Wailuku, Maui

April 12, 1851

"Watch your footing, Brother George!" Jonathan Napela called out. "The pathway has many rocks and tree roots."

George understood the Hawaiian words and called his thanks. He watched his companion maneuver the path with effortless agility, seeming to gain strength from the dirt under his bare feet and grace from the trees that overshadowed the path. George too felt his spirit quickened by the craggy, forested cliffs rising up on either side of the valley.

The Iao Valley was created by water—water that cascaded off the Hamaluka peaks to form rivulets and streams that flowed into two rivers. These courses ran down either side of the valley creating a ridge in the center. Along the spine of this ridge the kanaka and the haole ventured. George felt the draw of discovery pulling him along the winding path, ever deeper into the heart of the mountain. He glanced up at the gray clouds swirling amidst the peaks of the pali, and worried that rain might ruin their hike. He stumbled over a tree root for lack of attention, righted himself, and forged ahead, trying with little success to keep up with Brother Napela's pace. The man was familiar with the track and he was strong. Over the weeks of staying in the Napela's home, George had learned much about Brother Jonathan's strengths: he had a heart filled with childlike joy, a spirit open to faith, and an astute mind ready to evaluate new ideas.

George was also grateful for Brother Jonathan's sagacity. He was a support during the first meeting with Reverend Conde at the Ka'ahumanu church. Napela had introduced him to the reverend after the Sunday services, and George remembered how his stomach churned as he tried to organize his thoughts. The man was polished and intelligent and obviously knew something about the Mormons, for the first thing he questioned was the idea of Joseph Smith digging up another Bible out of the ground. George tried to explain about the Book of Mormon and that the members of the Church did not take the book in place of the Bible, but proved one by the other. He then tried to offer him the missionary tract, "The Voice of Warning," but the reverend refused, and condemned it without reading it. George found himself silenced by the man's disdain, but Brother Napela stood close by him, and, against the reverend's warning, declared that he would listen to what the Mormon missionary had to say. If the preaching went against the Bible, he would reject it; if it did not, he would consider it.

Reverend Conde and others in the church council were not pleased with that pronouncement. George knew it was because Jonathan held a high position in the community. As a district court judge and a descendant of Hawaiian royalty, he was influential, and many would give credence to his choice.

George smiled as he looked at his hiking companion. In his work pants, simple cotton shirt with the sleeves rolled up to the elbow, and bare feet, he did not seem much like a judge or the son of a chief. George shook his head. They made quite a pair—he with his fair skin, pale blue eyes, and sandy colored hair, and Jonathan with his brown skin, brown eyes, and wavy black hair. One was a child of the land; one was hoping for adoption.

A rise brought them momentarily above the trees, and George caught his breath as a shaft of sun shot through the lowering clouds, illuminating the side of the distant mountain. The sunlight exposed deep clefts in the cliff face, where three silver ribbons of water plunged a thousand feet to the base of the pali. There the water was lost in the thick vegetation.

Jonathan came to stand beside him.

"This is heaven," George whispered, the Hawaiian words coming easily.

"Do you think heaven looks like this, Brother George?"

"Oh, I hope so," George said, with such longing that Jonathan laughed.

"Come, let us sit and eat our food, and talk about heaven."

They settled themselves under a koa tree with unobstructed views of the cliffs and the waterfalls. They drank from their canteens and ate the fish and poi wrapped in ti leaves. George peered down into the valley, trying to catch a glimpse of the river running below. All he saw were the light-colored leaves of the kukui trees and the bright red flowers of the lehua.

"It is such a peaceful place," George said in English.

"What is the word *peaceful*?" Jonathan asked.

George tried to think of Hawaiian words that had the same meaning. *Maliʻe*. Calm. *Maʻlu*. Quiet. He relayed these words to Napela who gave him a crooked smile.

"Well, not always calm and quiet. A great battle was fought in this valley."

"Oh, yes?" George said, a note of anticipation in his voice. He loved the stories that Jonathan told, and over their weeks together, he had heard many. Listening helped him increase his Hawaiian vocabulary and learn much about the Hawaiian culture.

Jonathan sat back against the koa tree and began talking, his voice taking on a mellow tone and smooth cadence. "It was called the battle of Kepaniwai and in it, my grandfather, the chief and warrior Kihakaulia, fought bravely. He was a young man, and it is said he could cast a spear through the eye of a boar. The year was 1790 and the great warrior chief, Kamehameha, brought many canoes into the bay of Kahului. The conch shell blew, the drums beat, and the call went out for the warriors of Maui to come and fight for their leader, the high chief Kalanikupule. My grandfather, with a large group of fighters, ran over the mountain from Lahaina. They ran for many hours on this very path until they reached Kukaʻemoku, the great peak of the god Kanaloa."

George closed his eyes and imagined the ferocious warriors running along the path with their wooden spears and stone clubs.

"When my grandfather and his men reached the great peak, Kamehameha's warriors had already pushed the army of Kalanikupule far into the valley. Kamehameha had learned the weapons of the white man and brought muskets and cannon. Many of the warriors of Maui were killed, but many more fought on, their shouts of defiance echoing off the cliffs. In the end Kamehameha was victorious, but there were so many killed on both sides that their bodies clogged the stream. That is why it is called the battle of Kepaniwai—the damming of the waters."

George did not like to imagine that scene. "And your grandfather?"

"He lived. He returned to tell the villagers at Honokawai that now Kamehameha, the warrior chief from Kona, would be the chief over everyone on Maui. And after more battles, Kamehameha would be the aliʻi nui over all the islands."

"And now his grandson is the aliʻi nui."

Jonathan shook his head. "Another of Kamehameha's sons. You must remember that Kamehameha the Great had several wives, Brother George. King Kamehameha III was young when he came to the throne, and he has reigned twenty-five years."

"Do you think there will always be Hawaiian kings and queens?"

"Always? Always is a very long time, my young friend." Jonathan stretched his back. "Change is the only thing you can expect, Brother George. Look at the Hawaiian people. We began with chiefs and the worship of the four gods. We had the kapu system and the chanting of the oli. We had our fierce king, Kamehameha, with his many wives and his sacred heiaus—his temples. Then came his son, Kamehameha II, who did away with the kapu system and ordered the destruction of the heiaus. The world began sailing to our shores, and the word of Christ Jesus came to our ears. We looked to the British for our government and how we dress. We learned to speak the English and to write down our history with letters. Kamehameha III, brother to Kamehameha II, then changes the land divisions, and foreigners begin to look at our paradise home for the raising of crops and the grazing of cattle." Jonathan took a drink from his canteen. He stared at the sky with its billowing clouds and patches of blue sky. He sighed. "My friend, David Malo, who is a great man of letters, says that soon we will not know the islands of our birth."

"Does that make you sad?"

Jonathan looked at him. "Yes, but one cannot go backward, Brother George. I would not want to go back to the kapu system or living without Jesus in my life. Besides, if we were to go back, the Scotsman would not have come, and I would not have my beautiful wife, Kitty." George smiled. "And the Mormons would not have come, and I would not have my friend, George Cannon."

It was a guileless pronouncement, and George felt honored to be called the friend of this good man. "Thank you, Brother Jonathan."

Jonathan smiled and made himself comfortable with his back to the tree. "Now, you need to tell me more about Joseph Smith and the Book of Mormon."

For the next hour, George tried to answer Jonathan's many questions and explain the story of the first vision and the coming forth of the Book of Mormon. Finally his brain and tongue grew tired trying to think of and speak all the Hawaiian words. He lay back on the grassy knoll and clamped his hands around his head.

Jonathan laughed. "I am sorry, Brother George. That was a lot of Hawaiian."

George groaned. "My brain feels like poi."

Jonathan laughed heartily and then sobered. "You honor us to learn our language. It shows respect. I wish more of the newcomers were respectful of the Hawaiian people."

"God loves all his children equally, Brother Jonathan. Can we do less?"

George's eyes were closed so he did not see the look of awe on Jonathan's face. After several minutes where there was only birdsong and the rustle of leaves, Jonathan spoke. "Do you think more Mormon missionaries will come?"

George sat up slowly. "Yes. I think they will."

"And it is difficult to learn our language."

George rubbed his temples. "It is. Most of the missionaries who started this mission have gone home because they could not or would not learn the language. Most of the others who have stayed agree that it will take a year to learn even a little."

Jonathan shook his head. "That is too long." He looked at the distant mountains. "There has to be a way for them to learn more quickly."

George chuckled. "You are not even a member of the Church, Brother Jonathan, and you worry about the missionaries learning the language?"

Jonathan chuckled with him. "Yes. And, I have a great desire to read the Book of Mormon in my language too."

"Now that is a tall order," George said in English.

Jonathan nodded. "I know that English—tall order. My father-in-law, the Scotsman, says that all the time." He stood and slung his canteen over his shoulder. "It is a tall order, but it should be done."

George stood and dusted off his pants. He grinned at Jonathan. "There is much I admire about your people, Brother Jonathan. They have a joyful innocence about them and a simple wisdom and faith." He hesitated, not knowing if he could find the Hawaiian words to make sense of this next thought, but he tried. "Did you know that the Church believes that the Hawaiian people are descendants of the ancient Israelites?"

Jonathan looked surprised. "The ancient Israelites?"

George thought he was going to mock his statement, but a wide grin planted itself on his companion's face.

"That is what my friend, David Malo, thinks!"

Now it was George's turn to be surprised. "Really?"

"Yes, David is a great scholar of the Bible and ancient civilizations, and he says that many of the traditions of Hawaii nei are exactly like the Israelites of the Bible."

George shook his head in wonder. "Well, how about that? I wish I could meet this David Malo."

"I will write you a letter of introduction. He lives at a place called Ukamehame. It is on the way between Lahaina and Wailuku. He is a fine Christian man and I am sure he would be interested in speaking with you."

"I would like that. Does he speak any English?"

"A little." Jonathan smiled at George's look of discomfort. "Do not worry, Brother George, you speak well enough. Soon your brain will not feel like poi when speaking my language." He looked up the trail. "So, do you want to go on or go back?"

George brightened. "I say we go on for a while! And as we go, you can practice your English."

"My English is good."

George smiled at his attempt at the language. "Yes, but your English can be better."

"My English can be better." Jonathan started off down the path. "Now, let us go walking."

George chuckled. "Very good! Our hard work will pay off."

"In Hawaiian."

George took his time, and then said slowly, "Aia ke ola i ka hana."

Jonathan nodded. "Good, Brother George. Good."

Notes

- In the days prior to the coming of Captain Cook, the islands were divided into ahupuaʻa. These tracks of land extended from the summit of the mountains to the reef, and varied in size from 100 acres to over 100,000 acres. On March 8,

1848, Kamehameha III set apart the larger part of the land as government lands, which were intended to produce revenue for the operation of the government. It is referred to as the Great Mahele.

- "The Voice of Warning" was a missionary tract written by Parley P. Pratt in 1837.
- Jonathan Napela began language training sessions in his home with the early LDS missionaries. He would immerse them in the language for two to three months—a timetable used today in the language training centers of the Church.

CHAPTER 14

Wailuku, Maui

April 13, 1851

George awoke to the sound of arguing voices. He lay for a moment trying to clear the sleep from his tired brain, hoping to make out some of the words coming from downstairs. He couldn't decipher what was being said, but he was fairly sure one of the voices was Jonathan's and one was Reverend Conde's. Several women's voices inserted comments, and, whether they were adding to the contention or trying to subdue it, George couldn't tell. He did have a strong impression that he was at the center of the disagreement.

George closed his eyes and thought about the dream he'd had in the night. He'd stood in a place where there were many small stones from the size of an egg and up, and several men were pelting him with these stones, but he wasn't hurt by any of them. George smiled to himself as he remembered returning the assault with hearty good will. He threw very straight, and many of the men were hurt and began to run away. Then the place changed, and he was leading a small company of folks down a muddy descent, as though it had been raining. The dream ended there, but he remembered feeling encouraged.

A few more strident pronouncements jumped up the stairs to George's ears, erasing the dream and its tranquil shelter. He sat up. He had known it would come to this. Over the weeks, Jonathan and Kitty had been assuring him that the opposition to him being a guest in their home was slight and manageable. This did not sound manageable. George slid out of bed and dressed.

When he arrived downstairs, he found that the company had departed and the house was quiet. No one was in the main room, so George went to the kitchen. He found Kitty cutting the rind from a red melon. She turned to him as soon as he entered.

"Good morning, Brother George."

"Good morning, Kitty Napela."

"I am sorry you were woken from your sleep by that horrid noise."

George grinned at her. "I am sorry you had to hear that horrid noise because of me."

Tears jumped into Kitty's eyes. "Jonathan is on the porch. He would like to talk to you. I will have something for you to eat when you are finished."

George nodded and turned away. A cold feeling surrounded him as he moved through the parlor. It was as though the words that had been spoken there had left ill will floating in the air. It was the feeling of mobs and hatred, and it made George shudder. He moved out onto the sunny porch and was grateful for the warmth. It made him feel hopeful. He found Jonathan sitting on the steps and went to sit beside him. The man's face was filled with anger, so George just sat without speaking. Finally Jonathan sighed heavily and laid his hand on George's shoulder.

"I do not understand men," he said. "I wish my father were still with me. I would ask him his thoughts. He would give me a good answer."

George felt a tightening in his throat. "My father too, he could always make sense of things."

Jonathan patted him. "Well, here we are, having to figure this out by ourselves." He took his hand away. "If we were in Oloalu, my wise mother could give us counsel. But, she is getting old and does not like to talk much anymore."

"The Reverend Conde was here to warn you against me and my preaching, wasn't he?"

"Yes. He and his wife. They want us to put you out of our house. They want us to stop listening to your words. They say you do not preach the true doctrine of Christ. They say you preach lies."

George did not answer and the two men sat silent, listening to the call of the orange 'akepa bird in a nearby tree.

Finally George spoke, working hard to keep his tone even. "And what do you say, Brother Jonathan? Have I ever taught you and Kitty, or any of your friends, anything that I did not back up with proof from the Bible?"

"No, Brother George. We love the words you teach us. But that is not the trouble. The council has warned us many times against your preaching, and always I tell them to mind their own business. I am free to listen to what I like and to keep whatever guest I want in my home. But . . ." He hesitated and George waited. "But now they threaten to take away my judgeship."

George was stunned. "What? How . . . how can they do that? Do they have the power to do that?"

"The church holds a great influence in the government, Brother George. And since I received my first training at the Lahainaluna Seminary School, they feel I should give them my loyalty."

George just shook his head as his heart beat against his ribs. "But can they make a case against you for listening to my preaching?"

Jonathan actually smiled. "Oh, they will bring other things against me. They have warned me about my drinking many times. That could be a charge for dismissal."

"But you are trying to stop."

"Yes, Brother George, since you taught us the words of wisdom, I have been trying, but it is not easy. I am aliʻi and grew up drinking the awa at special occasions. And now, it does not help that the merchant ships bring in rum and whisky from around the world."

George could not find the Hawaiian words to express his feelings. He stood and walked out into the yard. Anger and disappointment squeezed his heart into a tight knot. He walked. He walked about the yard, his emotions too intense to allow for the blessed release of tears. *Why, Father? Why would you send me to this wonderful man and his wife only for the work to be frustrated? He will never join the Church. He cannot give up his position and his livelihood. I don't understand. I have been working hard to learn the language. I have been prayerful. I have heard your voice prompting me. I have been led here. Why?* He passed a ginger plant, and the pungent smell of the blossoms stopped him in his tracks. George closed his eyes, as sweet and comforting words swirled into his jumbled thoughts. *My ways are not your ways.*

Wait upon the Lord. Go to Lahaina and check on the mission. Leave things here in my hands. George nodded his head in acquiescence and slowly opened his eyes. When he turned, he saw a group of people standing around Brother Napela: Kaleohano, William Uaua, and several members of Kitty's family. Most of the group was trying not to glance in his direction, but Kitty's younger sister, Nele, was staring right at him with a look of chagrin. *Wonderful. How long have I been walking about, totally unaware of anything but my own worries, and how long have they been observing my strange antics?* George took a breath and tried to put on an air of nonchalance as he approached the house. *Now none of them will want to listen to me, not a madman out stomping about the yard and mumbling to himself.* He attempted a smile, as Kitty's brother, John Richardson, stepped forward and reached out his hand.

"We understand that the Condes were here this morning," he said in English.

George took John's hand and shook it. "News travels fast."

John smiled, but his eyes remained sober. "It is a small community. So, the Condes had something to discuss?"

George looked at Jonathan, knowing that he understood much of the English. "Yes, it seems they are not too fond of me."

"Well, they want to make sure that wolves don't enter the flock."

George swallowed. He wished John's English were not so good. He had always been intimidated by John Richardson. He was a district judge, like Jonathan, but unlike Jonathan, who had a ready smile and sense of humor, John Richardson was cautious and austere. George swallowed again. "And is that what you think of me, Brother John, that I am a wolf?"

A slight smile brushed the edge of John's mouth. "Well,

maybe a fox." He translated to the group what was said between him and George.

Jonathan stepped forward. "He is not a wolf or a fox. He is a young man with a good heart."

"But a good heart can be fooled," John answered in Hawaiian.

George understood every word, and righteous indignation flared in him. "Is that truly what you think of me? That I have been fooled by the man Joseph Smith and his fantastic claims about angels and gold bibles?" John translated the words into Hawaiian, and from the several downturned faces that would no longer meet his gaze, George knew that was exactly what they had been thinking. He clenched his teeth to quell his emotion. He looked directly at John Richardson. "Mr. Richardson, if you would be so kind to translate for me, I would like to say a word or two about my faith." John nodded his acceptance, and George gave him a level look. "I will know if you are giving the right meaning to my words." John's eyes narrowed, but George did not back down. He had to take several deep breaths to bridle his frustration before he could begin. He prayed for the Spirit. "I knew the Prophet Joseph Smith and his brother, Hyrum. They were decent men. They worked hard and gave the thousands of Saints under their care every possible opportunity to prosper and achieve. The gospel, restored to us through the Prophet Joseph, is the same as the primitive church in Christ's day. This you know, because I have taught you from the Bible; everything I have ever taught you from baptism, to priesthood authority, to revelation has come through the Bible."

"Then why do we need another religion or *another* Bible?" William Uaua interjected.

"The scriptures say 'one Lord, one faith, one baptism,' but

which one? Is it the baptism of sprinkling or immersion? Is it the faith of continuing revelation or that the heavens are closed? Are there prophets and apostles in any other church today?"

William stepped back as John completed the translation.

George's voice took on a quiet intensity. "The scriptures say, 'by their fruits ye shall know them.' Well, if you had seen the miserable swampland on the Mississippi that by industry and miracle was turned into the beautiful city of Nauvoo, then you would know the fruits of this Church and its people. If you had stood as I did and watched them bring the bodies of Joseph and Hyrum from Carthage Jail, and had seen the thousands of weeping people, then you would know the love the people had for them." George looked at each of their faces. "You know me. You know my heart. I am not a boaster. I am not a cheat. And I do not bear false witness."

Jonathan and Kitty and several others were weeping.

"What I have told you is true. Please, please, dear friends, do not let the false stories of Reverend Conde turn your hearts. Please, if you value your souls, promise me that you will not reject my words until you can understand them for yourselves."

John Richardson's voice broke as he translated the last of George's words. His face had lost some of its tension, but the tone of his voice was still reproachful and stiff. "I am worried for my sister."

George went and put his hand on the man's arm. "I know, Brother John, and the last thing I want to do is cause trouble for Jonathan and Kitty. Over the weeks they have come to mean much to me. They have been good and generous in letting me stay with them, but now, I feel prompted to travel back to Lahaina. Perhaps if I am gone, things will settle."

Jonathan wiped at his tears. "But I do not want you to go."

"Thank you for that, Brother Jonathan, but this will be a good time for me to check on my missionary companions and report the experiences I've had on my trip around the island." He hesitated. "I will speak favorably of my meeting with all of you." Several more faces took on a cheerless look.

"And will you return, young George?" Kitty asked.

George looked into her beautiful face, and a sharp point of pain went through his heart. "I do not know. We will leave it in God's hands." He turned and went into the house to pack his few belongings in his small valise.

Early the next morning, George stood on the same spot he had the day before, but today he was not preaching but leaving. Kitty handed him bananas to put in his satchel and a canteen full of water. Jonathan handed him a letter of introduction to David Malo.

"He is a fine old fellow. I am sure he will like you very much."

George's words felt like dry paper in his mouth. "Thank you, Brother Jonathan."

"You will come back?"

"We will see what the Lord wants."

Jonathan nodded. "Sometimes I go to Lahaina or Honolulu on court business. I will see you then."

"Yes, I would like that." George felt awkward. After all the weeks of conversation, he did not have words to say to them. "Thank you for your kindness to me. I . . . I will try and get back to see you."

"Yes. We will hike again into the sacred valley."

George felt the pressure of tears in the back of his throat, so he turned and started for the gate. When he reached it, he turned, and waved.

Jonathan and Kitty waved back.

George walked out the gate and down the road. His mind sought out scripture to bring him peace. *"Trust in the Lord with all thine heart, and lean not unto thine own understanding. In all thy ways acknowledge Him and He shall direct thy paths."*

CHAPTER 15

Ukamehame, Maui

April 15, 1851

George walked beside the stately Hawaiian man as he concluded business with the government land surveyor. George listened to the rolling cadence of the language as the meaning came to his mind in English. David Malo was taller and thinner than most Hawaiian men, with a high forehead and a thick shock of hair that he wore combed back. He was in his late fifties, but his carriage was straight and his movements refined. George thought of many a high-ranking man he'd seen on the streets of Liverpool who did not carry themselves half as well as Mr. Malo. His voice was soft and accommodating, putting the surveyor at ease—just as he had George when the two had met and George had handed him the letter of introduction from Brother Napela.

The conference with the surveyor concluded, and Mr. Malo sent the man on his way. He turned to George and smiled. "I apologize, Mr. Cannon. I did not mean to neglect you, but when one has a government worker in hand, one must make use of him."

George grinned. "Of course, I understand. I was the one who came without a meeting time." He hoped he used the correct Hawaiian words that would approximate his meaning.

Mr. Malo nodded. "You are welcome anytime. A friend of Napela's is a friend of mine." He gave George a smile and turned toward his home. "Shall we return to the house and have something to eat?"

"Thank you. That would be good, if it's not too much trouble."

"No trouble at all, Mr. Cannon. My daughter, Aa laioa, who you met when you first arrived, loves to cook for me." He began walking, and George kept pace beside him. "So, how is my friend, the judge in Wailuku?"

"He is doing well, Mr. Malo, except—" George hesitated, debating how much he should say and anxious to find the words to explain the situation fairly.

"Except?"

"I fear I caused trouble for them."

"You do not look like someone who would cause much trouble, Mr. Cannon."

George looked over at the man. "I am a missionary for The Church of Jesus Christ of Latter-day Saints, Mr. Malo. The Protestant missionaries do not take kindly to the doctrine I preach."

"I know your church, Mr. Cannon."

"You do?"

"Yes, the Mormons. You see, I read much. There have been writings in the newspapers. Good words and hateful words about your prophet Joseph Smith." He stopped and evaluated George. "I do not suppose you knew him?"

George felt the Spirit race through his body, causing his eyes to well with tears. "I did, Mr. Malo. I did know him."

"Well, my, my. I would very much like to speak with you, Mr. Cannon. Very much. I always like to get my information firsthand." He began walking again. "Let us have our meal and talk the day away."

George hurried to catch up.

When they reached the house, Mr. Malo made arrangements for Aa laioa to bring the food and drink to a table outside. The spot was shaded by a large banyan tree and overlooked the ocean. She brought roast pork and poi.

"Would you prefer something other than poi?" Mr. Malo asked. "Most haoles do not like it."

George reached to daub some poi from the big bowl into his own calabash cup. "Oh, no thank you, Mr. Malo. I enjoy eating poi." Aa laioa gave him a curious look. "Really, I do." She nodded and turned to leave. "Is she not eating with us?"

"She is going to beat the kapa cloth. Soon you will hear the pleasant sound of the wooden club as it beats upon the log. My daughter makes beautiful kapa."

"Is the kapa cloth used much anymore?" George inquired.

"Some, but use is not the only reason the women beat the kapa." George looked confused, and Mr. Malo pointed to a black and yellow bird sitting on a branch of the banyan tree. "Do you see that bird, Mr. Cannon? That bird is new to our islands. It was brought here. Many new things have been brought here: new tools, books, and laws—many things, even cloth. Most of the new things are good, but many of the ancient things are good too: our love for the land and the ocean, our strong braided rope, our dance and song, and our beautiful kapa cloth. The making of the kapa is part of my daughter's memory.

It is part of her hands and heart. She will pass the knowledge down to her daughter, and her daughter will again pass it down. Do you understand this?"

George nodded. He did understand. "My father has passed down the love of crafting wood, and my uncle John passed down the love of the written word. These are things I hope to pass down to my sons and daughters."

Mr. Malo nodded. "As well as your culture and history."

"Yes."

"As well as your faith."

"Especially my faith."

"So tell me of the Prophet Joseph Smith and the Book of Mormon." When George hesitated, Mr. Malo said, "Is something wrong, Mr. Cannon?"

"I just wish I knew the language better, Mr. Malo. My heart has so much truth to tell you, but my tongue gets in the way."

Mr. Malo chuckled. "I am amazed by you, young Mr. Cannon. You say you have been in the islands for only four months, and yet you know so much of our language already. Do not worry. Tell me your story now, and in a few more months return and tell me more."

George smiled at him. *What a gracious Christian man.* George prayed for the Spirit, and then, for the next hour he spoke of the restoration of the gospel as it had been in the time of Christ, of Joseph Smith's first vision, and of the translation of the Book of Mormon. Mr. Malo asked him many questions and was intrigued by it all. He seemed particularly fascinated by the belief that the Hawaiian people were descendants of the ancient Israelites.

"I think there is some proof to that, Mr. Cannon," Mr. Malo said. "We have many things in common with the ancient

Hebrews: circumcision, the presenting of the first fruits to the gods, confinement of a woman after childbirth, places of sanctuary."

Now it was George's turn to be intrigued as he listened to the Hawaiian scholar talk of the similarities between the Hawaiian and Jewish customs. The older gentleman also spoke of the legends of the seafarers of Tahiti crossing the open oceans to the islands, and of the aloha aina—*the people's deep love of the land.*

The last ray of sun flashed green on the edge of the ocean, and Mr. Malo paused in his narrative to take in the beauty. He stretched his back. "Ah, the days are getting longer and so are my stories, Mr. Cannon."

"It is fascinating, Mr. Malo. Thank you."

"You must stay the night with us, Mr. Cannon. We cannot have you stumbling to Lahaina in the dark."

"That is very kind."

Mr. Malo stood. "Well, actually, it is sensible on my part. I fear my friend Judge Napela would have me in court if I allowed anything to happen to you." George gave him an amused smile. "Now, I am going back to the house to write down some of the things you have told me. You should go to the ocean to swim."

George brightened. "I think I will."

Mr. Malo smiled at his boyish enthusiasm. "Would you like me to teach you an ancient Hawaiian prayer to the gods that you can chant before you swim?"

"I would."

"Now, I know we are Christian men, Mr. Cannon, but we can honor the customs of the past, yes?" George nodded and Mr. Malo continued. "When you enter the water take a piece of limu—you know this word?"

Belonging to HEAVEN

"Yes, the seaweed we eat."

"Yes. Take a piece and break it in two. Throw one piece up on the shore, offering it to the land gods, and say, ko uka, no uka no ia—*of land for land is this*. Then toss the second piece into the water as an offering for the gods of the ocean, and say, ko kai, no kai no ia—*of ocean for ocean is this*. Do you understand?" George repeated the words with ease, and Mr. Malo gave him a skeptical look. "I think perhaps you are hiding a Hawaiian tutu in your family line, Mr. Cannon." He chuckled and turned toward his house.

George stood and watched the genial man as he walked away. He heard the sound of the wooden club beating out the bark of the mulberry tree. "Mai pale i ke a 'o a ka makua." *Do not set aside the teaching of a parent.* He turned and walked to the ocean, feeling the air against his skin and the dirt under his feet.

Notes

- David Malo was a Hawaiian scholar and the writer of a book on Hawaiian history, *Moʻolelo Hawaiʻi* (*Hawaiian Antiquities*). He attended Lahainaluna Seminary at the age of thirty-eight and graduated with Jonathan Hawaii Napela.
- Hawaiian rope and cording is made from the strong fibrous bark of the olona tree.
- Kapa cloth is made from the beaten bark of the wauke or mamaki plant.
- Tutu is an endearing term for an older female family member or aunt.

CHAPTER 16

Lahaina, Maui

April 17, 1851

Dear Mary,

 I have returned to my grass hale in Lahaina. I found my three companions doing well, and I think they were happy to see me. Elder Farrer was out hoeing the garden and saw me coming down the road. He hollered for the others, dropped his hoe, and ran out to meet me. Soon I was surrounded by Elder Bigler, Elder Keeler, Keala, Pau, and Nalimanui. It was a happy reunion. Nalimanui kept patting my cheek and saying, "keiki, kieki." I think she feared that I had fallen off the pali, or had been eaten by a wild boar.

 I have been resting the past few days. The trip around the island was tiring, but filled with adventure and learning. I feel my command of the language is growing, though there is still frustration at not being able to explain things the way I would like. My speech is halting, especially when it comes to preaching the principles of the gospel. I find it impossible to gather my *thoughts and come up with the vocabulary to express myself. I will keep working.*

If you are not tired of my stories, I will share the last weeks of the trip with you. Please tell the children that I have seen the great volcano mountain of Haleakala. From the plain of central Maui, it raises its head ten thousand feet into the sky. Most of the time a crown of clouds sits on its summit. Brother Napela told me he would take me to the top someday. I hope we will be able to do that.

I met the most amazing Hawaiian man on my trip. His name is Mr. David Malo, and he is a friend of Brother Napela. People told me that he knows more about the ancient Hawaiians and their culture than anyone else in the islands, and now that I have met him, I believe it. We had the best talk about the Bible, the Book of Mormon, Hawaiian history, even Hawaiian plants and animals. The man knows everything. He was very respectful and even asked me to return for another talk. I stayed the night with him and his daughter. The next morning he gave me thirty-seven cents. I tried to give it back, but he refused. He is a true gentleman. His openness and lack of guile remind me a little of Hyrum Smith.

I have cultivated a great love and respect for the Hawaiian people, Mary. They are truly God's keiki. I so want to teach them the truths of the gospel, and I know things will improve when I can speak to them in their language. I do not know if I will see Brother Napela and his wife again. We did not part under the best of circumstances. Will you and the family please continue to pray for me and for the people of Maui—indeed all the people of the Sandwich Islands?

I pray for you every night. How is the planting going in the valley? Have you planted any of your garden yet? I hope you have a good harvest. Do you ever see Sister Hoagland? I will attempt to write to her. I will also write to President Young and Uncle John and Aunt Leonora. I hope my strength returns soon. I am tired down to my toes.

Ann, Angus, David Henry, and baby Leonora, please mind your older sister and her husband. They have care over you and you must honor them. If I ever get to the top of the mountain Haleakala, I will secure a small lava rock for each of you.

Aloha,
Your loving brother, George

Notes

- George Cannon wrote in his journal of his meeting with David Malo, and that the man gave him thirty-seven cents.
- David Malo writes of the similarities between the Jewish and Hawaiian cultures in his book, *Moʻolelo Hawaiʻi*.

CHAPTER 17

Lahaina, Maui

May 2, 1851

"This seems to be a favorite place for settling the problems of the mission," Brother Bigler said. "I like it."

As the sun slid behind them into the sea, the four men stood with their feet in the ocean as they looked up at the mountains and discussed the affairs of the mission.

Brother Farrer chuckled. "I could bring my fishing line and catch dinner at the same time."

Brother Cannon liked the thought of that efficiency. He looked around at his companions and found much to admire. They had all been working hard: providing for their physical needs, studying the doctrine, preaching when possible, and learning the language. Most of the men found this last task a tedious business, especially Brother Bigler. George thought back to his hike into the Iao Valley with Jonathan Napela and the wise suggestion he'd made about establishing some sort of school to train the missionaries in the language. He chuckled to himself as he imagined the scene of his friend Jonathan attempting to mold Brother Bigler's harsh accent into the soft rolling sounds of Hawaiian. A tinge of sadness normally accompanied thoughts of Wailuku and Napela, but today they confirmed George's resolve. For several days the prompting had come to return to Wailuku and continue his preaching to his friends there, regardless of what Reverend Conde had to say. The Mormon missionaries had permission from the Hawaiian government to preach, a call from Brigham Young, and, most important, a mandate from the Lord.

As he paused to gather his courage, George watched an agressive uaʻu bird searching for small fish in the shallows. He cleared his throat. "Brethren, I feel directed to make some changes in the mission, and I want to discuss these with you." He paused for reactions, but the others merely waited. George cleared his throat and began again. "We have talked about Brother Bigler and Brother Farrer traveling to Molokaʻi to preach, but now that Brother Clark and Brother Morris have left Oahu, I feel that that is the field in which you should labor. What do you say?" The two men nodded, and Brother Bigler voiced their feelings.

"If that is your prompting, Brother Cannon, we will follow your edict."

George nodded. "And I feel prompted to go back to Wailuku and continue my work with Brother Napela and his family and friends."

"And what of the persecution there?" Brother Bigler asked.

"I believe persecution will find us wherever we preach," George answered. "We know the adversary does not want this work to go forward on the earth."

"Amen to that," Brother Keeler said. He picked up a stone and tossed it out into deeper water. "And what of me, Brother Cannon? Where will I be serving?"

"I feel you should leave Lahaina for a time, Brother Keeler, and travel over to the koolau side of the island, to the towns of Keanae and Hana."

Brother Keeler's face brightened. "I have been praying for such a journey. Thank you, Brother Cannon."

George was aware of the trouble Brother Keeler would have communicating with the Hawaiian people. The man worked diligently at trying to learn the language, but it was difficult for him. He could converse about everyday necessities—food, directions, and tasks of living—but struggled with deeper conversations or preaching the doctrines of the Church. But the word of the Lord had been specific concerning the call, and George knew he dared not question. He was heartened by the courage Brother Keeler exhibited, being not only willing but excited to take a journey alone into unknown territory.

George dug a stone out of the sand and flipped it to him. "You will do well, Brother Keeler. We have all felt that the Lord is aware of his sons and daughters on these islands and that miraculous things can be accomplished."

"One miraculous thing would be for me to learn the language," Brother Keeler said.

"Amen!" Brother Bigler responded. "I wish I had been born with a tongue for the twelve letters."

Brother Farrer agreed. "It's what we all wish—except for Brother Cannon. When he speaks, he sounds like one of the kahaku maoli." George burst out laughing, and Brother Farrer turned red. "What? What did I say?"

"You just called me a full-blooded trespasser. Kahaku maoli. I think you meant, kanaka maoli, which means full-blooded Hawaiian."

Brother Farrer laughed with him. "Full-blooded trespasser!

I like that. I will have to remember that if I ever need to use it someday."

The men spent the rest of the late afternoon bathing, figuring out travel finances, and practicing their Hawaiian. George knew he would miss all of them keenly, but these were not the days of ease and reflection, but of work, work, and more work. Spiritual harvesting took prayer, love, and grit.

It was warm inside the Kaʻahumanu Church, and was made more so by the preaching of Reverend Conde. He had taken the text for his sermon from Romans 1:18: "For the wrath of God is revealed from heaven against all ungodliness and unrighteousness of men, who hold the truth in unrighteousness." Half of his discourse had been in hotly detailing these sins to his sweltering congregation, but then his gaze fixed on the Mormon missionary.

"I say to beware of the Mormon missionaries who fall into this category of unrighteous men."

George's body stiffened with anger, and Jonathan looked over at him. The slander stung so badly that George could not return his friend's gaze, but fixed his sight on the man in the dark robes at the dais. *This man does not know how well I understand his Hawaiian words. He thinks he is speaking only to his native parishioners.*

"Five men have come to these islands preaching a false doctrine," the reverend continued. "The leader of their church, one Joe Smith, pretends to have seen an angel and to have had some plates delivered to him that he translated into a book. This book is supposed to give account of the American Indians." The preacher's eyes narrowed as he looked at George. "Now, Smith says that these plates, these *gold* plates, were taken away by an angel, but that is just evidence to me that it is a lie. Had they been real, Smith would have kept them for the world to see. He is a liar and a cheat. He built a city called Nauvoo, in the state of Illinois, and the people of that city stole so much money and broke the law so often that the citizens in the surrounding area would not take it anymore. This Joe Smith, this prophet of the Mormons, was killed fighting the good citizens of the area. He was a wicked man, and the Lord punished him for his sins."

George gripped the seat of the pew to keep himself from leaping up and crying out against this injustice. Many in the congregation were staring over at him, and he wanted to stand up and rip to shreds the lies the Reverend was preaching. The Spirit warned him that disrupting the meeting would not have the desired result, and he knew that it was contrary to the law, so George kept to his seat, but his heart ached and his stomach felt full of rocks.

"Now, I say, if this Smith had seen angels, why did they not come down and save him from death? Does this not show that the wrath of God came down and consumed this wicked man? In fact, all of the wicked Mormons were run out of the state."

George took a deep breath and clenched his jaw to stifle the angry tears. His mind thought of the exodus from Nauvoo in the dead of winter—of bloody footprints in the snow. He saw again the homes deserted to the mobs and children dying from exposure. The lying voice of Reverend Conde grated on his sensibilities.

"There are four of these Mormon men living in Lahaina, and one of them comes frequently to Wailuku and stays in the house of Napela." Reverend Conde looked directly at Napela and the young man sitting next to him. "Perhaps they are friends, which could be a very dangerous thing."

A low growl rumbled in Jonathan's chest.

"I warn you not to be deceived by these Mormon missionaries. Yes, this is the enemy. I warn you to keep to the truth."

Before the singing or the prayer, George and Jonathan stood and left the chapel. When they reached the outside, George walked away from the church and Jonathan followed. It took George several minutes to calm his breathing enough to speak.

"How . . . how can he say such things when he knows they are lies? He knows they are lies! 'Ae 'enemi keia. *Yes, this is the enemy!* Isn't that what he said? Isn't that what he called me?" George looked over at Jonathan, who was standing with his head bowed. "Oh, Brother Jonathan, I am so sorry for the trouble this has brought you. It was a mistake for me to come back."

Jonathan looked up. "It is nothing you have done, Brother George. You wish only to preach your doctrine, and you have the permission of the government." He looked toward the church and waved to several of his friends as they exited the building. He walked toward them and George followed. "It is Reverend Conde who has made the mistake," Jonathan said in an aside. "Speaking out against me in church was not wise."

William Uaua, Kaleohano, and many other of Jonathan's friends surrounded the two. Their faces were filled with anger.

"He should not have spoken out against you in the sermon!" Kaleohano said heatedly.

William Uaua was so agitated he could not keep his body still. "By denouncing you, he tries to bring shame on your family and on your friend, George Cannon. He also brings shame on us, for we are your friends." He smacked the flat of his hand on his Bible. "We can think for ourselves. Do we not have the right to find out what is true and what is not?"

Jonathan stood stoic as their indignation swirled around him. George was amazed by his composed demeanor and delighted by the support and sympathy he himself was receiving. It seemed the reverend's sermon had conjured the opposite effect it intended. George felt his own anger subsiding, until he saw Reverend Conde emerge from the church. The sting of being maligned quickly returned, and George began walking toward the man.

"Brother George!" Jonathan called. "Where are you going?"

"I just want to speak with Reverend Conde," he answered in perfect Hawaiian.

When the reverend saw him approach and heard him speak Hawaiian, his face paled and he looked about anxiously.

Please be with me, Heavenly Father, George prayed silently as he went. *I just want to stand up for the truth. Please help me be a David.* As he approached, the reverend turned away from him, and George called out in English. "Reverend Conde, might I have the privilege of speaking a few words with you?" George knew that the reverend would have to stop as duty and manners dictated.

The man turned back and stood straighter. "Of course, Mr. . . ."

"Cannon. Elder George Cannon. We have been previously introduced."

"Yes, I remember."

"I will speak to you in English as my speaking of the Hawaiian is halting at best, but, I assure you, sir, my understanding of the language is perfect."

The reverend gave him a spurious smile. "My compliments."

Jonathan and his friends drew near, as did a third of the congregation.

"What is it you want, Mr. Cannon?"

"I want to tell you the truth of the gospel I preach, and then I want you to tell the people that you have told them lies."

The reverend's eyes narrowed. "I do not believe them to be lies. From all I have heard about your church, I have told these people the truth, and I will not tell them differently."

"There is not one doctrine we preach that cannot be proved from the scriptures. We preach faith, repentance, baptism by immersion, which were the means practiced in Christ's church. We also preach the giving of the gift of the Holy Ghost by the laying on of hands. That also was practiced in the primitive church. I dare you, Reverend Conde, to prove Mormonism false from the holy scriptures."

"I am sure that would be an easy task."

"No, sir, it would not, for everything we preach is truer to the primitive church of Christ than any of the doctrine preached by the reformed churches." The reverend glared at him. "I do not mean to offend you, sir. I have always been respectful of the spiritual leaders in all churches. You have done a great work to bring Christ into the lives of the people, but I ask the same respect from you. Allow me to preach freely and do not poison the mind of the people with falsehoods. Let the doctrine speak for itself, and let the people decide."

"I do not teach falsehoods, Mr. Cannon, and I will not let *you* poison the hearts of this people with wicked lies." Contempt colored his every word. "The man, Joe Smith, who you call a prophet, was a liar and a cheat."

George looked directly at Reverend Conde and leveled his voice. "Do not tell me about the Prophet Joseph Smith. I knew the man, and he did not die fighting the people of Illinois." George's voice grew in intensity. "He was killed by a mob of a hundred men as he sat innocent in a jail. My uncle, John Taylor, was there with him. He watched . . . he watched as the prophet and his brother were slaughtered." George's voice broke. "My uncle was terribly wounded in the same act of butchery." Jonathan came to stand beside him, and Reverend Conde stepped back. George looked at the stricken faces of the native people and realized that although most could not understand the words, they understood his passion, and felt the truth. Though George's strength was spent, he knew there was more of his testimony to give. "I knew the Prophet Joseph Smith. I knew him. I walked with him and heard him preach. I have read the revelations that have come through him from the Lord. I have read the Book of Mormon and know that no mortal man of limited learning could write such a book. I, along with thousands of others, bear witness of the truth of Joseph's first vision. Either he was a prophet and followed the directives God gave him, or he was a total fraud and deceived thousands of people." Passion colored his words. "I knew him, and I tell you Joseph Smith was no fraud. I also tell you sir, if you do not take back your words, I will stand as a witness against you at the judgment seat of God for having told this people lies, when you knew them to be lies."

Reverend Conde did not answer. George turned and walked away leaving the reverend to stand among his uneasy and murmuring flock. Napela and his friends followed George from the churchyard.

When George reached the Napela's garden, he wept. Hands on knees, bent double, he wept like a little child. All of the pent-up anger, sorrow, and weariness poured from his body as the tears flowed. Jonathan and Kitty stood on either side of him, each with a hand laid gently on his back. Inside the house Kitty's brother, John, retold the gathered friends the words that had passed between George Cannon and Reverend Conde. Many looked out at the young missionary during the telling and wept with him.

Note

- The persecution of the LDS missionaries in Hawaii and of the Hawaiian converts by the Protestant clergy was well documented in many of the Mormon missionary journals, written edicts, and newspaper articles of the day.

CHAPTER 18

Wailuku, Maui

May 11, 1851

Dear Elders Bigler and Farrer,

    I write to you from Wailuku. I pray that you have settled in Honolulu and that the work of the Lord is moving forward. There is a spirit of contention here, and I know that the adversary is not happy that we have come to this blessed land to preach the gospel. I feel if we honor the message, that one day soon the work will take hold in the hearts of these good people, and the Church will prosper. Continue with your study of the language. I feel it is a key.

    I did not go with the others to church today. I stayed at the house to study and pray. When Napela returned from the service he looked like his warrior grandfather ready to throw a spear through the eye of a boar. Reverend Conde had again spoken out against him in front of the congregation. He warned him that if he did not put me out and take in a new boarder, a Dr. Coon, then he would have no recourse but to turn him out of the church. Poor Napela. He is being buffeted on every side. He wants me to stay, but fears his position of judge being taken away from him. They have already brought him to trial for drunkenness and associating with a man who had been turned out of the church a few weeks ago. Kitty is also troubled. She does not want her husband to lose his place. Napela is a chief and well regarded in the community. He does not wish to have that influence tarnished. I love him, but I know he must be willing to sacrifice all for the Lord. Those of us who witnessed the atrocities of Nauvoo know much about sacrifice.

I have been led by the Spirit to travel to the area of Kula. It is up on the side of the great volcano mountain, Haleakala. When Jonathan heard of my plans, he was relieved. He has property there where they grow Irish potatoes. He sat down and wrote a note of introduction to the man who runs his affairs in Kula, Akuna Pake, advising him to take me in and give me whatever I need. He is also loaning me a horse.

Mrs. Napela is washing my clothes for the trip tomorrow. She is a good woman, but I think she will be glad to see the back of me.

Brother Keeler is still in Lahaina preparing for his travels to the other side of the island. I hope he can stop in Wailuku on his way to Hana and make the acquaintance of the Napelas and some of their friends. He sent a letter that he is anxious to be off on his new adventure. His enthusiasm for the work lifts my spirits.

I hope you are doing well. I will continue on in the faith that our hard work will bring in a harvest. You may not hear from me for a while as I will be getting settled in this new area. A neighbor of Napela's, when he heard that I was going to the Kula, warned me not to go. He said it is a difficult place. I told him I was used to difficult places.

*Your brother in the Lord,
Elder George Q. Cannon*

CHAPTER 19

Kula, Maui

June 1851

George hefted the large bucket to the next withered potato plant. He lifted the ladle and poured water onto the wilting leaves. Two more ladles and on to the next plant. Flies buzzed around his sweaty head, while his stomach grumbled with hunger. He would almost rather starve to death than eat any more mealy potatoes. For nearly three weeks now it had been nothing but mealy potatoes—sometimes with molasses. Was the Lord making him humble, like John the Baptist in the wilderness? George moved on to the next plant. Three ladles of water, pick up the bucket, and trudge to the next plant. He poured one of the ladles over his head, took out his handkerchief and wiped his face. *Kula, upcountry, the dry land,* George thought ruefully. *Dry and desolate.* He looked out across the plains of West Maui to the ocean. Oh, how he wished he was back in Lahaina with his three companions, standing in the cool ocean water, and eating bananas. His stomach rumbled in protest. Well, here is where the Lord wanted him, so here he would stay until given other directions. He sighed and poured another ladle of water on his head. Parts of the Kula district were beautiful, with large stands of trees and open, green grassland, but other parts were dry with cacti and rocks. Napela's land was a combination of the two. George was bending down to pick up the bucket when he saw Akuna Pake approaching from the farmhouse. The land caretaker was a head shorter than George, but with strength enough to carry a large pig under each arm. He had reliable common sense, a quick humor, and a good work ethic. His wife, Honua, was grumpy. George figured she had every right, as they lived mostly on mealy potatoes with an occasional windfall of fruit, poi, and fish.

Pake waved. "Mister George! Mister George! You have visitors at the house!" He hurried to George's side. "The judge has come with his cousin Kaleohano. They bring gifts for you."

"Gifts? What sort of gifts?"

Pake chucked. "Oh, you will like these gifts. We all like these gifts. Even my wife is smiling." He picked up the bucket. "Come. We will finish the watering later."

George trudged after the eager man, not sure he knew what to say to Jonathan or Kaleohano. He was trying not to be discouraged, but taking care of potato plants was not the type of harvest he wished for. He had spent a good deal of time traveling around the small villages in the Kula area without much success. The field was not white, and it was not ready to harvest. *Oh, George,* he chided himself, *stop murmuring.*

As he approached the small house, he saw Jonathan Napela and H. K. Kaleohano in the front yard giving water to their horses. Both men were the sons of chiefs and carried themselves with an easy grace, but all George saw at that moment were his friends, and it was good to see their familiar faces. A smile jumped to his mouth.

Jonathan saw George and Pake coming in from the field. He moved around his horse, took five long strides, and scooped George up in a hug. He stepped back and put his forehead on George's. "Aloha. Aloha, Brother George. I have missed you."

"I have missed you too, Brother Jonathan. I hope you are well." When he did not receive an answer, he stepped back. "Are you well?"

"I will tell you all about myself later. I have much to discuss with you." He held out his hand to Kaleohano. "Kaleohano wanted to come see you too."

George smiled at him. "Aloha, Kaleohano."

"Aloha, George Cannon. How are things in Pulehu?"

"Quiet, and full of potatoes."

Akuna Pake laughed. "Full of potatoes! This young one makes me laugh. O Kula i ka hoe hewa! *Kula of the ignorant canoe paddlers, because we are uplanders, far from the sea.*"

George smiled at the man and turned back to Kaleohano. "How are things in Wailuku?"

"Too quiet without you."

George scoffed. "More peaceful, you mean." Jonathan looked at the ground, and George was instantly sorry for his surly reply. "I am sorry, Brother Jonathan. You and Kitty have always been thoughtful of me."

Kaleohano interceded. "And that is why we are here. We bring you supplies: flour, salt, dried fish, kalo to make poi, breadfruit, bananas, and coconuts." George was stunned. His stomach growled in anticipation, and the others laughed.

"My father's stomach used to talk like that when food was being prepared," Jonathan said fondly.

"This is such a gift," George said. "Thank you."

Pake rhythmically clapped his hands and began chanting a happy song about food.

"Oh, there is more," Jonathan said. "We found another gift for you on our doorstep and thought we would bring it along."

From around the corner of the house stepped Brother Keeler.

"Brother Keeler! What are you doing here?" George yelled as he ran to give his missionary brother a hug. "What a surprise!"

"I am on my way to the other side of the island. Off on my grand adventure. I stopped in Wailuku, but they said you were here."

Kaleohano nodded. "It was fortunate we were coming to see you today."

"So fortunate," George said in Hawaiian.

"I suggest that we have something to eat, and then we have another surprise to show you," Jonathan said. "I think it will be something you like."

At the moment George could not imagine something he would like better than seeing his missionary companion—or having something in his stomach other than potatoes.

George loved taking a ride in the afternoon gloaming—the breeze picked up, sweeping away the scratchy heat of the day, and the birds trilled their evening revelry. For the first time in weeks George felt calm, and he and Brother Keeler, who rode with him on the sorrel mare, added their voices to the birdsong. They sang the hymns of Zion and a few pioneer ballads, and then listened in wonder as Kaleohano sang hymns in Hawaiian, his rich baritone voice seeming to still the twilight with its beauty. *Someday I will sing the hymns in Hawaiian,* George promised himself. He looked over his left shoulder to watch the huge golden sun as it settled like a crown on the island of Lanai. The golden sun of Maui—Maui the demi god—Maui the trickster. He urged his horse up next to Napela.

"Did you know that when I met with Mr. David Malo one of the topics we discussed was the similarities between the ancient Hawaiian culture and that of the Israelites."

Both Jonathan and Kaleohano nodded. "Oh, yes, it was a topic we used to discuss when we were classmates at Lahainaluna Seminary."

"I loved the story where he compared Joshua from the Old Testament with the Hawaiian legend of Maui the trickster."

"That sounds like a fascinating story, Brother Cannon. I'd love to hear it," Brother Keeler said.

"Well, I'm sure I can't tell it like Mr. Malo did, but I'll give you an idea. I hope my Hawaiian does it justice." He sat quiet for a moment, organizing his thoughts. "The story goes that Maui's mother wanted more daylight so she could beat the kapa cloth, and, being the loving son that he was, Maui secured a strong rope, climbed to the top of Haleakala, and flung the rope around the sun, stopping it in its place for several hours. The connection is to the story of Joshua when, with priesthood power, he stopped the sun in its course."

"And over the years it has melded into the stories of the Hawaiians?" Brother Keeler questioned.

"Well, that's the theory."

The party came over a small rise, and George saw a large open-sided hale. Several men were working on the roof to secure the new thatch.

Jonathan grinned at him. "So, here is your third surprise,

Brother George. I have had my men build you a hale for preaching." George sat staring at the building, which was large enough to hold fifty people comfortably. He did not speak, and Jonathan shifted in his saddle. "Do you not like it?" George still did not speak, and Jonathan tried to mollify his disappointment. "Someday soon we will build a proper wooden chapel here, but I thought for now this could be a covering for you. We could even put a stone basin in the ground nearby, deep enough for your immersion baptisms."

George pulled his gaze away from the hale to look at his friend. "Why did you do this, Brother Jonathan? After all the trouble I've caused you?" His voice thickened with emotion. "You are not even of our faith. Why did you give us this great gift?"

"You are my friend, Brother George, and you work hard at being a missionary. You deserve a place to preach."

"This is extremely good of you, Mr. Napela," Brother Keeler said. "Very generous." He thumped George on the shoulder. "Come on, George, shall we go and take a closer look at it?" He slid off the rump of the horse and began walking to the hale.

"Now there is a man of practical sense," Kaleohano said. He dismounted and followed, leading his horse along.

When Kaleohano was several paces away, George turned to Jonathan. "Thank you, Brother Jonathan. I will pray to the Lord to bless you for this kindness."

Jonathan nodded. "Blessings for Kitty too?"

"Of course. I pray for you both daily."

"That is good to know." Jonathan leaned over and patted his horse's neck. "The persecution continues against us. Some already call me a Mormon for my association with you."

"I will also continue to pray that the Lord will give you the strength to stand against your trials and to decide."

Jonathan attempted a smile. "That is one of the things I came to discuss with you, Brother George. Can I not take a center course between the Protestants and the Mormons?"

George shook his head. "There is no center course, Brother Napela. One Lord, one faith, one baptism. I know that you have felt the truth of the words I have taught you. There is light in you, but that light will become darkness if you do not obey what the Lord wants you to do."

"But it is difficult."

George's horse stepped sideways and George reined him in. He felt acutely his youth compared with Napela and the fact that he was without rank or position, yet the Spirit worked on him so forcefully that he knew he had to speak the truth. "There is no easy way in this. Do you think life was easy for the Jewish men who Jesus called to follow him? Do you think it was easy for the fifteen-year-old Joseph Smith to stand against the doctrine and preachers of the day? Do you think it is easy for me to be here, far from home, eating potatoes, and struggling with the language?" Tears of frustration coursed down his cheeks. "Do you think it was easy for the Savior to carry his cross to Calvary? If you wish to belong to heaven, Brother Jonathan, there is no easy way."

A look of pleading stamped itself onto Jonathan's handsome face.

George reached over and laid his hand on his arm. "I am sorry, dear friend. I wish there were words I could say that would comfort you. I wish I could make the decision easy for you and Kitty, but there is no center course." And with another

Belonging to HEAVEN

look at his friend, George dismounted his horse and headed for the hale.

❦

The next day, George paced outside the newly built hale, while a dozen Hawaiians gathered inside. These dear native people had come to hear the Mormon preacher tell them of the doctrine of The Church of Jesus Christ of Latter-day Saints, in their own language, and George could not remember a word.

Brother Keeler came out to console him. "Can I do anything for you?"

"Take my place."

"Sorry, I would only be able to greet them, say a prayer, and direct them home."

"I can't do this, Brother Keeler. My Hawaiian is hemahema."

"What does that mean?"

"Clumsy."

Brother Keeler scoffed. "*My* Hawaiian is hemahema. Your Hawaiian is beautiful."

George shook his head. "Perhaps when I'm speaking to one person, but you know how I am about speaking in front of a crowd."

Brother Keeler looked over at the hale. "Well, I'd hardly consider twelve a crowd."

George scowled at him. "I feel like a prisoner under the sentence of death. I've only spoken to a few people in congregation, and that was in my mother tongue, and now I'm supposed to give these good people a grand sermon in their own language?"

Brother Keeler watched him pace. "So, don't give them a

grand sermon. Just teach them a few simple truths and let the Spirit take it to their hearts."

George stopped and looked at his companion. "Thank you, Brother Keeler. That is wise counsel." He took several deep breaths and headed for the little church building. As he stepped into the hale, everyone turned to look at him, and he felt the momentary urge to run. Instead, he walked to the front of the assembly and looked into the beautiful brown faces. He saw Kaleohano smiling at him. He knew that Napela would not be in attendance, as he'd left before dawn to return to Wailuku. George said a silent prayer for the Lord to bless the good man and his family. He then said a prayer that the Lord would be with them in this little gathering in Pulehu. *Where two or three are gathered in my name.* He felt the comforting peace of the Spirit filling his soul. He opened his mouth and haltingly began teaching about faith, repentance, and baptism.

Notes

- Potato cultivation in the area of Kula was a good enterprise during the California gold rush. When the gold rush declined, so did the market for Kula-grown potatoes.
- One of the first LDS meetinghouses in Maui was located in Pulehu. The original grass hale was replaced by a wooden chapel near the location. It is still standing and can be visited by the general public.

CHAPTER 20

Keanae, Maui

July 1851

Dear Mary,

It is the end of July and I am temporarily at a village called Keanae. I traveled here with Brother Keeler, Kaleohano, and Napela. Keanae is on the windward side of the island, which means it gets a lot of rain. It is more beautiful than I can describe. It is thirty or so miles from the Kula area. Brother Keeler has been trying to preach to the people here for a month. They are very interested, but his Hawaiian is still awkward. I already wrote to you about the hale that Brother Napela built for us. Well, we have had several baptisms, and I expect a few more when I return. It seems a bit of light has come through the darkness.

On this side of the island, hundreds of small streams and rivers pour down from the mountain Haleakala. These rivers cause deep gorges, and it makes travel very difficult. Some of the pali are so steep that we have to get off our horses and lead them. And if the stream is swollen *with water from the rain, we have to swim across. There is no other way to get to this side of the island except to walk or ride a horse as the trail is not big enough for a wagon. Everything the people need on this side of the island they have to carry in on their backs. I suppose one could go by canoe on the ocean, but as I am prone to seasickness, I will gladly walk or ride my horse.*

This area, Mary, reminds me of scenes I had pictured out in my imagination—vegetation of the most luxuriant description, with the timber in general covered from the root upward in living green vines that run over everything. I have never seen anything to compare with it. We met a good many travelling on the road—very often rounding a point we would see two or three dusky faces peering round to catch sight of us—the females, with very few exceptions, wore garlands of flowers upon their heads. I would like to see you, and Anne, and Leonora with such garlands in your hair.

There was a great excitement among the people when we descended the steep trail into Keanae. It seems they had been watching for us, and seeing us approach from a long distance, they had gathered to meet us. Had we been princes, Mary, they could not have treated us with greater consideration and honor. They are anxious to hear our words. Even with my feeble preaching, they drink it in like water on dry ground.

A miracle occurred the second day we were in Keanae, Mary, and I feel like shouting Glory, Glory, Glory to the Lord God of Israel for his goodness to me—a poor weak instrument, a mere boy. As I stood to preach that second morning, I felt weak and empty. I requested their prayers, and I was truly blessed. I never preached with such power—the language came with ease and fluency, and I was filled with the Spirit with words and ideas. After the meeting we baptized thirty-one people. This day was as happy a day as I ever experienced, Mary. The Lord is truly aware of us.

I thought of you and the family on the 24th of July. Was there a celebration? It seems like a long time ago when I first saw the valley. It must be very different now with so many more Saints gathering to Zion. I will hardly know the place, or any of you when I return. Thank you for sending the Deseret News. *It makes me feel close to you when I read what's going on. Thank you for your prayers. You are in my prayers every day. Children, help Charles and Mary harvest the garden. The world has no use for a drone.*

> *Your loving brother,*
> *George*

CHAPTER 21

Oloalu, Maui
October 1851

Jonathan Hawaii Napelakapuonamahanaonaleleonalani stepped from the carriage, and the people of the village gathered around him—anguish and expectation washing their faces. Jonathan looked for the face of the old kahuna and for Ipakula the wonderful dancer, but knew he would not find them for they had walked the rainbow years ago. Jonathan reached out, and several came to lay their hands briefly on his arm. He walked slowly through the village, and the people followed. He saw the thatch of many of the hales in disrepair. He did not hear the sound of the kapa beaters or see the women weaving the nets. Memories flooded in of his years spent here. He thought of the games he loved as a boy—na hei, *string fingers,* and ho'olele lupe, *kite flying.* He thought of the competitions of pae i ka nalu, *surfing, or spear throwing.* He thought of his mother making him balance on the round stone.

"You can stay up there a little longer! Balance, balance, boy with legs like sticks! This will make your legs strong for running and climbing the coconut tree."

Jonathan pulled his mind from the past and continued his walk to his family kauhale. As he neared the lava stone wall surrounding the compound, he found it was the same, but his mother's New England gate sat askew on a broken hinge. He hadn't noticed that the last time he visited. Perhaps he should stay awhile and put things in order. He walked to the gate and carefully pushed it to the side.

"This gate needs fixing."

One of his mother's serving women stepped to the stone wall. "We are sorry, Judge, but your honored mother did not want us to touch anything."

Jonathan looked at her and nodded. "Of course, forgive me." He continued on across the courtyard to the halenoa, while the rest of the people stood on the other side of the stone wall. Jonathan prepared himself for a sorrowful scene as he chanted the words that announced his arrival and called for permission to enter. He was glad when he heard the low mellow notes of his mother's voice sending back words of welcome. He walked through the door and found the chiefess lying on her bed of mats, with many small pillows propping her comfortably into an almost sitting position. She beamed when she saw him.

"Ah, 'oni kalalea ke ku a ka la 'au loa." *A tall tree stands above the others.* She reached out her arms to him, and he went into her embrace. He laid his forehead on hers.

"Aloha nui, my dear mother. I see that Lono has been here to visit you and brought you some life."

She chuckled. "Do you think so?"

"I do."

"Bring over some mats and sit by me." When he was settled, she readjusted a few pillows under her arms and laid back. "Look at all the new pillows the missionary wives have made for me. They want me to be comfortable before I walk the rainbow."

"You will not walk the rainbow for a long time," Jonathan encouraged.

"Actually, the god Lono comes to whisper in my ear that night is coming, but that I must not to be afraid. He says that my aumakua, my spirit owl, will come and carry me to the rainbow on silent wings. And then I will go into the valley and meet my Lord Jesus." She closed her eyes and rubbed her fingers over the soft fabric of one of the pillows. "This is my favorite. *The Lord is my shepherd, I shall not want.*"

"That is one of my favorites too," Jonathan said, thinking of the scripture as he admired the careful work of the stitching. "The missionary wives have always been very good to you."

Chiefess Wiwiokalani opened her eyes and smiled at her son. "They have." The smile faded. "But why does that make you sad?"

"I am not sad."

"You are. There is a storm cloud on your face."

Jonathan weighed his words carefully. "Mother, you know that I have always admired the Protestant missionaries. They have given me much."

"Yes."

"And I have tried to live by the precepts they taught us."

"Of course, you are a Christian man." He did not answer. "You drink a little too much for their liking, but you are a good man and you believe in the Lord Jesus."

"I do." He patted her hand. "And I am trying to put the drinking aside."

"You are? Well, that is a wonderful thing."

He noticed that her breathing was labored. "Is there anything you need, dear one?"

"I have what I need here before me." She smiled at him and then gave him a mother's look. "But, you have not told me the reason for your sadness."

Jonathan lowered his head. "I have had my judgeship taken from me."

Wiwiokalani's voice was calm. "Tell me."

"The charges were my drinking and that I had been associating with a man who had been dropped from the church."

"But you are putting aside the drinking."

"Yes."

"And being a friend to a man is no reason to take away your position. The ministers have powerful influence in the government, but they do not have that much power."

Jonathan nodded. "But, I believe there is another reason. A reason they will not admit."

"And what is that reason?"

"I have been listening to the words of a preacher from another Christian church."

"There are many Christian churches."

"Yes, but this faith is different, and the Protestant ministers do not like it."

"Tell me."

"One of the missionaries of the new faith, Brother George Cannon, has become my friend. He is a missionary for The Church of Jesus Christ of Latter-day Saints."

His mother smiled. "That is a long name."

"Many people call them Mormons."

Wiwiokalani shifted slightly on her pillows and frowned at

him. "I know this name. Some of the people in the village have listened to the words of a man named Keeler."

"Yes. He is one of Brother Cannon's companions."

"And our church does not like their teachings?"

"No."

"So perhaps there is a reason. Perhaps you should not listen to these men. Our ministers teach us about Jesus. Is that not enough for you?"

"I thought it was, but—"

"What has made you doubt?"

"There has been much persecution from all of the ministers. They refuse to let the Mormon missionaries preach in their buildings, and they spread lies about them; they threaten the people with dismissal from their jobs for even listening to the words of the Mormons. Some people have even been threatened with jail. I just wonder why the ministers are so angered by the preaching of the Mormons?"

Wiwiokalani was silent for several moments. "It sounds as though they are afraid."

Jonathan was grateful for his mother's simple wisdom. "Yes, that is what I think. There have already been over three hundred of our people baptized into the Church—many in the Koolau area and in Kula, where Brother Cannon is preaching. He speaks our language like one of us."

"Brother Cannon, your friend."

"Yes."

"He is a man of age and much learning?"

Jonathan smiled. "He is a man of twenty-four and no learning."

Wiwiokalani's brow furrowed. "How long has he been on the island?"

"Ten months."

"Impossible. Ten months and he speaks the language like a child of the land?"

"He works very hard and I think the gift of tongues has been given to him."

His mother shook her head. "Ten months and they have baptized over three hundred?"

"Yes."

"No wonder the ministers are afraid. And you are interested in the teachings of Brother Cannon?"

"I am. He teaches that the gospel of Christ's primitive church has been restored."

"Tell me."

For the next hour Jonathan explained the story of Joseph Smith and the Book of Mormon, the first principles of the gospel, baptism by immersion, and the call of prophets and apostles. Wiwiokalani was alert to all the words, but when he spoke of eternal sealing, her face filled with awe.

"E lei kau, e lei hoʻoilo i ke aloha." *Love is worn like a wreath through the summers and the winters.*

"Yes. Love is everlasting. That is what the Church teaches. With the priesthood authority, what is bound on earth will be bound in heaven. It is like our belief in the ao ʻaumakua."

"The place in the spirit world where the family lives together."

Jonathan's throat tightened with emotion. "Yes, we can all be together. Ohana. *The family of God.*"

"This alone is a wonderful teaching." The air in the hale grew warm, and Wiwiokalani's eyelids began to droop.

"I have tired you with my much speaking," Jonathan said.

She smiled at him but did not open her eyes. "No, I am

thinking of angels, apostles, and my Hawaii Waaole." She opened her eyes. "The words seem true to me, but perhaps that is only because my son speaks them with such passion." She looked into his eyes. "I do not want you to be led away, my son."

"I believe Brother Cannon to be a man who loves the Lord and speaks with a true heart."

"And your sweet wife? What does Catherine Keliikuaaina think?"

"She too knows the goodness of George Cannon."

"But you are both afraid."

Jonathan stood and paced the floor. "They have already taken my judgeship from me. What more can they do?"

"They can keep you out of heaven."

Jonathan stopped and stared at her. "They do not have the power to do that."

"If you believe in your heart that they do, then they do."

Jonathan went to the door of the hale and looked out. "There is also the persecution that would follow us. We would give up much if we joined with the Mormons."

"Jonathan, you are ali'i; they cannot take that from you. They cannot take the land the king has granted you, and they cannot take your voice."

"But how would we live?"

"Sell some of your land to the people who are coming to grow sugar."

Jonathan nodded. Again his mother's simple wisdom.

"You and Kitty are wise and strong people. You will take your time to make this decision, and if it is right, you will find your way."

He sighed. "Yes, but now there is more to consider." He turned back to his mother, a look of wonder softening the worried lines of his face. "There is a child coming into our lives. A child to be born in March."

Wiwiokalani sat up, and Jonathan hurried to her side. "Ah, dear one, you must be careful."

She had a difficult time catching her breath, but she smiled through the pain. In starts and stops, words of an ancient prayer of thanks came to her lips as the tears flowed. Finally she calmed, and Jonathan helped her to lie back on the pillows. He took out his handkerchief and dried her tears as she ran her fingers through his hair. "You have waited long for this blessing. So long."

"Yes, but the blessing is shadowed by the death of our sons. There is much worry."

"Of course, I understand. You must be watchful of Kitty's health."

"Yes. Nothing must upset her."

Wiwiokalani closed her eyes and chanted an oli of strength. The sound filled Jonathan's body with peace. He would take that peace and strength back to his wife. His mother finished the chant and opened her eyes. On her mouth was a crooked grin.

Her look made Jonathan smile. "What is it?"

"Hala ka hoʻoilo, ua pau ka ua." *Winter is gone, the rain has ceased.* "Do not worry, my son. You will have a keiki to love and to teach."

Jonathan took his mother's hands. "Your mana is strong. I feel the truth of your words."

"Each life has its own kind of wisdom. And you are wise to be careful about your decision." Wiwiokalani closed her eyes, and Jonathan could see that she was dealing with pain. Finally she spoke. "The ancestors are whispering to me that this child will be beautiful like her mother."

Jonathan sat forward. "You think it will be a girl?"

"I see bright eyes and graceful hands. I see her dancing the hula, the maile leaves about her neck, and a crown of lokelani flowers on her head. Kings will recognize her beauty." The chiefess took several painful breaths. "I think this girl and I will pass each other on the rainbow." Jonathan wept. Wiwiokalani opened her eyes. "Do not weep, my son, for this child will bring you much joy. For this one you will choose the gospel of eternity."

Notes

- Jonathan Napela's full last name is Napelakapuonamahanaonaleleonalani. It is his royal last name that was chanted by the kahuna (priest) when he was born. The meaning of the name is: Of the sacred way of Namahana attracted to fly through the air and belong to heaven.

- The god Lono is the god of peace, nature, life, and fertility. Legend says that when Lono came to the islands he brought the techniques of the farmer and the herbal doctor.

- Aumakua are the family ancestor gods or spirits that are able to keep in touch with their descendants on earth through dreams.

CHAPTER 22

Pulehu, Maui

January 7, 1852

Dear Mary,

 I wish to glory in the Lord's goodness and to tell you wonderful news. Two days ago, my friend Jonathan Hawaii Napela came to be baptized. His wife, Catherine Kitty Keliikuaaina Richardson, did not join him, and that is a sadness to me, but she stood with him by the seaside, holding his hand, and watching as several others stepped into the ocean and had the sacred ordinance performed. A large crowd of people gathered to watch as this prominent Hawaiian aliʻi joined himself to The Church of Jesus Christ of Latter-day Saints. His cousin H. K. Kaleohano was there as well as his land supervisor, Akuna Pake. These two have already been baptized, and I think they have been sending prayers heavenward for this day. William Uaua has accepted the gospel but has waited to see what Napela would do before committing to baptism. Many wept when Brother Napela came up out of the water. The spirit was strong, and the people *felt to rejoice. The next night there was a total eclipse of the moon, and many of the superstitious Hawaiians thought it a sign that a great occurrence had taken place.*

Prior to this day, I had returned to Wailuku several times but did not stay with Jonathan and Kitty. I preached instead to others in the town who were eager to hear the words of the gospel. One day I was prompted to return to Napela's house, but felt uneasy because of the way he and I had parted. But the Spirit persisted. I made my way to the home of my friend only to find him in heated conversation with some four or five natives—one of these was named Samuel Kamakau, a member of Parliament, and said to be the best orator and one of the smartest natives on the islands. They were questioning Napela about our principles, arguing with him upon them, and he was defending them to the best of his ability. My arrival seemed most opportune; he was glad to see me and soon transferred the conversation to me. We conversed until the roosters crowed for morning. I was blessed with fluency, and the Lord enabled me to answer all their questions to their satisfaction. They were (especially Kamakau and one named Naiapaakai) the best-read natives of the Bible that I have conversed with. Toward the last they sat and listened and quit objecting or arguing. They wrote down some of our leading objections to the sects, together with the proofs showing their deviations from the ancient gospel pattern. After they got through with this, I called upon them to show us our errors from the scripture, as I said no doubt the ministers had endeavored to prove us false from the scriptures. They said they could not do it. Napela told them not to go behind our backs and talk about us, but if they had any objections now was the time to make them as I was present and could offer a defense.

I think, dear Mary, that this was the commencement of a great work in this region, for since then hundreds have been gathering to hear the message. The minister who preached such falsehoods against us has been deserted by most of his congregation. I do not wish him harm, but I hoped for the day when his followers would see the truth.

I apologize for the length of this letter, Mary, but my heart is overflowing. I am now back in Pulehu, sitting here by myself under a large tree, and looking at the wooden church we are building at this place. I marvel at the power of the Lord, as I think of the hundreds of natives who have joined with us. I am continually grateful. He revealed to me that it was my duty to remain on the islands, acquire the language, and bear testimony of His great work to the people. He has given me many promises connected with this and I feel how true His words have been. I now feel eager to begin translating the Book of Mormon into Hawaiian. Brother Napela will be a great help. Jonathan and Kitty have asked me to return to live with them in Wailuku, and in this I see another tender mercy from the Lord.

I told you about the arrival of the three new missionaries at the end of August—Brothers Lewis, Hammond, and Woodbury. Brother Lewis has been given the responsibility of the mission as Brother Clark is gone. He and his wife moved to Honolulu. Brother Hammond and his wife and baby remain in Lahaina, *as does Brother Woodbury. When they arrived they brought newspapers, letters to me from home, and even a daguerreotype likeness of my Elizabeth Hoagland. I received a letter from President Young congratulating us on the success of the mission, and a letter from Angus saying that he has gone with Brother George A. Smith to make a settlement in the Little Salt Lake. It is hard to believe that he is seventeen, and that in a few days I will be twenty-five.*

Aunt Leonora wrote that Uncle John will soon be released as president of the mission in France, and returning home to you in the summer. I hope you are not too disappointed that I will not be released this year. I feel I must stay and do everything I can to magnify my calling before returning home. If we stay busy in our work, then the time will go quickly.

Stay well. My prayers are always with you.

Your loving brother,
George

Notes

- The story of George Cannon's interaction with Kamakau and his friends when they confronted Napela is taken from Cannon's journal.
- A daguerreotype is an early photograph produced on silver or a silver-covered copper plate.
- Little Salt Lake referred to the town in southern Utah known as Panguitch.

CHAPTER 23

Iao Valley, Maui
March 1, 1852

The Rainbow Maiden was dancing on the sheer cliffs of the Iao Valley. She shimmered in and out of view as she attempted to beguile the angry clouds that swirled among the mountain gorges. George was awed by the breathtaking sight and wanted to share it with his hiking companion, but his Hawaiian friend was lost in the shadow of mourning. For hours they had walked deeper and deeper into the sacred valley, and Napela had not lifted his head for the entire journey, staring only at the path in front of him. Even when scattering rain covered him, he did not stop to seek refuge under the sheltering trees. Periodically a deep moan of sorrow escaped his body, and startled birds would dart from the nearby trees. Napela's mother, the chiefess, had died five days before and was buried in the Protestant cemetery. Upon his return to Wailuku, after the funeral, Napela was hardly recognizable. He would not eat, and the skin on his face sagged with misery. Kitty did not try to cajole him into a different temperament, but George noticed that her eyes often followed her husband's movement as he paced the garden or when he sat slumped over in his chair. She would move beside him and let her hand gently brush against his arm or back. This morning, when he had announced that he was walking into the valley, Kitty simply filled two canteens with water and packed a satchel with food. She had laid her forehead on his and whispered. "Aloha nui, kuʻuipo." *I love you, sweetheart.*

The two men had ridden horses up to a certain point and then abandoned them for the solace of walking. George wanted to find beautiful Hawaiian words to comfort his friend, but he could find no words in either language tender enough, so he kept silent and walked.

Rain came again, this time pelting and cold, and Jonathan stopped. He looked back at his companion and his shoulders sagged.

"I am sorry, Brother George. We should get out of this."

George nodded. They found a fallen koa tree whose root base spread out wide enough to shelter the two men. They sat silently listening to the hiss of rain as it fell among the foliage, turning the green leaves shiny. The smell of the dark earth, the sound of the rain, and the sight of the clouds on the pali filled George's senses. He knew he would never be the same. The island and the people had changed him forever. He was so deep in his thoughts that he almost did not make out Jonathan's words when he spoke.

"My mother said that she and my daughter would pass each other on the rainbow."

"Your daughter? But, your child isn't born. Did your mother think the baby would be a girl?"

"Yes. She said that the ancestors whispered to her about our child." George nodded. "You do not find this a superstation, Brother George?"

"I believe in personal revelation, Brother Jonathan. I believe in dreams and visions and angels appearing to prophets." Jonathan looked at him in wonder as he continued. "During your mother's last days I think the veil was very thin between this life and the next."

Jonathan put his head in his hands and wept. "Thank you for bringing me this gospel, Brother George," he said between sobs. "I love this gospel."

"I know you do. You were the man prepared, remember? E ka haole! *Oh, the white man!*"

Jonathan let go a soggy chuckle and wiped his face with the palms of his hands. "Who would have thought that such a young one would bring this great message?" He took a deep breath, and George watched as some of the sorrow drained from his face. "The last time I was with my mother I told her about The Church of Jesus Christ of Latter-day Saints. I was glad I was able to share that with her."

"And what did she say?"

"That it was a long name for a church." The two men chuckled together.

"Your mother was wise."

"Yes. Her people loved her."

"Wasn't she concerned that you were leaving the Protestant church?"

"She was. At first she did not like the idea."

"But then?"

"I told her about Joseph Smith and the Book of Mormon." A single tear rolled down his cheek. "I told her about eternal sealings."

"And what did she think of that?"

"She was glad. She liked the idea of the family of God, and the cords that could tie her and Hawaii Waaole together." He extended his arm out from under the shelter of the tree and let the rain splatter on his hand. "No waimaka o ka lani."

George looked over at him. "The tears of the sky?"

"Heaven."

"The tears of heaven. What does it mean?"

"Rain is the affectionate tears of the gods. They weep with me because I have lost my mother."

George also held out his hand to feel the rain. "Beautiful." His voice became wistful. "It rained at sea the day my mother died."

"Tell me."

A wave of nostalgia broke on George's tender feelings, pushing his thoughts to an image he worked hard to avoid. For a moment he was on the deck of the ship as the rough seamen consigned his mother's body to the deep. He saw his sister's hair whipping about in the wind and his little brother Angus clinging to his father's leg. He saw his father's stricken face. George spoke to clear the picture from his mind. "My mother believed the words of the gospel as soon as they were preached. My father too."

"Preached by your uncle John Taylor?"

George brought his hand in and shook off the water. "Yes. He was married to my Aunt Leonora, my father's sister." He pulled his knees closer to his chest. "My mother and father embraced the gospel not only with their hearts, but with their commitment. They left everything they knew—everything—and followed the Prophet's call to gather to Zion." George fought hard against the press of tears behind his eyes. "She died on the rough crossing. I was fifteen."

"You were young to lose your mother—and later your father."

"I was." George pressed his lips together and watched the rain. After a time he spoke, his voice low and husky. "I just thank heaven for the truth of the gospel."

"Yes, thank heaven for that." Jonathan put his hand on George's arm. "And thank heaven for you, George Cannon. You have given me much."

George shook his head. "I am grateful to you, Jonathan Napela, for your friendship and help with the language. And you and Kitty have given me a home in which to live . . . a home . . ." His voice trailed off.

"But you miss your home with your family."

"I do. But I want to return to them having served well."

Jonathan chuckled. "There is no worry about that."

George's mind jumped to another subject. "And just think what we are accomplishing with the translation of the Book of Mormon! I could never have done that without you."

"Someone else could have helped you."

"No. I think the Lord has chosen you for this, Brother Jonathan. You are well educated. You are a descendant of the old chiefs of the island of Maui, and in your family the language has been preserved and spoken in the greatest purity. Besides, you have thoroughly studied the principles of the gospel. Few in the nation are as well qualified to help me in this work."

Jonathan shook his head, looking ill at ease with the praise. "It is a gift for me to help."

George smiled. "A gift, is it? Well then, I say we get back

to the work! We have the translation to do, a conference of the Church to prepare, and a chapel to build."

Jonathan smiled. "I think there is some Calvinist in you, Brother George."

"Why is that?"

"You agree with their sentiments that 'idle hands are the devil's workshop.'"

George smiled. "I wonder if President Brigham Young was a Calvinist before he converted."

The rain stopped, and the two friends came out from under their shelter. Jonathan stretched and lifted his arms to the sky. A snatch of sunlight broke through the clouds and shone briefly into the valley.

"Ka hana a ka makua, o ka hana no ia a keiki," Jonathan chanted.

What parents do, children will do, George translated silently. It was a fitting tribute for Jonathan's beloved mother. She had taught her son well, and there was no doubt in George's mind that Jonathan would, in turn, teach his child well.

CHAPTER 24

Iao Valley, Maui
April 6, 1852

Brother Cannon stood in conversation with the Maui missionaries and several of the native converts in a beautiful place in the lower part of the Iao Valley. A bold mountain stream tumbled down from the mountain swirling past a grove of kukui trees, whose pale leaves fluttered in the wind. Normally, the trees afforded a delightful shade against the sun, but on this day, sun was not the problem. George had seen these dark, bellied clouds often enough to know that rain was inevitable.

"Brethren, I know we have been fasting and praying for a fair day that we might hold our conference outside in nature's beauty, but these clouds threaten rain."

"And at any moment," Brother Keeler said.

George nodded. "Therefore, I think we should direct the Saints to a building in Wailuku where we can hold our meeting." He turned to go, and most of the men followed, except Jonathan Napela, Kaleohano, and Akuna Pake. George glanced back and stopped, noting the puzzled look on Jonathan's face. "Brother Napela?"

"You are not going to hold the meeting under the beautiful kukui trees?"

"Well, we would love to, but the rain makes it impossible."

Jonathan looked at the sky. "Impossible?" He looked George squarely in the face. "Brother Cannon, did we not pray to the Lord for good weather for our conference?"

"We did, but . . ."

"And should we not have the faith that our prayers will be answered?"

Jonathan asked the question simply without any hint of judgment or condemnation, but George felt the rebuke. He was about to say that sometimes the Lord says no to things requested, but the Spirit restrained him. Instead he gave his friend a slight smile. "Of course, Brother Napela, you are right. We will trust the Lord and hold our meeting where we have planned."

As the congregation moved off toward the grove, George and Brother Keeler went to walk with Jonathan and Kitty. Kitty held their baby daughter in a soft cotton quilt. Jonathan smiled meekly as the two missionaries approached. "I am sorry for questioning you brethren," he said sincerely.

"We are not offended, Brother Jonathan. We all need a reminder of our faith," George said.

Brother Keeler smiled timidly at Kitty Napela. "How are you and your beautiful daughter?"

"We are well, thank you, Brother Keeler." She looked over at George and then to her husband. "Little Kaiwaokalani has come to ask you for a gift, Brother Cannon." She kissed the baby's forehead and waited for her husband to speak.

Brother Napela smiled. "We are having a gathering of

friends at our home after the meeting, and we wondered if you would like to give our Hattie her blessing and speak her name."

George beamed over at Jonathan. "It would be such an honor, thank you."

"What is the name you've given her, Brother Napela?" Brother Keeler questioned. "If you don't mind my asking?"

Jonathan reached over and ran his finger gently over his daughter's cheek. "Her full name is long, but her missionary name is Hattie, and we call her Panana. Harriet Panana Kaiwaokalani Napela."

"Panana? What does it mean?" Brother Keeler asked.

"One who guides. It was the name given her by King Kamehameha III."

Brother Keeler looked impressed. "The king gave her a name?" He turned to George for explanation.

"Don't look at me. I have not heard this story either."

The two waited for further explanation, but Brother Bigler came to them at that moment, and they were distracted with business for the meeting.

"I will tell you the story after the meeting," Jonathan said as he and Kitty went off to settle themselves under the trees with the rest of the congregation.

When George stood at the front of the gathering, two hundred faces looked up at him, yet he did not feel like running or passing along the responsibility of speaking to someone else; this time he felt only to bless them, tell them of his love, and preach to them the simple truths of salvation and the principles of the gospel that would unite them.

"Brothers and sisters, we meet together as one family—the family of God. We are pleased to see so many with us today, and we feel blessed . . ." he looked over at Brother Napela, "that our weather is good." Brother Napela smiled. "Today is an important day. Twenty-two years ago, April 6, 1830, our Prophet Joseph Smith, stood in a small home in Fayette, New York, and, under the direction of the Lord, organized The Church of Jesus Christ of Latter-day Saints. At the time there were six members of the Church—think of it, only six, and now there are thousands from many parts of the world who have heard the truths of the restored Church and are coming as sheep into the fold. Through all the persecution the Saints of the Lord have endured, the work has rolled on and will continue to roll on until the kingdoms of this world will become the kingdom of our God and his Christ." He paused and looked over the congregation. "And now the kingdom is being established in these beautiful islands. We have five hundred members of the Church on the island of Maui and five branches, one at Waiakoa, Keanae, Wailua, Waianu, and Honomanu."

He looked at Brother Bigler and Brother Keeler. "Those of us who came to these islands as the first missionaries felt deeply that the gospel should be preached to the native people—a people whose hearts are pure and open to the truth. Since that time many have been baptized, and many men have been called to the priesthood. Today we will ordain Brother William Uaua and Brother Jonathan Napela as priests in the Aaronic Priesthood. We will also call Brother Uaua and Brother Kaleohano as clerks." In the congregation many heads nodded, and Brother Cannon felt the power of their commitment. "Many of you have suffered persecution because of your decision to join with the Church." He glanced at Jonathan and

Kitty. "It is not easy to be a member of this Church, and some who have joined with us have turned back because of the falsehoods preached against us and the threats made against their person and property." George's words caught in his throat as he thought back to that horrible day in Nauvoo. He saw again the throng of weeping Saints, and the wagons carrying the bodies of Joseph and Hyrum Smith. His voice thickened with emotion as his focus came back to the attendant faces of the congregation. "I know something of persecution and sacrifice. I saw what Joseph and Hyrum Smith gave for their testimonies of this gospel. They gave their lives. Can I offer less? Those of you who have felt the spirit know that there is no other choice. There is no other choice but to join with us and meet the challenges. Others may falter, but we pray for you. We pray that you will find the strength to be faithful."

The Hawaiian words flowed with grace and power. Brother Cannon spoke the language like one of them, and they loved him for it. The people listened carefully to the words as they came from this haole boy with his tattered shoes and pale blue eyes. He did not speak with arrogance or superiority, but with caring and kinship. He brought into their minds and hearts their place in the Lord's kingdom. Ohana. *All God's children.*

The meeting continued long into the afternoon with singing, preaching, and the teaching of new principles of the doctrines of the kingdom.

The clouds hovered, but rain did not fall.

A heavy rain caused the imu in the Napela's backyard to steam and smoke, but the guests inside the house were not concerned. The roasted pig, chicken, fish, and sweet potatoes were safe inside the pit, and sharing the meal together would be a glorious finish to a glorious day. In their meetings they had been taught the principles of fasting, prayer, and tithing. They had been called to lift themselves above the world and to prepare themselves to receive the Book of Mormon in their native language. Many rejoiced, knowing that this would be a great blessing. Several of the native brethren had given powerful sermons and testimonies, and Napela and Uaua had been ordained priests in the Aaronic Priesthood.

George now sat in a chair on the lanai, enjoying his meal, and thinking of the blessing given to Hattie Panana Napela. She would grow to be a woman of grace and influence of whom Jonathan and Kitty would be proud. George stared out at the rain and thought of the Lord's goodness. He shook his head. Here he was eating poi and roasted pig, surrounded by native Hawaiians, and feeling as much at home as if he were sitting in Aunt Leonora's kitchen and eating boiled potatoes, Yorkshire pudding, and sliced beef. From inside the house came the beginnings of a comical mele about a man in love and his attempts to win the girl of his dreams. George smiled and sang along with his brothers and sisters.

Notes

- The faith manifested by the Hawaiian elders concerning holding the meeting outdoor in spite of the threat of rain is written in Cannon's journal.
- Missionary name: After 1850 the Protestant missionaries mandated that Hawaiian mothers give their children Western names. Many adhered to this practice, but also gave their children secret Hawaiian names.

CHAPTER 25

Wailuku, Maui

April 8, 1852

Dear Mary,

 We have just held the first conference of the Church in Hawaii and I thought of you and the family and the Saints in the Great Salt Lake Valley also gathering to unite the Church. I am sure our meetings were very different as we did not meet in a building, but within a grove of beautiful kukui trees. And we did not have President Young or members of the twelve apostles to speak to us, but heard good words of counsel from the missionaries and several of the native brethren. Their faith is strong, Mary, and they so desire to do what the Lord requires, but many are tied to the superstitions of their old culture or the teachings of the Protestants. Many struggle with tobacco and drink, but are attempting to put away their pipes and shun the bottle.

 We taught them the law of tithing and Brother Napela gave a stirring address on following every word that comes from the mouth of the prophets. He pledged *that he would embrace this new law. My heart felt to rejoice, dear Mary, for the spiritual strength of my friend. His wife Kitty has not yet come into the waters of baptism, but she treats me and the other missionaries kindly and we feel to bless her for that. I wrote you about the birth of their daughter, Hattie, and today she was blessed and received her name. I will write the name out for you, so the younger children can practice their Hawaiian. Her name is Harriet Panana Kaiwaokalani Napela. The name Panana was given to her by King Kamehameha III. It is said that when the king met Kitty Napela, he was so taken with her beauty that he could look at no one else in the crowd of people. He made Kitty promise that when a child came to them, that he would be allowed to give the child a special name. It seems that promise has been kept. Panana means compass, or one who guides, and she is a darling infant who I am sure will grow up to be as beautiful as her mother.*

  The work is moving forward at such a pace. Often we are baptizing and confirming twenty or thirty people at a time. The people have been blessed with dreams and miracles. I will relate one miracle to show you their faith. Since I hear that Angus and David Henry are lagging a bit in their commitment in the Church, perhaps you can relate this to them. One of Brother Napela's friends, William Uaua, was away from his home for several days. When he returned he found people in his house wailing and lamenting that his wife was dead. She had died three hours prior to his arrival and the family and friends were mourning her. Brother Uaua took the blessed oil, anointed her, and by priesthood power called her back. Within moments, the spirit returned to her body. I know you can relate to this, Mary, having been pronounced dead when that wagon rolled over you. You were brought back to us by faith and the power of the priesthood. It is a mighty power and I rejoice that it has been restored to bless the lives of the people.

I am often humbled by the faith of the Hawaiian people. Just days ago I believed that a storm up in the Iao Valley would doom our outdoor conference, but by the faith of the native Saints, we had not one drop of rain.

The work progresses, Mary, and we seem to be busy day and night. There are times I wake in the morning to find people standing at the door waiting to be baptized. With all the activity, letters may be longer in coming. Know that I think of you in the Valley and pray for your success. Please share this letter with Uncle John and Aunt Leonora as I will not have time to write separately.

Your loving brother,
George

P.S. Please pray for the Saints in their acceptance of the law of tithing. We have fasted and prayed about teaching this principle as the people are mostly poor, but it is a command from the Lord, and has been through all the ages of time from Father Adam and Mother Eve. Some came into the Church because we required no subsidy from the members, only food and lodging for the missionaries when we needed. This was different from the Protestant ministers who require much from their members. Brother Napela says that some of the weaker

Saints will give up on us because of this principle, but that does not mean that we should go against offering it. He says it will be a way of tying the members more closely to the Church and to each other. He is a very wise man. He has written a letter to President Young, which I translated into English for him. I think the President will be pleased that we have such stalwart native members.

Be well, my Mary, and pray for my pants that they do not fall to pieces before I get a new pair.

Love again to the family.

CHAPTER 26

Wailuku, Maui

March 19, 1853

"And behold, the third time they did understand the voice which they heard; and it said unto them . . ." George put his finger on the verse and looked up. "Are we satisfied with the translation for that line?"

Jonathan nodded. "Yes."

"So, on to the next line: 'Behold my Beloved Son, in whom I am well pleased, in whom I have glorified my name—hear ye him.'"

Jonathan sat with his eyes closed, listening intently to the words Brother Cannon was translating. He mumbled the words *iloko ona aʻu i hoonani ai Koʻu inoa* several times. "Hoonani means to make something beautiful. Is that the proper word for glorified?" It was a struggle for him to say the word *glorified* in English, and George smiled.

"I think that is just right." George put down the pen, stretched his fingers and squeezed his eyelids together. His hand and eyes were sore from hours of translating. He looked down to his side and jumped. Hattie Napela stood staring up at him with alert brown eyes. "Oh my!" George barked. His abrupt words frightened the child, but instead of crying, Hattie squawked at him in gibberish and hit him on the leg with her little calabash cup. "Moku, moku, moku!"

Jonathan laughed. "She has been standing there for the past five minutes, hoping to distract you from your work. I suppose she thinks she can interrupt us because it's her birthday."

George picked her up. "Of course! It's your special day!" He put his hands on either side of her waist and balanced her on his legs. "I'm sorry, dear one. I get lost when your daddy and I work." He looked over at Jonathan. "Especially when we are so near the end."

Hattie smacked him on the nose with her cup and started in again with her scolding.

"Ow! I don't think she likes my excuse," George said, standing and holding her like a sack of potatoes. Hattie squealed with delight. He looked down at his borrowed pants and light cotton shirt. "Good thing we are already wearing our play clothes." Hattie burbled out unintelligible words, and George laughed. "I agree! Let's get on with our picnic at the beach."

Jonathan stood. "Yes. Perhaps I will teach her to surf on the waves."

Kitty came to the doorway of the room just in time to hear this last remark. "She is not quite old enough, foolish man. She is barely walking by herself. Give her time to get sturdy on her legs."

"We will just have to make her stand on the round stone ball like my mother did with me. That way her legs will get strong."

Kitty shook her head. "Come along, you two. Everyone is ready to go." She reached out to take Hattie, but the little girl squealed and kicked. George brought her into his arms, and she clasped him around his neck.

"Well, Brother George, I think you have a child to care for today," Jonathan said.

"That will be a treat for me!"

"You may not think so after an hour or two of demands," Kitty warned.

The three turned from the room and moved outside. As soon as they stepped from the house, the low mellow thrum of conch shells sounded. Six men in native costume blew long, haunting notes on the beautiful shells as two aunties came forward, one placing a tiny feather crown on Hattie's head and the other hanging a lei of flowers around her neck.

A fleet of carriages stood ready for the celebration guests. The people waited for Napela and his family to climb into the first carriage and settle themselves, and then everyone followed suit. George chuckled at the imperious way Hattie was acting, as though it were her tenth birthday, not her first. The little cherub seemed well aware that all the fuss was for her.

Hattie dug in the sand at the edge of the ocean, and George helped her make a hale out of sticks, sand, and seaweed. She toddled after an aggressive aeʻo bird, and George saved her from being pecked. She was nearly run over when the kukini, *swift runners,* came charging down the beach course in a very close foot race. George snatched her out of the way just in time. As the hours wore on, he helped her swim, gave her drinks of water, and made her a little canoe from ti leaves to push around in the shallows. Brother Cannon was Hattie Napela's willing kokua—*helper*—and even though the tiny girl seemed never to tire, he kept close to her side.

When Kitty finally took her away to feed her, Hattie yelped, whined, and cried for the missionary, but when she was later returned to his care she'd fallen asleep in two minutes. She now lay snuggled in a cotton quilt under the shade of a pandanas tree, her feather crown crushed in her fist. George watched her, a wistful look on his face.

Kaleohano came and sat in the sand beside him. "Are you sure you want one of those?"

"Without question. Perhaps six or seven."

"Six or seven? You are a brave man, Brother Cannon." Kaleohano patted him on the shoulder. "But I think you are up to the task. If you can manage several hundred Hawaiian children, then you can handle anything."

George knew Kaleohano was referencing the childlike qualities of his people: the inclination they had to cling to old ways and superstitions, to take things easy, to work, but not beyond a certain limit. And, although George knew that living the gospel brought great joy, he also knew it was demanding. He watched several men playing 'ulu maika, *rolling the stone disks,* and saw the mirth in their good-natured competition. He saw the people swimming, and looked again at Hattie's perfect face. He loved them, and he knew that God loved them. Here before him was a branch of the olive tree, and he knew the leaders of the Church would do all they could to preserve this precious part of the vineyard.

"Kaleohano?"

"Yes, Brother Cannon?"

"How do you think the members of the Church will handle trials and hardships?"

Kaleohano studied the missionary. "We have already suffered trials and hardships, Brother Cannon." George sat silently, watching the waves, and Kaleohano sighed. "But, you think greater trials will come."

"It is always the way, Kaleohano. The adversary sees spiritual strength growing in the Hawaiian people. Do you think he will leave that alone?" Kaleohano shook his head, and George continued. "No. The father of darkness will blow upon the faith of the people like the harsh Kona winds blow upon the banana tree."

"And you do not expect that we will stand?"

"I think the trials will be too harsh for many."

"But we will have the missionaries to help us."

George contemplated this. "Yes, but what if there is a time when the missionaries are not with you?"

Kaleohano gave him a worried look. "Do you think that will ever happen?"

George decided not to burden his friend with any more of his misgivings. "No. I wouldn't think so, but . . ."

"But trials will come," Kaleohano finished. George nodded. "This we know, Brother George. Napela, Uaua, and I have often spoken of it—of what we can do to keep the banana trees standing."

George grinned. He liked the thought of the three men discussing the health of the Church and the spiritual welfare of the members. Perhaps he was worrying unnecessarily. He picked up a twig and absently broke it into pieces.

Kaleohano looked at the young man with compassion. "There are some of us that will not fall, even if a hurricane comes, Brother George. The words of truth are planted deep in our hearts."

George took a deep breath. "Thank you for that, Brother Kaleohano."

"Now, why don't you go and swim?"

George looked over at Hattie. "But, I . . ."

"I will watch the little queen while she sleeps. You go and let the ocean waves take away your cares."

George nodded. He hurried across the hot sand and dove into the cool water. He joined Jonathan and Kitty in their carefree swimming, and, for a time, the responsibilities of the mission gave way to water and sky.

Note

- George Q. Cannon and Jonathan Napela began the translation of the Book of Mormon into the Hawaiian language on January 27, 1852, and completed the work July 22, 1853. The final reading of the finished manuscript was accomplished January 31, 1854. The book was published in San Francisco in 1855.

CHAPTER 27

Wailuku, Maui

July 10, 1853

Stop counting steps! George chided himself. *You will get to Wailuku in so many sweltering steps whether you count them or not.* For a time he heeded his own counsel, but then the counting began again.

He had been to Kula on horseback to conduct Church business, but the beast had acquired a limp, so had to be left behind. George wanted to stay behind too. He wanted to visit with the members, eat opakapaka, and listen to the resonant Hawaiian voices singing the mele as the crescent moon sailed over Haleakala. But a strong feeling had come to him to return to Wailuku as quickly as possible, and, since a horse was not available, his feet became the painful transport.

"Now *I* will have a limp from walking all these miles in worn-out shoes," George mumbled. He wiped sweat from his brow and shook his head. "Stop complaining, George Cannon. Someone seeing you now would never think you'd walked thousands of miles from Illinois to the Utah Territory."

As he crossed the flat plain by Kahului, the prompting

to hurry came again. The hills into Wailuku never looked so daunting. As he made his way up Main Street, he saw Brother Napela coming down to meet him. The skin on the man's face was gray, and his eyes were red-rimmed and tormented. When Jonathan saw his friend, he let go a howl of anguish.

"I knew you would come. I knew you would come." He gripped George's arms. "I have been praying you back. Praying and praying."

"Brother Jonathan, what's happened?" George demanded, his heart pounding in his chest. Jonathan's head swung back and forth as though attempting to shake away the horror that beset him. "Jonathan!" George said sharply.

"It . . . it's . . . Hattie . . . smallpox."

"No!" George grabbed Jonathan's arm and dragged him along in the direction of the house.

Strangled cries issued from Jonathan's mouth. "And . . . and Kitty . . . another seizure. I blessed her, and she's better, but . . ."

George let go of Jonathan's arm and ran; fatigue and battered feet forgotten for the fear that gripped his heart. He shoved open the gate and raced through the Napela's garden. The ginger flowers and trilling apukani bird held no allure. All he could see was the yellow flag posted on the front lanai. He passed several family members and friends standing in a miserable clump a safe distance from the house. When Kaleohano saw Brother Cannon he stepped forward.

"He said you would come!"

"Where is she?"

"Bedroom. Her mother is with her." George turned and Kaleohano grabbed his arm. "But, wait! Wait! Will you go in there with the plague?"

George did not answer, but broke free, and raced up the

steps. He burst in through the front door, moving quickly to the room, and opening the door. When Kitty saw him she stumbled over and collapsed at his feet.

"Save her. Please, save her . . . and me . . . make us well. I promise . . . I promise I will believe and be baptized if you make us well."

George knelt down and took her by the arms. "Kitty, stop. Stop! Look at me!" She did, and he was shocked by the horrible visage: eyes nearly swollen shut from crying, and a bloody lip that showed teeth marks. These features, framed by stringy, unkempt hair, assuaged his anger and frustration. His words sounded with more compassion then he'd initially intended. "Kitty, do not seek for a sign. Do not bargain with the Lord. Trust Him—trust His will and His goodness."

The words fell on deaf ears. "Make us well," she pleaded. "I cannot lose another child."

Jonathan staggered to the bedroom door, and George looked at him with pity and understanding.

"Jonathan, take her to the chair."

As Jonathan lifted his wife and moved her to the chair, George stood and went to the bedside. Hattie was not yet two, and she lay in her parents' bed. She looked like a small doll that had been tucked in carefully by a caring child. A hook of pain caught in George's heart and made him gasp.

No! No! Not Hattie. Not my little Hattie. His mind raced through all that he knew of the illness: headaches, backaches, high fever and chills, a severe rash, and physical disfigurement. Death. Hundreds dead in Honolulu where the scourge began. Hundreds buried in shallow graves. But that was Oahu, and Oahu was separated by sea and distance. Oahu was far away.

"She's had fever and chills?"

"Yes," Jonathan said in a choked voice.

"Headache?"

"Yes."

George took Hattie's hands and checked her palms and arms for any sign of rash. "But no rash."

"No. No rash."

Hattie did not move or open her eyes, and it hardly seemed she was breathing. George laid his hand on her head. It was burning with fever. He felt if he lifted his hand away, the skin would be red from the contact. Was the little angel so near death that the heat no longer caused her misery? Thoughts swirled in George's head. *The Lord can save her. He caused the blind to see, and He raised Jairus's daughter. But what if it is Hattie's time? What if the Lord is calling her home?* He shook his head. *She must have a calling to perform—a calling that will tie her to this earth. She must!* Suddenly the jumble of thoughts stopped, and a peaceful assurance settled into his mind. *It is not smallpox.*

"It's not smallpox."

Jonathan started. "How do you know that?"

George shook his head. "I just know. It's serious, but it's not smallpox." He turned to look at Jonathan. "Brother Jonathan, you now hold the Melchizedek Priesthood. Bring the consecrated oil and anoint your daughter."

The suffering man staggered to George's side and, with shaking hands, poured a few drops of oil on his daughter's head. After he said the pray of anointing, George placed his hands lightly on Hattie's head and pronounced the blessing. It was a powerful yet simple prayer. He called out Hattie's full name, and commanded the destroying angel to depart. Then, after several moments' pause, he promised the sufferer that, according to God's will, she would live to be a joy to her mother and father.

Belonging to HEAVEN

He also pronounced that many would know her name and be touched by her grace and beauty.

A stillness filled the room, and Kitty melted into tears.

George finished the blessing, and he and Jonathan slowly lifted their hands from Hattie's head. She took a deep, shuddering breath, and though she did not open her eyes, her small hand brushed absently across her face.

George sat by Hattie's cot as Jonathan and Kitty slept in the next room. An hour after the blessing, Hattie had opened her eyes and asked for coconut pudding. She'd eaten two bites and fallen back to sleep. Jonathan carried her to her cot, stumbling with exhaustion and relief, and George had sent him and Kitty off to their room.

It was just before dawn, and the house was still. George leaned closer toward Hattie and chanted. "Ua ala 'ula mai o kua, ua moku ka pawa o ke ao; a keokeo mauka a wehe ke ala 'ula a pua 'lena, a ao loa." *There comes a glimmer of color in the mountains, the curtains of night are parted, the mountains light up; day breaks; the east blooms with yellow; it is broad daylight.*

George ringed his finger in one of Hattie's brown curls, smiling at the thought that someday he and Elizabeth Hoagland might have a few of these little cherubs, mixed in with a parcel of rambunctious boys. George blushed at these nonmissionary thoughts of marriage and family, and he quickly fixed his mind on priesthood blessings and the Book of Mormon translation. *The Book of Mormon in Hawaiian!* He and Jonathan would probably have it finished by the end of the month.

Hattie smacked her lips and opened her eyes. "Wai." *Water.*

George gently sat her up and brought a glass of water to her mouth. She drank greedily, some of the water dribbling down her chin.

George moved the glass away. "Better?" She nodded. He took a corner of the quilt and dried her face. He laid her back on her pillow.

"Mama?"

"Sleeping."

"Makua kane?" *Father.*

"Sleeping too."

Hattie accepted this news without fuss, and as always, George was amazed by her unflappable nature.

She reached up and patted his mouth. "Mele. Mele."

George smiled. He envisioned the joyful faces of Jonathan and Kitty when they awoke to find their daughter nearly back to normal. He brushed a finger over Hattie's cool forehead and began to sing:

> *Lead kindly light amid the encircling gloom.*
> *Lead thou me on.*
> *The night is dark and I am far from home.*
> *Lead thou me on.*

As George sang, he felt loneliness, doubt, and fear float with the notes out the open window and into the soft glow of morning.

Notes

- The sickness and seizures that plagued Kitty Napela were documented in several of the missionary journals, including George Cannon's.
- The smallpox epidemic of 1853 began in Honolulu, but soon spread to the other islands. It is estimated that 30 percent of the native population perished.

CHAPTER 28

Wailuku, Maui
October 16, 1853

Dear Mary,

    Soon the whales will return to the Lahaina channel and I will say my good-byes to these islands. I do not know an exact date, but I feel that the time is growing short. Not that any of us missionaries will slack in our work, but home seems to be calling. Sister Hoagland sent a letter stating that if I were delayed much longer she was seriously thinking of packing a satchel and coming over to join me. I think she would do it. She seems to be a partner after my own heart.

    Elders Tanner, Karren, Johnson, and Allred are taking well to the work. They are grateful for the intense language lessons given by Brother Napela. He says that if he can have the new missionaries for two months, he can give them a good start with the language. It is a good method and very different from how we original missionaries had to learn. I feel to give thanks every day *for the blessing of learning the language so quickly. It was a miracle that I fully acknowledge.*

A group of us have just returned from a trip up the mountain Haleakala to see the crater. There were fourteen of us and seven Hawaiian guides. It was a three-day trip, and we saw glorious vistas and had some adventures. I am writing the story down in my journal, Mary, and will share it with the family when I get home. Please tell the children that I could not bring them lava rocks from the volcano because our guides said it would anger Pele, the goddess of the volcano, and we did not want any bad luck.

I wrote you of the devastating smallpox epidemic, dear Mary, and it wrenches my heart when I think of the beautiful Hawaiian people suffering so from this sickness. They are like newborn babies against diseases, and thousands died from this outbreak. The board of health is estimating that 30 percent of the Hawaiian population may have perished. I know we lost about that number in the Church. Many were saved by priesthood blessings, but many died. We lost several of the strongest native elders, and many of us missionaries struggled with why the Lord would take such stalwart men—those that were needed here to fortify the Church. We think that perhaps they were taken to preach to their brothers and sisters on the other side. I don't know. I do know that the Lord will sort everything out.

I have been to most of the major islands now in an attempt to raise money for the printing press to print the Hawaiian Book of Mormon and for passage money for the missionaries to return home. It is not an easy task as the people are mostly poor, but they do what they can. One man brought his family's only horse and gave it to me to sell. I was moved to tears by his faith and felt impressed to bless him and promise him that he and his family would have their temporal needs met. I know the Lord does bless His children here. When I first met Brother Napela, he was two thousand dollars in debt, and they were in jeopardy of having their house taken. He has born testimony many times that the Lord told him if he would care for the missionaries, that all would be well. And so it is. He has withstood much persecution and continues to progress in the Church. He is one of the best men I have had the privilege to know, and I will miss him when the time comes to depart.

We will be going to the island of Lanai in a few days to see if it would be a good place for gathering the Saints. I will also go to the island of Hawaii soon to check on the workings of the Church and encourage the members.

I know this letter is long, but since I have not written for a time I thought it would be all right. I know I will be amazed when I see all of you again and there will be much to share and discuss. You will probably be amazed when you see me. I hope I can find a new pair of pants before returning, or you will think me the most ragged of fellows.

You are always in my prayers.

> Your loving brother,
> George

Note

- On the return trip from looking at property on Lanai, the sea was very rough and there was no wind. They attempted to row, but to little avail. Brother Cannon and the other missionaries became deathly ill. Finally Brother Cannon called upon Napela to pray. He did, and within a few minutes a pleasant breeze picked up, which carried them into Lahaina.

CHAPTER 29

Wailuku, Maui

April 9, 1854

Jonathan Napela stood in the doorway watching Brother George as he slept in the large chair on the lanai. It was near midnight, but Jonathan did not have the heart to wake his friend. With his head laid back against the cushion, his hand peacefully sprawled on his open journal, he looked again like the vulnerable child.

"Ki 'ia ka hele a ka na 'au ha 'aha 'a." *Hesitant walks the humble hearted.*

In the years of their friendship, Jonathan had never seen boastful actions or heard bragging words come from Elder George Cannon. Yet, surely the man had reason to boast. From the time when he and his missionary companions first arrived in the islands, the work had come far. Upon their arrival, not one native had been taught the doctrines of the Church. The missionaries did not have literature written in Hawaiian to explain the doctrine nor one word of the language to tell the story of Joseph Smith or the Book of Mormon. And now there were over three thousand native members of The Church of Jesus

Christ of Latter-day Saints, representing all the major islands. The Book of Mormon had been translated into the language of the land and would soon be published as a book, native men held the priesthood and served as local missionaries, and several meetinghouses were built or under construction.

Jonathan looked out into the darkened garden and listened to the rain—a soft rain. "Ku ua ho 'opala 'ohi 'a." *The rain that ripens the mountain apples.* He was about to turn into the house when mumbled words came from his sleeping friend.

"Plum pudding."

Jonathan let out a bark of laughter, and George stirred. A light breeze lifted the pages of George's journal, and he opened his eyes. When he looked over, Jonathan gave him a sheepish grin.

"Sorry, Brother George, I did not mean to wake you."

George slowly focused on his surroundings and sat straighter in his chair. "Was I snoring?"

Jonathan chuckled. "Yes, like a wild boar." George looked embarrassed. "No! No! You were not snoring, but you were talking."

"Talking? What did I say?"

"Plum pudding."

George laughed. "I was dreaming of the plum pudding I had at the Robinson's house this evening. It was the best plum pudding I've ever eaten." He looked out into the dark yard. "What time is it?"

"Almost midnight."

George shivered. "How long have I been asleep?"

Jonathan secured a quilt from the back of a chair in the house, moved out onto the porch, and handed it to George. "I am not sure, my friend."

George placed his journal on the side table and accepted the quilt. His look became nostalgic as he ran his hand over the soft cotton fabric.

"What is it?" Jonathan asked as he sat down.

"The night before I met you, a kind woman placed a quilt like this over me." He spread the quilt over his legs. "That was over three years ago."

Jonathan studied his friend's face. "You are sad tonight, George Cannon."

"A little."

"And a little tired?"

George sagged back into the chair. "Yes."

"You have every right to be tired. We have just finished with a conference for the Church with over a thousand members attending. And for the past several months you have been all over these islands. You have seen more places than I have seen in a lifetime: Oahu, Kauai, Molokaʻi! It makes me tired just to think of it."

"And next month I will go to the big island of Hawaii."

Jonathan looked over at George. "You are trying to bring all the little chicks safely under the wings before you leave us."

George laid his head back against the cushion as a tear slid from the corner of his eye. "Yes."

"And you will leave us soon?"

It took George several moments to answer. "Yes." He brushed the tear away but more followed. "Yes. Word has come that we five original missionaries are to begin searching for the means to return to the Valley."

Jonathan put his head in his hands and wept. After a time, he took a handkerchief from his pocket, and dried his face. "I knew . . . I knew this day would come, but perhaps I was hoping it would not." He took a deep breath. "Perhaps I can be like the trickster, Maui. I will stand up on Haleakala, and hold time in its place."

George gave him an understanding smile. "Or perhaps we could see time the way the Lord sees it, the way it is in heaven—which is, that there is no time. No partings, no comings and goings."

"That is why heaven is heaven," Jonathan said softly.

For several minutes, the two sat silently, listening to the patter of rain on the leaves of the garden.

Jonathan sat forward in his chair. "Are you worried for us, Brother George?"

"What do you mean?"

"Worried that after you and Brother Bigler and the others leave us that we will go back to our old ways?"

"There is always a temptation for people to go back to their old ways."

"But you see us differently. You see us as the children of Abraham, and you have taught us to honor this great heritage—to keep the commandments of God. To keep the Words of Wisdom. To be morally and physically clean." He started laughing. "I remember the sermon you gave the one time about bathing and keeping ourselves free from lice and ticks like the aliʻi do—about putting the dogs, chickens, and pigs out of our houses. You said to build the livestock their own houses outside." The two laughed together.

"We lost some of the poorer Saints after that sermon," George quipped.

"Yes. They thought it was an extravagance to give an animal its own house!"

The two worked to control their laughter. They did not

want to disturb those sleeping in the house, but the gaiety and remembrance was a tonic for the melancholy of separation, and each wanted to stretch this time of lightness and aloha hoa hanau, *brotherhood.*

"There have been many good memories, Brother George. Even with all the work and struggle—many good memories."

George laid his hand on his journal. "Yes, and I have written most of them here."

"Would you read some memories to me?"

George hesitated and then picked up the journal. He languidly turned pages and looked at dates. "Remember the time we went strawberry picking in Kula?"

"I do. I remember very well. What did you write?"

George read. "Friday, 11 June 1852. We arose this morning very early with the intention of going to Kula on a strawberry frolic. Brother Gaston took a cart in which the sisters rode. Picking strawberries. We had a very pleasant time and enjoyed ourselves much. Brother Keeler was over from Kaupo, Brother Napela from Wailuku." He looked over at Jonathan, who was nodding his head.

"Didn't we have what you call a pick nick?"

George laughed. "We did, and we had strawberries every way we could think of: strawberry sauce, strawberry milk, strawberry pudding."

"That was a good day. Read something else."

George leafed through the book. "This was my first trip to Moloka'i—almost two years ago. It doesn't seem possible." He read. "Friday, 18 June 1852. We started early this morning in a whaleboat and had rowed to the point of the island before the breeze struck us. We then hoisted the sail and ceased rowing. Brother Perkins and I were very seasick."

"You and the ocean have never been friends," Jonathan said, a great deal of pity coloring his words.

George looked up from the journal and smiled. "Oh, I love the ocean, Brother Jonathan. *Boats* on the ocean are my enemy." Jonathan laughed as George found his place in the journal. "We met with Brother and Sister Woodbury and were very glad to see each other. This part of this island does not afford many facilities for cultivation, but sufficient to raise enough for the inhabitants—the mountains come almost close down to the water's edge—leaving but a narrow strip of land for cultivation with occasionally a small valley entering into the mountains. The water is not very good, not so good as the water in Wailuku. There are a great numbers of fish ponds along the shore that produce great quantities of fish for which this Island is noted. It is quite a pretty Island and no doubt very healthy as there is a constant breeze blowing."

"Were you not amazed by those fish ponds, Brother George?"

"I was. The amount of fish they hold is remarkable."

"And they were built in ancient times."

"Which proves the brilliance of your people."

"Thank you for that," Jonathan said. He studied George's face. "Are you too tired to read something else?"

"I'm not tired at all anymore," George answered. He turned pages and paused at a few before stopping. He ran his finger along the words. "This is from Tuesday 17 May, 1853, but I won't read you the entire thing because much of it talks about receiving letters from home."

Jonathan gave him a crooked smile. "Letters from Elizabeth Hoagland, the teacher you often speak of?"

"Do I . . . speak of . . . really?"

For the sake of his friend's feelings, Jonathan contained his mirth. "It is only natural to speak often of those we love."

George blushed and took a detached stance. "Well, from several reports, I hear she is turning into a fine young woman." He narrowed his eyes at his friend. "Now, if you'll let me continue, I think you'll find this interesting as it concerns your friends." Before Jonathan could come back with a teasing reply, George read. "I also was much rejoiced to read some letters from Honolulu containing cheering news of the progress of the work there; the whole city was all excitement, they had baptized about 148 and there had been from 1,000 to 1,500 spectators to witness the baptisms; they had baptized as many as fifty-six one Sunday. They had ordained Brothers Uaua and J. W. H. Kauwahi elders and I. W. Kahumoku and Toma Paku priests, and several teachers and deacons. They speak in high terms of Elders Kauwahi and Uaua and of their speaking. Brother Johnson calls them sons of thunder, and says if I have any more children like Brother Uaua, to send them along and they would find employment for them."

Jonathan nodded. "Those two are powerful Saints."

"Indeed. When I was on Kauai, Brother Kauwahi helped Brother Farrer read over our translation of the Book of Mormon. Did I tell you that?"

"Yes, you told me. They were perfect for that job. Brother Farrer speaks the Hawaiian very well now, and Kauwahi is a brilliant son of the land."

George turned pages. "Yes, a famous lawyer known from one end of the islands to the other."

Jonathan smiled. "And known not only for his smartness but for his wildness and tricks—his drinking and rowdy ways."

"To put it kindly," George said candidly. "But since he

joined the Church and obtained the priesthood, his course has been exactly opposite. His voice is always raised to warn his brothers and sisters."

Jonathan sobered. "The gospel has a way of changing people—in spirit and body. It is powerful." He looked straight into George's face. "It changed me. How grateful I am that it changed me. When I think of all the things I have seen, Brother George, and all the miracles of healing—the woman who could not stand straight, the young boy with the broken arm, Uaua's wife coming back from the dead. I know that these are sure evidences of the power of the priesthood."

George nodded.

Jonathan leaned over and placed his hand on George's arm. "So, do not worry for us, Brother George. We will keep the gospel in our hearts. We will honor the great gift that you have brought us."

George brushed a tear from the corner of his eye and closed his journal.

Thoughts of sleep were forgotten as Jonathan Napela and George Cannon sat up far into the night telling each other stories, talking about doctrine, and evaluating the branches of the Church. They were just two men sitting on the lanai of a house in Wailuku—two men, two Saints, two brothers.

CHAPTER 30

Wailuku, Maui

June 26, 1854

Hawaii nei lived in his blood; it spoke in the sun and ocean, it sang in the splash of streams from the pali, and it whispered in the pink of sunrises and the ginger of sunsets. He was the son of chiefs and a thousand years of mana tied him to the land, yet when Jonathan Napela looked into the eyes of George Cannon, he saw the blue waters of the sea, the dark wood of the koa trees, and the red dirt of Honokahau. This keiki who had learned to love poi and speak the native tongue as though his ear had heard it from his birth was dear to him. Jonathan thought back to the day, over three years ago, when the young man in the light suit passed his home. He was rumpled and retiring, but he carried in his mouth the words of hope and in his heart the testimony of God's authority brought back to earth. The man and the message were dear to him.

As they walked the yard together, Jonathan knew it would be the last quiet time he would have with his friend. At the feast he would be surrounded by hundreds of members, and on the road to Lahaina there would be the other departing missionaries as well as the Hawaiian elders. Never one to miss a teaching opportunity, Brother Cannon had suggested the Hawaiian elders should ride along and he would give them final instructions and answer questions.

"I like your new pants and vest," Jonathan said.

"And shoes," George added, showing them off.

"How are they?"

"Good. Better than the ones I had before."

Jonathan scoffed. "The ones you had before were tattered bits of leather."

George looked up and grinned. "Ah, but they were comfortable."

The two men laughed together.

"Yes, we are grateful for the new missionaries coming to our islands to preach, but perhaps you are more grateful for the ones who bring their wives who cook and sew."

George nodded. "Truer words were never spoken. If Sister Hammond hadn't sewn me new pants I would have been heading home in rags."

The words "heading home" cast a cool shadow on the bright day, and the two friends continued their amble in silence.

Finally George spoke, keeping the conversation in the realm of Church business. "I hear there's a man offering his land on the island of Lanai as a gathering place for the Saints."

"Yes, a high chief, Levi Haalelea."

"And he is offering it at no charge?"

"Yes, for four years he says we can go and try it. Then if it works, a price can be negotiated."

"I think we need to be careful."

"I agree. I hear that Haalelea is a very good businessman, and that there is not much water on Lanai." Jonathan picked a ginger flower and breathed in its fragrance. "If only the king would let us gather to the Great Salt Lake Valley."

George shook his head. "I think the king is wise to keep his people together. Your numbers are few and you are susceptible to outside diseases. Think how many died with the smallpox."

Jonathan nodded and shuddered at the memory. "Yes, but the Hawaiian Saints need to be together in a place where we can strengthen each other in the gospel."

"And escape persecution."

"And escape persecution."

"This is President Young's vision: bring the faithful from the four corners of the earth to live united in faith, industry, and righteousness."

"I have not met President Young, yet I know that he is a prophet and a great man."

"I can testify of that, Brother Jonathan."

"Perhaps I will meet him someday."

George smiled at him. "Perhaps you will."

Hattie Napela came tottering around the side of the house. Seeing the two men, she squealed, and stumbled forward, holding out her arms, not to her father, but to Brother Cannon.

"She knows her favorite," Jonathan said as George picked her up.

Hattie patted his face. "Mele! Mele, mikanele!" *Song! Song, missionary!*

Jonathan chuckled. "You captured her with your singing when she was sick, and now you must pay the price."

George smiled and laid his forehead on Hattie's. "I will miss you when I go."

Jonathan felt a wave of melancholy flood his body. He excused himself and walked quickly toward the house.

"Where are you going?"

"To the house. Kitty and I have a gift for you. Do you think Brother and Sister Hammond are the only ones who can give you gifts?"

"Kohuole makuakane," *silly father,* George said in exaggerated tones. He made a funny face that sent Hattie into a fit of giggles.

Hattie pulled his ears. "Mele! Mele!"

"Ow! You are one determined little girl, aren't you?"

"Mele, kohuole mikanele!" *Song, silly missionary.*

"And smart."

As the afternoon withdrew, Elder George Cannon danced Hattie Napela around the yard, singing the hymns of Zion in soft, flowing Hawaiian.

Jonathan and Kitty watched the two from the front window, their faces filled with loss.

In the evening when the sun hovered over the island of Lanai and the sweet scent of flowers filled the air, more than a hundred people crowded into the open-sided hale, and said aloha to the Mormon missionaries. The Saints wore their best clothing—the women in their brightly colored holoku dresses, and the men in their European shirts with maile leis around their necks. The women wore strands of flower leis and crowns of flowers on their heads. Napela was proud of how beautiful they looked, and he greeted each member of the company with tenderness, and encouraged them to find a place at one of the tables. Four low tables were covered with ti leaves and spread with food: calabashes of poi, roasted kalo and potatoes, and packages of beef, fish, pork, and fowls done up in banana leaves that came hot from the imu. There were steamed crabs, grilled eel, and seaweed. There were bananas, mountain apples, and watermelons, as well as coconut pudding. It was indeed a feast of honor.

When the guests settled, Jonathan gave a welcome and said a blessing on the food; he then went from table to table visiting and making sure all was well. Brother Cannon and the other departing missionaries sat on mats around the low tables trying their best to enjoy the bounty of food and the companionship of their Hawaiian brothers and sisters, but Jonathan noticed that they did not eat much, and that beneath their smiles were tears.

Brother Hawkins was there from the Big Island, and Brothers Bigler and Farrer from Oahu. They had come for a final conference of the Church and to report their numbers. Jonathan smiled as he set another calabash of poi on one of the tables. There were now over three thousand members of The Church of Jesus Christ of Latter-day Saints on the islands—most on the islands of Maui, Oahu, and Hawaii, but some on Moloka'i and Kauai. There were Hawaiian men who held the priesthood and served as missionaries. The Book of Mormon translation was complete, and Brother Cannon was taking it to a Church-owned printing press in San Francisco to have the copies made. Many miraculous things had been accomplished in four years, and Jonathan felt humbly grateful to have been a small part of it.

A group of Saints at the far end of one of the tables began singing a lovely mele about the flowers of the islands, and Jonathan saw George leave off his conversation with Kaleohano and turn his head in the direction of the music. Leaving would be hard for him. The festivities began to take on a somber tone, and suddenly Akuna Pake was on his feet and begging the crowd for their attention. He went to the center of the hale, turning in circles, and clapping his hands.

"Here is Akuna Pake, the great storyteller of Maui!" People jeered him. "But, he will not tell you stories of Wakea and Papa our first parents. He will not tell you stories of the four gods Lono, Kane, Kanaloa, or Ku. He will not even tell you stories of the Mormon missionaries who came here to teach us the gospel of Christ, and who wore out their shirts, and shoes, and pants in doing this." He looked at Brother Cannon as everyone laughed and made fun of him. "No! Akuna Pake will tell you the dog story." Everyone quieted. "Once, long ago when the native people considered dog a great delicacy . . ." Several people pushed their neighbors knowing they *still* considered dog a great delicacy. "Long ago," Akuna teased and the people laughed. "Long, long ago." The people laughed harder. "Some haole merchants were invited to a feast. They had meats and fish of every kind at this feast, and among all this bounty there were a number of roasted pigs and dogs. One of the clever natives suggested, as a good trick, to sever the heads of the pigs and put them with the dogs, and take the dog heads and put them with the pigs." Chuckles ran around the room, and Akuna Pake paused dramatically. "This they did!" Many looked over at Brother Cannon to see how he was enjoying the story and were happy to find a broad smile on his face. Akuna Pake continued. "Of course the merchants did not want to eat dog meat and would not touch any of the meat where the dog's heads were, but they ate heartily of the meat that they thought was pig. The natives tried to get them to eat the other meat. 'Oh no,' they said, 'these delicious pigs are good enough for us,' and they would not touch the other. When the feast was over, the natives told them what they had done, and the merchants ran to the ditch and let go of their dinners." The people roared with laughter.

"What a terrible waste of good meat!" Brother Farrer called

out, and the people laughed louder, and those around the missionary thumped him on the back.

Akuna Pake sat down to much adulation, and Brother Napela moved to the center of the hale. Though still smiling, everyone quieted because of the respect they held for the royal son. Napela looked around at the missionaries, and when he spoke his tone was sober.

"I wish to promise you something from all of us." A hush fell over the group, and the smiles left the missionaries' faces. Napela put his hand over his heart. "We did not serve you dog meat tonight." Kind-hearted laughter filled the room, and when Napela caught George's glance he saw his face beaming, and his eyes filled with tears. Jonathan pushed down his emotions. "And now we will give our dear missionaries time to say good-bye." This time the stillness in the room was complete.

Brother Hawkins spoke first. He expressed his love for the Hawaiian people, and bore his testimony of Joseph Smith and the restoration of the gospel. Brother Bigler then stood to thank the people for being patient with his awkwardness in speaking the language and for putting up with his rough manners. In tears, he told them of a dream he'd had that he would be called to serve a mission in the Sandwich Islands. When he was called instead to dig gold in the California goldfields, he had been discouraged and upset, but decided to go where the Lord had called him. If he had not accepted that call, he would not have been in California when the call came to serve in the islands. He gave them words of love from Elder Keeler who was detained on the Big Island. Next, Brother Farrer spoke of the miracles he had encountered while serving on Maui and Oahu. He told them to be careful with the truths they had been given and to be a strength to each other. When he shared how grateful he was that he had not gone home early, a flood of tears accompanied.

When it was his turn, it took Brother Cannon a long time to stand. He looked around at the people, many of whom had their faces in their hands, weeping bitterly. He took a deep breath and Jonathan knew he was praying for strength. He had seen that look many times before. He added his own prayer to that of his friend's. George reached into the pocket of his suit jacket and brought out a letter. His voice was husky, and he had to clear his throat several times before he could actually form words.

"I . . . I bring you news from the prophet of the Church, even President Brigham Young." Many stopped crying and looked steadfastly at the young man. "At the last general conference of the Church, twenty men have been called to serve as missionaries in the Sandwich Islands."

For several moments there was stunned silence, and then praises were voiced and the weeping began anew. Brother Cannon put strength into his voice to quiet the din.

"I know many of these men: Joseph Peck, Orson Whitney, and Joseph F. Smith, the son of Hyrum Smith."

Jonathan melted to tears as he thought of the great love the leaders of the Church had for the Hawaiian people to entrust them with such a treasure as the son of Hyrum Smith.

George smiled. "Now, many of you thought I was a child when I first arrived."

"You are still a child!" someone called out.

"Thank you, ancient one," George called back, and chuckles echoed around the room. "But, I am old compared to these. Many have not reached twenty, and Joseph F. Smith is only fifteen." The faces of the people were filled with awe. "These will need the same love and care you have given us, and they will need your strength." Many heads nodded in commitment to this call, and George felt a wash of emotion pour through his body. He tried to stanch the tears, but it was no use. "We . . . we are all sons and daughters of God. Ohana. One family. I will keep you in my prayers and heart." Tears streamed down his face, and many of the Saints wept openly and loudly. George looked at Kaleohano and Napela. "You have the priesthood, you have your branch presidents, you have each other. All of these things will help you to be strong. Stand fast in the faith so that even if I do not see you again in the flesh, we will see each other in the spirit when this life is over." All the people felt the love he had for them. "I will miss you so very very much." George wiped his eyes with the sleeve of his shirt. In so doing, he looked like a young child, and Napela broke into sobs. The emotion ran like waves through the hale, and not even Akuna Pake could cajole them out of their sorrow.

Kitty Napela stood and came to Brother Cannon, holding Hattie in her arms. The woman and the little girl put their foreheads on his and wept with him. Hattie kept patting his face as she blubbered. A line formed behind them, and long into the night the Latter-day Saints of Maui said their good-byes to Elder George Cannon and the other dear missionaries who had sacrificed so much to serve them.

Jonathan had gone with George as he said his good-byes to Keala, Pau, and Nalimanui in Lahaina, and although they had never joined the Church, Jonathan could tell they held a deep love and respect for Brother Cannon. Keala and Pau were entranced by the beautiful way George spoke the Hawaiian, and the way he'd matured since they first knew him. But, Nalimanui kept calling him keiki, and scolding him for not coming more often to see her. She made him promise that he would return to see her before she walked the rainbow, which made George weep. He placed a crown of lokelani flowers on her head and thanked her many times for her kindness to the missionaries. It was only when Jonathan reminded him of the time of the boat's departure that George turned and walked from the hale and his friends.

Now, as they stood on the busy dock at Lahaina, Jonathan watched as his friend stared out across the channel to the island of Lanai. Jonathan wondered if he was actually seeing the water and the land, or if there were other scenes flowing past his vision: scenes of clouds and rainbows in the Iao Valley, of dozens of Hawaiians standing at the water's edge waiting for baptism, or of Hattie's brown eyes.

Brothers Bigler, Farrer, and Hawkins came to say their alohas, and Jonathan helped them load their things in the small rowboat that would take them out to the sailing ship. They would stop in Honolulu for a time and then on to home. Jonathan turned to find Brother Cannon looking at him, holding up his new valise, and smiling a brave smile.

"Thank you again for the gift. The only problem is that Brother Bigler wants to trade his old one for mine."

Brother Bigler called from the boat. "It's only fair, don't you think? He about wore mine out on his trip around the island!"

Jonathan chuckled and brought his focus back to George. "You have done well, Brother George." He paused. "Only one slight sadness—that we could not get my Kitty into the waters of baptism."

George gave a slight nod. "Each person must follow their

own path, Brother Jonathan. She is a good woman, and has been so gracious in taking care of the missionaries."

"And she says she will go with me, no matter where the gathering takes us."

George smiled. "See, that is a brave thing for her to do. Do not worry, Brother Jonathan, her time will come." He set down his case and took Jonathan's hand. "Watch over the members. Your strength will be needed, especially when it comes to the gathering. Keep a careful eye on the policies and procedures to make sure things are in order."

Tears filled Jonathan's eyes as he gathered George into his arms. "Looking out for things, even to the last."

George put his forehead on Jonathan's. "Aloha nui loa."

Jonathan's voice was only a whisper. "Owau, o Nepai, ua hanauia mai la e na makua maikai." *I, Nephi, having been born of goodly parents.*

"Ready to shove off!" the boatman called.

Elder George Cannon picked up his valise, took one last look at his friend, and joined his brethren in the boat. His heart ached. He knew the cords of aloha, woven through his spirit, would eventually loosen, but for now the mele of the land, sky, and people tugged him back.

He squeezed his fingers around the handle of his valise and set his face Zionward.

Note

- In reference to Akuna Pake's story, the clever Hawaiian man who switched the pig and the dog heads was actually Jonathan Napela.

Hope
1868–1872

CHAPTER 31

Salt Lake City, Utah

June 1868

"Brother Cannon!" The sturdy voice of Brigham Young came from his office to the ears of his secretary, and George Cannon nearly knocked over his inkwell. He secured it before it had the chance of spoiling the paper he'd been working on for the last hour. President Young came to the door of his office, and Brother Cannon looked up. "Are you nearly finished with that translation?"

"Yes, President, I'm nearly finished." The outer door to the offices opened, and Joseph F. Smith entered. George brightened immediately. "Aloha, mikanele!" *Hello, missionary.*

"Aloha! Pehea ʻoe?" *Hello. How are you doing?* Brother Smith answered.

"Maikaʻi loa." *Very good.* George glanced over to President Young. "Paʻahana." *Busy.*

President Young scowled good-naturedly. "All right, that's enough of that. I'm not being blessed with interpretation of tongues, and I won't have you gossiping right in front of me." The two younger men chuckled at the President's counterfeit annoyance. "Brother Smith, come wait in my office. I don't need you distracting Brother Cannon when he has work to do."

Brother Cannon stood and picked up several papers. "I can actually come now, President. There's only a line or two left, and Brother Smith and I can translate that easily."

"Well, come ahead then. We have much to discuss."

President Young ushered the two men into his office and shut the door. George headed to his usual seat, and Brother Smith took the chair adjacent.

As soon as the President sat down behind his desk, he began speaking. "Brother Smith, we have received a letter from Brother Jonathan Napela at Laie, Oahu, and Brother Cannon says the content refers to crops, debt, and the status of the people gathered there. I have some concerns about the mission, and after Brother Cannon reads the letter, we are going to have a very frank discussion about the prospects of our continuing the work." George's heart dropped, and he knew Brother Smith's heart was experiencing similar distress. "Now I know the feelings you two have for the Hawaiian people. You know their character and goodness, but you also know their shortcomings. That is why I want your counsel." He looked at each man squarely. "You have both been ordained Apostles of the Lord, and, as such, it is your duty to look after the health and welfare of the Church. So, like I said, after the letter, we will have a frank discussion." He sat back in his chair. "Please read what you've translated, Brother Cannon."

George organized the papers. "May 2, 1868. To B. Young, Latter-day prophet and a great leader to all the people around the world, respectfully: May it please you. My very dearly beloved friends, Alama and Green, are leaving. We have come to know them through a long and pleasant friendship as they have come and gone often, but they are now leaving with their families. We all love them both. Therefore only Ilae and B. Kalapa remain to assist us with my president, G. Nebeker, as he does not understand our language.

"My current work is here in Laie, where I encourage my brothers to cultivate sugarcane of which there is close to eight acres and done by hand, not by plow. The cane is now growing and G. Raymond has begun using a plow. My desire is to end our poverty as we are in deep poverty. Alama and the others are leaving with nothing. I now believe that if we had the same kind of food that you have, small grains, then we would not be healthy. Our food, the taro, is large in size, and there is also the delicious sweet potato. So we survive and do without nice homes or clothes. But all the brethren are hopeful that we will benefit in the near future from the sugarcane we are planting. We are hoping that our cane will get to you through the efforts of our President G. Nebeker and that we will receive payment from him in order to buy clothes and homes. Our Father, please do not take away our President G. Nebeker.

"When we were dining together in Laie, my brethren there are accustomed to eating with their fingers to put food into their mouths. My and all our hope is to realize eating at a table with knives and forks and so forth, and a desire to end uncivilized ways in the manner of dress and socializing, whereas my brethren have received the Christian faith and no longer live as pagans. However, there is still much ignorance in their manner of dress, talking loudly, not knowing how to sit and socialize pleasantly upon chairs or sofas and eating with knife and fork. Most of the brethren are like this. Very few are accustomed to behaving in a civilized manner. However that will end in the future when our material needs are met. I continue to instruct my brethren to put an end to uncivilized ways such as wearing the native loincloth.

"The brothers are making a strong effort in cultivating food, sugarcane, and whatever tasks the President tells them to do.

"From what I have reported to you above, that the ignorant ways among my brethren have not yet ended, therefore I request that you ask our fellow brethren over there to aid us in prayer that this ignorance, in regard to their physical behavior, come to an end.

"This was my thought to you."

George leaned over and showed Brother Smith the last lines of the letter that hadn't been translated. Brother Smith studied the words for a moment, and then read.

"Farewell to you, our Father. May almighty God prolong your life on this earth to do God's work. Amen. J. H. Napela."

President Young sat for the longest time, his eyes closed, his fingers tapping. The two young apostles knew better than to interrupt his thinking, so remained silent with their own less weighty contemplations. Finally the president looked at them.

"Brethren, when I sent Hammond and Nebeker over to buy land for the new gathering place for the Hawaiian Saints, I did so with some concern. As you know, I'd written to King Kamehameha V about our plans to purchase land to gather the Saints. I told him our desire to instruct the people not only in spiritual matters, but also temporal matters. We view no system of salvation as being complete that does not provide means for the welfare and preservation of the body as well as the salvation of the Spirit."

"Practical salvation," George offered.

"Exactly right, Brother Cannon. Practical salvation." He clasped his hands over his stomach. "Three things bothered me at that time. First, although King Kamehameha gave us permission to buy land, we were not allowed to send out our missionaries to preach the gospel. The Protestant advisors in his government had convinced him that we were not Christians under *their* definition." George noticed that the president looked as though he were biting back a bitter response to that nonsense. "Of course, that edict has never really been enforced, and the gospel message is going forth in the islands." He gave each man a satisfied smile and continued with his concerns. "Second, I was severely disappointed in the fiasco that happened on Lanai with Mr. Gibson." Brother Smith nodded his head in agreement; an action President Young noted. "Yes, we will certainly be discussing that matter in relation to the settlement at Laie." He gave Brother Smith a perceptive look and stood. He walked to the window. "And third, I do not know if our Hawaiian brothers and sisters will ever be faithful enough to merit the fullness of the gospel." Brother Cannon and Brother Smith protested at once, and President Young chuckled. "Yes, I thought that might get you going." He turned to them. "So let us discuss this last concern first. Brother Cannon, do you disagree with what Brother Napela said in his letter about the uncivilized state of many of the Saints?"

"I do."

"Disagree?"

"Yes."

President Young returned to his seat. "Convince me."

"I found that the missionaries who were most successful with the Hawaiian people were those who respected their goodness and culture, the ones who acknowledged their simple faith and openness. I think we need to appreciate how far they've come from their first contact with foreigners."

"That is reasonable, but what of Brother Napela's concerns?"

"I think Brother Napela is an intelligent man, and I believe he sees the vision that we see for the future of this sacred people, but I think he is trying to please the leaders of the Church. I think he is anxious for the changes to come quickly."

"But you do not feel this urgency?"

"No. I think the nicety of eating with a knife and fork is something that will come, but I do not think it should be the criteria for judging a person's fitness for the kingdom. When the Lord dipped the bread in the sop, was he not using his fingers?"

Brother Smith grinned, and President Young grunted. "And what about their manner of dress, Brother Cannon?"

"Must all men dress alike? Because the Lord wore robes and sandals, should we wear robes and sandals?" Brother Smith coughed to cover a chuckle. George ignored him and went on. "As long as they are modestly covered, is that not pleasing to the Lord?"

Brother Smith cut in. "If I may, President?"

"Of course, Brother Smith."

The twenty-nine-year-old sat straighter. "I think their manner of eating and the way they dress are side issues. Your question was if the Hawaiian Saints would ever be faithful enough for the fullness of the gospel."

"Yes, and there is the question of their moral behavior." President Young fixed Brother Smith with the eye of a prophet. "Do you not think their moral behavior should be called into question?"

"Of course, but they have come out of a society who, prior to the Protestant missionaries, had a"—he looked at Brother Cannon—"*unique* moral foundation."

George watched a flush of color creep into Brother Smith's face.

President Young leaned forward. "You are not suggesting that we bend the doctrine of chastity for their *unique* moral foundation, are you, Brother Smith?"

Brother Smith turned even redder, but he held his ground. "No, not at all. All I'm saying is that those who truly embrace the gospel are extremely faithful, President. They work diligently to give up the old ways and to be obedient to the doctrines."

The President turned his gaze to Brother Cannon. "Brother Cannon?"

"The faith of the stalwart Hawaiian Saints is a mighty thing." His voice grew thick with emotion. "If you had the chance to walk among them, President, you would see their faith in priesthood power and miracles."

President Young nodded. "I have heard such reports from several of the missionaries who served in Hawaii, Brother Cannon, but from 1857 to 1865 we saw a drop in membership from 4,000 members to 300. Where was the faith of the Saints? Where were the stalwart members?" Both young apostles hung their heads, and George heard a softer tone come into President Young's voice. "I need to know what happened, so if we continue this missionary effort and the gathering at Laie, we won't make the same mistakes." He hesitated. "Brother Smith? You were sent to the Hawaiian mission when you were fifteen."

Joseph F. Smith looked at his leader. "Yes, President."

"And you learned the Hawaiian language in one hundred days." Brother Smith nodded. "Would you say that was a miracle?"

"A miracle, a gift of the Spirit, and a blessing." He and

George shared a look. "Brother Napela was also instrumental. I could not have done it without his teaching as well as the help of many others of the native Saints."

"And you felt that the Lord was with you in the work?" President Young questioned.

"Very much so."

President Young fixed the young man with an uncompromising look. "So, what happened?"

Brother Smith swallowed, and George was glad he wasn't the one under the prophet's scrutiny. "Well, the gathering to the island of Lanai was difficult for them."

President Young didn't blink. "Go on."

"I think it's important to understand the Hawaiian people's attachment to the land, President. They are kamaaina—children of the land—and they are attached to the places of their birth, so asking them to uproot themselves to another place is difficult. Only the very strong members abandoned their homes to go to Lanai, which left the branches in other areas weak."

The President turned his gaze to Brother Cannon. "What else?"

George's mind raced to form an answer. "The missionary work done by the native brethren is impressive, President. Elder Napela himself is responsible for hundreds of his brothers and sisters joining the Church. They are faithful and committed to the work." He hesitated.

"But . . ." President Young adroitly assessed.

"But the calling of all the American missionaries home in 1857 caused a great upheaval."

President Young rubbed his hands over his face, and a growl rumbled from his chest. "There was nothing for it. I had the

U.S. government breathing down my neck, sending out troops, and threatening our people here in Utah."

"Without question, it was a necessary action, but it left the Hawaiian Saints like sheep without shepherds."

"And they need shepherds."

"Yes. I don't think it's very different from the rest of us. Look how many of the Saints in Nauvoo lost faith after the deaths of Joseph and Hyrum."

Brother Smith concurred. "Napela and some of the other native elders did the best they could during that time, but things were difficult on Lanai: water was scarce, crops were damaged or destroyed by vermin and worms, and they didn't have transport to get what they did grow to markets in Lahaina and Honolulu. Many of the members slid back to an easier way; many returned to their homes on the other islands."

"And into that muddle steps Mr. Gibson."

George looked over at his friend Joseph, and noted the expression of disgust that stamped itself onto his face. He felt the same. It turned his stomach to think that a priesthood bearer could be so full of avarice and self-glory that he would take advantage of the trusting Hawaiian people. Mr. Gibson had taught them false doctrine, sold priesthood offices, and put land titles under his name—bilking the Saints out of property to which they'd contributed. His actions had caused a stain on the reputation of the Church—a stain that the Protestant ministers flaunted with utmost satisfaction.

Brother Smith spoke at once, and there was flint in his normally genial voice. "Mr. Gibson is a swindler and a rogue, and I say good riddance to his excommunicated hide."

President Young laughed. "Well said, Brother Smith, but I

must take responsibility for some of that calamity. I gave him permission to check on the Lanai colony."

"To check on it, not to become the self-proclaimed king," Brother Cannon answered. "Besides, you had your share of work to attend to at that time."

"No excuse for being a poor steward in a part of the Lord's vineyard, Brother Cannon."

"But as soon as the native elders sent the letter detailing Mr. Gibson's devilish behavior, you took action immediately."

He gave Brother Smith a half grin. "Yes, Brother Cannon, it seems the brethren I sent to Lanai sorted out the mess as efficiently as could be expected." He sobered. "But unfortunately, by that time many of the Hawaiian Saints were discouraged and had fallen away. I do not wish that to happen again."

George prayed for insight, and, with the silence in the room, he knew his brethren were doing the same. A memory floated into his mind and filled him with the Spirit. "I was present at a prayer meeting we missionaries held prior to a Church conference in Wailuku. At this meeting, Elder Woodbury spoke in tongues and Brother Hammond translated. In the blessing, Brother Woodbury indicated that holy temples would someday be built upon the islands to bless the lives of the people." George looked steadfastly at President Young. "I have no idea when this will take place, but I do believe the Hawaiian Saints are some of God's dearest children, and, as Woodbury's vision indicated, they deserve *every* blessing of the restored gospel."

"I feel the same, Brother Cannon. They are a sacred branch of the vine of Israel," President Young said. "That has never been in question. But can we pull them away from the world, brothers? Can we expect this gathering to be successful?"

"Yes. It will be successful," Brother Smith said simply. "But it will not be the same kind of gathering as we have here. I think if we strengthen those who choose to gather to Laie, and also strengthen the good members in their individual towns and villages, then the entire Church in the islands will flourish."

President Young chuckled. "A partial gathering."

"To go along with a practical salvation," Brother Cannon added.

"Just so, Brother Cannon. Just so." President Young paused and looked at each man carefully. "So, you think we should go on with our work in the islands?"

They both said, yes—enthusiastically.

"And I should consider a request from President Nebeker for the Laie colony?"

"What request?" George questioned. As President Young's secretary he was privy to most correspondence, but was unsure about this piece of business.

"Under the advice of Elder Napela, President Nebeker has requested that the Church consider building a sugar mill at the colony. That way we would not have to pay the other large sugar growers to process the sugar we grow."

"I think that's a grand idea," Brother Cannon said immediately.

"Do you?"

"Yes, President Young, a grand idea."

"At first I thought cotton would be the way to go, but it seems sugar is a better crop for the climate."

Brother Smith nodded. "I agree, President. And it seems as though Brother Napela has some insight into the possibilities."

President Young grinned. "Oh, I have no doubt that our Brother Napela has his eyes and heart on all the possibilities for his brothers and sisters in the islands." He sat back in his chair and George thought he saw a look of contentment soften his features. "Mahalo, brethren. You have given me much good counsel and much to pray about."

Brother Cannon and Brother Smith shared a grin at President Young's pronunciation of the word, *mahalo*. He'd pronounced "halo" like the crown of light around an angel's head. They found his attempt at the language endearing.

The meeting ended with prayer, and the three men each headed home to family and supper. George Cannon walked past Cannon and Son's Bookstore and publishing house, debating whether or not to stop in for a few minutes to check on a few orders. He shook his head. No, he was anxious to get home and share news with his wives, and hug his children. Work would still be there in the morning. A cool evening breeze tugged at his hat, and George felt invigorated. He thought back to the windy days when he and Brother Napela had ridden horses to Kula, or through the cold winds and rain along the beautiful coast of Koolau. He knew that the years had brought change for them both, and he sent out a prayer of gratitude for his Hawaiian brother. He also sent out a blessing for the new venture at Laie's sugar plantation.

Notes

- Brother Cannon was called to be an Apostle in 1859 at the age of thirty-two. He served as a counselor to Brigham Young, John Taylor, Wilford Woodruff, and Lorenzo Snow. Brother Joseph F. Smith was called to be an Apostle in 1866 at the age of twenty-eight.

- Joseph F. Smith was called to the Sandwich Islands Mission when he was fifteen years old. He served from 1854 to 1857.

- Walter Murray Gibson made himself the "king" of the Lanai settlement. In a quotation from his diary he writes: "Who or what shall I fear when I am King—and I shall keep within my Kingdom . . . I am King; not of oceanica, not of Malaysia, not of Hawaii nei, not of Lanai, but of Palawai on this day of grace. But this is but the baby of my Kingdom. Oh smiling Palawai, thou infant hope of my glorious kingdom."

- Elder Woodbury's vision of temples in Hawaii was truly fulfilled when in January of 2000 the second temple in Hawaii was dedicated in Kona. The first temple was dedicated in 1919 at Laie, Oahu.
- George Q. Cannon had six wives and forty-three children.

CHAPTER 32

Honolulu, Oahu

October 21, 1868

Hattie Panana Napela grabbed her boater hat off the peg at the back of the classroom, flung her satchel over her shoulder, and headed for the door and freedom. Her instructor's voice caused her only a moment's hesitation.

"Miss Napela, a daughter of high standing should act with more decorum."

"Yes, sir," she said as she moved outside without stopping. She quickly navigated the wooden landing, which ran the length of the second story, and hurried down the steps on the side of the building. She'd built up so much momentum that she had to grab the railing at the bottom to keep herself from falling. Even with this action her feet began to slide and she smashed into a young man attempting to ascend the stairs.

"Hemahema!" *Clumsy.* "Watch where you're going!"

Hattie righted herself and looked up. "Sorry. I'm so sorry."

When the young man saw the girl's face his irritation turned to embarrassment. "Miss Napela! No, really, I'm sorry. I . . . I should have been more careful."

She laughed. "Kamuela Parker, are you apologizing to me for my lack of decorum?"

"You know my name?"

She gave him a quizzical look. "I know everyone's name. Oahu College is not that big of a school, Mr. Parker." She put her hat on her head. "Besides, aren't you the boy who is always giving candy and flowers to all the girls?"

Kamuela was taken aback by her straightforward manner but managed a smile. "I believe all women should have flowers and candy."

Hattie began walking and Kamuela followed. "Admirable, Mr. Parker, but such actions do tend to make a name for a person." He tried to respond, but she went on. "And, *you* know my name, and I have done nothing of note to make a name for myself."

The boy stood straighter. "But, you are you."

"And what does that mean?"

"The daughter of a royal Maui family."

Hattie stopped. "And how do you know that? Aia a pai 'ia ka maka, ha'i 'ia kupuna nana 'oe." *Only when your face is slapped should you tell who your ancestors are.* She looked at him straight on. "I don't go blabbing my pedigree to everyone."

"No . . . no, of course not, Miss Napela," Kamuela stammered.

Hattie scoffed. "It's all foolishness, anyway. Isn't your grandmother the granddaughter of Kamehameha I?"

Kamuela stammered. "I . . . well, I . . ."

She started walking again. "Never mind, Mr. Parker, as my father says, we are all only little fish in the big Moloka'i fish ponds."

Kamuela walked casually by her side. "I like that. Your father is very wise, Miss Napela."

She gave him a wry grin. "Of course, with your family, you wouldn't be fish; more likely you'd be little cows on a big Waimea ranch."

Kamuela laughed. "So, you are aware of my ancestry too." Hattie gave him a half smile, and he was brash enough to wink at her. "Actually I knew your face before I knew anything about your background."

Hattie stopped again. "And how is that, Mr. Parker?"

"Your cousin, Mary Ellen Richardson, showed me a picture of you before you arrived here."

"Oh she did, did she?"

"Yes. And it was a grand picture, but it did not do you justice."

Hattie felt heat rise into her face. "What nonsense." She moved off quickly. "And now I must run, Mr. Parker. I am done with school for the day."

Suddenly he was beside her. "You are leaving school early?"

"I am."

"Where—where are you going?"

Hattie could tell he wished those words back in his mouth. "Aia no i ke au a ka wawae," she replied. "Do you wish to jinx my trip before I begin, Mr. Parker?"

"No, of course not, Miss Napela."

She took pity on him. "I'm meeting my parents by the main gate. We are going to Laie for a celebration."

"Laie is a long way away."

She kept up her rapid pace. "Only thirty some miles. We will probably spend the night in Kaneohe and go the rest of the way tomorrow."

"Do your parents live at the Mormon settlement?"

These interruptions were becoming irritating. Hattie stopped and gave him a narrow look. "Yes. Do you see that as a bad thing?"

Kamuela looked crestfallen. "No! No, of course not. I've just heard my uncle talking about the work going on there—cotton, cattle, and sugar."

"My father is in charge of the sugarcane plantation," she said, a bit too imperiously. "And now, I really must be on my way." She turned and started off down that path, glad that the young man did not follow. He was a nice enough sort of boy, but she wanted the day to herself with her mother and father. With her boarding at the school, and them living at the colony, she did not get to see them as often as she'd like.

"Have a safe journey!" the boy called.

Hattie raised her hand in the air and kept walking. As she came around a large planting of hibiscus bushes, she saw her father's small two-horse carriage waiting at the main gate. Hattie ran. Decorum was forgotten. She picked up the corner of her skirt, put her hand on top of her straw hat, and ran. She called out to them, and her mother stepped down from the carriage and waited with open arms.

Hattie flew into her mother's embrace, the two women laughing with the joy of reunion.

Jonathan watched the two with a look of perfect contentment. "A 'ohe mea 'imi a ka maka." *Everything I desire is in my presence.* "So, daughter, how are your studies?" he asked in a mock serious voice.

Hattie stepped back from her mother's arms. "I would expect as well as your work with the sugar."

Jonathan laughed. "And of course neither of us is going to

be as arrogant as the poloka *frog* who croaks its name all day long to no one."

"That would be a tedious waste of time."

Jonathan raised his eyebrows, and Hattie giggled. She went to her father and he leaned down, placing his forehead on hers. "I have missed you, my little guide."

"I think of you every day."

Jonathan was about to say something else when Kitty spoke.

"I hear the wind singing in the Nuʻuanu Valley," she said softly. "I think it is calling us to be on our way."

"Yes, we should be off," Jonathan replied. "I want to be over the pali and into Kaneohe before the sun sleeps." He helped his ladies into the carriage and settled himself into his seat. He picked up the reins and glanced back at Hattie who was making herself comfortable in the tight space of the back seat. "Are you all right, Panana? I know it is a small space."

"I'm fine, father. I know the road is narrow over the pali. I would rather be cramped than to have the carriage wheels slide over the cliff."

"Wise thinking." He slapped the leads on the horses' rumps and gave the command to walk on. Soon the horses were cantering along Nehoa Street and nearing the backside of the Puowaina crater. Jonathan looked back at his daughter and smiled. "As we pass the ancient volcano, Panana, do not let your imagination run away with you."

"I like my imagination to run away with me. And I like the old stories. Tell me the old stories, Makua kane. Tell me the stories of the aliʻi bones that are hidden in Puowaina crater and of the kapu breakers that were sent there for human sacrifice in the ancient times."

"Hattie Panana Napela!" her mother protested. "Have you not outgrown ghost stories?"

"Well, . . ."

"Wouldn't you much rather hear a story of love?" Hattie gave a disgruntled look to the back of her mother's head, but did not comment, and Kitty continued talking. "Soon we will pass by Mauna 'Ala and the Royal Mausoleum."

"Another place for bones," Hattie grumbled.

"What was that?" her mother asked.

"Another great story of love! Queen Emma and King Kamehameha IV."

"And dear little Albert," Kitty said, a motherly tone creeping into her voice. "If heavenly beauty ever came to rest on any two children of the land, it was surely on King Kamehameha IV and his gentle queen, Queen Emma."

Jonathan and Hattie shared a look, as Kitty always said the same thing when this story was told.

"Well, I say heavenly beauty came to rest on my parents too," Hattie pronounced.

"Silly girl," Kitty said, but Jonathan saw a grin brush the corner of her mouth.

"And the royal couple held beauty not only in their features, but in their hearts," Jonathan added.

"Everyone knows this story," Hattie said, leaning forward and patting her father's shoulder. "Let me tell the next part." She cleared her throat dramatically, and Kitty and Jonathan laughed. "The king and queen were very young when they married, but their love was deep."

"They had known each other from childhood," Kitty offered.

"They had known each other from childhood. But their

desire was not for pomp or the things of the world; their desire was to help their people. So many Hawaiians had died from sickness that the king and queen wanted a hospital where the children of the land could get the best of care." Hattie stopped her narrative. "Makua kane, many died from the smallpox when I was a little girl, right?" Jonathan nodded. "But, I didn't die."

"You did not have the smallpox."

"But, I was very sick."

"Yes."

"But you and Mekanele Cannon gave me a priesthood blessing."

"Yes, I have told you that story many times." He turned his head to glance at her. "Do you have memories of Brother Cannon? You were very young when he left."

Hattie brightened. "I think I remember that he sang to me, and that he helped me build a little sand house down by the water."

Jonathan's voice filled with tenderness. "Yes, that was on your first birthday. You are a clever girl. I cannot believe you remember that." He clucked to the horses who were slowing their pace. *"I* don't remember much before I was nine or ten."

"Were you ever a little boy?" Hattie asked in a shocked voice. "I always thought you were born old."

"Hattie Panana Napela! Be careful in your teasing," Kitty counseled. "You must always honor your father."

"I do, mother. I do honor him." She laid her hand on her father's shoulder. "You know that I honor you, don't you, Father?"

"Of course, my little guide."

They turned up into the Nu'uanu Valley, and the heat from the lowlands began to dissipate. Hattie took off her hat and let the cool breeze dry the moisture from her forehead.

"So, what happened to our love story?" Kitty asked. "We were just getting to the part where a child comes into the lives of the royal couple."

Hattie piped up. "I don't want to talk about this anymore. The ending is too sad with the little prince dying, and then just over a year later his father dying of grief and a broken heart."

Kitty turned to her daughter and nodded. "Hmm. Perhaps you are right, Panana. It was devastation for Queen Emma to lose all that she loved. And, for a time, her grief overwhelmed her."

Hattie let out a sharp breath of air. "So sad."

"But there is a lesson to be learned from our great queen," Jonathan said. "She did not let grief keep her in the dark valley. She honored those she loved by getting out and serving her people. It has only been five years since the tragedy, but we hear all the time of the queen's involvement in some new service."

Hattie put her face toward the breeze. "I know. She is kind and brave." She looked back and forth between her parents. "I don't know if I could ever be so brave."

Kitty turned sideways in her seat. "We do not know how strong we are until we are tested," she said with a gentle smile.

Jonathan encouraged the horses to a faster pace. "And Queen Emma has her faith. She knows that heaven and her family are waiting."

"It still has to be lonely without them," Hattie said on a sigh.

The three sat in silence for the next few miles, experiencing cooling shadows as the forest thickened, and listening to the clop clop of the horses' hooves on the hard-packed road. Jonathan liked that he and his girls could chatter about many subjects, or sit in comfortable quiet, not needing conversation to tie them together. Kitty hummed a mele, and Jonathan wondered if she would sing it at the celebration. Perhaps she and Hattie would dance! He glanced at Hattie in the backseat. She had taken a book from her satchel and sat dozing and reading in turn. How he loved them. He thought of what his daughter had said about Queen Emma—about how lonely she was without her husband and little boy. Jonathan knew he would feel the same, for even though his mind understood the precious doctrine of eternal sealing, he was sure his heart would languish with the pain of separation.

The sky was clear and the breeze was increasing as they traveled up the valley. Jonathan thought ahead to when they would come to the crest of the mountain, the cliff dropping away a thousand feet to the valley floor. If a person dared, and the wind was not too forceful, one could go near the edge of the precipice and look out for miles over a lush, carpeted valley to the ocean. Hattie always wanted to see the view, much to her mother's worry. Today they would not have time to stop. They would reach the top of the cliff and follow the narrow road to the right. The packed path hugged the face of the cliff and precariously wound its way to the valley floor. Today there was no rain and the road would be dry. That would assure good footing for the horses.

"Be careful, Makua kane!" Hattie suddenly said in an excited voice. Jonathan and Kitty jumped, and Hattie laughed.

"Ah! Little trickster!" Kitty scolded. "We thought there was danger."

"There is danger," Hattie warned, her voice becoming slow and mysterious. "We will be to the Nu'uanu Pali very soon, and we must be on the lookout for mo'o wahine." She laid her hand on her father's shoulder. "Especially, my father. There are many lizards here, and any one of them could be moʻo wahine."

"I do not fear the lizard demon even if she is transformed into a beautiful woman," Jonathan answered.

"Oh, but the lizard woman must be feared, especially because you are a man. The beautiful lizard woman hates all men. She would lure you to the edge of the cliff and throw you off! She would throw you down into the mist, and your body would fall and fall until it smashed on the rocks beneath."

"Hattie Panana, that is enough!" Kitty scolded.

Hattie ignored her. "Your bones would mingle with the bones of the six hundred warriors who fought the last battle of Oahu, and your cries would join their cries of anguish that howl up over the pali like rushing wind!"

Jonathan laughed, and Kitty scolded him too. "Do not encourage her."

"I like her story, "Jonathan defended. "Besides, moʻo wahine cannot tempt me, for I have the most beautiful women here with me in this carriage."

"Do not try and turn my thinking," Kitty stated. "No more stories about evil lizard women, or bones, or howling."

"But, what of the gruesome story of the last battle? I am sure our daughter would like to hear of the fierce warriors of Oahu fighting bravely against Kamehameha I," Jonathan teased.

"No. Our daughter may not have lapu, *ghost,* dreams in the night, but I do not wish the angry spirits to visit me."

"Oh, the trip will be so boring now," Hattie lamented.

But, it wasn't. When they reached the barren heights of the Nuʻuanu Pali, Jonathan turned the horses onto the narrow, descending road, and soon the carriage transported the family into a wonderland of trees, vines, flowers, and waterfalls. The cooler air of the heights soon disappeared, replaced by warmer air saturated with the smell of leaf and flower. The three sang together: songs of the kings and queens, songs of the ancient ways, songs of their Maui home. And when the steepest and narrowest part of the road was behind them, Jonathan stopped the horses under a stand of kukui trees by a stream, and Kitty brought food out of the calabash pot.

"Rice balls!" Hattie exalted, taking the succulent food from her mother.

Jonathan agreed. Soft sticky rice mixed with grilled fish and pineapple. He had liked rice from his first tasting, even though most natives did not care for the starchy grain. Asian workers, immigrating to the islands to work on the burgeoning sugarcane plantations, had brought with them a disparate culture and unique food, and although he could not embrace some of the flavors, Jonathan found rice delightful. As he munched away on his supper, he thought of all the changes that had come to the islands—even in just the short sixteen years since Hattie had been born: the arrival of new faiths, cultures, and languages, new buildings and industries, the rise of parliamentary government, and the diminishment of the Kamehameha dynasty. Like many Hawaiians, Jonathan worried that the land and the Hawaiian sovereignty was seeping like sand through the hands of the kahaku maoli, *children of the land,* but he also knew that pushing back change was as impossible as pushing back the huge winter waves at Kawela.

The late afternoon sent long shadows into the clearing, bringing Jonathan from his reverie. "Time to be on our way. Brother and Sister Winston expect us before nightfall." He chuckled to himself as he saw brightness come into Hattie's face.

"We're staying at the Winstons' for the night?"

"Yes, and they still live in the big house by the ocean—the big house that has a water closet with a bathing tub."

"Oh, piffle. I don't care about any of that," Hattie protested. "I just like their funny old dog."

Kitty gave her an odd look, but Jonathan laughed.

"Hattie Panana Napela, you are sunshine."

After a night at the Winston's with a good meal, a moonlit swim in the ocean, happy conversation, and singing, all went to bed tired and content. Jonathan awoke before dawn and, with the old dog as his companion, he went out to the seaside to say his prayers. He thanked the Lord for his many blessings, for the increased production at the Laie plantation, and for the celebration day, which had dawned fair. There was a cool breeze blowing and no threat of rain.

Upon his return to the house he found the others awake and busy. Sister Winston was organizing her troops for the trip to Laie. Her four children, who ranged in age from four to ten, were scrubbed, schooled in their mother's expectations of behavior, and set to tasks. Hattie had also been assigned to help cook breakfast, and to pack the handiwork in the wooden crates. In preparation for the celebration of the new sugar mill, Sister Winston had sewn tablecloths, table runners, wash cloths, dresses, baby clothes, pillow cases, and quilts for use by the members of the colony. Idle hands were considered worse than cursing in the Winston household.

Jonathan liked Sister Winston. She was demanding, but never harsh, and her family seemed to thrive under her command. Brother Winston was a quiet fellow who admired his wife's abilities.

Hattie was hauling another box of handiwork to the Winston's wagon as Jonathan approached. She gave him a narrow look. "And where have you been all morning?"

"Prayers," he answered coolly, smiling at her. "And it's only been an hour."

"A'ohe lolena i ka wai 'opae." *No idlers when there is work to be done.*

Jonathan chuckled and took the box from her, putting it in the back of the wagon. "Where is your mother?"

"Doing dishes. I think she's kept some breakfast for you."

"Good. I'm hungry."

"Well, eat quickly and get to work."

"Bossy as the Kona winds," he answered, turning to go into the house and nearly bumping into Brother Winston.

The haole man stammered an apology. "Oh! Brother Napela! I am sorry. I . . . I was just on my way out to the hog shed. Sister Winston says we're to bring along three young pigs to replace the ones eaten at the feast."

"That's not really necessary, Brother Winston. We have quite a herd of pigs at Laie now."

Brother Winston seemed momentarily perplexed. He blinked several times. "Well, Sister Winston thinks it's a good idea." He edged off. "So . . . I'd better just go and get the pigs."

"Perhaps that is best. Your wife is a wise woman." He saw a smile plant itself onto Brother Winston's mouth.

The next half hour was filled with activity as the rest of the things were loaded, and everyone readied themselves for departure. Jonathan, Kitty, and Hattie climbed into their carriage, while the Winston family loaded into their wagon. The four-year-old sat on the buckboard with her mother and father, while the rest of the Winston children sat in the back of the rig with the food baskets, boxes of handiwork, the old dog, and the pigs.

"We are all ready here!" Sister Winston called, waving a white hankie in the air.

Jonathan gave the horses the command to walk on, and the procession started. He was excited for the day. It was a beautiful ride along the seacoast and, in three to four hours, they would be with the Saints in Laie. It had been a good year for rain, and the crops had done well. He and President Nebeker estimated that the mill could produce eighty to ninety tons of sugar and five thousand gallons of molasses, which would help them through much of their debt and possibly leave a surplus. They hoped to market the sugar to the Saints in Utah, thus having it be mutually beneficial to all involved.

Jonathan looked to his left, to the Koʻolau Loa mountains, and was enchanted by the sight of a pearly mist swirling within one of the ravines. It made him think of the hikes he and Brother George had often taken into the Iao Valley. That time seemed ages ago, and Jonathan pondered the many changes that had occurred in each of their lives. Upon returning to the Salt Lake Valley, George had married his Elizabeth Hoagland, and shortly after that, the couple had been called to serve a mission to San Francisco. It was then that his friend worked on publishing the Hawaiian Book of Mormon. *Ka Buke a Moramona.* Brother George had sent him one of the first copies, and Jonathan would never forget tearing off the brown mailing paper and holding the precious book in his hands. He'd opened the cover and run his fingers over the sacred words, weeping to see the words in his language, weeping as the Spirit testified of its truthfulness. That truth had brought him to the gathering place in Laie, and the call to be the foreman of the sugarcane plantation and sugar mill. Jonathan felt pleased to be able to serve the Lord and his fellow Saints at Laie, and, though he knew that most of the six thousand acres the Church owned was underutilized and somewhat barren, he could see progress and potential. They had forty-five acres of sugarcane planted with a hundred more waiting for the plow; there were kalo fields, pasture land for grazing the cattle and sheep, a plot of corn, and individual gardens. The actual settlement was a mixture of native thatched huts and wooden framed houses, and it was growing at a slow but steady pace. The two hundred or so Saints who lived at the colony were faithful, even though life at Laie was difficult. Jonathan thought over past discussions with President Nebeker about bringing water down from the mountains in canals or a flume and digging a series of artesian wells. When such plans were in place, they would not be at the mercy of the rain, and they could have an abundance of trees, plants, and flowers right down to the edge of the ocean. Jonathan grinned. An Eden setting would bring a sense of stability and serenity to the hearts of the people.

"Makua kane?"

Jonathan brought his thoughts to the present. "Yes, Panana?"

"How far to the plantation?

They had just passed Kahana, which was a sure marker of the distance. "What do you think?"

"Two miles?"

It was their old game. "More than two, but less than twenty."

"Five miles?"

"More than five, but less than fifteen."

"Seven miles?"

"More than seven, but less than nine."

Hattie leaned forward and put her arms around her father's neck. "Mahalo, Makua kane. I will try to be patient for eight miles."

"Why don't we sing a song?"

Hattie brightened. "We can sing about Opele ka moemoe!"

"I like that one," Kitty said.

And so, for the next eight miles, the Napela family sang not only of Opele-the-sleepy-head, but of the magical menehune, and many other mele of mirth and wonder. As the music floated back to the Winston family, they joined in when they knew the song, and the miles passed agreeably for all.

Soon the company arrived on the outskirts of the colony. They passed acres of sugarcane, saw the sugar mill on a slight rise above the field, and continued on toward the settlement. Jonathan headed the horses toward their small frame house, where they would settle Hattie's things and rest before the celebration. Brother Winston, on the other hand, turned his rig in the direction of the Mission Office. Sister Winston was determined to deliver the handiwork and the pigs to President Nebeker before even a word of celebration was spoken.

Jonathan had shown Hattie and the Winston family the sugar mill, explaining the machinery and how it worked and answering all the children's questions. The young ones were especially interested in the twelve mules that were the mill's power source. Hattie made everyone laugh by giving each mule a name like: Holoholona, *brute*. Or Pipi kauo, *ox*.

After the tour, their small group joined the assembled crowd at the front of the sugar mill for the dedication ceremony. Jonathan and Brother Hammond gave speeches, and President Nebeker gave the dedicatory prayer. It had been a grand afternoon, but Jonathan was glad to have the serious part finished. As the congregation dispersed, many of the men from the work crews came to thank him for his words and his leadership. It embarrassed him. Out of the corner of his eye, he saw his Kitty and Hattie smiling at his discomfort.

As the sun set a scarlet crown of lehua flowers on the head of the Koʻolau Loa mountains, Jonathan walked to the feast with his sweethearts. He felt happy. He looked forward to the food, the singing, and the dancing. He tried to keep plans and projects out of his mind—for tonight he would think only of the roast pork, the sweet poi, his daughter's delightful voice as she sang the mele, and his wife's graceful hands as she danced the hula.

The next morning when Jonathan and Kitty awoke, Hattie was gone. Her kapa covering was neatly folded on her bed of mats, and her clothes had obviously gone where she'd gone. Jonathan went to look for her, thinking the ocean might have beckoned her for an early morning swim. He finally found her riding a mule around the sugarcane field. She saw him approaching on his horse and waved to him.

"Good morning, Makua kane!" She called.

He called back. "Good morning, Pulelehua." *Butterfly.* He stopped his horse and watched with delight as Hattie manhandled her little mule to do her bidding. He was glad that his

Panana did not let her pampered upbringing tarnish her unspoiled nature. When she and Kitty spent time at the big house in Wailuku, Hattie was treated like an aliʻi princess. As Hattie grew up, Kitty had insisted that her daughter be placed in the charge of the Protestant missionaries at the exclusive Mauna Aliʻi Seminary at Makawao. Hattie was never allowed to wear the loose-fitting holokus, but was always regally dressed in tight-fitting clothing of the European style. Kitty had also arranged for her to have a beautiful horse and to be taught to ride sidesaddle. It wasn't surprising then that Jonathan laughed out loud as Hattie reached his side, sweaty faced and triumphant, astride her unimposing little mule.

"Is this the same quiet pulelehua who flew so softly out of the house this morning?"

Hattie laughed with him. "I wanted to take a closer look at the sugarcane."

Hattie slid from her mule as Jonathan dismounted. "Inspecting my work, are you?"

"Well, someone needs to keep an eye on you and make sure you're doing a good job."

Jonathan tied his horse to a sturdy bush, and Hattie did the same. Hattie slid her arm through her father's, and they began walking. "And I must keep my eye on you, daughter. You are getting to the age when others will see the beauty of your character *and* your face."

Hattie scoffed. "There is no need to worry about that."

"Really?"

"Definitely not."

"There are no young men at your school who talk with you or want to walk with you to classes?" Hattie hesitated a split second too long and Jonathan grinned. "See. I knew there would be someone."

"Makua kane!" Hattie protested. "I only have *friends*."

"Well, friends are good. Now, tell me about this one boy who is your friend."

"Really, there is no one." Jonathan raised his eyebrows. "Well, there is this one boy, Kamuela, who watches me and wants to talk to me, but I barely know him."

"Is he a nice person?"

"I guess so, but I barely know him."

"And does Kamuela have a last name?"

Hattie blew out a breath of air. "Kamuela Parker, if it matters."

Jonathan stopped walking. "Kamuela Parker? Of the Big Island Parkers?"

"Yes."

"He is a very wealthy young man, Panana."

"Well, his family is," Hattie countered.

"No, little sweet potato, Kamuela Parker has been raised by his grandfather, Mr. John Parker, and just a few months ago this grandfather walked the rainbow."

"I am sorry to hear of Kamuela's loss. I will have to tell him so when I see him." She began walking again.

Jonathan walked with her. "Do you not know what that means, Panana?"

"That the young man has inherited his grandfather's property."

"Well, half of it. The newspaper articles say Kamuela's grandfather left half his property to his son, John Palmer Parker, and the other half to his grandson."

"But why are you telling me all this, Makua kane? It doesn't make any difference to me."

"It does, Panana. If this boy is interested in you, then I must be sure of his character. And often wealth does terrible things to a person's character."

Hattie stopped and gave her father a narrow look. "I do not know Kamuela Parker very well, but I think he is a good person. He did not say one word about his property or wealth when he talked to me; in fact, he seemed to like it when I told him we were all little fish in the big Moloka'i fish ponds."

Jonathan laughed. "You told him that?"

"I did." She took her father's arm again. "So, stop worrying about me."

"Ah, Panana. I am afraid that is not possible."

They walked up to the sugar mill and stood looking over the field of cane. Hattie complimented her father on the good crop and the progress that was being made at the colony.

"So, you *were* up early to inspect my work," he teased.

She smiled. "Well, that, and . . ." She reached inside her satchel and brought out several stalks of cane. As she showed them to him, Jonathan watched as her smile faded and her look become thoughtful. "I . . . I wanted to plant some of these in your field. I want to be a part of your great work, Makua kane." Jonathan immediately felt the press of tears and could not speak. Hattie put the stalks back in her bag and laid her hand on his arm. "Will you show me how to plant them?"

Jonathan nodded. They headed toward a small stone cistern by the side of the field. It was a receptacle for rainwater and was nearly full. Jonathan filled a bucket, and the two continued their journey. He took his daughter to the end of a row of new plantings where slender green shoots had recently poked through the dark soil.

He cleared his voice of emotion. "Here is a good place. No one will bother them, and, if we give them extra water and pray over them, perhaps they will catch up with their taller cousins."

"Wise thinking," Hattie said.

Jonathan got down on his knees, and his daughter joined him. With his hands he dug a trench and extended the row, as Hattie got into her satchel and brought out five stalks. Jonathan took one from her.

"See these bands around the stalk?" She nodded. "Look for one that has a bulge or bud. That's where the new shoot will come from."

"Mine has one!"

"Good. Lay the stalk in the trench, long ways—like this." He laid down his plant, and Hattie copied. "We will give it a little water, and cover it with soil, and let God do the rest." Jonathan sat back on his haunches. "Now, you do the others."

He watched as Hattie took the bucket and the other stalks to her piece of ground and carefully completed the planting. She came back to join him, a happy smile on her dirt-smudged face.

"Thank you for not laughing at my silly wish," she said softly. He nodded, wiping the dirt from her cheek. "And, now it is time for the oli." Her face held great expectation.

Jonathan stood and pulled Hattie to her feet. "I am not the best chanter," he stated.

"Well, you are the best we have," Hattie said bluntly.

Jonathan laughed and hugged her. He took a deep breath and calmed himself. Looking out over the field to the ocean, he let the chant pour into his heart. He felt the mana of his parents, Hawaii Waaole and Wiwiokalani, and the power of the land. He called for a blessing on the new plants, on his wife and his daughter, on the unknown future that lay before them. And though he knew that life was uncertain, at this moment Jonathan felt that goodness surrounded him.

Notes

- John Palmer Parker, paternal grandfather to Samuel (Kamuela) Parker, was born in Massachusetts in 1790. He came to the Sandwich Islands in 1809 and settled on the island of Hawaii. He became influential as a cattle rancher, and in the cultural and political aspects of the islands.

- The battle of Nuʻuanu took place in May 1795. It is one of the final battles in Kamehameha I's war to unite the islands. The army of Kamehameha pushed the Oahu defenders up into the valley that led to the Nuʻuanu Pali. Caught between the army and the precipice, it is estimated that between 500 and 800 Oahu warriors were pushed to their deaths.

- In January 1865, Francis Hammond was authorized to purchase 6,000 acres of land at Laie from Thomas Dougherty for the sum of $14,000.

- In ancient times a portion of the area of Laie had been a "city of refuge." Often a person who violated a kapu was put to death, unless they could reach a puʻuhonua, or place of refuge. Here they could be absolved of their crime by a kahuna (priest) in a purification ceremony.

- Menehune are mythical little folks of Hawaiian lore. They live in the deep forests and hidden valleys, and are said to be gifted craftsmen.

CHAPTER 33

Salt Lake City, Utah
January 26, 1869

George Cannon was daydreaming. It was an occupation he rarely employed, but his office at Cannon and Son's Publishing was cold this morning, and the snow stuck to the window in frosty patterns. This dream warmed him, and he closed his eyes again to recapture the clement atmosphere. He was standing in the ocean with Brothers Bigler, Farrer, and Keeler. Their thatched hale stood at a distance, and Nalimanui waved to him from the garden. The scene changed, and he was walking past Napela's house in Wailuku, and Kitty Napela was calling out to him. He saw Brother Jonathan coming from the house and into the garden. He was carrying baby Hattie, and he looked joyful. George tried to breathe in the smell of the ginger as he moved into the garden to meet his friend.

"Elder Cannon?"

George opened his eyes and looked up into the face of the mail clerk. The young man looked uncomfortable. "I'm sorry, sir. I knocked, but there was no answer."

"Not to worry, Brother Richardson. I was just tired of going over the accounting ledger. Letting the eyes rest a little."

"Yes, sir." Brother Richardson moved to the desk and verified the addresses on the envelopes before depositing the bunch into Elder Cannon's mail tray.

"Anything interesting?"

"Something from the Sandwich Islands, looks like?"

George sat forward immediately and reached for the stack of letters. "Really?" He went through the envelopes quickly, coming upon the one he wanted. "Ah, it's from Elder Napela at the Laie plantation. Probably writing to tell me how well the work is going."

"Your time in the islands must have been a wondrous adventure," Brother Richardson said.

Brother Cannon opened the letter and sat back in his chair. "That is exactly what it was, Brother Richardson—an adventure into paradise." He gave the mail clerk a crooked smile. "Now don't think it was all eating bananas and swimming in the ocean. It was challenging and we worked hard."

"Knowing your work ethic, sir, I wouldn't question it." The young man moved to the door. "I'll get back to *my* work now, and leave you to your letter."

George did not reply. He had opened the pages and was already absorbed in the first precious words from his friend.

Aloha, my dear Brother George,

I have news that might bring you joy. President Nebeker has counseled with me about traveling with him to the valley of the Salt Lake. We are bringing sugar and molasses to the Saints in Utah. We wish to show our dear Prophet Brigham Young that we have been working hard to build up our little piece of the kingdom. The rain has been good this year, and the sugarcane drinks in the water and the sun and grows. It is still a struggle in Laie, but we work with hope and patience because we love the Lord, and we love what The Church of Jesus Christ of Latter-day Saints offers us. I have held in my heart a desire to take upon me the higher ordinances of the House of the Lord, and that is another reason President Nebeker says I should travel with him to Salt Lake. I would then have the endowment, and I would be able to tell my Hawaiian brothers and sisters of the great joy of being sealed to heaven. Kitty will not be traveling with me. She is fearful of crossing the great ocean, and she does not have the same desire to see the beloved Prophet and the city of the Saints. I do not know if my dear companion will ever become a member of the Church, Brother George. Perhaps she will not in this life, but she has always been a support to me.

I have received special permission from King Kamehameha to travel to America, and I am to make a report of my trip to him when I return. He is very interested in this great man, Brigham Young, who led so many people across the wilderness of America. President Nebeker and I will leave the island near the end of June and arrive in Salt Lake City sometime in July. President Nebeker thinks I should see the big celebration that is given for the pioneers who came into the valley on July 24. I hope we will be there in time. I am excited to cross the great ocean. I think I will feel like the ancients of my people who crossed the dark water thousands of miles to find a new home. I am tied to the land of my birth, Hawaii nei, but I am also tied to the kingdom of the Lord. It will please me to make a report to our great prophet and thank him for his kindness to the people of Hawaii.

I long to see your face, my dear friend. Is it truly almost twenty years since you set your feet upon the islands? How grateful I am that your feet found their way to Wailuku. Hattie desires to travel with me, but it is not possible. I know that she has written you letters, and that you have written to her. She remembers you singing to her and helping her build the house of sand on her birthday. She will be seventeen in March, and I think you would like her, Brother George. She is becoming a true compass, and many look to her for guidance. What I admire is that she does not croak her name like the pompous poloka frog.

We are working hard to make sure everything is ready for the voyage. I hope you are happy with the news that I will soon be in Utah.

> *Your brother in the Lord,*
> *J. H. Napela*

Happy with the news? George was elated! He read the letter two more times, crying and laughing with the correspondence and the memories the words evoked. He dried his face on his handkerchief, picked up his coat, hat, and gloves, and headed for the door. Ledgers and accounts could wait; he was much more interested in finding Joseph F. Smith and William Farrer and bringing them the happy news from the islands.

CHAPTER 34

Honolulu, Oahu

June 22, 1869

"Shove to!" the voice of the dockhand shouted, and Hattie Napela and Kamuela Parker scrambled out of the way of the rumbling pushcart. It was loaded with metal pipes and fittings, and the worker seemed more concerned with getting the goods to their destination than with the people he might crush along his way.

"So much chaos!" Kamuela said loudly to be heard over the noise of the dock. He shifted the package he was carrying as he maneuvered his way through the crowd.

Hattie took his arm and guided him out of the mainstream of turmoil. She called out to a man pushing a wheelbarrow of fish down the way. "Excuse me, sir!" she called in English. The man glanced in her direction. "Excuse me!" He stopped. "Could you please tell us where the *Murray* is docked?"

"Hey?"

"The sailing ship—the *DC Murray*. Do you know where she's docked?"

He pointed. "There a way. Jos kep walken'. Yall come to 'er." He moved off.

Hattie gave Kamuela a blank look. "Did you understand a thing he said?"

The two laughed, and Kamuela mimicked. "Jos kep walken'. He pointed. "There a way."

They walked in the direction the man had pointed, and soon Hattie saw her father. He had his back to them, and seemed to be supervising some men who were hoisting several large barrels onto the deck of the ship.

Hattie dodged around several people and a baggage trolley. She raced to her father's side calling out, "Makua kane!"

Jonathan started at the sound of his daughter's voice and turned to greet her. "Aloha nui, my Panana!" he said, gathering her into his arms. "Aloha nui."

She slipped a lei of green leaves around his neck. "I brought you a maile lei for remembrance. Please do not forget me, Makua kane."

"How could I forget a piece of my heart?" Jonathan looked about. "But did you come by yourself? How did you get here?"

Hattie chuckled. "You know very well I did not come by myself. I told you that Kamuela Parker was bringing me to see you off. He has a carriage and horses from his Honolulu estate."

Jonathan looked around. "Well, where is he? He should not leave you alone in this type of crowd."

Just at these words, Kamuela came to Hattie's side. "You are right, sir. I'm sorry."

"Oh piffle," Hattie said. "Was it his fault that I ran off like a wild boar with Pele's fire on my tail?"

Jonathan laughed and held out his hand to the young Mr. Parker. "She is a bit difficult to keep in line."

Kamuela adjusted the package and took the proffered hand. "Actually, I find her charming."

Jonathan saw a blush rise into his daughter's cheeks, but she straightened her back and attended to her duty. "Father, this is my friend, Mr. Kamuela Parker. Kamuela, this is my dear father, Jonathan Hawaii Napela."

"I am very pleased to meet you, Mr. Parker," Jonathan said.

"And I am honored to meet you," Kamuela answered with a brush of reverence in his tone. "I have heard much about you and the splendid work being done at the Mormon colony."

"Really?"

"Yes. My Uncle John has heard that the king and queen are very impressed by the number of children you have at Laie."

"Oh, yes?"

"Yes, they worry for the diminishing population of their people due to disease and the dwindling number of births." Jonathan saw Hattie raise her eyebrows and roll her eyes. He coughed to hide a chuckle as Kamuela continued. "And that the Mormon colony seems to be the only place where there are many births and many young children."

"Interesting."

"Yes. And my Uncle John says he is also impressed by the way you run the sugar plantation."

Hattie broke in. "Kamuela."

Kamuela blinked and looked over at her. "Oh. Oh . . . am I talking too much?"

Hattie and Jonathan said yes and no at the same time.

Jonathan chuckled. "No, Mr. Parker. You are not talking too much. I appreciate the fact that you and your uncle have a favorable impression of our little colony at Laie."

"Yes, sir, we do. My Uncle John thinks it's admirable that

you do not make your workers sign binding contracts like the other sugar plantations do. Is that true?"

Jonathan smiled. "At Laie, we are all brothers and sisters in the gospel, Mr. Parker. We try very hard to treat each other with respect. We wish to make none of the men working at the plantation bond-slaves. We contract with them by the month. They are free at the end of the month to leave if they wish to do so."

"Does that work well?"

"It seems to," Jonathan answered with a grin. "And does your operation on the Big Island work well, Mr. Parker?"

Kamuela gave him a half grin. "I am just learning the ways of the ranch," he said unassumingly. "I will return there in a few weeks for the summer. My uncle is a good teacher, Mr. Napela. I only hope to be as wise as he is someday."

Jonathan was impressed with Kamuela's openness, but before he could ask another question, President Nebeker came to his side. "Hello, Miss Napela!" he said brightly in English to Hattie. "Are you here to see your father off to America?"

"Yes, President. And I have brought you a gift for your departure." She stepped forward and placed a maile lei around President Nebeker's neck.

"Well, how very kind. Thank you." He turned to Jonathan. "The captain says we're departing soon. The last of the sugar is being loaded, and the tide is turning, so listen for the call. You wouldn't want to miss the boat to America." Belatedly he noticed the young man standing close to Hattie. "And who is this fine fellow?"

"This is my friend, Kamuela Parker. Kamuela, this is President Nebeker. He is the mission president at Laie."

They shook hands.

"I'm glad to meet you, President Nebeker. I hope you have a safe journey to San Francisco."

"Thank you, son." He clapped Jonathan on the shoulder. "We need to be on board in about fifteen minutes, my friend." He tipped his hat to Hattie. "Always a pleasure to see you, Miss Napela. Keep that singing voice of yours in good tune, will you? I would love a song or two when we return."

"Of course, President."

"See you on board, Brother Napela." He turned and walked to the ship's gangplank.

Kamuela stepped to Jonathan and held out the package. "A gift for your friend, George Cannon. It is not much, just a set of calabash cups. I thought it might remind him of the islands."

"How thoughtful, Mr. Parker. Thank you."

Kamuela turned to Hattie and placed his hand on her elbow. "I will leave you and your father to say your alohas."

Hattie looked anxious. "But . . ."

"I will be just over there watching the final preparations." He reached out his hand to Jonathan. "Have a good trip, Mr. Napela. I am very happy to have finally met you."

"I feel the same, Mr. Parker. Take good care of my Panana while I am away, will you?"

Kamuela looked awed by this assignment. "I . . . I will do my best, sir."

After he was gone, there was a moment of silence. Finally Hattie looked up into her father's face. "You will be gone many months."

"Yes."

She straightened the collar of his suit coat. "Now, do not worry about your English. You know enough words to understand most conversations."

"Yes."

She took a deep breath and lightened her tone. "It will be good for you to meet President Young. You have waited a long time." Jonathan smiled at her attempt at cheerfulness, but emotion kept him from speaking, and Hattie continued. "It will also be good for you to see all your missionary friends." He nodded. "And I know you will make many new friends in Utah."

"Thank you, Panana." He looked to the ship and back to her face. "I wish you were going with me. I would love us to see America together."

She sighed. "Perhaps another time." She reached quickly into the pocket of her dress and brought out a letter. "Oh! Will you give this to Mikanele Cannon for me, along with my aloha?"

Jonathan took the letter. "Of course. He will love to have this."

Hattie shifted from one foot to the other, and Jonathan looked over at the ship, and then out to the ocean. Finally Hattie spoke.

"This summer while I am in Laie, I will be sure and watch over the sugar plantation for you."

Jonathan chuckled. "Good. Good. It will keep you busy and out of trouble."

"I never get into trouble." Jonathan raised his eyebrows. "Besides, Mother will be there part of the time to keep her eye on me."

His visage grew tender at the mention of Kitty's name. "And while she's at the big house in Wailuku, perhaps you can go and visit the Winston Family in Kaneohe. Their old dog likes you."

"That is a good idea!" Hattie looked over at Kamuela who was talking with a young deck hand. "It was nice of Kamuela to bring the gift, wasn't it?"

"Yes, it was." Jonathan smiled at his daughter. "It was a mature thing to do for one his age."

"He will be sixteen tomorrow," Hattie said, with deference. Jonathan grinned. "Is that so?"

"Yes, and don't tease me just because I know his birth date."

"I would not think to tease you, Little Guide." He tugged at one of her long curls. "In fact, I think Kamuela is a good man."

"He seems to think the same of you."

A whistle sounded, and a call came from the boatswain that all passengers should board. Hattie flew into her father's arms.

Her voice was ragged with sudden tears. "I hope you have smooth seas and a fair wind, Makua kane."

"Thank you, Panana." He stepped back and lifted her chin. "Do not worry about me. All will be well."

She nodded bravely, but tears washed her cheeks. "Will you write to me?"

"Of course. I will tell you all about my adventures."

The boatswain blew the whistle again and the final stragglers began moving toward the gangplank and onto the ship. Jonathan gave his daughter one last hug and stepped back. "The months will go by quickly, Panana."

"To me they will ride on the turtle's back."

Kamuela came quietly to stand by Hattie. "Ho ʻi hou i ka iwi kuamoʻo." *Return to the homeland.*

Jonathan nodded and then gave Hattie a crooked smile. "I hope my stomach is better on the large water than poor Brother Cannon's."

Hattie laughed. Through her tears, she laughed. That bit of gaiety undid the tie of reluctance and gave Jonathan the release he needed. He turned and walked onto the ship.

The crossing had been difficult. Three weeks of capricious winds, fierce squalls, and rolling water had tested the doggedness of the most seaworthy individual. Jonathan had fared better than most, but as he stood now on the San Francisco dock, he was struggling to keep his balance. He knew he was on solid ground, but the land seemed to sway under his feet.

President Nebeker approached, and Jonathan stood straighter. "Are you getting your land legs, Brother Napela?"

Jonathan frowned. "Land legs?" After a moment's reflection, he smiled. "Ah! Land legs! I am getting my land legs slowly."

"Not to worry, it takes a while."

Jonathan looked at the President's gaunt face. "You were very sick on the voyage. Are you better now?"

"With my feet on terra firma, I am a new man."

Jonathan did not know the meaning of terra firma, but he didn't have the energy to ask. He took a deep breath. "So, what work is there to be done, President?"

"Load your trunk in the wagon, and then help supervise the dock hands loading the sugar and molasses. Do you feel up to that?"

"Yes, of course."

President Nebeker nodded. "I have to get the paperwork done at customs. We will send the goods today to Sacramento, and they'll hold them in the warehouse until we get there on Monday."

"Will we stay in San Francisco for many days?"

Brother Nebeker gave him an understanding look. "Only three. Now, I know you're anxious to get to Salt Lake, Brother Napela, but I am in need of a few days' rest. Besides, I must wash some things, get mending done, and find a new shirt or two."

Jonathan grinned. "I need socks, and a bath."

Brother Nebeker laughed. "Well, there you go!" He picked up his satchel and headed for the customs house. He turned back. "Do not worry, Brother Napela, Salt Lake isn't going anywhere. I'll meet you back here in an hour."

Jonathan steadied himself on his feet and walked to the wagon. He deposited his trunk, and then went to where the men were offloading the sugar crates and molasses barrels. Jonathan hoped he would not have to do much directing, as his English was mediocre at best. As he neared the site, he was pleased to see that the men were capable and their foreman exact in his discipline.

As the men worked, Jonathan surveyed the portion of San Francisco he could see from his position. He remembered the thrill he felt upon catching sight of the coastline after weeks on a rough sea. A cold, grey fog had obscured the shore mid-morning, but as the mist began to rise, Jonathan found that the ship had moved into a large harbor. Steep hillsides rose from the ocean's edge, most covered by buildings and a bit of foliage. Many of the structures seemed hastily and poorly built—ready at any moment to slide from their tenuous foundations. He knew that the great gold rush of 1849 had brought thousands of prospectors to California from around the world, and it seemed the city of San Francisco was thrown up overnight to accommodate them.

Jonathan could tell that several of the men offloading goods were Asian—most likely Chinese men who had come to work for the prospectors and to provide cleaning and cooking services. When the gold claims began to give out, many of the foreigners, especially the Chinese, signed up to work on building the Transcontinental Railroad. That amazing feat had only been accomplished two months prior, and Jonathan felt honored to be one of the rail line's first customers. It would be his first time on a train, and he could not wait to write Hattie about the experience.

Jonathan saw President Nebeker returning at a brisk pace. He wore a broad smile, and Jonathan surmised that the man's good humor came from well completed business, coupled with the fact that he was glad to be off the torturous ocean. The President stopped to deliver some papers and instructions to the foreman, who nodded with understanding and turned back to his work. President Nebeker then came to Jonathan.

"Everything is taken care of, Brother Napela! We can be on our way to the hotel." He thumped Jonathan on the shoulder. "Ah, bath and bed! It will feel remarkable to sleep in a bed that does not sway."

Jonathan's stomach grumbled. "Perhaps we could eat something, and then bath and bed?"

President Nebeker laughed. "Of course! What was I thinking? Food first!"

As Jonathan followed the president from the dock, he wondered what food they would eat, what the hotel room would look like, and how his retiring nature would blend with the more gregarious American temperaments he would meet along the way. He told himself not to worry. "Nana ka maka; hoʻolohe ka pepeiao; paʻa ka waha." *Observe with the eyes; listen with the ears; shut the mouth.* Yes, he would learn much and tell his adventures to his dear ones. In fact, perhaps it would be: food, bath, *letter,* bed.

Belonging to HEAVEN

Note

- The Transcontinental Railroad is considered the greatest technological feat of the nineteenth century. The Union Pacific workers laid 1,087 miles of track beginning at Omaha, Nebraska. The Central Pacific workers laid 690 miles of track beginning at Sacramento, California. The two teams met at Promontory, Utah, on May 10, 1869.

CHAPTER 35

Truckee, California
July 19, 1869

My dear Panana,

I know that I have already sent you two letters from San Francisco and one from Sacramento, but I must tell you about the train and the train ride over the Sierra Mountains. We have stopped overnight in a small town called Truckee, and they have postal service, so this letter should not be delayed in getting to you, even though it must travel through rough and desolate country. It is hot and dry, but it is also beautiful. The mountains are high and they do not have broad-leafed trees like the kukui or the ulu. The trees here are mostly pine, and, instead of leaves, they have green needles. They are not needles like we use for sewing, but that is what people call them, because they are narrow and long. Here is a little drawing of a pine tree.

Hattie, I know you have seen pictures of trains, but to actually ride inside one is thrilling and frightening. The metal engine of the steam train has a huge smokestack that billows white steam. There are metal wheels that go on metal tracks. The sound is clack clack clack as the train moves along. The engine pulls a line of cars—some are for people, some for animals, and others for baggage and cargo. From Sacramento to Truckee our train had to pull up steep mountainsides mile after mile. At times it seemed we were hardly moving. We went through tunnels and over wooden trestles that hung over deep gorges. How could anyone build such a thing? It is remarkable to me. And the American people finished it only four years after their great Civil War. That says something for their strength and determination. Some people do not like the change that the train will bring, but things always change, my dear Panana. One must treat change with careful respect, for it can bring destruction or improvement.

This railroad stretches almost all the way across the country, and it has only been operating for a few months. I feel very lucky to be one of the first passengers. It will take us four or five days to get to northern Utah, where it would have taken weeks. Perhaps someday there will be trains in Hawaii and we can take a ride together.

There was a young boy on the train who asked me if I was an Indian. I told him that I was not an Indian, but that I was Hawaiian. Then I told him I was the son of a chief, and he gave me such a confused look. The poor little fellow could not figure it out.

It is hard to believe, dear daughter, that soon I will be in the great city of the Saints. My heart cannot contain the joy to think I will be seeing Brother George.

I hope he will have some time to spend with me as he is such a busy person now.

I have written to your mother about my travels, so now, when the two of you are together, you can talk about the new things I am sharing with you. I miss you both very much.

When you ride the mule out into the sugarcane, my Panana, please think of me.

Your loving Makua kane

CHAPTER 36

Kaneohe, Oahu

August 30, 1869

Brother George went with me into the Endowment House to be the translator for the important words of heaven. All the symbols of the endowment lesson teach me how to be a better person, my dear Panana, and I so want to be a better person. In the ceremony I wandered from the lowly earth to the splendor of God's kingdom.

Hattie Napela put down the letter and looked into the attendant eyes of the old dog to whom she had been reading. "See, I am still his dear Panana even after two months of absence." The old dog cocked its head from side to side as Panana spoke to it. She laughed. "My father is a very spiritual man, old dog. In the ancient days, if he had not been ali'i, he would probably have been a kahuna."

Hattie and the old dog sat together on the Winston's wooden pier, enjoying the morning quiet and watching turtles poke their heads out of the turquoise water. Hattie also dabbled her feet in the cool water as she read her father's letters. The old dog was not capable of these last two occupations, but he seemed not to mind.

"Now, let's see—where was I?" The old dog lay down, and Hattie found her place in the letter. "Now pay attention to my father's wise words." She read. "I have tied myself to heaven, and I have also done the work of tying for King Kamehameha I. What a grand time it will be if we are all in heaven together." Hattie stared down at the dog. "I wonder if that includes you?" The dog grunted and Hattie laughed. "You are not very respectful of my father's words." She laid her hand on the koa wood box that sat next to her on the pier, and thought of all her father's letters inside. The wood had been polished to a soft luster, and Hattie ran her fingers back and forth over the surface, thinking of the months before her father would return to her. She shook her head and continued reading.

"Our king, Kamehameha V, is very interested in the Prophet Brigham Young, and I will have much to report about the great Utah leader when I return home. There is no location in the territory where his words do not fall. Every year he makes two trips to all the areas of the land to check on the people—to watch for their needs and to make sure they are doing right. He is very interested in education, and all the young go to school, and everyone can read and write. I have found the Latter-day Saint people to be good. There is no stealing, adultery, fighting, talking at night, or drunkenness. On the most part, I find them gentle like the Hawaiian people. If they are walking along and see a gate open they will go and close it. Even the children do this. I think it is the gospel that makes them so. And everyone has been very kind to me. The merchants are always trying to give me something for free."

Belonging to HEAVEN

Suddenly the old dog sat up, its tail thump, thump, thumping on the wooden boards. Hattie jumped.

"Oh, dog! You scared me." She turned to glance at what the dog was looking at and saw Mrs. Winston standing at the back of the big house, waving her handkerchief. Hattie could barely make out her words, as her voice came from a distance.

"Woohoo! Woohoo! Miss Napela, you have a visitor!"

The dog stood and barked.

"A visitor? Who knows me here?" she grumbled to the dog. But then, Kamuela Parker stepped out of the house to stand next to Mrs. Winston.

Hattie's heart beat like the drums of a fast hula. She put her hand on her chest. "Oh, silly." She stood and began walking—quickly, but not too quickly. The old dog trotted along beside her. Hattie saw Kamuela shade his eyes against the morning sun. As soon as he saw her, he began walking too. They met under the shade of a banyan tree.

"Aloha, Panana Napela."

"Aloha, Kamuela Parker."

"What . . ."

"I . . ."

"When did you . . ."

"I thought I would . . ."

Kamuela bent down to pat the old dog, and Hattie took a deep breath.

"It is good to see you, Kamuela. How did you know I was here?"

He straightened up. "I didn't. I was on my way to Laie to see you." Hattie's heart drummed again. "I knew the Winstons were your friends, so I stopped for water and to say hello to them."

"Ah. That was lucky."

"Yes."

Now it was Hattie's turn to pat the old dog. "What are you doing on Oahu? I mean, it isn't time for school yet."

"My Uncle John had to come to Honolulu for business. I came with him."

"Ah." Hattie was suddenly aware of her casual appearance. She wore a loose-fitting holoku dress (which she never wore, except away from her mother's presence), no corset, and no shoes. Her hair, which she'd hastily pinned on top her head that morning, had been tousled by the morning breeze, and now curls of dark hair framed her face and fell onto her shoulders. Mr. Parker, on the other hand, wore a pair of light linen trousers, a white shirt, a pair of handsome suspenders, and stylish European shoes. *Where was his jacket?* "Where is your jacket?" she blurted out.

"Sorry?"

Hattie inwardly growled at herself. *Why am I being so stupid? I have never had this problem talking with Kamuela before.* She reminded herself that she was a year older than he was. It didn't help. Right now she felt as though she were five. "I just wondered where your jacket was."

"Oh. Mrs. Winston insisted I leave it in the house, in case I wanted to go swimming."

Hattie brightened. "Would you like to?"

"Yes, that would be wonderful. It was a long ride over the pali this morning."

They began walking toward the ocean. "You must have started early."

"Before sunrise, but my horse decided it wanted to go slow." He smiled. "I'm going to need a nap."

Hattie smiled back. "Well, at least you don't have to travel all the way to Laie . . . unless there was another reason you were going there."

"No," Kamuela answered, a mellow softness in his voice. "A 'ohe mea 'imi a ka maka." *Everything I desire is in my presence.*

Hattie's thoughts became a jumble, and she swallowed hard. "Ah . . . how is your ranch? Have you been working hard?"

"Very hard. I don't know if I will ever love the life of a cowboy."

Hattie laughed. "Perhaps you can be the manager and come up with all the good ideas."

"That might suit me better."

They reached the edge of the water, and they stood for a moment letting the breeze brush against their skin, and listening to the swoosh and hiss of the waves on the shore. Hattie looked down at the crumpled letter in her fist. "Oh, silly me!" she chided, attempting to smooth out the wrinkles in the paper.

Kamuela looked over at her. "Is something ruined?"

"No. I've just crushed my father's letter. I was reading it when you arrived . . . and . . . I didn't finish."

"Please, you must get back to it."

"Really? You wouldn't mind?"

"Of course not, Panana. I don't need to be entertained every moment."

"Well then . . . ," she took a few steps away from him. "I'll just be sitting over there on the pier."

Kamuela stepped forward. "May I sit with you while you read?"

"Well, that will be boring for you. What about your swim?"

"Maybe we can swim together after you're finished reading."

The thrum of drumbeats started again in her chest. *Wili i*

ke au wili o kawili. Now this is confusing, she chided herself silently. "I'm a silly poʻo uli bird!"

"What was that?"

Hattie looked up, surprised that she'd spoken out loud. "Ah . . . nothing. I was just thinking that I could read some of his stories to you, if you'd like."

Kamuela smiled broadly. "I would like that very much. I would like to hear about your father's adventures in the wilds of Utah."

The two began walking to the pier, the old dog following. "I keep all his letters in a box. You probably think that's silly."

"Not at all. The words of a father are important. I never knew my father. He died when I was very young."

"I'm sorry, Kamuela."

"But my grandfather raised me, and he was full of words." He chuckled. "Mostly about work and business."

They moved onto the pier and sat down. Hattie picked up the koa box, took off the lid, and deposited her letter inside.

"Aren't you reading that one?" he asked, as he busied himself taking off his shoes and socks.

"I was nearly finished with it." She rummaged through the letters. "I want to read you the one where he went to this big pioneer celebration. I think it's very interesting."

"Pioneer?"

"The members of the Mormon Church who were forced out of their homes. They came in wagon trains across most of America—thousands of miles. Brigham Young was their leader." She took her father's letter out of the envelope. "My father has met him—Brigham Young."

"Why were they forced out of their homes?"

She opened the letter. "I don't know, really. I can tell you what my father told me."

Kamuela nodded. "Yes, I would like to hear."

Hattie spent time telling him stories that her father had told her about the persecution and violence against the Mormon people. She finished with the mob killing of the Prophet Joseph Smith and his brother, and the governor of Illinois forcing the people out of the city of Nauvoo.

Kamuela looked troubled. "I don't understand. I thought America was a place of protection for the people and their beliefs. I thought they had freedom of religion."

"Not for the Mormons, it seems." Hattie scanned the letter until she found the place she wanted. "So these pioneers traveled for thousands of miles, and arrived at the Great Salt Lake Valley on July the 24th. And every year on that day they have a big celebration."

"I guess I'd celebrate too, once I got the chance to stop walking."

Hattie laughed. "Yes, *they* walked across a country, and I complain when I have to walk from the Winston's house to the ocean."

Kamuela nodded. "I'm afraid I'm the same." He scratched behind the old dog's ears. "We are too used to being pampered, aren't we, boy? I live with my Uncle John and Aunt Hanai now, and my auntie spoils me terribly." The old dog wagged its tail and Kamuela chuckled. He turned to Hattie. "You must be proud to be part of such a strong group of people."

Hattie felt a twinge of regret. "Well, I haven't actually been baptized."

"Really? But, your father is such a leader in the Church."

"He is honoring my mother's wishes. She feels doors would be closed to me if I were a member of the Mormon Church."

"Oh, I see."

"But, my father has taught me many good things."

"Of course." There was an awkward silence, and then Kamuela smiled at her. "So, are you going to read to me or not?"

"Yes! Let me find the place." She scanned the letter and began reading. "Today I went with Brother Cannon and his family to the Pioneer celebration. We all dressed in our finest and walked to the Temple Block to watch the procession. There was great excitement in the city with the buildings draped in the national colors of red, white, and blue, and children waving small American flags."

"Wait!" Kamuela interrupted. "They honor the country's colors—the country that did not protect them?"

Hattie put down the letter. "My father says the Mormon people love their country."

"Even after all they suffered?"

"I guess so."

"Hmm. I probably would have headed off into the wilderness and made my own country."

Hattie laughed. "King Kamuela." She found her place and read. "I sat in the stands where Brother Cannon, the other Apostles, and the prophet were sitting."

"I'm sorry to interrupt you again, Panana, but I have another question."

"Of course, Kamuela. I don't mind."

"The Mormon Church has Apostles like those in Christ's day?"

Hattie gave him a puzzled look. "Is that unusual?"

Belonging to HEAVEN

"Well, no other Christian church has Apostles, Panana, not that I know of anyway."

Hattie just shrugged, and went on reading. "I was with just a few others at the beginning, as Brother Cannon's children wanted to stand by the roadside with their friends, and the Brethren had to go and walk near the front of the procession. After they made the circuit they all came to sit in the stands and watch the rest of the pageant. At precisely half past eight, the procession started. It was thrilling, my dear daughter! First came the national flag . . ." Hattie saw Kamuela shake his head, but she continued. "Next came a brass band, and after them the Pioneers of 1847 with a big banner. Some of the pioneers were old and feeble, but they marched proudly. Next was President Brigham Young with his counselors and the Twelve Apostles. Then came companies of men, women, and children representing different modes of immigration: wagons, horses, and handcarts. One little tike had a boat built around him and he was paddling along." Hattie giggled. "I wish I could have seen that." Kamuela nodded. Hattie ran her fingers along the words until she found her place. "The entire crowd was moved by the next group of marchers. It brought many to tears. There were twenty-four young gentlemen walking solemnly along, carrying a large U.S. flag between them. Behind them were men of the Mormon Battalion. These men of the Church and their families had been driven from their homes when Governor Ford refused to acknowledge the Saints' right to exist in the state, and yet they mustered into the United States service in July of 1846. That was barely two years after the Prophet Joseph was murdered by a bloodthirsty mob. It is difficult for me to imagine, Panana, how the Church members have not become bitter and turned their backs on the country of America."

"That is what I say," Kamuela agreed.

"They suffered much for their faith."

"And your father?"

"My father?"

"Hasn't he had to give up much to be a member of the Church?"

Momentary sadness moved across Hattie's face. "Yes. I know it has been hard for him. I think it is one reason he is so happy to be among the Saints in Utah. His letters are filled with not only his adventures, but with his feelings." Kamuela nodded and Hattie went back to reading.

"I know I am going on and on, Little Guide, but I just want to share every moment with you. And, I know you would have liked the twenty-four young women who came next in the parade. They carried the banner for the Deseret University, and they were dressed in pretty white dresses with blue sashes. I thought of you when I saw them. Finally there were the good people of the valley: farmers, merchants, professional people, and families walking, riding horses, or in carriages. It was a grand sight to see." Hattie sighed and looked up. "It sounds wonderful, doesn't it?"

"It does," Kamuela answered. He ruffled the top of the old dog's head. "Is there more?"

"Oh, only about attending a meeting afterward in the Tabernacle."

"And what is that?"

"It's a big meeting hall. Father said it can hold 7,000 people. Can you imagine that?" She folded the letter and put it back into the envelope.

Kamuela shook his head and looked out over the shoreline

to a simple grass hut. "Salt Lake sounds like a very sophisticated city."

"I think it is, from what my father writes." She sighed again. "Maybe he won't ever want to come home."

"There is no worry about that, Panana. His heart is tied to you, your mother, and Hawaii nei."

Hattie's eyes filled with tears and she turned away to put the letter into her koa box. "I hope so," she mumbled.

Kamuela stood and took off his suspenders. "And I say it's time we took our swim."

"I think so too!" Hattie said, gaiety returning to her demeanor. She took the pins from her hair and let it cascade down her back. She stood and brought fabric from the back of her dress between her legs, and held it gathered in front. She looked like she was wearing a large pair of bloomers, but she didn't care. The day was growing hot, and the water looked inviting.

Kamuela pushed her from the pier, removed his shirt, and dove in after her. Hattie put on a show of outrage when she surfaced, but couldn't keep up the pretense when Kamuela swam close and the drumbeats sounded again.

Note

- The Tabernacle is a large dome-shaped meeting hall that sits on the west side of Temple Square in Salt Lake City, Utah. Construction of the building began in 1863 and was completed in 1867.

CHAPTER 37

Laie, Oahu
September 1870

Jonathan sat on the side of the stone water cistern, sheltered from the rays of the setting sun by a small pandanas tree. It had rained an hour ago, and the atmosphere was oppressive, but it didn't matter. He needed to be out of the house—away from Kitty's sadness, away from the settlement, away from people. He listened to the gentle rustle of the wind in the sugarcane and the lonely trill of the sea bird calling for its mate. He tried to listen to things beyond mortal hearing—voices of instruction and expressions of solace. One hand brushed tears from his cheeks, while the other ran absently over the pages of his Bible. His mind wandered through images of his life with his daughter: Hattie building a sand house with Brother George, Hattie learning the hula at her mother's side, Hattie's exuberant face the first time she went off to school. Jonathan looked out to the end of the cane rows and thought about the day when she'd planted her sugarcane in the field. Now she was eighteen and far from that young girl who had longed to be part of his work.

The sun was setting behind the pali, sending a shimmer of

coral to brush the underside of the clouds, but today Jonathan's heart did not joy in the beauty—today his heart was filled with feelings of failure and loss. He stood and walked toward the mountains. Movement seemed like the only thing that offered any relief from his melancholy.

"What have I done wrong, Father? How did I fail my Panana?" Anger and frustration made his voice strained and raspy. "Have I not been a stalwart servant? Did I not teach her?" He wiped the tears with the back of his hand and looked down at his Bible. "Kitty is so angry—angry and disappointed." He shook his head. "Why can I not find the answers?" He was so lost in his distress that he did not hear the soft rustle of footsteps approaching behind him on the path.

"Makua kane?" An anxious voice whispered.

Jonathan turned quickly and frowned at the speaker.

Hattie stepped back. Her face was blotchy from crying, and her eyes were filled with fear.

"I do not wish to speak to you right now, my daughter."

"I know, but my heart is breaking and . . ."

"And so is mine." He turned to go.

"Please."

Jonathan hesitated. "I do not want to speak sharp words to you out of my pain."

"But, I want to hear them. I need to hear them."

Jonathan's shoulders sagged. There was a long silence before he spoke. "Come, there is a small stream where we can sit."

He walked up the trail, and she followed. The sun set behind the mountain, and a cooling breeze blew down from the canyon. The fiery red blossoms of the lehua trees quivered in the breath of air, and Jonathan felt a slip of pain release from his heart. *Dear Father, how will we figure this out?* As they walked, he was glad Hattie did not speak. He needed the time to sort out his thoughts and feelings.

They came to a slight rise, and Jonathan felt his heart pump as he climbed. Age was finally beginning to mark his body with inadequacies, but he did not dwell on this inevitable occurrence; he was more concerned with the inadequacies of his spirit. Jonathan paused at the top of the hill and looked down into the bowl-shaped depression where trees, bushes, and flowers clustered around a natural spring of water. A small hand was placed on his back, and he moved off, feeling the fingers linger and then slide away. His heart twisted in his chest, and tears of regret slid down his cheeks.

By the time they reached the place where the spring bubbled from the hillside, Jonathan had secured his bitterness enough to think that talking might be possible. Hattie went to the small pure stream, took a long drink, and splashed water onto her face. The action was so childlike that Jonathan's heart twisted. He wanted to reach out and take her in his arms, but he shook his head and hung onto his disillusion.

He found a rock on which to sit, and Hattie sat near. Neither seemed able to find the words to break the isolation, but the certainty of oncoming darkness pressed them to try. Hattie reached for her father's arm, drew back, and folded her hands in her lap.

"E 'ao lu'au a kualima," she said softly. *Offer young kalo leaves to the gods five times.*

Jonathan took a breath, but did not speak. How often as a young boy, before the Lord Jesus came into the life of his family, had he heard his father, Hawaii Waaole, speak those words to him? How many times after he'd made a mistake had he been sent to the kalo patch to gather the young leaves? How often had he offered them to the gods for forgiveness? But the old gods were gone, and more was expected than the offering of young kalo leaves.

"Did I not teach you from the scriptures what is the best way to live your life?"

"You did."

"Did I not teach you from my heart that you were precious to me?"

Tears rolled down Hattie's cheeks. "You did."

"Mai kapae i ke aʻo a ka makua, aia he ola malaila." *Do not set aside the teachings of one's parents for there is life there.*

Hattie hung her head and nodded.

Jonathan's heart melted. "Perhaps my words were weak. Perhaps I spent too much time away from you, paddling my canoe against forceful currents."

"No!" Hattie said abruptly. "You taught me well, Makua kane. It was just that Kamuela and I had such a strong love for each other. We overstepped the boundaries."

Jonathan nodded with understanding, and silence again fell between them. Finally Jonathan spoke, his voice low and somber. "Somehow, we will figure this out."

Hattie looked at him and wept. "I am sorry, Makua kane. I am sorry. I am sorry. I am sorry." Intakes of breath came between each sob. "Can you ever love me again?"

Jonathan quickly picked up his scriptures. He turned the pages until he came to the place he wanted. He read, "I will arise and go to my father, and will say unto him, Father, I have sinned against heaven, and before thee, and am no more worthy to be called thy daughter; make me as one of thy hired servants. And she arose, and came to her father. But when she was yet a great way off, her father saw her, and had compassion, and ran, and fell on her neck, and kissed her." Hattie's face lifted, watching her father intently as he read. "And the daughter said unto him, Father, I have sinned against heaven, and in thy sight, and am no more worthy to be called thy daughter." Jonathan choked on his emotion as tears streamed down his face. "But the father said to his servants, bring forth the best robe, and put it on her, and put a ring on her hand, and shoes on her feet, and bring hither the fatted calf, and kill it, and let us eat, and be merry. For this my daughter was dead, and is alive again; she was lost, and is found."

Through his tears, he smiled at her. "Panana, I will love you forever."

She rushed into his arms.

For several minutes they cried together. Jonathan felt the grip of sorrow release from around his heart. Repentance, forgiveness, and love were the only answers. When he taught people the gospel, did he not teach of the great atoning sacrifice of the dear Lord Jesus? Had he not needed that blessed atonement in his own life? Was there a person living or dead who had not made a mistake and needed the wondrous assurance that sins of scarlet could be made white as snow?

Hattie's tears subsided, and she sat close beside him, laying her head on his shoulder. "Mother will never forgive me," she said meekly.

Jonathan noted the loss in his daughter's voice. His wife and daughter were precious to him, and he lamented the tearing of their relationship. He knew Kitty had inherited her father's stubborn pride, but she'd also been blessed with her mother's gentleness. He put his arm around his daughter's shoulder. "Your mother loves you, Panana. Right now she is upset and disappointed. Give her time."

Hattie buried her face in her hands. "She says that I have brought disgrace on the family, especially since we are of such high standing."

Jonathan took her hands away and looked straight into her eyes. "Enough of that, Panana. The Lord does not care about high standing. He cares only how we are preparing for His kingdom. He cares about our hearts, and how we can make things right."

"But, can I ever make this right?"

Jonathan felt peace pour into his heart. "Yes. You and Kamuela will marry, and you will love your child. And you will be a guide to your family. That is how you will make it right."

"But mother says she refuses to let us be married. She says we are too young."

Strength came into Jonathan's voice. "You will marry. You say that Kamuela loves you."

"Yes."

"And that he wishes to marry you."

"Yes, it is our greatest desire. We want to spend our lives together."

"Then there is no more to be said." Darkness was surrounding them, but there was just enough light for Jonathan to see a stillness soften his daughter's features. He reached out and took her hand. "Come, we must go before darkness overtakes our feet."

She hesitated. "I will take my mat and sleep in the mission office. I do not think mother wants to see my face tonight." She looked sadly at her father. "It will be quieter for you if I am not there."

Jonathan ran his finger across her cheek. "We will put this

in the Lord's hands, Little Guide. He will take us where we need to go."

The two started off down the path, being careful to avoid stones and tree roots that hindered their way. The lights from the Laie settlement winked from a distance and spoke of home and haven but, as darkness blanketed the landscape, Jonathan knew that he would need wisdom and patience from the Lord Jesus to bring light back into his home.

CHAPTER 38

Wailuku, Maui

August 23, 1871

Jonathan Hawaii Napela was aliʻi, the son of a chief and chiefess. He was a graduate from Lahainaluna School. He was a judge, and one of ten mission leaders for The Church of Jesus Christ of Latter-day Saints in Hawaii. He was the head of the sugar plantation at Laie. King Kamehameha V had personally asked him to run for the state legislature, a race he had lost by only forty votes. Such a background would have caused many men to strut around like a rooster, or feed on the slop of popularity, but such conceit was not in Jonathan's nature. The mana that upheld him was strong like the koa tree, but it was also quiet like the wing stroke of the forest owl.

Today he needed the mana from all of his ancestors as he stood in his finest suit and feather cape at the back of the chapel of the Kaʻahumanu Church. He held the trembling hand of his daughter, and, in spite of the dark circles under her eyes, which spoke of troubled sleep and worry, Hattie Panana Hianaloli Kaiwaokalani Hailau Aala Napela, was a beautiful bride. Her wedding gown was pale dove gray silk in the European fashion:

tight fitting at her small waist and flaring out to the floor. A pleated sash of cream circled her waistline, while the bodice was adorned with silk flower rosettes and delicate ribbons in all shades of grey, cream, and white. She wore her small feather cape, and her hair was piled softly on her head and adorned with a crown of yellow mamo feathers and ginger flowers. Jonathan smiled down at her, and she attempted to smile back. The sentiment barely brushed her pale lips before it was lost again in a tight line. He prayed a silent prayer of strength for his Panana. The weeks and months leading up to this day had been fraught with great sorrow.

Jonathan's mind wandered back to the day that Kitty had come to him and Panana with her counsel concerning the baby. The offering came in tones of concern and love, but Jonathan sensed Kitty's firm resolution concerning the decision.

"My younger cousin and her husband on Kauai have longed for a child for many years, Panana. The blessing of hanai, *adoption,* would bring great joy to them and would take away the cares that come with this child."

Jonathan watched as Hattie's eyes filled with tears. "But, Kamuela and I are going to marry. It is announced."

"I know. It seems you are set on this, but I still say you are too young. And you are especially too young to raise a child."

"But, we . . ."

"And you both come from high-standing families. This is something you must consider." Kitty took Hattie's hands. "I am sure Kamuela would agree. The child will be loved and well cared for. And there will be times when you can see the child. It is the best possible solution."

Hattie had turned to him. "Makua kane?"

"It must be your decision, Panana. It must be your decision."

And Hattie had decided. Under Kitty's urging, Panana and Kamuela had decided on hanai. Kitty had then agreed to accompany her daughter to their home in Wailuku for the birth of the baby, but only after she'd garnered the promise that the birth would be kept a secret. The two would arrive at the big house a short time prior to the birth, and Kitty would tell friends and relatives that Hattie was suffering from typhoid fever and could receive no visitors. Only one trusted elderly tutu and the doctor would be allowed to see her.

Jonathan put Hattie's trembling hand in the bend of his arm, and laid his big hand over it. For the hundredth time the words flowed into his mind. *I should have said more. I should have been more of a support if she'd wanted to choose another way.* Regret battered his heart. There was some solace in the way Hattie lived her life during the next several months. She seemed to be at peace with her decision, and she worked to calm her emotions for that day of parting. Even so, he could not imagine his daughter's sorrow when, after weeks of concealment, she'd given birth to a little girl, only to have to relinquish her into the hands of the tutu. Hattie had insisted that she be allowed to name the child. She had taken the baby in her arms, kissed her face, and whispered in her ear that her name would always and forever be Mary Kihalaninui Parker. Jonathan forced back his emotion. Just days after the birth, Kamuela Parker arrived from his home on the Big Island to console his sweetheart. The boy may have been young in years, but not in character.

The music altered, and Jonathan felt a tug on his arm. He looked down, and Hattie gave him a brave smile.

"I think it's time for us to walk," she whispered.

Jonathan nodded and the two stepped forward. As they walked slowly down the aisle, Jonathan considered the time and circumstance that separated him from this place. He was grateful for the Protestant missionaries who had taught him and his parents the love of the Lord Jesus. He was grateful for his training at Lahainaluna Seminary. He was grateful for the lessons of heaven that he'd heard from the preachers at this very pulpit, but he also thought of the face of his friend, Brother George, and the words of truth that had come from his lips. Jonathan's heart swelled as he remembered the day Brother George stood with him in the Endowment House at Salt Lake City, explaining certain things and translating the promises of eternity into Hawaiian. Jonathan's days were now filled with service and certainty, and even though threads of disappointment, sacrifice, temptation, persecution, and heartache were woven within the fabric of his gospel life, the words of his young missionary friend had proven true—if you wish to belong to heaven, there is no easy way.

Jonathan's thoughts were brought to the present as he felt Panana's body stiffen at his side. He looked around and saw that they were walking by Kitty. His wife did not look at the two of them as they passed, and Panana did not look over at her mother, instead she looked straight ahead—straight into the smiling face of Kamuela Parker.

As the newly married couple emerged from the church, a cheer went up, conch shells sounded, and the friends and relatives threw rice at the bride and groom for good luck, and hung leis about their necks. For the first time in the day, Jonathan saw a genuine smile from his daughter, and noticed that a look of bemused joy had stamped itself onto Kamuela's face. As the company moved to the place of celebration, Kamuela paid loving attention to his bride and her needs. Jonathan was glad. The worry he'd carried for his daughter's happiness lifted slightly, and he found it possible to hope for a good life for the two youngsters.

Many came to congratulate him and Kitty for the happy day, and Kitty responded with quiet gentility. None but he and the bridal pair knew of her actual sentiments. Jonathan took Kitty's arm, and the two moved with the crowd from the churchyard toward their home. Friends and relatives filled the air with the sweet sound of aloha as a cooling breeze blew down from the Iao Valley.

Hattie's Uncle Kuikelani, who was a very high chief, decided that the important couple should have a marvelous wedding celebration, and so it was. Carpets were laid from the church, across the street, to the gate of the Napela's big house. Two large imus were filled with kalo, breadfruit, sweet potatoes, pig, chicken, and many kinds of fish, and crab and octopus were cooked to perfection. The low tables were covered in ti leaves and laden with bananas, pineapple, papaya, coconuts, mountain apples, and guavas. There were calabash bowls filled with poi and Hattie's favorite—coconut pudding.

There was an open-sided hale where the musicians and the dancers performed, and a similar but larger hale, where the tables were set. This gathering place was festooned with delicate red kokio ʻula flowers, and the vines of the nuku ʻi ʻiwi and the maunaloa. The main table for the bridal party was of regular height with chairs and sat facing the other tables. Jonathan sat next to Hattie with Kitty on his right. Kamuela's Auntie Hanai, sat next to him with Uncle John Parker on her left. All who looked to the top table could see open joy on most of the faces. Uncle John Parker and Chief Napela waved at many people while they were being seated, and Auntie Hanai kept reaching over and taking Hattie's hand, or patting Kamuela's face. Only Kitty Keliikuaaina Napela seemed estranged from the festivities. Many people presumed that she was not feeling well, and soon the whispered rumor spread among the party goers that the mother of the bride had a stomachache.

"Onaona i ka hala me ka lehua," the singers chanted. *Fragrant with pandanas and lehua.* "He hale lehua no ia na ka noe." *It is a house of lehua made by the mist.* "O kaʻu no ia e ʻanoʻi nei." *There is that which I desire.* "I liʻa nei hoʻi ʻo ka hiki mai." *Which I indeed have a yearning for and that is the arrival.* A hiki mai no ʻoukou." *And indeed you all have come to me.* "A hiki up no me ke aloha." *And you have come together with hearts full of love.* "Aloha e." *May love be with you.* "Aloha e." *May love be with you.*

Kamuela Parker stood. He was only eighteen, but out of respect for his status as a major land owner, and now as husband to Harriet Panana Napela, the guests quieted immediately. Jonathan saw his new son-in-law swallow several times and knew the young man was nervous, but when he looked at his bride, he stood straighter and gave her a tender smile. Kamuela moved his gaze to the gathered friends and family.

"Before we begin the feast, I would like to tell you a story. When I was in Honolulu at the Oahu College I was known for giving gifts to some of the girls—candy and flower leis."

"And I don't know where he got the money," his Uncle John broke in. "I only sent him twenty-five cents a week pocket money."

The guests laughed, and Kamuela gave his auntie a wink. She had been known to sew a ten-dollar gold piece into the lining of the linen suits she sewed for him.

"I also had a horse that I would let people ride, if they

wanted. One girl who liked to ride into Manoa Valley was my friend, Mary Ellen Richardson." He looked over to where Hattie's cousin was sitting. The girl blushed furiously as a smile jumped to her mouth. Her relatives teased her good-naturedly. "One day Mary Ellen showed me a picture of her cousin from Maui who would soon be arriving to attend school at Oahu College."

"That was a mistake!" William Uaua called out.

Everyone laughed, and Mary Ellen received another round of teasing. Kamuela smiled at her kindly. "Yes, I was fascinated with the picture, and I said to myself that this girl would one day be my wife." He took Hattie's hand, and she gave him a look of unadulterated affection. "When she arrived at the school it was love at first sight . . . for me anyway." Many people chuckled at that admission. "But she was so popular and so kind to everyone that I figured there was no chance for me. At times I would follow her and try to talk to her."

"He even tried to give me candy," Hattie stated.

"Which she would not take," Kamuela returned.

The two smiled at each other, and Jonathan felt another lifting of his heart.

"Little fish in the big Moloka'i fish ponds," Kamuela said quietly, and Hattie nodded. He worked to control his emotions, as he turned back to address the gathering. "Panana Napela became everything to me, and I wanted to be a better person, hoping that someday she might care for me. And one day, she did care for me. And now she is my bride." He picked up his calabash cup. "In the style of Europe I will raise my cup to my beautiful Panana."

Everyone lifted their calabash cups to the beaming bride. Kamuela leaned over, kissed her on the cheek, and said softly, "E lei kau, e lei hoʻoilo i ke aloha." *Love is worn like a wreath through the summers and the winters. Love is everlasting.*

Jonathan was near enough to hear the tender sentiment, and emotion caught in his throat. He remembered his mother speaking those same words to him and Kitty on their wedding day, and now it seemed her voice whispered a blessing over his daughter's marriage. "Mahalo, mother," he said quietly.

Servers began depositing huge platters of food on the tables, and people began to eat and talk. The music started, and the mellow voices of the singers sent out the beautiful mele to the ears and hearts of the assembly.

Kitty stood. "I'm not feeling well. I'm going to my room."

Jonathan and Kamuela stood together. Kamuela spoke first. "I am sorry that you are not well. Is there something I can do for you?"

Kitty looked at him and shook her head. "No . . . thank you. I am just tired." She moved to Hattie, who stood slowly. Kitty took her daughter's hands. "I wish you peace. Loaʻa ke ola i Halau-a-ola." *Be happy again. Healing and contentment after the struggle.*

Hattie's grip tightened on her mother's hands, but strong emotion had taken away her voice. She looked into her mother's beautiful face and nodded. Kitty Keliikuaaina Napela withdrew her hands and left the hale. Hattie turned and went into the arms of her new husband.

NOTE

- *Hanai* is the Hawaiian custom of adoption. Hanai is a deep tradition in the Hawaiian culture, where a child is taken in and raised by a relative or friend. It is also common to take in needy children who are of no relation.

CHAPTER 39

Salt Lake City, Utah
November 18, 1871

Dear Mikanele Cannon,

Mr. Parker and I wish to thank you for the beautiful crystal glasses you sent to us for our wedding. They made the journey over land and ocean with no breakage, and we have them now at our home, Mana Hale, on the island of Hawaii. As we have many visitors, they are much used and appreciated. I think you would like my house, Mikanele Cannon. Kamuela's grandfather built it after the style of New England and inside it is all koa wood. I feel like I am living inside a tree. It is higher up the mountainside, and it gets very cold in the winter. Does it seem strange to you that it can be cold here in the islands? You should come for a visit and see for yourself. You and your family would be welcome to come any time. Kamuela and I love to entertain people and we would surely make room for such a dear friend of my father.

George Cannon lowered the letter and chuckled. He

wondered what the accommodating Parkers would do with the abundant Cannon family, numbering now past thirty. The tired man closed his eyes, and for a moment the work and demands fell away as his imagination and heart returned to the islands: the soft feel of the air, the smell of ginger flowers, and the taste of poi. He hiked again into the sacred valley with his friend Napela, watching the rainbows dance on the sides of the pali. He heard the sweet voices of the Hawaiian Saints singing the songs of Zion. Tears pressed at the back of his throat, and George opened his eyes to stop the emotion. He did not know if he would ever return to his beloved Hawaii. For now, service to his family and the Church took every moment of his life, and it was rumored that next year might see him a delegate to the United States Congress. He pinched the bridge of his nose to squeeze away the tiredness and went back to reading his letter.

> *My father is back in Laie now, taking care of the sugar and going on his missionary trips. Mother spends her time between the house in Wailuku and the small house at the Laie settlement. I am perfectly content with my life here on the ranch. It is a little remote, but like I said, we have many visitors. I have two Japanese servants who work for me. They are not the paniolo cowboys who work on the ranch, but are here only to help me around the house. Tomi is my cook and he can cook anything we want. He also bakes bread that disappears the moment it comes out of the oven. Toko is the steward and he does many of the tasks around the house. He has helped me to plant a beautiful garden.*
>
> *It is interesting, Mikanele Cannon, that even though I have not seen you since I was a child, I have always felt near to you and cherish the letters we exchange. I want*

to thank you for your words of comfort when I shared my feelings about our Mary. As you tenderly shared about the loss of your five little ones, you reminded me that the Lord is aware of all our sorrows and that we do not always comprehend His ways. I must trust, as you counseled, that all things will work out well. And I must share with you that life is becoming sweet again, Mikanele Cannon. I have found that another child is coming to join our family, and my heart is filled with the voices of many birds. I will write you when the child is born and tell you all about it.

I must end my writing as I hear Kamuela coming to fetch me in the wagon. We are going to town for supplies. Normally he goes with one of the paniolo, but I want to buy a new hat. I hope you will think about coming to visit us. You could go hunting with my dear Kamuela, and you could sing to me again.

Thinking of you fondly,
Hattie Panana Napela Parker

George Cannon carefully folded the letter and slid it back into its envelope. He looked out his office window at the gathering clouds that threatened snow. *You could sing to me again.* Where had all the years gone since he was a young man walking the trails to Makawao and Hana, the years that took him from a boy in England to a man of business and responsibility, the years that took Hattie Panana from a baby to a woman in her own home?

Apostle Cannon sighed. For a brief moment he would like to stand in the ocean at Lahaina, feel the warm sun on his back, and once again have Nalimanui pat his face and call him keiki, but he knew that change was the constant and that the river of life was moving them all forward into unknown destinies.

CHAPTER 40

Wailuku, Maui
December 1871

The teacup fell.

Jonathan stood frozen in the kitchen doorway, halted by the sight of the falling cup, and the shaking in his wife's graceful hand. "Have the seizures come again?"

Kitty slowly shook her head—her eyes fixed on the broken pieces of the cup. "I am being punished."

Jonathan shook himself from his confused thoughts. "What?"

"God is punishing me."

Jonathan moved into the kitchen and Kitty stepped back, pressing herself against the dish cupboard. Jonathan stopped. "Kitty, God does not . . ."

She cut him off. "Don't! Don't tell me what God does and does not do. He is punishing my pride and conceit."

Jonathan looked stricken. "Kitty, stop. Stop. You don't know what you're saying." He walked to her and took her hands.

She snatched them away. "Do not touch me!"

"What is it? Why are you so upset? Tell me."

Her expression showed defiance and dread. "I am sick."

"Are you having seizures again?"

"I told you, no," she snapped.

Jonathan's heart pounded in his chest, but he forced gentleness and love into his voice. "Tell me."

Kitty glared at him a moment, then stooped down, and picked up a broken shard of the teacup. With one deft stroke she drew the sharp edge across the fingers of her opposite hand.

Jonathan cried out in shock and pain. "No!" He ran to her and grabbed her bleeding hand, pressing it against his chest without thinking. Blood blossomed on his white shirt. "Why? Why did you do that?" Fear clamped itself around his heart. *Mad. Has she gone mad?* He dragged her to the sink, pumping water into the basin and forcing her hand under the cool water. Water and blood swirled together in the sink as Jonathan's mind slid sideways with panic. He grabbed a white dish cloth and bound it around Kitty's fingers. *This will help. This will help.* His mind echoed. *This nice white dish cloth from Sister Winston—this will fix things. Good Sister Winston has given us many dishcloths. Good Sister Winston and her old dog.* Jonathan shook his head to throw out the incoherent thoughts and forced himself to focus. He looked into his wife's face and saw desolation. Tears jumped into his eyes as he cradled her hand. "My love, why . . . why did you do this?"

"Do not fret so much, Jonathan. I did not feel a thing," came the cold answer.

"How could you not feel that?"

Kitty tried to wrench her hand away. "Would you like me to show you again?"

Jonathan held her wrist firmly. "No."

"I have the sickness," she said flatly. "He ma'i makamaka 'ole." *The disease that deprives one of relatives and friends.*

Leprosy.

"Impossible," Jonathan whispered.

Kitty stared at him with a blank look. "I know the signs." She pulled back the sleeve of her blouse to expose the flesh of her arm. Smooth, discolored patches of skin were clearly evident. "These are the marks," she said harshly. "Now do you see?"

Jonathan stepped back. Terror scraped at his mind with sharp claws. "Auwe! Auwe! Auwe!" he cried.

Kitty's eyes flew open in shock. The fierce lament ripped away her refuge of anger and defiance. She slumped to the ground sobbing.

"Auwe! Auwe!" Jonathan continued. He could not stop the grief that flooded from his body, the grief that found expression in the ancient Hawaiian cry of pain. He knelt on the floor rocking back and forth. He was not a judge, elder, or ali'i. He was not a man, or a father, or a husband. He was a child who had been shoved into a dark pit. He could not breathe. Darkness was smothering him. He had to escape from the dark place. He had to fly to the height of Haleakala—to the place where the sun lived. When the sun came streaming onto his face, he remembered innocent scenes from his childhood: racing along the beach with his friends, learning his letters at Lahainaluna school, fishing for opakapaka from his small canoe. "*Father Hawaii Waaole, come and guide me. Mother Wiwiokalani, come and give me wisdom. Send my spirit ancestors to take me into the mists of the Iao Valley. Come and show me the way to walk the rainbow.*"

"Husband."

The word bound him to the earth. He sat up and looked at his wife. Her eyes were filled with loss and terror.

"Will you leave me?"

Jonathan's heart broke at the question. "I will never leave you."

"Even when Kalawao calls my name?"

Jonathan thought of the leper colony established on the island of Moloka'i, and tears washed his face. "Even then." He took a deep breath and sat flat down on the floor. Kitty crawled into his arms. He stroked her hair. "And perhaps we can keep Kalawao from ever calling your name."

"How can we do that?"

"I will build us a lovely grass hale close to the feet of the mountains in Laie. I will be your kokua, *helper,* and I will care for your every need. When it becomes necessary, we will keep you hidden from the world."

"Laie—a place of refuge," Kitty said quietly, a note of hope coloring her words.

"Yes. And just like in the ancient days, you will be safe there."

Kitty was still for a long while. "And you do not think God is punishing me?"

"No. This is a sickness, my dear one." Jonathan grieved at the death that had come to his people through the coming of foreigners to the shores. And now his Kitty was suffering the fate of so many of the kama'aina. His words caught in his throat. "The . . . the Hawaiian people are like children to these sicknesses." Jonathan closed his eyes and saw again the light shining on the top of Haleakala. "We will find a way through this. I know that God loves His children."

"Even his wicked children?"

"You are not wicked, my Keliikuaaina."

She pressed herself closer to him. After a long silence she spoke. "My prideful heart does not understand your faith. Even after you have voyaged through a rough sea, you still believe?"

Jonathan pondered the question as he thought about Brother George's words from long ago. *"Do you think it was easy for the Savior to carry his cross to Calvary?"* He felt the Spirit move through his body, and commitment settled into his heart. The voyage through the rough sea had made his faith stronger. He would never go back. He would never choose a different path. His answer to his dear Keliikuaaina was simple. "I do believe."

NOTE

- King Kamehameha V issued a decree January 3, 1865, that called for the segregation of leprosy patients (even children) from their families and communities. When family members hid the diseased instead of relinquishing them to authorities, the government took more drastic measures. The isolated peninsula on the north shore of Moloka'i was chosen as the area for forced internment. Kalawao sat on the eastern edge of the peninsula, and Kalaupapa on the west. Both names evoked terrifying images of separation and loneliness.

CHAPTER 41

Laie, Oahu
September 1872

Jonathan lay on the hu'oli mats and listened to the wind and rain beating against the thatch of their simple hale. He moved from the side of his wife, who slept the sleep of exhaustion, and went quietly out the door to stand on the covered lanai, and watch the fierceness of the storm. The house's position faced the verdant mountains, and as Jonathan emerged into the dark night, a streak of lightning cut across the pinnacle of the rugged pali, illuminating the deep ravines and the ghostly sheets of rain. Ho iku mai ke lani. *The light that cuts the sky.* A crack of thunder followed and the air vibrated. The tempest thrashed the tops of the coconut trees, sending many large palm fronds crashing to the ground. The buffeting rain found its way onto the lanai, soaking Jonathan within minutes, yet he did not move, but stood like a stone image, chanting out words of defiance.

For many months Jonathan had kept his wife safe and secluded from the settlement and well-meaning inquiries. When the idea of building an isolated hale had first come to him, Jonathan had thought long about the reasons he would present to President Nebeker. The mission leader was a man of sense and would certainly inquire why the Napelas wanted to change their dwelling place from the center of the settlement to a remote location closer to the mountain.

"I want to spend time working on the water supply system."

President Nebeker's brow furrowed as he looked across his desk at his sugar plantation foreman. "Well, it's a needed project, Brother Napela, but what of the sugarcane and the milling?"

"I will continue with those tasks, President. The new hale would not be far from the cane field and the mill. I could ride to the fields every day, and in the evening I would work on the water system."

In the end the president agreed and even had some of the field workers help Brother Napela build his new hale. Jonathan did not confide to his leader the main reason for the move, which bothered his conscience, but for Kitty's sake, he would not take any chances. The board of health was mandating stricter orders about the detainment of persons with leprosy and their separation from loved ones. The thought of such an occurrence brought Jonathan nightmares in the darkness.

For the past nine months he and Kitty had lived in their remote paradise, enjoying walks and working together in a small garden. They read the Bible and rode horses into the beautiful valley. Kitty even helped him with ideas for the water system. The peaceful surroundings seemed to bring a remission of the disease, and the swelling in Kitty's face and legs diminished. She took on reflections of her former beauty, and Jonathan saw a welcomed lessening of her anxiety. Most days he would supervise work at the sugar mill, go over business with President Nebeker, and pick up items from the company store. When friends asked about Kitty, Jonathan would say that, after their daughter's wedding, she was in need of a bit of solitude, and those who knew Kitty Napela's high-strung personality did not question the truth of it.

Lightning flashed, illuminating the underbellies of the dark swirling clouds, and Jonathan lifted his face to the sky and chanted. His chant spoke of ancient days when the great seafarers of his people navigated the open ocean. It spoke of their bravery against the storm—of their fierce strength that carried them over the dark water. As his mouth sang the words, his heart prayed for the Lord Jesus to ease his worry, and, if it were possible, to heal his dear wife. Jonathan believed in miracles. He had seen them many times when the Utah missionaries had been in the islands, when the Hawaiian Saints expected answers to their simple prayers, and at those times when a miracle of healing had happened directly beneath his hands.

The wind and rain beat at his face, and Jonathan chanted louder. He prayed for understanding and strength. He would not question God's will, but he knew he needed strength to endure the fiery furnace.

"Jonathan?"

A crack of thunder sounded, and Jonathan turned to look at Kitty as she shrank back into the hut. He held out his hand to her. "Come out with me."

She hesitated. "Are you feeling well?"

"I am. The water dries my tears! The wind fills my lungs! The lightning helps me to see!"

He held out his hand to her again, and Kitty stepped out onto the lanai. A gust of wind blew her hair away from her face, and rain soaked her nightdress as she came to stand beside him.

"Why are you out here?" she called against the wind.

"I am fighting with the little gods of the land!" he called

back. "The four hundred are trying to stand against me, and I am challenging them!" He put his arm around her waist. "Come! Challenge them with me!"

"I am not strong enough," she said as the wind whipped her hair about.

"I will chant and you will dance," he told her. "Your dancing will delight the four hundred and they will give you whatever you desire!"

"There is much I desire."

"Then dance!"

Clear and strong, Jonathan began the chant of their ancestors, and Kitty danced. At first her dancing was unsure, but as the strength of her husband's voice filled her body, her movements became powerful. The sway of her body told of the ocean waves in the fierce storm, her hands told of the strength and bravery of her people, her arms told of their longing.

The storm swirled about them, and their mana grew.

A desperate knocking came to the door of the hut, and Jonathan sat up quickly. *No one ever comes to our hale,* he thought in a panic. Kitty sat up at his side, a gasp strangling in her throat. Pale morning light came through the small windows, and Jonathan was glad for the thin pieces of cloth that blocked the view in. He motioned for Kitty to be still and stay behind the screen that separated the living area from the sleeping area. He struggled to calm his breathing as he went to the door. The knocking had continued, and now a voice added its urgency.

"Brother Napela! It's President Nebeker!" Jonathan opened the door to the mission leader. He face was haggard and his body taut. He spoke immediately. "There is a man here from the board of health, and he's brought two policemen and a doctor with him."

Kitty rushed out. "No! Oh, no! No!"

Her hair was disheveled, and her look was that of a wild animal in a trap. President Nebeker stepped back at the sight of her, but Jonathan reached out and drew her close.

"Come in. Come in, President." As soon as the man was inside the hale, Jonathan shut the door. "Where are these men?"

"At the mission office. They came late last night, but the storm kept them inside. The man from the board, a Mr. Bowen, says they're here to check the entire settlement for signs of leprosy." His eyes flicked to Kitty's face and then back to Jonathan. "I . . . I wanted to tell you, dear friend."

Jonathan nodded. "How long have you known?"

President Nebeker put his hand on Jonathan's arm. "A while."

"Yet you did not say anything."

"The Lord did not prompt me to pursue the matter."

Jonathan's eyes filled with tears. "We are so grateful for this time we have had together."

Kitty began pacing. "But, what are we going to do? What are we going to do now? I could run. We could run into the mountains."

Jonathan's shoulders sagged. "I will not have them hunting you like a common criminal. Some of these policemen shoot the sick ones who try to run away." He rubbed his head as though trying to push a solution into his brain. "Maybe you could just not go down to be examined."

Kitty hesitated. "But . . . but people know I'm here."

"Perhaps the Church members will not say anything," Jonathan encouraged.

President Nebeker drew a deep breath. "I'm afraid some of the Saints are not saints, Brother Napela."

Kitty brushed tears from her cheeks. "And they are afraid."

President Nebeker looked at her with pity. "Yes."

She stood straighter and looked at her husband. "Tell me what I should do."

The tears rolled down his cheeks. "I don't know. I don't know." He took her into his arms. "President, if you will give us some time? We need to pray about this."

"Of course, Brother Napela. Of course." He moved to the door and opened it. The doorway framed a beautiful picture of dazzling green mountains and clear blue sky that made Jonathan's heart ache. The president turned back to them. "You both have my love." He left, leaving the door open.

As the sun climbed toward noon, the Saints of the Laie settlement watched as Jonathan Hawaii Napela, son of the chiefs of Maui, and his beautiful wife rode to the mission office on their horses. They came, like the others, to be examined for leprosy. But unlike the others who stood outside the makeshift medical building, they were dressed for travel and had secured small suitcases behind their saddles; these held the few earthly possessions they would take from their Laie home. They would leave the ancient city of refuge to obey the modern law of King Kamehameha V.

Jonathan and Kitty dismounted and walked to the building, past the gathering of silent friends—friends who did not step back, but forward, gently laying their hands on the arms and shoulders of the aliʻi couple.

Everyone knew that Kalawao was calling.

Charity
1873–1879

CHAPTER 42

Kalawao, Moloka'i
April 26, 1873

Towering two thousand feet above the desolate Makanalua Peninsula, the ancient volcanic cliffs stood as barriers to hope for the lepers on the deck of the sailing ship, *Warwick*. Jonathan and Kitty Napela gripped the railing and stared at the flat hand of land that reached its lava fingers into the pounding surf. Waves hit the craggy shore, sending white sprays of water fifteen feet into the air.

"It's too rough. The boats can't go all the way in," Jonathan overheard the first mate report. He turned his head sideways to take in the man's countenance as he spoke to the captain, and saw neither pity nor concern on either face. Jonathan figured the ship and its crew had made the journey from Honolulu to Kalawao so many times since the first disposal of lepers in 1866 that a callous detachment had replaced their humanity.

Feeble sunlight was attempting to break through a bank of ash and pearl clouds, but a somber shadow encased the barren landscape. As the ship drew on toward the east side of the peninsula, the wayfarers saw a bit of grass and a few stunted trees on the sloping land that rose to the crest of the Kauhako crater. For some reason, that slight bit of nature eased the pain in Jonathan's heart.

Kitty shivered as the ship hit into a wave, sending a cold spray over the rail to mock the miserable passengers. Jonathan put his arm around his wife as her numb fingers struggled to find purchase on the wet wood.

The captain came to stand beside them. "Mr. Napela, may I have a word?" Jonathan nodded, but the captain hesitated. "Alone?"

Reluctantly, Jonathan let go of Kitty's waist, and she sat down on the deck. A young boy took up a place beside her, the symptoms of leprosy showing clearly in his swollen face covered by a smattering of pea-sized nodules. Kitty did not react to his presence with either repulsion or compassion but stared blankly at the inhospitable terrain. Jonathan turned his attention to the captain and moved with him away from the earshot of the dispirited passengers.

"Mr. Napela, the board of health has made you the assistant superintendent of the colony under Rudolph Meyer, correct?"

"Yes, sir. I will be the luna."

"Then, it is my duty to inform you that the longboats will not be able to make it all the way to shore because of the conditions."

Jonathan stared at him. "What does that mean?"

"We will take the patients as far as safety will allow and then lower them into the surf. They will need to swim the remainder of the way to the beach."

Jonathan looked over to take in the waves pounding on the beach of smooth rocks. Panic seized him as he thought of the numbness in Kitty's hands and legs, the inability of some to swim, and of the young ones without parents or family to assist them. His thoughts were torn back to the day before—the scene of desolation and fear on the dock in Honolulu. He closed his eyes to block the memory, but the images assaulted.

"Makua kane!"

Jonathan turned to see his dear Panana moving down the pier to meet him. Striding beside her was her husband, Kamuela, and in her arms was their darling baby, Eva Kalanikauleleaiwi. Panana's face held the fierce determination of her warrior ancestors, but as she neared, tear tracks betrayed her resolve.

Jonathan walked away from the containment area where the leper patients were being held prior to boarding. He walked to health and life, taking Panana in his arms and breathing in the smell of her. "My guide has come to show me the way," he whispered.

"I do not know the way through this, Makua kane. On the path there is only shadow."

"Look higher, Little Guide. Look to where there is sunlight on Haleakala." Fifteen-month-old Eva squawked from being held too tightly between the two, and Jonathan stepped back to stare at the child, an expression of wonder on his face. "I tried not to hope that I would see her." He held out his hand to Kamuela. "Mahalo. Mahalo nui, for bringing them."

Kamuela hesitated and then took his father-in-law's hand. "You're welcome."

Hattie shifted Eva to her other hip. "Do you think anyone could have stopped me from coming?"

Kamuela nodded. "She is the Kona wind blowing up from Waimea."

Jonathan smiled and reached out to gently drag a finger along Eva's cheek.

"Would you like to hold her?" Hattie asked, holding the baby out to him.

Jonathan stiffened. "Well, I don't know if—"

Hattie cut short his reluctance. "You are a kokua, Makua kane—a loving helper. You do not have the disease." Jonathan still hesitated. "Well, do you?" Hattie pressed.

"No, I do not have the disease."

"Then hold your granddaughter." Eva's legs kicked out into the air as she dangled in her mother's hands. "Hurry, she is heavy!"

Jonathan took her. Eva stopped kicking and looked steadily into her grandfather's face. "Is she going to cry?" Jonathan asked, a note of panic in his voice.

"No, she is not going to cry. But it's better if you hold her close." Hattie shook her head. "You would think you'd never held a baby before."

Jonathan brought Eva into his arms. "Well, I haven't had much practice for many years," Jonathan answered, brushing the soft brown curls off Eva's sweaty forehead.

Hattie put her arms around both of them. "Makua kane, I was wondering if you would give our daughter a blessing?"

Jonathan's eyes flicked to Hattie's face. "I will do what you want, but it must truly be your wish."

"Yes. I want the comfort of your prayers."

Jonathan nodded. "Let us step back from the crowd a little." He moved off to the side of the group, and Hattie and Kamuela followed. They all stood close together, and Jonathan had to clear his voice several times before beginning. "Dear Lord, maker of the islands and the oceans, creator of the ginger flowers and the sunlight—I take this infant girl, Eva Kalanikauleleaiwi Parker, into my arms to give her a blessing under the power of the priesthood. I bless her with health and a kind heart. I bless her that she will be a joy to her mother and father—her brothers and sisters. I bless her that in her journey, she will find the peace of the Lord. In Jesus' name. Amen."

Hattie patted her father's arm. "Mahalo. Mahalo, Makua kane." She gave him a weak smile. "So you think there will be brothers and sisters for our little Eva?"

"I believe you and Kamuela will have a large and wonderful family, Panana."

Tears gathered in Hattie's eyes, and she turned quickly to move back into the crowd.

Kamuela stepped to Jonathan's side. "She does not wish to show you her grief."

"She has always tried to be the koa tree, when she is actually the pikake flower," Jonathan said, turning to his son-in-law. "Please watch out for her while I am away."

Kamuela nodded. "Ka malu halau loa o ke kukui." *I will shelter her like the kukui tree.*

Jonathan looked at Eva, who looked right back at him. Her serious expression made him smile. "She is considering everything, isn't she?"

"She is a thoughtful one," Kamuela concurred.

At that moment Eva reached up to tug on Jonathan's hat, nearly pulling it from his head. "Oh, my!" Jonathan yelped.

"And she is strong," her father said proudly.

Jonathan secured his hat and kissed his granddaughter's forehead. "I can see that." She reached for his hat again. "And she is determined like her mother."

"I think she wants the feather lei on your hat."

"Then she shall have it," Jonathan said, taking off his hat and allowing Kamuela to remove the lei. After returning his hat to his head, Jonathan took the lei, and slipped it over Eva's head. Immediately the little hands stroked the soft feathers.

Father and grandfather smiled.

"He lei poina 'ole ke keiki." *A lei never forgotten is the beloved child.* Jonathan glanced again at his daughter, observing that she paid no attention to the hat incident, but stared fixedly at the containment area. He went to stand beside her. "What is it, Little Guide?"

"Where is she? Where is my mother? Why can't I see her?"

"She sits at the back, out of sight."

"I want to see her."

The anguish in his daughter's voice sent a spear of pain into Jonathan's heart, and he had to grit his teeth to push down emotion. He handed Eva to Panana. "I will go and see if I can get her to come forward."

Jonathan walked to the containment area without restriction. The guards from the board of health knew this man's place as luna of the colony, and afforded him freedoms not offered to the other persons on the pier. As Jonathan neared the area separated off by a fence and wire caging, he noticed the eyes of a child peering just over the top of the fence slats. His small fingers were clinging to the mesh, and a forlorn mewling sound formed behind closed lips.

Jonathan knelt down to him. "What is it, son?"

The kind voice made the boy weep outwardly. "I'm going to the colony."

"Yes, I know. I'm going with you."

The boy looked at him. "You are?"

"Yes. I am being sent to take care of you."

The boy took a shuddering breath. "I am scared."

"Of course, but there are many who will look out for you."

The boy nodded, and Jonathan patted the slender fingertips poking through the mesh. "Your name is Kepola, isn't it?"

The boy looked surprised. "Yes. Kepola."

"And how old are you?"

"Seven."

Jonathan swallowed hard. "What else troubles you, Kepola?"

The boy pointed. "My mother and father are there. They are trying to talk to me, but they are far away. I cannot hear their words."

Jonathan looked back to where Panana and the other families of the patients stood. He went to talk to one of the guards, and after some discussion, returned to address the group. "I have received permission for you to move closer to the confinement area." Some people began to move forward immediately, and Jonathan stopped them with his voice. "Wait! Please wait, friends. You must abide by certain rules, or we cannot let you closer." The people stopped and waited for Jonathan to tell them what to do. "You cannot go all the way to the confinement area. You must stop where the guard tells you. You must not reach out to try and touch the patients. If there is something you wish to give the patients, give it to me, and I will deliver it." He paused. "Do you understand?" The people nodded. "All right. You may move forward to where the guards tell you to stop."

Surprisingly, the people moved forward in an orderly manner, positioning themselves opposite their loved ones in the cage. Fifteen patients vied for a bit of space at the front, and Kepola had to struggle to keep his place. His parents were already talking to him.

"Be a good boy, and do what the luna tells you to do." The boy nodded bravely, but Jonathan could tell that all he wanted to do was climb into his mother's arms. "We will send you special things whenever we can." She held out some string to Jonathan and he took it. "Here is some string for the game you like to play." Jonathan put the gift into the boy's hand and moved away. The cacophony of voices rose in pitch, and Jonathan looked over to Hattie. She was trying to find her mother, but was finding only unfamiliar faces. Jonathan went to the side of the cage and called out to Kitty to come forward. Kitty's shadow, and then Kitty herself, moved ghostlike from the back recesses of the containment area. Hattie impulsively stepped forward, but the guard held his rifle in front of her.

"Only to here."

Hattie nodded. When her mother lifted her eyes to find her, Hattie was shocked by the swollen appearance of her face. Her skin did not carry the marks that others wore, but still it was unsettling how much her mother's face had changed since the last time they were together. Hattie pressed her lips together and lifted Eva higher on her hip. "Mother, this is our little Eva," she called out. She looked over at Kamuela. "We have all come to see you and to give you our love." Kitty was silent. "We are doing well at the ranch. There is always so much work. I have a garden, and there is company almost every week." Hattie gave her father a desperate look, and he whispered to Kitty through the cage.

Kitty put her hand on the wire and stared out at Eva. "She is a beautiful girl. Protect her."

"We will, Mother. We promise."

Kitty's eyes moved from the child's face to her daughter's. "I love you, my Panana, and I am sorry for any grief I have caused you."

Jonathan heard the gasp of breath and turned to see Hattie's body sway. Kamuela held her arms and she straightened. "Mother, I . . ."

"You were just so young. I thought it would be better." Kitty's voice held tears. "But, I see that your love is bound with strong cords." She looked at Hattie and then at Jonathan. "I hope there will come a time when you can forgive me." She turned to go.

"Wait! Wait, Mother! I do forgive you," Hattie called, desperation and sorrow coloring every word. "And you must forgive me too!"

Kitty turned and gave her a tender smile. "There was never anything to forgive, my sweet Panana." She moved back to her hiding place.

"Mother!" Hattie called. "Mother!" She shoved Eva into Kamuela's arms and rushed forward. "Mother!" Jonathan caught her around the waist before the guards reached her. "Auwe! Auwe!" she lamented. "He maʻi makamaka ʻole! He maʻi makamaka ʻole!" *The disease that deprives one of relatives and friends.* "Auwe! Auwe!"

Hattie's anguish rippled through the crowd, and other voices began wailing. Many of the patients wept loudly.

An administrator from the board of health came from the ship onto the pier. He viewed the scene with disgust. "Guards, get these people back." He glared at Jonathan. "And you get the patients under control. We're ready to get them onboard."

As the guards shoved back the families of the unfortunates, Jonathan went to the cage and spoke to the patients in a soothing voice. They stopped shouting and wailing, but many still called out words of parting and shed tears of loss. Kepola pressed his face against the wire, unaware of the damage it would do to his numb flesh. His mother kept calling out to him to be a good boy.

As the doctors came to escort the patients onto the ship, Jonathan walked to the families. He held his weeping Panana in his arms and spoke to the others. "As luna I will do my best to care for your loved ones, and I am sure the board of health will see that we have all the supplies we need at Kalawao." A few heads nodded. He looked down at his Panana. "And now I must leave you," he said slowly, holding back his emotion with every ounce of strength.

Her hands gripped the lapels of his suit coat and would not let go. "Auwe! Auwe!"

The man from the board of health approached. "Mr. Napela, you must come onboard."

Jonathan stepped back, but Hattie would not release her grip. He put his hands over hers and worked gently to pry away her fingers. "Aloha. Aloha nui loa."

"Auwe! Auwe!"

"Mr. Napela!"

"Aloha nui, Panana. Aloha nui." The fingers came away from the cloth, and Kamuela stepped forward to take his wife's arm. She slumped to the ground.

"Auwe! Molokaʻi aina o ka ʻeha ʻeha!" *Molokai, island of distress.* "Auwe!"

Jonathan stumbled back.

"Mr. Napela, now!"

"Mr. Napela?" It was the voice of the ship's captain.

Jonathan opened his eyes and saw the deck of the *Warwick* and felt the rocking of the ship. "I . . . I'm sorry, Captain. I . . ."

"Are you well, Mr. Napela?"

Jonathan focused. "Yes. Yes, captain. I . . . I was just trying to figure how we could get them safely ashore. It is a long way for the weaker patients to swim."

"We have had to do it a few times before, Mr. Napela, and that was without a luna to guide the people." Jonathan stared at him. "I am sorry, but there's no other way for it. Most times the longboats can make it all the way to the beach, but not today. We will get you as close as we can. You need to get the patients organized." He turned abruptly. "Men! Prepare the longboats!"

Jonathan went over and sat next to Kitty. He ruffled the hair of the little boy sitting next to her. "Are you doing well, Kepola?"

"No, luna sir. My stomach has been sad on the water."

"Well, soon we will be on the land, and the land will not move."

"I would like that."

The patients were drawing near, and Jonathan evaluated their fitness. Two young male patients seemed strong—barely showing signs of the disease—while several others had kokua with them. Jonathan took Kitty's hand. "Because of the waves, the longboats cannot take us all the way to the shore." He spoke on, not giving them time for a response. "How many can swim?" Seven of the fifteen raised their hands. Jonathan looked at a middle-aged man who was more than two hundred pounds. "And you, Makana? Can you swim?"

"Oh, luna, before the sickness I was a great swimmer and rider of the surf, but now my hands and feet do not work so well. I will pray to the Lord Jesus that I can be like Peter walking on the water."

Jonathan smiled at the big man, grateful for his calm faith.

"We will certainly need the Lord to watch over us, Makana. He turned to look at each patient. "So eight will need help."

A hapa haole woman spoke in a panic, as if finally grasping what Jonathan was telling them. "We have to swim in the rough water? I . . . I cannot swim in the rough water. I will not make it to the shore!" She tried to push herself away from the railing, but the inability of her legs and hands to function normally testified of the damage of the leprosy. "I cannot swim! I cannot! I will stay on the boat!"

The ship hit into a trough, and the woman tumbled sideways, knocking her head on a crate. Several people lost their balance and toppled into each other, crying out in pain and fear. Jonathan said a mighty silent prayer, and lunged for the panicked woman, attempting to keep her from any more harm. She had a cut on her forehead, but she was conscious.

The ship steadied, and Jonathan spoke loudly. "There are barrels here of paʻi. These barrels are not overly large, but they will float. Those of us who are strong and can swim will help those who cannot." He looked at the worst cases. "We will help you hold on to the barrels." The cries quieted. "I will make sure the boatmen get us as close to the beach as possible, and I promise you that we will all make it to shore."

A somber resignation engulfed the company. Jonathan stood, and the two young men came to his side. "We can swim. We will help." The kokuas also came forward.

The wife of one of the patients looked compassionately at Kepola. "I am here with my husband as kokua, but he can swim, so I will help the boy."

Jonathan set his jaw against the swelling of emotion that threatened to overtake him. He needed every bit of strength to get through this ordeal. He tried not to doubt himself, but he was a man of sixty and his body had seen too many sunrises and sunsets. He made the assignments, matching size and strength, and went to tell the captain of their plan.

As the ship drew along the eastern side of the peninsula, two small islands rose up out of the churning surf. Jonathan found the plant-covered hillocks singular: one looked like the rounded top of a head, as though a giant were walking in the deep water, while the other seemed to be his pointed hat that had been snatched off his head by a mischievous wave.

The booming voice of the first mate jerked Jonathan away from his momentary escape. "Mokapu! Okala! Look to the land!"

"Prepare to weigh anchor!" the captain commanded.

Please Lord, help us, Jonathan prayed in his heart.

The longboats were lowered, and the ladder let down. Jonathan saw many patients studying the ladder with apprehension. He gave Kitty a reassuring hug. "Shall we be the first? Then I can help the others from below." To his relief, Kitty nodded and started for the ladder. Jonathan went in front, careful with his footing as he descended. Kitty followed, methodically grasping one rung and then the next, making sure that her hands had purchase before she moved her feet. She made it the twenty feet into the longboat without incident. One by one the fifteen patients and five kokuas made it into the two boats, despite the sprays of water and the pitching of the ship. Even Makana made it safely, although when he settled himself in the second boat, it tipped dangerously, causing several women to scream. The third longboat was filled with barrels of pa'i and other miscellaneous crates and burlap bags. The four sailors in each boat took up the oars and began the crossing toward the beach.

Jonathan watched the captain on the deck of the ship, and, although he stood unmoving and did not call commands, Jonathan could tell he was scrutinizing every action of his crew. When the drag of the waves began to pull at the hull of the longboats, the crew members put up their oars.

"Time to disembark," the senior oarsman said to Jonathan.

Jonathan heard the crash of cargo hitting the water and turned to see the men of the third boat tossing barrels and boxes overboard. There was no time to delay. "Swimmers, bring over the barrels." Without hesitation the two young men and the four kokuas slid out of the boats into the treacherous water.

The hapa haole woman began to wail, her small reserve of fortitude used up. Jonathan moved to her, caught her around the waist, and took her over the side with him into the dark water. Luckily, when they surfaced, the kokua assigned to the woman was there. He helped his now mute charge onto her barrel, and began pushing her to shore.

"Kitty! It's time!" Jonathan called. She slid into the water, and he was beside her. He secured a barrel and she steadied herself on it. "Are you all right?" She gave him a slight nod. Jonathan tried to check that all his people were making their way toward the rocky beach, but the rolling of the waves, and the drag of the current made it impossible. Once he caught a glimpse of Makana, his barrel submerged under his weight, being pushed along by one of the young men.

As he struggled through the surf, Jonathan wondered if this might be his jail cell in Carthage, his crucible of the cross. Images of Brother George came into his mind: the two of them hiking in the Iao Valley, sitting together translating the Book of Mormon, his friend singing to Hattie in the garden. Jonathan wrenched his thoughts back to the sea and the shoreline. He could not calculate how long they'd been in the water; he only knew that his legs were beginning to cramp, and it was hard to catch his breath.

Kitty began to slide off the barrel, and he tried to push her up, but he had no strength.

"Kitty, hold on," he gasped.

"Just let me go," came the weak reply. "Please, let me go. It will be better."

Jonathan did not answer her; he only pushed harder against the barrel. Suddenly he felt the drag of a wave rolling back from the beach and heard the roar and the crash of the incoming surf on the smooth rocks. He looked up and saw the white spray of the cresting wave, which caught them in its power and flung them forward toward the treacherous shoreline. Kitty was ripped out of his arms.

No!

Jonathan frantically reached out for her, but his hands and arms were assaulted by hard stones as the wave dragged him up onto the beach. He tried to find purchase to crawl, and to call out her name, but his strength was spent, and bitter water filled his mouth. He wept with exhaustion and failure. Just as another cruel wave came to claim him, Jonathan felt strong hands grab his arms. He was pulled up the beach and set on dry stones. He rubbed the salt water from his eyes and tried to focus on his rescuers. They were moving back into the surf to pluck another victim from the arms of the sea. Jonathan opened and closed his eyes several times, sure that they were playing tricks on him. One of the rescuers was a young kamaʻaina, naked except for the traditional malo, and the second man was his own grandfather—his grandfather who had walked the rainbow fifty years before. His grandfather with his long, white hair and beard, dressed only in his malo, his brown skin wrinkled, his hands strong.

"Kupuna kane," Jonathan whispered. Dazedly he looked around and saw other survivors scattered along the curve of the beach. *Kitty!* Jonathan staggered to his feet. He tried to call out her name, but his voice was only a harsh croak. He turned this way and that searching for her—her familiar form—her blue holoku. Someone pointed, and he looked behind him. Kitty sat propped against the hulking form of Makana. Jonathan stumbled over to them, sitting down and taking his wife into his arms. While they were silent, Makana spoke.

"The kama'aina have saved us, luna, and now many more of the children of the land, as well as patients, come down to look at us."

Jonathan looked slowly around. "How many have survived, Makana?"

The big man smiled. "I think all of us, luna. I think all of us. We walked like Peter on the water!"

Jonathan wept. He knew that many hardships would come, but at least he had kept his first promise to patients. They were alive on the shores of Kalawao.

NOTES

- When the leper colony at Kalawao was first established in 1866, there was no dock or landing for the ships that arrived to drop off patients. In the 1870s a dock was established on the west side of the peninsula at Kalaupapa where the shoreline was less treacherous.
- Most patients were rowed to shore, but occasionally when the sea was rough, patients had to swim.

CHAPTER 43

Kalawao, Moloka'i

April 27, 1873

The old kama'aina who had saved the lepers on the beach was not Jonathan's grandfather—that had been a vision of exhaustion and longing. The man, Ahele, was a child of Moloka'i, and for generations his family had fished the ocean in their outrigger canoes, raised pigs, grown sweet potatoes, and built fences of black lava rocks that crisscrossed the peninsula from Kalawao in the east to Kalaupapa in the west. Before the coming of the lepers, the people of Ahele's village spent the summers in the great valley of Waikolu, growing their precious kalo in terraces built by a people who lived long before the great uniting of Kamehameha I.

For 1,200 years the ancients had walked the land of the Makanalua Peninsula, worshipping at the sacred heiaus their gods Kane, Ku, Kanaloa, and Lono, as well as the forty, and the four thousand. They honored Laka, the goddess who gave birth to the hula at Ka'ana Moloka'i, and they listened carefully to the visions of their revered kahunas. Moloka'i pule O'o. *Moloka'i of the powerful prayers.*

Belonging to HEAVEN

With the coming of the lepers, the healthy kamaʻaina of the peninsula had been mandated to leave—forced to abandon their thatched hales, their kalo patches, and their pigs. Many had followed the order, but many had refused, relocating to the Kalaupapa side of the peninsula and leaving Kalawao to the sick. They left their fishing area of Kalawao Bay and their kalo patches and summer hales in the valley of Waikolu.

The first lepers cast ashore sought refuge in this valley, but winters in Waikolu were cold and inundated with nearly constant rain. This inclement weather brought colds, sore throats, tuberculosis, and pneumonia, and many weakened sufferers walked the rainbow from these illnesses. The refugees able enough left the valley and braved the rocky shoreline for the flat plain of Kalawao, but here there was little food and no water. Water could be ported from the valleys of the Waialeia or Waihanau, but without enough kokua to help, the supply was limited.

The board of health had built a few houses and thatched huts, along with a small hospital compound and storehouse. They also sent limited food, seed, and supplies, confident that the patients would fend for themselves. But with hands and fingers swollen to uselessness, no bucket could be carried, no garden could be planted, no home could be built, and no fishing net could be thrown out to gather the bounty of the sea. Kalawao became a settlement of survival, where the strong preyed on the weak.

With the help of the young kamaʻaina and Ahele, the newly arrived sufferers made their way into the valley Waikolu, where they found a few of the old thatched huts. These dwellings were broken and dilapidated from years of neglect, but still offered meager shelter to the exhausted newcomers. While some found a place on the hard-packed floors, others simply lay down under the protection of the kukui trees and dropped into sleep.

Jonathan made sure Kitty was sleeping and then went to the stream to drink and wash the salt from his head and face. He sat down on a rock ledge, and Ahele came to join him.

Jonathan did not try to stop the tears that ran down his cheeks as he addressed the venerable old man. "Mahalo, Ahele. Mahalo. Your mana saved many of us today." He placed his hands on the man's shoulders and scrutinized his face. It was deeply lined and weathered, but the eyes were clear and held a deep wisdom. "I am Jonathan Hawaii Napela, and I have come to Kalawao to serve the people as luna."

Ahele nodded several times. "It is good to meet you Luna Napela. The sick peoples here need a strong leader to help them."

Jonathan sighed and folded his arms across his chest. "Will you tell me what you know, Ahele?"

"In the beginning there were only a few sick peoples." He held out his ten fingers to indicate the few. "Then more boats come with more people. They died pretty soon. Then some men come and build houses like the haoles build and houses like the kama'aina build. The church men come and build a church. Two churches. But these church men do not stay. They too afraid they will catch the sickness."

"I have been told of these churches. One is for the Protestant believers and one is for the Catholic believers."

Ahele looked over at Jonathan. "Is the luna a church man?"

"I am, Ahele. I am a Mormon."

Ahele frowned. "I never hear this word."

Jonathan smiled at him. "I am not surprised." He looked out at the ocean and the little pointed-hat island of Okala. "I believe in the Lord Jesus and in following His ways."

Ahele smiled broadly. "I too believe in the Lord Jesus! Many years ago, missionaries came to our village from topside."

"Topside?"

Ahele turned his body and pointed to the top of the cliff. "That is what the haoles call the land that sits above us."

Jonathan studied the height. "Is there a way to topside, Ahele?"

"There is a trail in the Waihanau Valley, luna, but it is very difficult. Sometimes the sick peoples try to go topside, but they fall. They do not walk on steady legs, and the trail is narrow."

Jonathan was sickened at the desperation that would compel such an attempt. "And who buries the dead?"

Instead of answering right away, Ahele held out his hand with the palm down. "Here is our land, Luna Napela." With his other hand he indicated the space surrounding his hand. "This is the great water. On this side of the land is Kalawao. On this side is Kalaupapa. You understand?" Jonathan nodded. Ahele now pointed at the center knuckle of his hand. "This is the crater Kauhako, the ancient mouth through which Pele's fire came. It is the creator of our leaf of land. At the bottom of the wide hole that opens to the sky is a great pool of water. Some say there is no bottom to the pool. Sometimes the bodies are put there. Sometimes the sick who have strength dig shallow graves and the kamaʻaina help them. But, often the wild pigs find these places."

Jonathan felt overwhelmed. There was so much to do. How could he possibly make a difference? "And what of the superintendent?" Ahele gave him a confused look. "The luna from topside."

"Ah! Luna Meyer from Kalae. He comes sometimes. He and his sons bring cattle down the steep pali trail for the sick peoples. But he is here only a short time, and after he goes those naʻu ʻino, *evil-hearted,* call out ʻA ʻole kanawai ma keia wahi!' *In this place there is no law!*"

A breeze came down through the valley, rustling the leaves

of the kukui trees. Jonathan closed his eyes and felt the motion of the cool air on his skin. He needed to pray for helpers. There were now over eight hundred patients living at Kalawao and scattered throughout the peninsula. Even with the kokuas, there were not enough healthy hands for the work. There needed to be doctors, carpenters, gardeners, men to keep the peace, and religious shepherds. "Auwe," Jonathan said softly.

"Do not worry, Luna Napela. The Lord Jesus will help you."

Though Ahele's words brought him some comfort, Jonathan was tired; he felt it in his arms that were tired from paddling his canoe through rough seas; he felt it in his heart that was tired of suffering. He nodded at the old man. "Mahalo, Ahele."

"And tomorrow when the tide is low, my grandson and I will guide you along the shore to your home in Kalawao." Ahele stood. "We will go now and find you food, and you must rest, luna. The wind and the waves have drawn away your mana."

As Jonathan lay back against one of the kukui trees, he felt the truth of Ahele's words. His soul was tired, perhaps more tired than his body. He closed his eyes and felt the dappled sunlight playing through the leaves of the kukui trees. To the sound of the rushing stream, he fell asleep.

NOTE

- Rudolph Meyer was born April 2, 1826, in Hamburg, Germany. He arrived in Hawaii in January 1850. He settled on Moloka'i where he met high chiefess Kalama Waha, who later became his wife. Meyer was a man of intelligence and industry and began many profitable endeavors such as cattle ranching, coffee and sugar growing, and running a sugar mill. He became a steward for the Kamehameha royal family and oversaw much of their land and properties on Moloka'i. Rudolph Meyer was named the first superintendent of Kalaupapa in 1867 and served in that capacity for thirty years until his death in 1897.

CHAPTER 44

Kalawao, Moloka'i

May 11, 1873

Kepola was in the lead, anxiously tugging on Jonathan's jacket. "Come on! Come on, luna! You need to see the little haole man in the dress. He is sleeping under the hala tree."

"Kepola, stop pulling at my jacket," Jonathan barked. He did not mean to sound so gruff, but to be woken before the rising of the sun by an impulsive menehune did not make for an agreeable temperament. He was tired. But, as he thought about it, he was perpetually tired. The past two days had been especially trying as Kitty had experienced a great deal of pain, and Jonathan had stayed vigilant by her side. The toe of his shoe caught a rock, and he stumbled.

"Wake up, luna!" Kepola called out to him. "It is not good to sleep and walk at the same time."

Oh, how Jonathan wished that were possible. The days had melded into one another since their arrival on Kalawao. The kama'aina, Ahele, and his grandson had led the new arrivals from the valley of Waikolu to the plains of Kalawao and had helped settle the patients at the receiving station and in newly deserted hales and houses. He had then taken Jonathan and Kitty to the wooden house set aside for the resident superintendent of the settlement. It was a simple but suitable dwelling with a front living area, a bedroom, and a kitchen. The furnishings were sparse but acceptable. The home sat on a rising slope of land, and faced the road that ran from Kalawao to Kalaupapa. To the back of house rose the towering, forbidding cliffs. At the front of the house there was a lanai where one could sit and look out to the distant shoreline and the ocean. On a clear day it was likely that one could see the beckoning spectral that was Oahu. On the east side of the house was a shed where the stores sent by the board of health were kept, along with a wagon that sat abandoned for want of a horse. On the west side of their dwelling, at a distance, was a larger unoccupied house. At the time of their settling in, Jonathan thought it strange that no one had claimed the structure—perhaps it was saved for the doctors or clergy who made periodic visits to the settlement. Down the road a quarter mile to the east was the hospital compound and receiving station, and a quarter mile beyond that were the two churches. Houses for the patients were scattered nearby these structures on the opposite side of the road. The hales and houses were inadequate in number and function, and many patients had no choice but to sleep out in the open, or by the side of a lava rock wall against which they leaned a pandanas mat for scant protection.

Day after day, Jonathan became aware of these inadequacies as he assessed the needs of the settlement, knowing he must first attend to the most critical situations. The only problem was that every situation was critical. The bug-filled hales were putrid with rotting thatch. There was a scarcity of good food and clean water. In the dilapidated hospital, the terminally ill lay on thin dirty mats with no doctor to attend or comfort them in their dying, and there was little medicine or bandages to cover the ulcerous sores of the suffering patients. Added to this were the thuggish attacks and thievery by the brutes of the settlement. Luckily there were only a handful of these wretches, and they tended to be wary of Jonathan's size and authority.

"There is my hale," Kepola announced as they dropped down into the area of the settlement by the two churches.

Jonathan chided him "Yes, and that is where you should be—still sleeping."

"I do not like to sleep that much," Kepola replied.

Jonathan grunted, but grinned at the same time. Kepola was indeed the busy one of the settlement. The leprosy that scarred his face had not as yet attacked his youthful limbs, so he took every opportunity to use them. In the two weeks since their arrival, Kepola had investigated the settlement of Kalawao, met most of the people, ventured into the valleys of Waialeia and Waihanau, and been to the top of the crater to look down into the brackish pool of water at its bottom. This last bit of adventure he had accomplished with his kokua mother, Malia. Malia and Kono had taken the boy into their care from the moment the kokua woman had hauled the boy safely from the churning surf and onto the rocky beach. Jonathan was glad. The image of Kepola's face as he was torn from his parents on the wharf in Honolulu frequently haunted his dreams.

"And did Malia scold you for getting up so early?"

"Of course not, I went out as quiet as a mouse. I did not wake them."

"Ah, but you woke me."

"You are the luna," he said nonchalantly as if that were

explanation enough. He stopped abruptly and pointed. "See! There under the hala tree," he whispered. "The man in a dress."

Jonathan squinted to make out the distant form. With his old eyes it was difficult to see in the murky predawn light. It seemed to be just a bundle of black cloth. "Are you sure it's a person?"

Kepola gave him an impatient look. "Yes, I am sure. He came yesterday on the boat."

"I did not see the boat."

The impatient look deepened. "I know, luna. You were inside your house with your sick wife. But he came yesterday. There was another haole man with him. He was old and he wore a dress too, but he went away on the boat and left the other one."

"Are you sure that they wore dresses?"

"Yes, long black dresses."

Jonathan's heart lifted. "Perhaps it wasn't a dress, Kepola, but a cassock."

"What is a cassock?"

The s's were hard for him to say and Jonathan smiled at his attempt. "It is like a long coat. The priests of the Catholic Church wear them." Jonathan squinted again at the bundle of clothes. *Perhaps it is a Catholic priest, he thought. Perhaps he is a priest and a doctor.* He was well aware of the caring and capable priests and nuns of the faith who were sent out to minister to the world. It was just what Kalawao needed. Had the Lord sent this man to be a worker and a helper? Jonathan stepped forward quickly.

"Hey!" Kepola yelled, hurrying to catch up. "Wait for me!"

The crunch of their footfalls on the lava pebbles awoke the sleeping man long before the two visitors reached him, and

Jonathan felt a twinge of regret at having disturbed his rest. He knew what that was like. The young man stood, placing his cap on his head and rubbing the sleep from his eyes. He was indeed a priest, and Jonathan sent a prayer of gratitude to God.

"Good morning," Jonathan said in English.

"Aloha maikaʻi ʻoe," *a fine greeting to you,* the priest said, the Hawaiian words coming easily.

Jonathan's face lit with pleasure. "You speak the language!" he said in Hawaiian.

The priest smiled. "I have been in the islands a while now. I thought it best to know the language."

As Jonathan looked at the young face of the priest, his heart went back to his friend George Cannon, and he remembered conversations and sermons where the soft Hawaiian words flowed from his lips to the ear of the listener like the mist in the Iao Valley. Jonathan stepped forward and extended his hand. "I am Jonathan Hawaii Napela. I am the assistant superintendent of the settlement."

The priest gave a little bow, but did not take his hand. "I am Father Damien de Veuster of the Congregation of the Sacred Hearts."

Jonathan lowered his arm and smiled. He was not offended that the young man did not take his hand. He had probably been given orders by his superiors not to touch or mingle directly with persons who had the disease, and he was unknowing of Jonathan's status. "Have you come to minister to your flock, Father?"

"I have. I have also come to care for the other poor sufferers."

"Are you a doctor?" Jonathan asked hopefully.

"No, but I have been trained how to care for their basic

needs. The Catholic Church will also send stores of medicine, ointment, and bandages to supplement those sent by the board of health." He stood a little taller. "I also have building skills, and I know a little about horticulture. I will do what I can to help the afflicted who must live here."

"Then we are brothers in this work," Jonathan said. "I have come as kokua to my wife but also to take care of the needs of the patients." His voice grew husky with emotion. "Mahalo. Mahalo, dear Father Damien for answering God's call."

"You are a man of faith, Mr. Napela?"

"I am."

"Are you Catholic or Protestant?"

"I am an elder in The Church of Jesus Christ of Latter-day Saints."

"You are a Mormon?"

"I am. I have been a member just over twenty years, and, like you, I have a little flock of followers to shepherd here at Kalawao."

Father Damien looked back at the small building that was to serve as his church. "Do you have a building in which to meet?"

Jonathan smiled and shook his head. "No, for now we meet in nature." A look of shock came to Father Damien's face as he surveyed the bleak and barren landscape. Jonathan laughed. "There is a beautiful grove of trees on the mauka side of the crater." Father Damien did not look convinced. "I will show you sometime." Jonathan's heart lifted. "In fact, I will show you everything!" He felt a tug on his coat sleeve and looked down to see Kepola's frowning face. "Oh! Oh, I'm sorry, Kepola. I forgot your introduction. Father Damien de Veuster, this is my friend, Kepola."

Jonathan watched as the father gave the boy a tender smile. "Aloha maikaʻi ʻoe, Kepola."

Kepola beamed. "Aloha, Makua. I will also be glad to show you around. I know places that even the luna does not know."

"I wouldn't be surprised," Jonathan laughed.

"I would be honored to have you as a guide, Kepola."

The sky blushed a pale rose as the morning came on, and Jonathan figured it was time for him and Kepola to get to their homes for their scanty breakfast. "We will leave you to your morning preparations, Father Damien. Do you have food?"

"I do, Mr. Napela." He grinned. "I have no shelter and no extra clothing, but I do have a little food."

"We will need to build you a house by your church," Jonathan said.

"And, we will need to build you a church," Father Damien answered.

"Ah, but first we will have to pray for lumber," Jonathan quipped.

The two men laughed. Kepola joined in, although he wasn't quite sure what he was laughing about.

When Jonathan returned home from the predawn outing, he found Kitty still asleep, and many patients and kokua waiting with their calabash pots for their daily ration of food. Jonathan opened the barrels of paʻi and handed out the hard, beaten kalo, wrapped in ti leaves. He also had salted salmon, rice, and a bit of poi. Many of the patients refused the rice and took only poi. Jonathan understood. When the stomach becomes accustomed to one food as a staple, it is hard to get it to agree to anything else. He also handed out the buckets to the kokua and stronger patients who would make the trek into the Waialeia Valley for water for the settlement. When he returned to the house, Kitty was awake, but not feeling well. He brought her to the lanai and set her in her rocking chair. It had come on the last steamer to Kalaupapa, and it proved to be a great comfort to her. Also arriving were books, their parlor table, and some clean white linens from Sister Winston—the dear Winston family of Kaneohe with their old dog.

Jonathan had fixed Kitty some poi, put a shawl around her shoulders, and sat by her side on a creaky chair. They passed the time talking, resting, and saying aloha to people passing by on the road from Kalaupapa to Kalawao—most of the people walked, but some went on horses, and Jonathan wondered what kind of prominent position they had left behind. Of course, here on Kalawao, the regard for status that might have separated the people in other communities was nonexistent. Kitty had reminded him that the board of health had promised him a horse to help him get from place to place, yet it had not arrived on the last two boats. He told her he didn't mind walking. He also told her about the arrival of Father Damien de Veuster, and how he had the feeling the young man was going to be a dedicated kokua. They sat silently, watching the waves crash on the rocky coastline. When they looked farther out to sea, they could see the hazy outline of Oahu, and Jonathan was positive he had located the bay at Hanauma. Kitty told him he was dreaming—that his old eyes could not clearly see the house next door let alone Hanauma Bay.

As the sun drew high into the sky, Kitty complained that her headache was worsening, so Jonathan took her back to her bed, put water and dry biscuits on her side table, and went off to find Father Damien. He found him standing hunched over outside the hospital.

Jonathan went quietly to stand beside him. "Can I do anything for you?"

The father slowly shook his head. He did not stand up or look at Jonathan. Finally after several minutes, he straightened. He stepped away from the side of the building. His skin had a chalky pallor and he blew out puffs of air. "I went in to see if I could give last rites to any of the dying. I . . . I was not prepared for what I saw, or smelled."

Jonathan nodded. "I wear a strip of cloth around my neck that is soaked in camphor. That helps. I've also been told that if you smoke strong tobacco from a pipe it blunts the smell."

"I have heard that too. I brought a pipe with me, but I did not want to offend them by smoking it."

Jonathan was touched by the father's compassion. "Oh, Father Damien, they are so grateful to have someone care for them. They will not be offended."

Father Damien nodded and took a deep cleansing breath. "It deepens my love for the Savior." Tears filled his eyes. "He actually put his hands on them to cleanse their putrid flesh."

"Yes. 'We love Him because He first loved us,'" Jonathan quoted. "Nui ke aloha mamua o ka maka 'u." *Great love over fear.*

"Great love over fear."

Jonathan looked down the roadway toward Kalaupapa. "Do you feel up to a walk?"

"Yes. I would like a healthy walk," Father Damien answered.

"Good. I say we walk to Kalaupapa. It is only three or four miles, and I can point out things along the way."

"Perfect."

Jonathan began walking, and Father Damien moved with

him. "There are not many patients at Kalaupapa, but the kamaʻaina villagers keep some in their hales."

Father Damien looked surprised. "The healthy villagers take in the sick? Don't they realize they can catch the sickness?"

"Great love over fear," Jonathan said softly, and Father Damien nodded.

The two men walked past houses and hales, and Jonathan told the priest what he knew about the inhabitants and their condition. As he had only arrived at the settlement two weeks prior, his knowledge was limited, but it was comforting to share what he did know with another kokua—another kokua who was not just there for one patient, but for all.

Note

- Belgian priest Father Damien de Veuster arrived at Kalawao May 10, 1873. He was thirty-three years old at the time and would spend the next sixteen years of his life tenderly serving the patients of the leper colony. He died of leprosy April 15, 1889, and was buried under the shade of the hala tree under which he first slept upon arriving at Kalawao. On October 11, 2009, Damien was canonized a saint in Rome by Pope Benedict XVI.

CHAPTER 45

Salt Lake City, Utah
June 20, 1873

Elizabeth Hoagland Cannon found her husband weeping in the parlor. It was long past time for him to be at work, and the expression of sentiment was so uncharacteristic that it made her pause in her busy daily schedule, close the parlor door, and sit next to him on the sofa.

"George, what is it?"

He laid his hand over his wife's. "I know, I should be at work," he said slowly.

"Do not trouble about that," the practical Elizabeth responded. "Cut your sorrows in half by sharing them with me."

George sat back, wiped the tears off his face with his handkerchief, and blew his nose. "My sweet Elizabeth."

"I believe you are overwrought, George. Here you have just returned from being a delegate in Congress, where you had to suffer through all the anti-polygamy fury, and now you're called as a counselor to President Young." She shook her head. "Not to mention editing a newspaper, taking care of the publishing business . . ."

"And being burdened with my many wives and children," George added with reserved good humor.

Elizabeth sat for a few moments with her mouth opened, and then she grinned. "Here I should be consoling you in your sorrow, and I'm parading your burdens before you." She lay back in his arms. "I'm not a very good wife."

"You are the best of wives."

"It's just that I'm worried about you."

George gave her a little squeeze. "I know, my dear. But you need not worry about my busy life. I do not consider any of the things I am called to do a burden. Just the opposite is true. I feel very blessed. All my callings are a great joy to me."

"*And* they keep you out of trouble."

George chuckled. "Well, yes, that too. I don't care much for idle hands, do I?"

"No," Elizabeth said, sitting up. She turned to look at him squarely. "So, if it is not your hectic life, Elder Cannon, then what has you weeping this morning?"

"The letter I received yesterday from Brother Jonathan."

Elizabeth nodded and took her husband's hand. "Ah, that would do it. Was the news difficult?"

"I have not brought myself to read it."

"Then how do you . . ."

"Just seeing the envelope brought back all the heartache we received from his first communication from the leper colony." George stood and went to the fireplace, reaching onto the mantle and retrieving the letter. "From the agonizing day when Joseph and Hyrum were killed, through all the mob violence against the Saints, to all the bodies buried on the plains, I have learned not to question the Lord." Tears came into his voice. "I have learned to surrender to the Lord's will." He shook his head.

"But the suffering of the Napelas at Kalawao has made me want to raise my fist to the air, Elizabeth." His voice broke. "It has made me want to shout in protest!"

Elizabeth was silent, respecting her husband's anguish. Slowly he moved back to sit beside her, and she took the letter from his hand. "Should we read his words? Perhaps your friend will school us about faith."

"That would not surprise me."

Elizabeth opened the flap and removed the letter, handing it to her husband. George unfolded the letter and focused on the beautiful Hawaiian words. His mind began to translate the meaning as he began to read.

To my dear Brother George,

Aloha!

Kitty and I send love to your family.

For the three weeks we have been at Kalawao, Kitty has not been well. The sadness of leaving loved ones, the rough crossing, and the struggle to get to the beach was very hard for the patients, and I think that some will not recover. Kitty is doing a little better every day and I believe that someday soon she will be able to walk the path to the ocean and plant a little garden. The soil is poor and one has to remove stones and hallow out a place to put some rich soil from the valley in order for the plants to grow. We can only give them a little water as it must be carried from quite a distance, and it is precious. I have been learning a few tricks from a Catholic priest who has come here to help. He is originally from Belgium and he is only thirty-three years old. That is very young.

Of course you were younger, Brother George, when you first came to our islands.

George looked up from the paper. "I *was* young. I don't know how I had the courage to do many of the things I did."

Elizabeth smiled at him. "Look at your own sons, George. When you're young, you don't realize you need to be cautious."

George chuckled. "That's true, isn't it?"

"But, more important, you were able to do the things you did because you trusted the Lord." She gave him a tender look. "I remember the letters you sent me—so filled with faith and conviction."

"Yes, and I also had the help of a remarkable Hawaiian Saint." He looked back to the letter. "I am glad he has a helper now."

"So am I."

George continued reading.

> *The priest's name is Father Damien de Veuster, but the patients call him Kamiano or Father Kamiano. He does not have the sickness, and yet he works closely with the patients so that they will trust him. He is on a rotation schedule with three other priests, and each will be here a few months and then return to their other fields of labor. Their superiors in Honolulu have given them strict rules to follow regarding contact with the patients, and that is wise if they are to go back out into the world. I am glad he is here for many reasons. He is someone to talk to, and he is a hard worker. Only days after he arrived there was a newspaper article about him in Honolulu, where the writer said that the priest was going to stay at Kalawao and sacrifice himself for the lepers. We*

have heard that it caused much talk, and people began donating hundreds of dollars for the cause of Father Damien. He was uncomfortable with the notoriety, but I am glad, Brother George. The money will be a great help to the colony.

I guess the government didn't want to be outdone, because the last two steamers have brought more supplies, food, and lumber. This is good, because between ten and fourteen new patients arrive every week. Many die, but many more come to take their place. We have had several patients come who are carpenters. Those who still have use of their hands will help Father Damien and me build coffins and houses. We will also make improvements to the hospital. We now have about fourteen members of the Church in the settlement, and we hold our Sunday meetings in a grove of trees, or in a member's house if it is rainy. I would like to build a church building near to the Protestant church, but I think we will have to wait.

I must tell you of something wonderful that came on the last steamer. A horse! Yes, the board of health has finally sent the horse they promised! Now I can ride to all the parts of the land to check on the patients and fulfill my job as luna. So, things are getting better, Brother George, and I am trying to serve wherever the Lord calls me.

Ships of every kind come once or twice a week bringing patients, goods, letters, and sometimes food. There is never enough food. We receive many letters from our dear Panana. They come on the boats that visit Kalawao and Kalaupapa, and sometimes they come overland from Kaunakakai, which is topside on the southern coast of Moloka'i. Panana writes that she and Kamuela are doing well, and little Eva is a healthy girl. They seem to have visitors all the time. She tells us that she writes to you, so you probably know all the news. Perhaps the board of health will let me leave the settlement for a trip to the Big Island. I would be very happy for that. But, for now there is much to do.

I received a letter from the board of health, instructing me to prepare the house next to ours for the arrival of a patient who is very important. He will arrive sometime the end of June. They did not give me the name of the person, and Kitty and I are very curious.

I am sorry for the length of this letter, but since I do not write that often, I figured you would forgive me. I hope you are doing well, my dear friend. I often think of the time we were together in Salt Lake City. Please send my love to our most gracious prophet, Brigham Young, and would you please ask him if he could send me another picture of him? I gave the one I had away, and Kitty is mad at me for doing it.

May your family be well. We look forward to your letters.

Your brother in the Lord,
Jonathan Napela

George sat for the longest time, staring at the paper in his hand, and ruminating about the vagaries of life. Life was difficult, but for some it seemed to be more difficult than for others. Some people suffered their challenges silently, while others made themselves verbose martyrs for the world's sympathy. And, here was his dear friend living in a leper colony and excited about a horse. A horse.

Elizabeth stood. "Are you all right now?"

He looked at her and smiled. "I'm better, yes. You were right. My friend's faith has given me some comfort." He stood up, took her in his arms, and gave her a kiss. "And I have decided something."

"Oh, yes? What is that?"

"No work today. No work for me, no cleaning for you, no studies for the children. We are going to load up the wagon and take a drive up the canyon. We will take a picnic and we will do nothing but loaf around and play games."

Elizabeth looked surprised. "No work for you?"

"No work, wife!" She laughed at his bluster. "No work! No work! No work! Now, off you go to tell the wives and children!"

"But what about the picnic?"

"I will help you with the picnic! I will help you harness the children! I will even help you put on your bonnet if it will get you going!"

Elizabeth was in a fit of giggles as she scurried out the door and into the hallway. George heard her calling orders and alerting the children to the amazing day ahead. In the squeals, questions, and general hubbub that followed, George slipped the letter from his friend into its envelope, sent out a prayer of strength and comfort to those far away in Kalawao, and went to change out of his cumbersome suit.

Note

- George Q. Cannon served four terms as the Utah territorial delegate to Congress. He was the editor of the *Deseret News*, and started a publishing company, Cannon and Sons, which would later become Deseret Book Company.

CHAPTER 46

Kalawao, Moloka'i
June 29, 1873

Since his arrival at Kalawao, Jonathan had never seen the people so excited about the arrival of a boat. The procession to the landing at Kalaupapa showed a bevy of adorned patients, wearing the best of their tattered clothing—clothing normally saved for Sunday wear. The kokua had gone to the valley with the first light of day and brought back leaves and flowers to be fashioned into charming leis. These ornaments now draped the necks and crowned the heads of the well and the disfigured.

"Are you sure you don't want to go with me to the landing to see the great man arrive?" Jonathan asked as he settled Kitty into her rocker on the lanai.

"No, too many people."

"I understand." He tucked a quilt gently around her legs. "Will you be all right without me for the afternoon?"

"Yes, of course. I can do some things for myself now."

Jonathan beamed at her. "Yes, you can! You are gaining strength every day."

"Well, you'd better be off," Kitty answered, a slight edge to her voice. She moderated her tone. "Did you and Malia get the house cleaned?"

"We did. It wasn't easy with Kepola running in and out."

Someone called to Jonathan from the road. "Aloha, luna! You'd better hurry or you will see only the backside of the boat as it returns to Honolulu."

Jonathan turned and waved. "I'm waiting for the priest. He's riding over in the wagon with me."

"Ah! The sick have to walk and the well get to ride," the caller said with good humor.

"You are welcome to ride if you are willing to do the work of loading the wagon when we get there."

The caller chuckled. "No, no! I had enough work just getting out of bed today."

Jonathan waved at the patient as he limped off down the road.

"Jonathan, look," Kitty said. "The father is coming now." She pointed off to the east, where Father Damien could be seen coming up the road. He walked with a cluster of patients who all seemed to be trying to talk to him at once.

"I will meet him at the wagon," Jonathan said, bending down to place his forehead on his wife's. She leaned back, and he chided himself for forgetting the painful condition of her skin. "Aloha nui. Is there anything else I can get you before I leave?"

She touched his face. "I am fine. Go and take care of the important patient."

"Here at Kalawao, there is no one more important than anyone else," Jonathan scoffed. "He will soon learn that." He turned and walked down the steps and off to the place where the horse stood patiently, already harnessed to the wagon. He raised his hand and Father Damien hailed him in return.

Jonathan saw him say a few words to those walking with him. The group called out words of parting and continued on their way, as Damien headed toward the wagon.

"Good day, Father!" Jonathan called out as the priest approached. "I hope one wagon is enough for all of the great man's things."

Father Damien chuckled as he came up beside the wagon. "How many things must one man have at Kalawao?" he asked.

The two climbed up onto the buckboard together and settled themselves into an affable companionship. "Walk on," Jonathan commanded, and the horse started off down the track that would merge with the main road to Kalaupapa.

"I have some news for you," Father Damien said after a few minutes of silence. His look was solemn, and Jonathan wondered what new bit of sadness troubled him. The work and the heartache were better shared than kept to a single burden.

"Of course, Father. We can work it out together."

"I have written to Bishop Maigret in Honolulu concerning the rotation with the other priests."

Jonathan's heart lurched in his chest. *Father Damien was going to leave them early. Leave them well before his three-month assignment was finished.* Jonathan held his disappointment in check. He well understood the crushing responsibility of Kalawao: the toll on body, mind, and spirit; the never-ending toil; the putrid death. He understood how a young man, even a young man of great faith and compassion, would struggle under the weight of hopelessness. Jonathan braced his emotions for the announcement.

"I have requested that there be no rotation. I have requested to live out the remainder of my days at Kalawao."

The force of the words hit Jonathan like a punch, and he

found it difficult to breath. He pulled the horse to a stop and stared over at the young priest. Emotion broke through his restraint, and tears coursed down his cheeks. "'Oni kalalea ke ku a ka la 'au loa," he said with great reverence. *A tall tree stands above the others.*

Many patients passed by the wagon on their way to Kalaupapa and wondered at the spectacle of the two shepherds weeping together. It was several minutes before either man could speak. Finally Father Damien took out a large handkerchief and wiped his face. He blew out a large breath of air. "It is what I have been called to do, Brother Napela. When the Lord speaks strongly, then we must obey. Do you understand this?"

"I do, my friend."

Father Damien sat straighter and looked Jonathan squarely in the face. "It would have been much more difficult to make the decision to stay if you were not here, Brother Napela. Do you understand this?"

Jonathan nodded. "I do understand. I am glad that we can work together. It means much to us here at Kalawao that you have made this choice, Kamiano. God takes note of your obedience and sacrifice." Before Father Damien could respond, Jonathan tapped the lines on the horse's rump and the wagon began to move forward.

On the way to Kalaupapa the two men discussed the newly arrived and the newly dead, the need for more medical supplies, and how they must pray harder for a doctor to join them at the colony—a doctor to administer to the sick. They debated about the best place to run the pipes that would bring water from the valley to the settlement, and they arranged a time when they would get together to build more coffins. By the time they entered Kalaupapa and saw the schooner *Kinau* weighing anchor, they had the affairs of the colony organized for the next several days.

Kepola came running to the wagon as soon as it came into sight at the landing. "Father Kamiano, Luna Napela! Where have you been? I have been here for hours!"

The two men smiled as they got down from the buckboard. "I have no doubt," Jonathan said, ruffling the boy's hair. "Are Kono and Malia with you?"

"Yes, of course. They wouldn't want to miss the exciting day."

Jonathan tied the wagon lines to a nearby tree. "They probably grew tired of your pestering."

Kepola gave him an impish grin. "Me? I am no trouble to anyone." The schooner's bell rang, and Kepola jumped. "Ah! Come on! Come on! They're putting down the longboats!"

"Well, run along then," Jonathan instructed as he secured the settlement ledger. "Father Kamiano and I will follow at a slower pace." Kepola turned quickly and ran off to join a group of boys standing at the very edge of the water. Jonathan watched him with affection. "That Kepola makes me laugh."

"He is one of the fortunate ones who found people to care for him," Father Damien said as they walked. "But I worry for the children. There are so many who are sent without parents to take care of them. I think more die from loneliness than from the leprosy."

Jonathan nodded. The plight of the unattended children wrenched the soul, and it was a worry often discussed by the two men. "We will pray for enough lumber to come so that we can build your house and also a house for the orphans."

"Your faith is strong, Brother Napela. You truly believe that if a man asks for bread the Lord will not give him a stone."

Jonathan smiled. "We cannot escape the trials of life, but our Heavenly Father loves us, Kamiano. This I know."

Father Damien looked at the many patients gathered at the ocean side watching the labor of the ship's crew. "Even when the sky is dark."

"Especially when the sky is dark."

They continued their way to the landing and arrived as two longboats came around the side of the steamship. One was loaded with goods, the other with people. Jonathan counted the number of patients, and then looked down at his ledger, frowning. "The letter from the board of health said that eight patients would arrive today, and I count only seven."

"Perhaps the queen's cousin maneuvered his way out of Kalawao. Perhaps they're keeping him in the Kalihi Hospital."

"Or some private facility," Jonathan concurred.

Just then there was a stir among the gatherers, and Kepola called out. "There! Look there! Here comes the prince. He is riding in his own boat."

Another longboat had come into sight, and the people on the shore strained to see the great ali'i who was fated to be one of them. Jonathan shook his head. It was obvious to him that Peter Kaeo, cousin to Queen Emma and a member of the House of Nobles, was determined from the outset not to be numbered with the sick. The big man sat in the back of the boat surrounded by an assortment of items: a polished koa trunk, a tall wicker basket, a silver lamp with a silk shade, two bird cages, a saddle, a small wooden wheelbarrow, and a young palm tree. Secured in the prow of the boat was a pig in one bamboo cage, and a dog in another.

Jonathan had met Peter Kaeo on several occasions when he'd gone to Honolulu on business for the colony at Laie. As part of the Kamehameha royal family and a member of the government, Peter Kaeo was well known by the lesser aliʻi from the other islands. Jonathan knew Peter Kaeo's face well, but he was sure the man would not remember him. Jonathan took a deep breath. As luna, he well understood the protocol of attending to a person of such importance, but as he looked at the other sufferers on the landing, his heart could not fashion a place of greater importance for the man in the boat.

"Has he brought birds with him?" Father Damien asked quietly.

"And a dog," Jonathan replied, a hint of humor in his voice.

"He'd better be careful with those things when the food supply begins to dwindle."

The two men chuckled together as the first boat of goods arrived. Jonathan called out to those in the work detail to begin the unloading, and Father Damien went to join them. The boat of patients came ashore, and Jonathan went to meet them and take down their information. As the four men and three women disembarked, Jonathan took note of the varying levels of the disease's advancement: most had the obvious signs of ulcerations, facial nodules, or enlarged ears, but two of the men showed smooth complexions. Jonathan gave a puzzled look at his ledger—there were to be five men (including Peter Kaeo), three women, and no kokuas. Who were these two men who showed no signs of leprosy?

Jonathan moved forward to greet the new patients, knowing they would be feeling lost in their strange new circumstances. Indeed, the women stared around at their bleak surroundings as though they had been sent to a place worse than purgatory, while the men looked tired and resigned. One of the men with unblemished complexion seemed determined to take control of his situation. He stepped in front of the others as Jonathan approached.

"Are you the resident superintendent?

"I am. I am Jonathan Napela. Welcome."

"Well, I hardly find that an appropriate greeting. Like being welcomed into a grave."

Jonathan tried not to be baited by the man's discourtesy. "And you are?"

"William Ragsdale."

Jonathan checked his ledger. "Yes, Mr. Ragsdale. I have your name—"

Mr. Ragsdale interrupted. "Is there no receiving station? Must we really stand out here in the open while the others stare at us?"

This time, Jonathan was taken aback by the man's abrupt manner. He looked to be hapa haole, but his demeanor did not hold the gentle patient qualities of his Hawaiian birthright. Jonathan looked at him directly. "Yes, Mr. Ragsdale, there is a small receiving station at Kalawao, but your boat landed at Kalaupapa and here we do not have a building."

"Well, that is inefficient. Why hasn't one been built?"

"It's up to the board of health to commission the building of another station."

"Well, they will certainly be getting a letter from me."

Jonathan had had enough of the man's arrogance. "If you will excuse me, Mr. Ragsdale, I have other patients to care for." He turned his attention to the other members of the group, taking down their information, and explaining the basic layout of the settlement. In a soothing voice he told them that they would be assigned a helper (another patient), who would guide them. They would have to share lodging with others until the planned dormitories could be built, and they would be given vouchers for food and supplies. Tension and sadness began to drain from their faces, and by the time their helpers came to collect them, two of the women were weeping with relief. Jonathan made sure they were attended to and then turned and began walking to the landing where Peter Kaeo's boat was being lugged ashore by the oarsmen. As he walked, one of the newly arrived patients came to his side. "Luna Napela, may I have a word with you?"

"Of course, Mr. Williamson, how can I help you?"

The haole man adjusted his hat to block more of the sun from his face. "Well, actually I'm hoping that I can help you. You see, I have worked at the Kalihi Hospital for several years."

Jonathan stared at the man. "Are you a doctor? The note from the board said nothing about a doctor coming to Kalawao."

The man smiled. "No, luna, I am not a doctor; I am just another patient. But, I was a doctor's assistant. I have worked with the patients at Kalihi and would love to help here." He hesitated. "My Hawaiian is halting, but if you could use me . . ." his voice trailed off.

Jonathan was stunned. "*If* we could use you?" He put his ledger on the ground and took the man by the hand. "You are a blessing to us, Mr. Williamson. A blessing. We need your help desperately. There is a small house by the side of the hospital. I will make sure you are housed there."

Mr. Williamson nodded. "Thank you, Luna Napela."

"No, Mr. Williamson. You are an answer to many prayers." Jonathan gently released the man's hand. "I will have someone show you to our hospital and I will meet you at the house later after I have settled the queen's cousin."

Mr. Williamson gave him a half grin. "Mr. Kaeo brought a dog and two birds, you know?"

"Yes, I know."

"And he insists he does not have leprosy, but some sort of skin disease."

"The board of health has written of that."

"Well, perhaps a few months at Kalawao will mold his character to a more humble station," Mr. Williamson said. He placed his hand on Jonathan's shoulder. "No worries about a guide! I will find my way to the hospital." He started off, then turned, and came back. "Oh, I would suggest that you be wary of William Ragsdale. He is a brilliant attorney. He worked for many years as a translator in the legislature. He speaks both languages expertly. He presented himself for exile before showing any symptoms. He's something of a celebrity with the board of health. I'm afraid he might find life at Kalawao a little boring." He tipped his hat and was off.

Jonathan was trying to figure the meaning of Mr. Williamson's warning about William Ragsdale when Kepola ran up.

"Luna! The important man is getting out of the boat, and they are unloading his things! I would be glad to help carry the birds to the wagon!"

Jonathan picked up his ledger. "I am sorry, Kepola, but Mr. Kaeo does not want his property touched by any of the patients." The smile left Kepola's face, and Jonathan understood his shame. "But it would be very helpful if you would carry the settlement book for me."

Kepola brightened. "I would be glad to do that, luna!"

"Now go and stand with the others and watch Father Kamiano and me as we work."

"Be careful, luna, for you are getting old."

Jonathan growled at him. "Off you go now!" He turned toward the boat, failing at his attempt to hide a grin.

Father Damien met Jonathan at the edge of the water as Peter Kaeo stepped from the front of the longboat onto dry land. He came forward with a smile on his face and his hand extended. "Napela! It is good to see you again. I wish it were under better circumstances. We in the family were sad to hear of your wife's illness. My cousin Queen Emma sends her best."

Jonathan was shocked by the exuberant greeting. "Mahalo, Prince Kaeo. We wish we could see your face at a different place." He tentatively took the man's hand feeling as though he may have misjudged him. When he looked over at Father Damien it seemed he felt the same. "Prince Kaeo . . ."

The big man laughed and thumped Jonathan on the back. "Ah, Napela, if you and I start quoting our genealogies we would have to call the kahunas, and we would be here all day. Just call me Kaeo and I will call you Napela."

Jonathan nodded. "Kaeo, this is Father Damien de Veuster. He has come to live his life at Kalawao serving the lepers. Father Damien, this is Peter Kaeo, cousin to our dear Queen Emma."

Peter Kaeo bowed to the young priest. "We hear your name spoken in Honolulu, Father Damien. It is a great service you give to my sick people."

"It is an honor to be among them. They are a good people."

Peter beamed. "Yes, they are, aren't they? I ask the Lord to bless them every day."

"So, you are a religious man, Mr. Kaeo?" Father Damien asked.

Peter laughed loudly. "I try, Father. I try."

"And are you Catholic?"

"No. Like my cousin Emma, I belong to the Anglican Church." He turned to Napela. "I must admit that she is much more devout than I am. She has sent me with instructions that I am to use the time here to polish my faith." He waved at a group of patients that were staring at him, and they waved back, clearly thrilled to be acknowledged by the great man.

"Well, we should get you to your house." Jonathan said. "It is all ready for you."

"And what about the family of kamaʻaina that the Queen arranged to take care of me?" Peter asked.

"Yes, they will come to the house this evening to help you organize your things and receive your instruction."

"Wonderful! Wonderful!"

Jonathan pointed to the horse and wagon, secured in the shade of one of the only trees in Kalaupapa. "If you would wait with the wagon, we will load your things."

"I would offer to help, but my foot is very painful at the moment."

Jonathan and Father Damien shared a look. "Do not worry. We will have the work done in no time," Jonathan assured.

As Kaeo hobbled to the wagon, Jonathan and Father Damien went to the shoreline to collect the unloaded possessions of the great man. Together they hefted the crated pig. "I have some good news to tell you," Jonathan said puffing.

"What is that?"

"One of our prayers has been answered."

Damien grunted. "Which one of the many?"

"The one about a doctor for the hospital."

Damien almost dropped the cage. "A doctor has come?"

"A doctor's assistant. Mr. Williamson worked for many years at the Kalihi Hospital."

They put the pig in the wagon and went back for their next load.

"Mr. Williamson? One of the patients?"

"Yes. He is a very nice fellow."

Damien smiled. "To stand in contrast with Mr. Ragsdale."

Jonathan shrugged. "Well, we can't have all our prayers answered." He noticed that Father Damien had stopped walking. He turned back to find him staring out to sea. "What is it, Kamiano?"

"If a man ask for bread, will I give him a stone?"

"What was that?"

Father Damien shook his head. "You think we can't have all our prayers answered? Just take a look at that, my dear Brother Napela."

Jonathan turned to look out at the *Kinau* that was still at anchor. What he saw made him catch his breath. Two additional longboats were headed to shore, loaded down with lumber—lots of lumber. Jonathan looked over at the priest and smiled. "Tomorrow I say we put up the framing for your house *and* the orphanage. What do you say to that?"

Father Damien smiled back. "Amen."

Notes

- Peter Kaeo, William Ragsdale, and William Williamson were all historical individuals who each played a role in the life of Kalawao and Kalaupapa and therefore in the life of Jonathan and Kitty Napela.

- During the years Peter Kaeo was a patient at the leper colony, he and his cousin Queen Emma exchanged many letters. These letters were eventually compiled into a book entitled *News from Moloka'i*.

- A later patient at Kalawao, Ambrose Hutchinson, wrote in his journal of Father Damien and Jonathan Napela, describing them as "the best of friends."

CHAPTER 47

Kalawao, Moloka'i
October 23, 1873

My dear Brother George,

   I write to you on a day of great sadness. I know that there is nothing you can do to aid me in my misfortune, for it will take weeks for this letter to reach you, and by that time the seas of trouble here will either be calm or rough. Still, I needed to pour out my sorrow to you, and to ask for your prayers. Just the thought of you praying for me brings calmness to my soul. The board of health has sent a letter that I am to give up my job as assistant superintendent. The assignment was what enabled me to stay at Kalawao to care for Kitty. With my place stripped from me, the board says that I must leave the island and return home. Home? I do not know where that is other than here beside my wife.
   In the dismissal the board says that they have received many letters of my incompetence, drunkenness, and laziness from William Ragsdale. All of these charges are outright lies, but I am not being given the opportunity

to defend myself. Mr. Ragsdale is a favorite of Mr. Hall, the president of the board of health, who takes every word he writes as the truth. The actual truth is that Mr. Ragsdale has wanted the post of assistant superintendent from the moment he set foot on the island four months ago, and he was not above telling falsehoods to achieve it. Well, he has achieved his goal, and I am to be sent away from Kalawao. I worry for my dear Kitty. She says that she will die quickly if I leave, and I do not think that Mr. Ragsdale will work well with Father Damien, or care for Kepola and the other children. He thinks only of himself, and he is mean when something is not done his way. The other day we were working with a crew digging the ditch for the water pipes, and Mr. Ragsdale did not think the men were working fast enough. He was yelling and cursing at them, and he picked up a rock to threaten them. I had to shout him down, and he did not like it. I have also reprimanded him on his immoral behavior. He lives with a kamaʻaina woman who cares for his every need, and he mistreats her. He is also angry that I sometimes give food from the storehouse to the kamaʻainas. I cannot help this. We have taken much of their land and they are starving. These are only a few of the many reasons Ragsdale does not like me.

  Peter Kaeo says that he will write to his cousin for me, but I do not want to trouble Queen Emma with such matters. She has enough to worry about with the political upheaval after the death of Kamehameha V. He did not name an heir, so the legislature elected Prince Lunalilo to serve in his place. Kaeo and Queen Emma have shared many letters over this appointment. Lunalilo

Belonging to HEAVEN

is not good at making decisions and he has drinking problems, but that is a letter for another time.

I mentioned that the native people of Kalaupapa are starving—well, most of us at Kalawao and Kalaupapa are starving. The kalo crops all over the islands are failing and there is a great shortage of poi. I have a bit of paʻi to offer the patients, but mostly it is salted meat or salted salmon, and rice. The Hawaiian stomach does not like such food, Brother George, and it often causes great problems with digestion. The food shortage is also something Ragsdale blames on me.

This is where I will end my complaining, dear friend. I am sorry for all the sad news, but I knew that it was safe to pour my sorrows into your heart. I have written a letter to the board of health asking that I be allowed to stay at Kalawao, even though my position has been taken away. I pray they grant my request.

Thank you for sending the picture of our dear prophet, Brigham Young, and for the Hawaiian Book of Mormon. The Saints here are grateful to have the words of Nephi, and Alma, and King Benjamin. I have my own copy, but it is getting worn. When I open the pages and see the words, I am back in my house in Wailuku, and we are working on the translation. Those were the days when the sun shone brightly on the top of Haleakala.

Mahalo for bringing the gospel to my life.

Your friend,
Brother Jonathan

Jonathan opened the storehouse door and heard the wind in the underbrush and the trill of the o-o bird, but he did not hear Kitty's weeping. Perhaps exhaustion had overtaken her frayed emotions and allowed her the release of sleep. His own emotions raged like a newly trapped animal. He was angry, fearful, and helpless all at once. He was angry at the board of health for taking Ragsdale's word without question, fearful that they would not consider his request to stay, and helpless against their power. He stepped out into the sunshine and closed the storehouse door. He had to trust that the Lord knew his heart and would answer his prayers. He walked to the house and quietly ascended the back stairs. One of the boards squeaked under his weight, and immediately Kitty called out.

"Jonathan, is that you?"

There were tears and a note of panic in her voice, and Jonathan hurried to the bedroom. He put his writing things on the side table and took her in his arms. She began sobbing. He held her lightly so as not to irritate her skin. "Hush, hush, my dear Keliikuaaina. I am here. I am right here with you."

"You cannot leave me. Please, please do not leave me."

"I am not going away."

"Who will care for me if you go?"

He gently brushed her hair away from her face. "Kitty, I am not going away."

"But, they will come for you, and I have no way to hide you like you hid me at Laie."

"You will not need to hide me, because they will not come for me."

She attempted to focus on his face. "How do you know this?"

Belonging to HEAVEN

Jonathan stood and went to his pile of papers. He selected one and turned back to her. "I have written a letter to President Hall and the board of health giving the reasons why I should be allowed to stay." He moved back to the bed and handed her his handkerchief.

"They must let you stay, Jonathan. They must."

"I think the words I have written are strong." He sat on the bed. "Would you like me to read them to you?" She nodded and he gave her an encouraging smile. He looked at the paper and read.

To E.O. Hall, President of the Board of Health

Dear Sir,

> *I received the notification from the board of health informing me of my termination as superintendent and ordering me to return to my home on Maui.*
> *I hereby thank the board with full gratitude. However, regarding the order that I am to return home, I humbly petition the board, and its benevolence as our father, to permit me to stay here with my wife as kokua, for the following reasons:*
> *On August 3, 1843 I took my wife as my legally married wife and on that same day I vowed before God to care for my wife in health and sickness, and until death do us part.*
> *From the time my wife arrived on Moloka'i, she has not been in strong and good health. Several weeks ago I stayed at home to be near her, and I had my subordinates come to my house where we worked on the tasks given me to administrate.*

I am sixty years old and do not have much longer to live. During the brief time remaining, I want to be with my wife.

He felt Kitty's body shudder and he reached his arm around her to hold her close. He continued reading, his voice low and soft.

My wife has also lived a long life, but with this disease, it will quickly shorten her life. Such is the reason for this petition.

Kitty began crying and Jonathan lowered the letter. "I just go on to say how I've been in close contact with the patients and that it would be a misjudgment on the part of the board to send me into the lives of healthy people when there's a chance the sickness could be in my body."

Kitty sat away from him. "It's not, is it?"

"No, but it is a good argument."

Kitty leaned back against her pillows. "Read me the rest."

"Are you sure?"

"Yes."

Jonathan found his place in the letter.

Many kokua have been permitted by the board of health to live here assisting their patients. With that same benevolence I ask the board to approve me.

I know that the patients dying at Kalawao do not have just leprosy, but also fever, stomachache, severe pain, dizziness, and so forth. When these symptoms strike, people are without medicine because there is no one to fetch medicines or assist in caring and serving those people afflicted. The result is usually death.

Belonging to HEAVEN

With the hope that I will encounter your favor regarding my petition.

I remain your humble servant,
J. H. Napela

Kitty closed her eyes and relaxed into her pillows. "It is a good letter."

Jonathan took the handkerchief from her and dried the last of her tears. "Rest now." At that moment he heard his name called from a distance. The young piping voice was drawing nearer, and Jonathan went quickly to the window to see who it was. *Kepola. I'll feed that boy to the sharks.*

Jonathan turned to make sure that Kitty was sleeping and then went quickly to the porch to intercept the intruder. As soon as Kepola saw him step out the door, he called loudly.

"Luna! Luna Napela! You must come quickly."

"Kepola, be quiet! My wife is not well."

Kepola rushed to Jonathan's side, moderating his volume but not his urgency. "Luna, you must come now to Father Damien's house. There is something wrong with him."

"What do you mean?"

"He is stumbling around his house, talking to himself, and crying."

"He is crying? Are you sure, Kepola? Father Damien is not one to cry."

"I am not making it up, luna. Others heard him too."

"Let me check on my wife. If she is sleeping, I will come with you."

Several minutes later the two companions were moving down the road toward the Catholic church and the newly built rectory. Gray mist clung to the tops of the cliffs, and a cold wind whistled down from the canyon. Clouds were gathering over the ocean, and Jonathan knew that soon a chilling rain would soak the barren landscape. He tried to keep pace with Kepola, but his joints ached and his breathing was labored. How good were the days when he ran up the trail into the Iao Valley! As they neared the single story house that was Father Damien's shelter, Jonathan noticed a gathering of patients standing behind the fence and staring in the direction of the structure.

"See, I told you," Kepola announced.

When they reached the gathering, the sounds of something amiss were clearly evident; there was indeed crying, along with periodic bangs and clatters coming from inside Father Damien's house.

Jonathan patted Kepola on the shoulder and spoke to the group. "Stay here, everyone. I will go and see what the trouble is."

Everyone seemed more than happy to have Luna Napela be the one to investigate.

Jonathan walked up onto the porch and called out. "Father Damien, it is Napela." He moved to the door and knocked. "May I come in?"

A ragged voice called out. "Yes, yes, come in. Come in."

Jonathan opened the door onto chaos: the bedding material was pulled off the bed frame and lay in a heap on the floor, the dishes were out of the cupboard, and papers were strewn everywhere. Jonathan stepped carefully into the room and shut the door. "What has happened here, Kamiano?"

"I've lost them! I've lost them!" He opened several drawers in his desk, which he had obviously cleared before, and ran his hand along the wood. "I just had them. I know I saw them yesterday."

Jonathan moved closer and spoke in a soothing tone. "What is it you've lost?"

Father Damien did not look at him but kept looking and weeping. "The food tickets. The food tickets. Several of the patients gave me their food tickets to keep safe, and now I've lost them." He gripped the side of the desk and sobbed.

Jonathan went to him and laid his hand on his slumped shoulder. This behavior was so uncharacteristic of his friend. "Kamiano, I am the resident superintendent. I trust that you had the tickets, and I will issue you new ones for the patients." Father Damien continued to sob. "Now, what really is the trouble?"

"Mr . . . Mr. Williamson told me about the letter you shared with him from the board of health."

"Ah."

"They . . . they can't really send you away, can they?"

Jonathan righted a wooden chair. "Here, sit down." Father Damien did, wiping his face on the sleeve of his cassock. Jonathan brought another chair and sat facing him. "They have taken away my place as resident superintendent." Damien looked at him with a face of loss. "And they have requested that I leave Kalawao."

"They can't! Oh, they can't!"

"Yes, they can." Damien started to rise in agitation, and Jonathan put a hand on his shoulder to keep him seated. "But . . . but I have written a letter to the board requesting that I be allowed to stay to take care of my wife."

"You have?"

"Yes. And, I have faith that they will grant my request."

Father Damien put his head in his hands and wept. It was a long while before he composed himself, and Jonathan waited patiently. Finally he looked up. "I would wish no one to stay here at Kalawao who had the opportunity to leave, but I do not know what I would do without you. You are my friend, Napela. My great friend."

"I feel the same, Kamiano." Jonathan patted the young priest tenderly on the shoulder like a father would a son. He went to the door and opened it, calling out to those still standing by the fence. "All is well! Father Kamiano had lost something, but now it is found. Go home before the rain comes!" He waved to Kepola. "Hey, Kepola!"

Kepola stopped. "Yes, luna?"

"Would you go and ask Malia if she will walk up to my house and check on my wife?"

"Of course. I will stay with Kono while she is gone."

The patients turned to leave, and Jonathan went back into the disheveled room. For the rest of the afternoon as the wind blew, and the rain pelted the tin roof, the two friends worked together to bring order back into Father Damien's house.

Notes

- In the fall and winter of 1873, the kalo crop on the islands failed. Because of this there was a shortage of poi, the staple of the Hawaiian diet. On the major islands and near towns and cities, it was not such a problem, but at Kalawao the result was starvation for many of the leprosy patients.
- The letter Jonathan Napela sent, requesting permission to stay on as Kitty's kokua, is in the archives of the Hawaii Board of Health.

CHAPTER 48

Kalawao, Moloka'i
November 17, 1874

The board of health had sanctioned Jonathan Hawaii Napela's request to stay on at the leper colony as his wife's kokua, and, although he no longer distributed the food or supplies or made daily rounds to check on the patients, little else had changed. Jonathan was regarded with respect as he cared for the people, worked on the water system, assisted Mr. Williamson at the hospital, and helped Father Damien with numerous tasks. The one thing that changed over the months following his dismissal was his increased loathing for William Ragsdale. Jonathan was usually patient with a person's weaknesses, but Ragsdale chose to be a bully and a reprobate, and because of his callousness the patients suffered.

When Jonathan thought of the past winter, his anger and frustration rose. So many had died—died from starvation because Ragsdale would not fight for them. There had been a failure of the kalo crops across the islands, and poi was scarce, but Ragsdale refused to insist that the board of health send sweet potatoes to supplement the loss. He would not even elicit

Superintendent Meyer to bring down more cattle for slaughter. Jonathan knew Ragsdale did this to make himself seem efficient in the eyes of his superiors. He gave the patients only small portions of salted meat or fish, and rice—a diet they could not tolerate. When Ragsdale did receive poi, he would give it to his friends and give the people rice instead. Often he just told the sickest patients to go away and die. And many did just that.

"Why do you wear a scowl?" Father Damien asked, looking up from the support stud he was nailing.

Jonathan shook his head in frustration. "Ah, I was just thinking of the hard time last winter."

Father Damien hammered another nail into place. "I try *not* to think about that time. It just makes me angry."

"Probably a good idea. Better to think about now."

"Indeed. Our gardens are growing, the orphanage is built . . ."

"And the dormitory."

Father Damien stood and brushed sawdust from his cassock. "And now we are finishing your chapel."

"Yes, and I am grateful," Jonathan said as he scrutinized the good work. "Are we ready to raise that final wall?"

"We are."

Jonathan called to the other carpenters, and they came to assist. As the wall rose, Jonathan felt a rush of emotion. The Mormon chapel was being built by Catholic, Protestant, and Mormon faithful, as well as a few pagans mixed in. Jonathan smiled. All were children of Father in Heaven. All were loved. Even with the dreaded disease, most of the people of Kalawao lived their lives with brotherhood and compassion. Perhaps it was *because* of the disease that they found a higher vision.

The wall stood, and the men went to work securing it. Jonathan looked around at what their effort had accomplished, and, although it was just a floor and walls at the moment, he loved the little chapel. It would not be as grand as the churches of the Protestants or the Catholics, but Jonathan did not care. It would house his little flock and be a place of refuge every Sabbath day. There would now be three houses of worship standing on the north side of the Kalaupapa Road—three sacred dwellings where people could go to gain strength for another day of living with leprosy.

A sudden wind blew down from the pali, snatching the hat from Jonathan's head and making the skeletal walls of the chapel shake. Jonathan looked out to sea. Clouds had been gathering all morning, but they hadn't seemed to predict a coming storm. Another gust made him sway sideways, and he stared up to the pali where dark clouds were billowing over the cliffs. He was troubled by how fast the clouds were moving and knew a strong Kona wind was the force pushing them.

Father Damien brought him his hat. "A bad storm is coming."

"Yes. We must send everyone home."

The two men held onto their hats as another strong gust blew past. This blast was of longer duration. It picked up small pieces of wood from the work site and whirled them into the air. The men bent low and covered their heads for protection from the flying debris. Jonathan yelled at the workers to secure their tools and head for home. They complied immediately.

Jonathan saw Peter Kaeo struggling along the road, leading his horse. He made sure Father Damien was safely on his way and then headed off to intercept Kaeo.

"Kaeo!" Jonathan called as he pushed against the wind toward his friend. He knew that the big man was unsteady on his pain-ridden legs, and he worried that a fall might bring on grim complications. The gust abated, and Jonathan moved quickly to Peter's side. He was hunched over and breathing hard when Jonathan reached him. "I am here with you, my friend."

Peter looked up and gave him a feeble nod. "Where did this come from?" he wheezed. "The god of weather is angry about something."

"We should move ahead while the wind is down," Jonathan encouraged.

Peter gathered his strength, and the two men moved off. A crack of thunder rumbled over the pali, and Peter's horse shied sideways. Jonathan calmed him and said a prayer that they would make it to their homes before the full force of the storm engulfed them.

The tempest lasted four days, and the final day was the most devastating. The fierce wind blew from the south and the west, shredding the plants in the garden, uprooting newly planted trees, and leveling many houses. An unceasing torrent of rain filled the rivers and created dozens of waterfalls that leapt over the pali and cascaded two thousand feet down the sides of the sheer cliffs. The ocean waves were so high that the entire coastline was engulfed in surge after surge of white spray.

The afternoon of the fourth day, the wind abated and the clouds broke apart to reveal snatches of blue sky. The people of Kalawao emerged from their insecure shelters to hope for sun and assess the damage. Jonathan ventured down to the village area to check on the people. He stood staring at the devastation left behind by the storm. The few trees in the village had been stripped of leaves, and one had been snapped in half, its splintered trunk pointing skyward. More than twenty houses had been flattened to the ground, while the majority of thatched hales had nothing left but the framing. People stumbled about in a daze. Their hearts, which they'd trained to be numb to the vicissitudes of wholeness and health, were now twisted alive by a sudden tragedy they could not reckon. Jonathan could not comprehend what he was seeing until his gaze fell on the house of Kono and Malia—or what had once been the house of Kono and Malia. Jonathan squinted his old eyes to focus on a rounded lump in the road. It was Kepola, squatting in the dirt and staring at the rubble. Jonathan moved to stand beside him, but the boy did not look up.

"Kepola?" Still there was no movement. "Kepola? Where are Kono and Malia?" Slowly the boy pointed to the wreckage.

"They have left me behind."

Jonathan's legs lost strength, and he sat down in the road next to the boy. They sat silently for a long time, while people passed by, and slivers of sunlight flickered through the clouds.

"Napela?"

Jonathan looked up into the weary face of Father Damien.

"We need your help."

With Father Damien's assistance, Jonathan slowly pushed himself onto his feet. "Come on, Kepola. I will take you home," he said, extending his hand. He looked over to Father Damien. "I will return as soon as he is settled."

Kepola took Jonathan's hand, and the two set off down the road. There were no words spoken until they reached the house, and Jonathan saw Kitty standing on the porch. "A tender bird has fallen from the sky," he called to her. Kitty shaded her eyes and waited. The two wanderers ascended the steps and stood on the porch, Jonathan catching his breath, and Kepola staring at his bare feet. Jonathan met Kitty's gaze. "Kono and Malia have walked the rainbow."

Kitty bit her bottom lip. "Anyone else?"

"I do not know. I must go back to help."

Kitty waited until Kepola looked at her. "Come. The storm is over now."

Kepola stumbled to her and laid his head against her stomach. Kitty put her arms around him as he cried.

"They need me to help," Jonathan said softly.

Kitty nodded. "We will be fine. I will make him a bed, and he can help me save the plants in the garden."

Jonathan's heart swelled with love. For a moment, his heart went back to his wedding day and the church in Wailuku. He saw again Kitty in her beautiful dress with a crown of flowers in her hair. He heard his words as he promised to love her in sickness and in health and Kitty's words after the ceremony as she whispered that she would always honor him. Those sweet promises had been a safeguard against misunderstandings and disagreements—a net when they were cast adrift in the challenging waters of life. Their life together had not always been perfect, but Jonathan knew that they lived in a fallen world and perfection could not be expected. As Jonathan looked at Kitty's hands, now swollen by the leprosy, he saw only beauty.

"Mahalo," he whispered. He went down the steps and headed off toward the settlement. When he turned once to look back, he saw Kepola still weeping in Kitty's arms, and Kitty looking resolutely out to the ocean. Jonathan had no doubt that his wife would stand like that until the boy had cried out all his tears.

Note

- Peter Kaeo wrote of this devastating storm on Moloka'i to his cousin, Queen Emma.

CHAPTER 49

Kalawao, Moloka'i

End of April 1876

"Hurry up, Father Kamiano! How can you get anywhere on that little mule?" Kepola called, pulling his big horse to a stop and waiting for the priest.

Father Damien rode to his side but did not stop. "We might be slow, but we are steady. Can we help it if the legs on Napela's horse are long?"

"And I like to go fast," Kepola said, catching up.

"And you like to go fast. Perhaps you will join in the horse racing today."

Kepola shook his head. "Sister Napela has already told me I can't. I'm to fetch Brother Napela from the boat and give him his horse."

"But surely you can stay and watch."

"Of course, I have a bet on Tom Riley and his scrawny mare."

"I'm sure Brother Napela would not approve of your betting on a horse race, Kepola."

"Aw, it's just for fun, Father Kamiano. It makes us cheer

louder for our pick." He readjusted his hat on his head. "Besides, I'm ten now. I can decide some things on my own."

Father Damien chuckled. "Ah, yes, ten is such a responsible age."

Kepola took the comment seriously and sat a little higher in his saddle. "I bet Brother Napela won't even recognize me after being gone a month."

"You have probably grown another inch or two."

"Do you think so?"

"At least."

"I've missed him," Kepola said simply.

"So have I," Damien concurred.

The two riders came over a rise at the southwest corner of Kauhako crater and saw the village of Kalaupapa and the boat landing. Kepola searched for the steamer and pointed out its approach about three miles out at sea. Since there was not a breath of wind, the ocean was calm, and the ship was making good time.

"I'm going to ride fast to meet it," Kepola said excitedly, urging the horse forward with a few heel jabs.

"It won't bring the ship to anchor any sooner!" Damien called after him. Yet, soon he found himself tapping the mule's rump with his riding stick and urging the beast to its fastest pace. Upon reaching the landing, he tied the mule to the tree alongside of Napela's horse, and joined Kepola at the water's edge. As always, there was a group of people at the landing, waiting to see the new arrivals, waiting to post mail or receive goods, or just to satisfy their curiosity or relieve their boredom. Mr. Williamson was there with the hospital wagon. Damien thought he must be expecting supplies from the board of health. That would be a welcomed surprise. Damien knew the board thought him a nuisance, as over the past three years of being at the leper colony, he'd argued with their decisions on many issues, and aggravated them with continual requests concerning insufficient housing, medical supplies, clothing, water, sanitary conditions, and food. He smiled to himself, knowing that Napela ran a close second to his pressure on the bureaucrats.

Mr. Williamson came to stand beside them. "Good day, Father Damien. Today is a good day."

"It is, Mr. Williamson."

Mr. Williamson put his hand on Kepola's shoulder. "And a very good day for you, young man."

Kepola's grin widened. "Oh, yes, sir." He stood staring out at the steamship as if willing it to travel faster. "I just hope he still sees the beauty of this place."

The two older men shared a look of understanding.

"I'm sure he will, Kepola," Mr. Williamson replied. "I'm sure he will."

Finally the ship set anchor, and the goods and passengers began the final leg of their journey. Kepola was bouncing up and down on the balls of his feet as the longboat shoved off.

"There! There he is!" the ten-year-old yelled, waving his hand enthusiastically.

In the first of the longboats, Jonathan Napela sat with regal ease. As soon as his eyes found Kepola, he smiled broadly and waved with just as much enthusiasm as his young charge.

"You know he wrote me letters while he was gone?" Kepola said proudly. "He wrote about the Church conference at Laie, about Honolulu, about seeing his daughter, Panana." He waved again as the boat drew near. "Hello! Hello, luna!" he yelled.

"Be careful," Mr. Williamson said with a smile. "Do not let assistant superintendent Ragsdale hear you call Napela luna."

"Aw, what do we care about him?" Kepola said candidly. "He's on his way to walk the rainbow any day now."

Father Damien looked shocked. "Kepola!"

"Well, he is. And I wouldn't like to be him when he meets up with the Lord Jesus on the other side." With that final statement, which left his older companions speechless, Kepola ran into the water to help bring the boat onto the landing. He kept reaching over the side of the boat to touch Napela's arm and face as the older man leaned down to place his forehead on the lad's. Finally the lead oarsman snapped at the boy to get back, as the boat was secured and the passengers began to disembark. Jonathan stumbled as he stepped over the side, falling onto his hands and knees. Kepola was by his side immediately.

"Luna! Are you all right?" He helped him to stand, as Mr. Williamson and Father Damien rushed forward.

Jonathan stood and gave Kepola a hug. "Yes, yes. I am fine. It has just been a long trip for an old man." He smiled and ruffled Kepola's curly hair. In turn he brought Mr. Williamson and Father Damien into an embrace. "I have missed you. How are things with the people?"

Father Damien smiled. "We have poi, and the fishing has been good."

Jonathan nodded his understanding and put his arm around Kepola. "It is good to be home." The boy beamed as Jonathan looked down at him. "And how is my dear wife?"

"She is doing well, luna. I change her bandages every day, and she has walked several times to the river in Waikolu Valley for bathing." Jonathan looked surprised. "Do not worry, luna. I make sure she is safe. She says the magic water of the river makes her feel better."

"You are a good boy, Kepola," he said, giving him another hug. "And now I would like to go to my home."

"Let me gather your things," Mr. Williamson said.

"Thank you, my friend. There is my trunk, valise, and a basket. And there is a box for Kepola."

"For me?"

"Yes. Your parents have sent some things. Your mother especially wanted you to have some new clothes. She fears you may be growing out of everything."

Kepola grew solemn. "How is my mother?"

"She is well, Kepola. She and your father have given me many words to tell you, and when there is time you will hear them all."

Kepola grinned. "My mother can speak many words."

Napela chuckled. "Yes, she can." Jonathan turned back to Mr. Williamson. "There is also a large basket for the hospital. Sister Winston from Kaneohe has made hundreds of bandages for the patients."

"I will gather everything," Mr. Williamson said. He looked at Jonathan's haggard expression. "And please ride with me in the wagon."

"Yes, I think I will. I am a little too tired to ride my horse." He turned to Kepola. "Kepola, would you mind . . ."

The boy answered before all the words were out. "I would be glad to ride your horse back to the house."

"Good, good. Then it's all settled." Jonathan moved toward the wagon and his gait was a slow hobble.

Father Damien walked beside him. "Are you all right, Brother Napela?"

"Oh, yes. I just wrenched my leg a little in the fall. Nothing to worry about."

Father Damien helped his friend onto the buckboard, making sure he was settled before moving off to secure his mule. As he mounted and turned back to escort the wagon, he carefully evaluated his friend's appearance. *Nothing to worry about.* The priest's mind kept repeating those words of reassurance, but the tremble in his heart kept the words from seeming true.

"So, now you are the district leader of your church over both Kalawao and Kalaupapa," Peter Kaeo boomed. Jonathan gave a self-effacing nod as Kaeo went on with his narrative. "It makes sense. I mean your congregation grows every time a ship arrives. You now have a fair-sized group of Mormons in both places."

"I think it is the only time when a Church leader wished for fewer members," Jonathan said solemnly.

"Indeed," Kaeo said clasping his hands across his expansive stomach. "You are right, of course."

The group of friends sat on the Napelas's front porch, enjoying each other's company and the stillness of the late afternoon. Peter Kaeo dominated the gathering with his engaging personality; Mr. Williamson made his quiet but astute comments; Father Damien observed and smoked his pipe, and Kitty sat content in her rocking chair with her husband by her side. She leaned forward slightly, looking down the road in the direction of Kalaupapa.

"Are you sure it was wise to give Kepola your horse for the whole afternoon?"

"He will be fine," Jonathan said. "He rides that horse better than I do."

"I just hope he minds us and doesn't try to enter the horse race."

"Knowing that boy," Father Damien interjected, "he'd probably win the grand prize."

Jonathan could tell that Kitty was pleased by the comment, but she kept up her pretense of disquiet. "Well, I hope he's on his way home for supper."

Peter Kaeo took a gold pocket watch from his vest pocket. "Yes, it is getting to be that time, isn't it?" He got to his feet. "It is a joy to have you back, Napela. Perhaps tomorrow we can go down to the ocean and do a little fishing."

Jonathan stood laughing. "You mean I'll do the fishing and you'll do the watching."

"Well, can I help it if you are better at it? From your stories, your father was a great fisherman. He must have passed it down to you because the fish almost jump into your hands." He slapped Jonathan on the back. "Besides, there may not be much time left for us to fish together."

Jonathan gave him a curious look. "And why would you say that?"

"Well, it may be that I will be leaving you soon." The company was suddenly alert and full of questions. Peter laughed and held up his hands. "Now, wait! Wait! I am not saying anything for sure. It is just that Queen Emma has written that the board is sending a team to reevaluate the condition of a few of the patients. I am one of them."

After a long silence, Jonathan spoke. "That is good news for you, Kaeo. I will pray for a good outcome."

Father Damien and Mr. Williamson stood.

"There are patients I need to visit," Williamson said, shaking hands with Napela. "I will write a letter to your Sister

Winston, thanking her for the bandages. They will do much good."

"I will walk with you," Father Damien said to Williamson. "Makana has asked that I read to him from the Bible. It comforts him."

"Big Makana—the great swimmer and rider of the surf," Jonathan said.

"What's that?" Damien asked, turning to him.

"Oh, just a memory," Jonathan answered. "Makana was on the boat with us when we arrived. Read him the story of the Apostle Peter walking on the water and how the good Lord lifted him up. He likes that one." Damien nodded and said his good-byes.

Jonathan watched as the three men walked to the road and parted ways—Peter Kaeo to his big house, Mr. Williamson to his small home by the hospital, and Father Damien to the unpretentious rectory.

"We are all little fish in the big Moloka'i fish ponds," Jonathan said with affection. He heard the crackle of paper and turned to see Kitty bringing the letter from Panana out from under her shawl. "Would you like me to read it to you again?" he asked, sitting down in the chair next to her.

"No, perhaps later. I am tired now." She handed Jonathan the envelope. "I would like to see the picture again."

Jonathan took the letter and slipped out the photograph. He scooted his chair closer. "There are Panana and Kamuela."

"Silly man, I know my daughter and her husband."

"Of course," Jonathan said with a chuckle. "So then, that"—he said, pointing—"is Eva. She is four now, and Helen"—he pointed again—"is two, and Panana is holding the baby . . ."

"John Palmer Parker."

"Yes."

"And you said that he is a good baby, but his teeth are coming in."

"Yes. He is not too happy about that."

Kitty ran her fingers lightly across the photograph. "It is a lovely family."

"It is."

"And another child is coming to join them?"

Jonathan nodded. "A month before Christmas."

Kitty sighed, and Jonathan wished there was more he could do for her longing. He had been able to spend time with his daughter and son-in-law at their home in Honolulu; he had walked the gardens and played with his grandchildren. He had witnessed the love that Panana and Kamuela had for one another and for their children. He had tried to give Kitty as much detail as possible, but it was impossible to relate the feel of the little ones in his arms or the smell of the ginger flowers that Panana had planted in their garden. Kitty took the photograph and struggled to hold it in her swollen hands.

"I have not always been the best mother and wife."

"Kitty, please."

"I need to share this with you, Jonathan. I need to ask you questions. Please, let me say what I must say."

"Of course."

"In the teachings of the Lord Jesus, a person can always repent of the bad they have done in their lives. They can always try and make things better."

"Yes. That is the blessing of the Atonement."

Kitty sat quiet, looking at the sunset. "I have often let pride and fear run my thinking. I have often closed my ears to good counsel and my heart to truth."

"Kitty..."

"I have sought to counsel the Lord, Jonathan. I have. And, yes, I am my father's daughter, there is pride in my veins, but there were times I could have made a different choice." She looked again at the photograph. "I could have made a different choice." She looked out to the rugged coastline. "I was lifted up, but Kalawao has taught me. The Lord blessed me with Kalawao to teach me." Jonathan put his face in his hands and wept. "And what of the gospel of Christ? All the years that you stood up for the gospel, all the years you preached the gospel and baptized hundreds of people, and I always held back."

Jonathan looked up quickly. "You have always supported me. You have always loved the teachings of the Church."

"Yes, but pride and fear kept me from the water. I did not want to give up my position. I feared people's criticism. And through everything you have loved me." Tears came freely. "And, what of my dear Panana? I kept many things from Panana." She looked into Jonathan's eyes. "Forgive me. Please, forgive me."

Jonathan stared at her for several moments and then nodded.

Kitty leaned over and laid her swollen hand on his arm. "Thank you, Jonathan. You are a good man. I will love you forever." She pressed her lips together in an attempt to control her tears. "Now, I need you to do something for me when I walk the rainbow."

"Kitty, please."

"There is a letter I've written. I wrote it nearly a year ago when I still had the use of my hands. It is in the side drawer of my desk under my bandages. It is a letter to my cousin, and it will help to correct a mistake. Will you promise to mail it for me when I am gone?"

"Yes, of course," Jonathan whispered.

Kitty took a deep breath. "Good." She sat back in her rocker and closed her eyes. "Good." She patted his arm. "Perhaps you should walk down the road a ways and call for Kepola."

Jonathan wiped his face with his handkerchief and stood. He went carefully down the steps and started off across the yard. His limp was worse, and he knew that the pain in his legs and feet had nothing to do with his fall earlier in the day. Jonathan looked out to the ocean and the coral clouds of sunset, and peacefulness engulfed him. *Be still and know that I am God.* Indeed, Kalawao had a way of teaching.

Kepola's voice called out to him, and he turned to watch the boy trotting toward him on the big horse. He wore a new calico shirt his mother had sewn for him, and he was waving his hat and whooping. Jonathan laughed. Through the strong emotion of the last hour, he laughed. He couldn't help it—the boy made him laugh.

"Hey! Brother Napela!" Kepola called. "We ran in the race and I didn't fall! What do you think of that?" He drew near and slid off the horse at Jonathan's side.

Jonathan put his arm around the boy's shoulder. "I think we'd better not tell Sister Napela."

Kepola nodded. "Good idea. No sense giving her something to worry about that's already done."

Jonathan chuckled. "Ah, Kepola. What am I going to do with you?"

"Feed me! I'm starving!"

"Well, supper is ready, but you need to put the horse away first."

Kepola looked stricken. "Couldn't I just . . ."

"No. Horse first. Sometimes we must do things that are difficult."

Kepola gave him a resigned sigh. "All right." He began pulling the horse along at a faster pace. "Do I get extra poi for not complaining?"

"Yes, yes. Get along with you now." Kepola whooped and headed for the corral. Jonathan shook his head as he watched him go. "Extra poi for not complaining." A sudden wave of melancholy washed over him as he moved forward and pain shot into his feet. "O ka 'aui aku no koe o ka la." *The sun will soon go down.* He looked up to see an owl float through the twilight sky. "Please, Lord Jesus. May there be someone to watch over Kepola when Kitty and I are gone."

Notes

- One of the first symptoms of leprosy is pain in the hands and legs as nerves deaden and joints swell.

- In June of 1876, the board of health sent a review committee to evaluate a few of the patients for release from the Kalawao settlement. Peter Kaeo was among the few whose case was considered. At first his petition was rejected. Then a letter came from Honolulu informing him that his condition had improved enough for him to leave Kalawao. He left the island the first part of July 1876 to a special care facility in Honolulu. He died four years later.

CHAPTER 50

The Parker Ranch, Hawaii
July 1876

When Kamuela Parker saw Tomi, his Japanese cook, riding out to the back paddock on Panana's horse, he knew something was wrong. He immediately left off speaking with his foreman and rushed to meet him. His thoughts were on one thing. *The baby. Has Panana lost the baby?* Tomi clumsily reined the horse to a stop and tumbled from the bare back. Kamuela caught him.

"Tomi, what is it?"

The little man was crying. "I no know Misser Parker, you come quick."

"Is it the baby?"

"No, no. Not baby. Missy Parker she scream and cry. She tear up garden."

Kamuela jumped onto his wife's horse and headed for the house. As he drew near the outbuildings he could hear his wife screaming. They were not screams of pain but of anger and sorrow. He slid off the horse and ran to the front garden. Panana was screaming and yanking at a hibiscus bush, attempting to pull it from the ground.

Kamuela grabbed her shoulders. "Panana! Stop! Stop!"

She glared up at him, her face streaked with dirt, her eyes red from crying. "Let me go!"

Kamuela's grip tightened. "No. You must stop! This is not good for the baby."

An animal sound came up from Panana's chest and she slumped to the ground. "My body will break from the sadness. It will break."

Kamuela knelt by her. "It must not break, Panana. It must not. What would the children and I do without you?"

"And what will I do without my Makua kane?"

"Your father? Has something happened to your father?"

She clutched at the grass. "Auwe! Auwe! He has sent a letter! He maʻi makamaka ʻole!" *The disease that deprives one of relatives and friends.*

Kamuela sat down hard on the dirt. There was nothing to do but mourn.

Salt Lake City, Utah

George Cannon was on his knees, pleading for strength, pleading for understanding. He knew the words—he knew the promises, but the solace of the Spirit was overwhelmed by the specter of the shadow of death. How could this be? His friend had just been made the district president. There was work for him to do. *For my thoughts are not your thoughts, neither are your ways my ways, saith the Lord.*

George opened his eyes and looked to heaven. "That does not help my heart," he lamented. He stood and picked up Brother Napela's letter. He folded it carefully and put it back in its envelope, knowing what he needed to do. He needed to find Joseph F. Smith and share the sorrow. It was nearing the end of the work day so he gathered his things and headed out of the building. He would walk through Temple Square and past the Endowment House. He would think about the day when Jonathan Hawaii Napela was endowed with power from on high. He would think on the blessings of the priesthood and the gift of eternal life. He would focus on doctrine until the pain in his heart lessened.

Kaneohe, Oahu

Brother and Sister Winston carried their baskets of lehua flowers to the small fishing boat. Before the sun rose, Sister Winston had insisted they hike into the mountain valley to gather the delicate scarlet blossoms. No letter of grief was going to derail her faith or keep her from offering a tribute that would honor the man.

Now she sat stoically in the prow of the boat holding the baskets of sacred flowers while Brother Winston rowed. "Out past the reef if you can manage, my love."

"I will do the best I can," Mr. Winston said, smiling.

"That is all anyone can expect," Mrs. Winston responded.

The boat broke through a light surf and continued on toward the reef and open water. Sister Winston called a halt in a place where the ocean was relatively calm, and the sun flickered in golden shafts through the turquoise water. Mr. Winston put up the oars, and Mrs. Winston handed him a basket. One by one the two haole Saints laid the puffy red blossoms on the water and sang in the best voices they could muster.

> *Come, come, ye Saints, no toil nor labor fear;*
> *But with joy wend your way.*
> *Though hard to you this journey may appear,*
> *Grace shall be as your day.*
> *'Tis better far for us to strive*
> *Our useless cares from us to drive.*
> *Do this, and joy your hearts will swell!*
> *All is well! All is well!*

Kalawao, Moloka'i

President Napela stood in front of his flock in their little chapel in Kalawao. His love for them was great. More than any other congregation with whom he'd associated, the Saints of Kalawao were patient, humble, and compassionate. He saw their swollen faces, the nodules, the ulcerated sores on their deformed hands, and the collapsed noses. They were all beautiful. He was given the gift to see them as God saw them. *Man looketh on the outward appearance, but the Lord looketh on the heart.*

Jonathan opened his Hawaiian Book of Mormon. "In Mosiah, we read about some of our responsibilities as baptized members of the Church: 'Yea, and are willing to mourn with those that mourn; yea, and comfort those that stand in need of comfort, and to stand as witnesses of God at all times and in all things, and in all places that ye may be in, even until death, that ye may be redeemed of God, and be numbered with those of the first resurrection, that ye may have eternal life.'" He looked up and saw Kepola wipe tears away with the back of his hand, as Kitty put her arm around his shoulder. "Be of good cheer, brothers and sisters," Jonathan said tenderly. "How glad we should be for the gospel of Jesus Christ that teaches us about resurrection and eternal life. What peace to know that God is aware of us and that He loves us. Our flesh may be imperfect, but we know a peace of the Spirit that others will never know in this life, for we truly do comfort those that stand in need of comfort. We truly do stand as witnesses of God at all times and in all things, and in all places—even until death." Several heads nodded. "We truly do mourn with those that mourn." Jonathan stood silent for several moments as gratitude overwhelmed him. "You are my friends, and I thank you for the comfort you have given me over the past months. Our bodies may be weak, but our spirits are mighty, and we will walk through our trials together."

As the Saints sang the final hymn, they looked at their leader and saw him, not as a chief separated from them, but as a brother. He was one of them, a child of God paddling his canoe through the fierce storms of life.

CHAPTER 51

Kalawao, Moloka'i
October 26, 1878

The cold rains of autumn had arrived with a chill that invaded the bones and could not be exiled. The shadow of the great cliffs shrouded the Makanalua Peninsula much of the day, preventing the outcasts of Kalawao from witnessing either sunrise or sunset, thus casting a pall over the ill-fated inhabitants.

Jonathan Hawaii Napela stood on the side of the Kauhako crater, looking down at the brackish pool of water at its bottom. The ancient practice of throwing the bodies of the dead into the pool made him think of graves—the extra graves that had to be dug at Kalawao and Kalaupapa in the winter months. He forced his gaze away from the trapped bit of sea and his mind away from morbid thoughts. Over the past two years, since the sign of leprosy had imprinted itself into his body, Jonathan had forced his spirit to override his flesh. Much of the time he was successful, but on gloomy days like today, his fortitude failed. Fragments of his past life haunted him. Where was the handsome young man who had won the attention of the beautiful

Belonging to HEAVEN

Kitty Keliikuaaina Richardson? Where was the strength of his hands that had once held the reins of his horse, or the strength of his legs that had once taken him into the Iao Valley?

Jonathan looked down on the ruins of the ancient heiau on which he stood. Legend said it was the most sacred of all the Moloka'i temples, and he tried to chant words that would pull the mana from the stone up into his body, but he could not. His throat was swollen with the disease, and phlegm blocked the once mellow voice. *Dear Lord,* he prayed silently. *Give me the strength to endure.*

The sound of footfalls met his ears, and Jonathan turned in their direction. Kepola was running over the barren landscape to meet him.

"Brother Napela!" he called.

The boy's foot caught on a stone, and he fell flat, but he was up again in a second and continuing his run. Jonathan could not keep from smiling. He needed to get the boy a proper pair of shoes so he wouldn't stumble so much. He decided to take him to the colony store that very afternoon.

"Brother Napela!"

Jonathan waved and waited for Kepola to reach him. The boy had a cheerful look, so Jonathan did not anticipate some new report of disaster. Kepola made it to his side and stood panting for breath. Jonathan waited patiently. Finally, with a big gulp of air, Kepola straightened and spoke.

"Luna, there are men who have come to see you," he said in a rush.

"Men? From where?"

"They have taken the trail from topside."

Jonathan shook his head. "That is not what I meant. Do you know who they are?"

Kepola was beginning to recover his breath. "They are from the Church."

"Which church?"

Kepola gave him an impatient look. "Our church." He took Jonathan by the arm. "Come on! They are waiting for you at Father Kamiano's house. I told them I would find you right away, and it's been an hour! You should never go off without telling someone where you're going."

As he was pulled along, Jonathan chuckled to himself. He rather liked being scolded like a child. After a few minutes, he had to stop. "You must go slower, Kepola. Remember, I am an old man, and the leprosy has caught up to me."

"Would you like me to run ahead and tell them you are coming?"

"Yes. That is a very good idea."

Kepola hurried off, and Jonathan began his slow trek. He passed a scattering of houses, the hospital compound, the bath house with its new water system, and the store. Several people who sat huddled in blankets on the lanai waved to him. He said his hellos and continued on. This was his life. All of this was familiar. He walked past the many new houses that had been built after the storm of '74. His legs were hurting, but he kept walking—past the LDS church, past the Protestant church, to the fence and the gate, and into Father Damien's garden. As he neared the porch, the door opened and Kepola rushed out, followed sedately by three men. Jonathan recognized them all immediately.

"Brother Richards, Brother Nehemia, Brother Kalawaia. How good to see you!"

Brother Richards stepped toward him. "Brother Napela?"

Jonathan stopped. He had forgotten that these men had not

seen him since the April conference in Laie, two years ago, and he was much changed. To them he must look like a monster.

Brother Richards continued to him, putting his hands gently on Jonathan's shoulders. "Aloha, Brother Napela. We have come to see you."

The Hawaiian brethren came forward with their greetings and love, but they did not touch their friend.

"I am sorry that you had to wait for me," Jonathan said.

"That was no trouble, dear friend. We have been visiting with Father Damien."

"How long will you be in Kalawao?" Jonathan asked hopefully.

"Four days. We wish to visit with you and Sister Napela and to assess the needs of the Saints."

Jonathan liked Brother Richards's efficient manner and how he treated him not as a leper, but as a Church leader. "Four days. That will be good. It is not a long time, but I am grateful. And where are you staying?"

"Father Damien suggested that we stay in the house vacated by Peter Kaeo."

"Oh, yes. That will work well," Jonathan said, looking over to Father Damien. "Thank you for that."

"So, we will visit, and you can show us the settlement and give us a report."

"Yes, there are many things to discuss."

"Good. And on Sunday we will attend church with you at Kalawao."

Jonathan brightened. "Yes, and then we must walk to Kalaupapa to visit with the Saints there."

"Well, if it will not overtire you."

"Oh, he can walk," Kepola blurted out. "You just have to go slowly."

Jonathan gave Kepola a measured look. "Brethren, this is Kepola—my mother."

Everyone laughed, and Jonathan felt his spirit lift. He looked into the faces of his friends, and saw a glimpse of heaven where there was family, brotherhood, laughter, and no sickness.

As they went to Kalaupapa for the Sunday service, Kepola walked ahead of the group with one of his friends. Jonathan noticed the shortness of his pants. He would have Kepola write to his mother to ask for a longer pair. Jonathan's mind continued to comb through a list of tasks: fix the broken window pane in the Kalawao chapel, hoe the weeds in the garden, check on gravesites in the Kalaupapa area, get Kepola to write to his mother . . .

"Napela?"

Jonathan turned his gaze from the road in front of him to the men walking beside him. "I'm sorry, did you ask me something?" He worked to clear his head of jumbled thoughts. "I guess I was preoccupied."

"As you have every right to be," Brother Richards said. "I do not think I could keep up with all you have to do."

"Well, there are many people who help, and, of course, Father Damien is a very hard worker."

"He feels the same about you, you know. In fact, when we were at his house the other day, do you know what he said about you?"

"I cannot guess."

"He said that you and he were yoke mates. That's what he said. Yoke mates. That many vital jobs were done when the two of you worked together."

"Well, that is kind of him, but recently I have not been much help."

"A time and a season, Brother Napela. A time and a season."

The group of men walked along in silence for a time enjoying the cool, rainless day. Jonathan felt at peace. It was good to be with these Church leaders who sacrificed their time to care for the members. They had also given money to make repairs to the hospital and purchase needed ointments and medicines for the patients. And, most important, their visit had brought new life to Kitty. She served the men simple meals, sat with them on the lanai, and joined in the conversations.

Jonathan decided that after the other brethren spoke in the afternoon meeting, he would give a few words on gratitude.

The four days had passed quickly, and now Jonathan stood at the base of the pali waving at the Church leaders as they began their ascent up the hazardous trail to topside.

"Watch your footing! Some of the places are narrow."

"Mahalo, Brother Napela! We will be careful!" Brother Richards called back. "We will write to you . . . and to Kepola."

Kepola waved enthusiastically. "Mahalo, good Brother Richards!"

Jonathan laughed. He did not know what the next months would bring, but for this day he felt fortified.

"Well, we should probably start back down to the valley to Kalawao, since you walk so slowly," Kepola said.

"When I was younger I could have beaten you in any foot race," Jonathan growled.

"A hundred years ago."

"Your legs are skinny. My mother, Wiwiokalani, made me balance on a round stone to give my legs strength."

"Balancing on a round stone? That's an ancient practice. See, like I said, a hundred years ago!"

Kepola ran forward laughing, and Jonathan picked up a kukui nut, and threw it at the back of the boy's head.

"Ow! That wasn't fair!"

"And a hundred years ago, my father, Hawaii Waaole, taught me to throw the kukui nut."

Kepola came back to him laughing, and rubbing the sore spot on his head. "Maybe you could teach me to throw the kukui nut."

"Maybe," Jonathan said, ruffling his hair. "Maybe I can."

Note

- Elder Henry Richards would recount his trip to Kalawao in his journal. He told of walking with Napela to Kalaupapa to check on the Saints there, and of his meeting with Father Damien where the priest referred to Jonathan Napela as his yoke mate.

CHAPTER 52

Kalawao, Moloka'i

August 6, 1879

He felt light. His face and arms and legs, so heavy with the leprosy, felt weightless as he floated in the cool waters of the Waikolu stream. The leaves of the kukui trees rustled in the slight breeze—the sound like the ti leaf skirts of the hula dancers.

"My son?"

He slowly turned his swollen face in the direction of the voice and saw his mother sitting cross-legged on a stack of hala mats. She smiled at him.

"Aloha nui, my son."

He smiled back at her. *Aloha nui.*

"Remember your wedding day when you and your beautiful Keliikuaaina came to receive my love and counsel?"

I do.

"The ancestors spoke to me that day. They gave me words about your life. They wanted me to tell you of the steep paths that you would have to climb, to warn you of the rough seas." Her graceful hands began to tell the story of her words. "But I would not tell you. That was a day of joy when you and your bride could see only the blue of the sky."

He returned to that day with the sun on his face and the sweet smell of ginger surrounding. He saw his bride in her white holoku, and her hair cascading down to her waist.

"This life must be lived one day and then another. The sun rises over Haleakala and sets into the arms of the ocean. The paddle is put into the water at the beginning of the journey and set aside when the next island is reached."

He nodded.

"Who shall make the sun to shine, the moon to walk its silvery path? Did we put the fish into the ocean or the birds into the sky? Did we make the red blossoms of the sacred ohi'a lehua tree?" She stood and came to the water's edge. "There is poi and fish waiting." She turned to walk up the trail.

Mother?

She did not stop.

"Mother?"

A hand was placed on his arm, and Jonathan felt the heaviness of his body. He groaned.

"Jonathan?"

Slowly he opened his eyes. He sat in his rocker on the porch. Kitty was beside him in her own rocker, her hand on his arm.

"Do not leave me."

He could not turn his head to look at her. He tried to say that fish and poi were waiting, but all that came from his mouth were unintelligible growls. He closed his eyes. He liked her hand on his arm and the sound of her voice.

"The steamship *Kinau* is coming to the landing at Kalaupapa tomorrow. Perhaps there will be a letter from Panana, or from Brother George. Perhaps Panana will send another photograph. Six children now. How is that possible?" Her hand patted his arm. "Am I tiring you with my much talking?"

A slight shake of his head. The sound of water falling onto rocks filled his ears. The smell again of ginger flowers.

"Jonathan?"

He grunted.

"We have walked together over many different paths. Will you leave me on this path by myself?"

He walked again in the sacred valley and saw the Rainbow Maiden dancing in the mist.

"I love you."

He heard the sweet trill of the o'o bird.

"I will always love you."

Tears.

"You came as my kokua, knowing that this might be your fate. If you must go then I will follow you soon."

A silver sheet of rain moved across the ocean leaving behind a double rainbow. He heard the tapping of the kapa beaters and the low tremble of the conch shells. His breath mingled with the breezes blowing down from the valley—out across the water to the edge of the rainbow.

"Jonathan? Please try and stay with me."

But he had stepped forward into the brilliant colors.

On the afternoon of August 7, 1879, as the steamship *Kinau* brought ten new patients to the shores of Moloka'i, hundreds of people walked behind the wagon that carried the body of Jonathan Hawaii Napela to its final resting place. The mourners wore their Sunday best—women in their brightly colored dresses and men in their calico shirts. They wore leis on their hats and around their necks. Long ropes of maile leaves draped the coffin, along with dozens of exquisite leis crafted by leprous fingers.

Kepola drove the wagon, and Mr. Williamson and Father Damien walked beside. As they passed Napela's house they took their hats off to Kitty Keliikuaaina Napela, who sat in her rocker on the porch.

She will follow him soon, Kepola thought. *And then I will mail her letter.*

The sound of conch shells drifted over the procession, announcing that a royal chief was approaching the spirit world.

Kepola turned the wagon north off the road that led to Kalaupapa and led the followers toward the Kauhako crater. Napela's body would not be placed in the cemetery at Kalawao or Kalaupapa, but would rest in one of the many caves within the walls of the crater, as befitting a son of the great Maui chiefs.

At a designated spot, Kepola stopped the wagon, put on the brake, and jumped down from the buckboard. Mr. Williamson approached him.

"Well done, Kepola."

"Thank you, sir."

Mr. Williamson noted the newly acquired stillness of the thirteen-year-old. He stood quietly as Father Damien said words of parting to his friend and as the congregants sang their songs of love. Only when the kahuna, and a selected few, came forward to take over the body, did the young man falter. As the burial helper climbed onto the buckboard and took up the reins, Kepola stumbled to the wagon and laid his hand on the coffin. No one heard his whispered words.

"Mahalo, Luna Napela. Mahalo. I promise to take care of

Sister Napela until it is her time. I do not think it will be long." He wiped the tears away with his shirtsleeve. "Can I ask you for something? Will you please come to meet me when I set my feet upon the rainbow? I do not think I will be frightened as long as I can see your face."

Kepola took a deep breath and stepped back, joining himself with the people of Kalawao, who sang and watched until the wagon passed over a rise and disappeared from their sight.

CHAPTER 53

Salt Lake City, Utah
September 1879

Elder George Cannon sat staring at the letter in his hands. He'd read it over several times, but now he could only see one word—rainbow.

Dear Mikanele Cannon,

My Makua kane walked the rainbow August 6, and I cannot stop my weeping. Please tell me that his words about eternal families are true. Ohana Iesu. One family of Christ Jesus. *I had a dream that my grandmother, Chiefess Wiwiokalani, walked upon the rainbow to greet him, and when I looked at their faces, they were young, and they were smiling.*

My head knows that it is better for my dear one to go, but my heart misses him every minute. Can we not go back to the days in Wailuku when you two were translating the sacred book, and I was being a little pest?

I have six children now. I guess I must keep going forward.

Belonging to HEAVEN

May the gospel help you dry your tears, Mikanele Cannon.

Aloha nui,
Your weeping Panana Napela Parker

George stood and dazedly crumpled the letter into his pocket. He opened his door and moved out into the entry office. His secretary glanced up, a look of confusion flickering across his face.

"President? Can I . . ."

George kept walking. He walked down the hallway and out the doors of the office building into the blazing summer day. People who saw him on the street, and knew him, were bewildered by his odd appearance. One never saw the counselor to Brigham Young in the public eye without his suit coat and hat. Several people gave him a tentative greeting, to which they received no reply.

George kept walking. He walked north toward City Creek Canyon. He walked away from the voices and the sounds of the city. He walked until he was alone. He walked on the narrow shadowed trail of the Iao Valley. He looked ahead and saw his friend in his casual pants and shirt, barefooted, and singing. Brother Jonathan's rich Hawaiian voice sang of waterfalls cascading down the face of the pali, of rivers and rainbows. George could see the Rainbow Maiden dancing in the mists of the valley. He could smell the ginger flowers, and hear the small piping call of the o-o bird. He stopped walking. He was standing in the shade of a koa tree. He looked up. No, it was a simple cottonwood tree, its pale leaves twitching in a breath of dry wind.

George hit his chest with the flat of his hand, hoping to

pound out some of the pain and grief. The strength in his legs gave out, and he slumped to the ground.

"Auwe! Auwe! Auwe!" The emotion of the ancients poured from his body.

George kept pounding his chest as the lament continued and slowly the pain eased and the tears ceased. Hawaiian words flooded into his brain. He staggered to his feet and continued his pilgrimage into the solitude of the canyon. Nature alone heard the words Brother George chanted for his friend—for his brother.

> *Na Au makua mai ka la hiki a ka la kau!*
> Ye ancestral deities from the rising to the setting
>   of the sun!
>
> *Mai ka hoo kui a ka halawai!*
> From the zenith to the horizon!
>
> *Na Au makua ia ka hina kua, ia ka hina alo!*
> Ye ancestral deities who stand at our back and at
>   our front!
>
> *Ia kaa akau i ka lani!*
> Ye gods who stand at our right hand!
>
> *O kiha i ka lani,*
> A breathing in the heavens,
>
> *Owe i ka lani,*
> An utterance in the heavens,
>
> *Nunulu i ka lani,*
> A clear, ringing voice in the heavens,
>
> *Kaholo i ka lani!*
> A voice reverberating in the heavens!

Eia ka pulapula a oukou, o Napela.
Here comes your child, Napela.

E malama oukou iaia!
Safeguard him!

George took out his handkerchief and dried his eyes. "Father, take him home to you. He is your good son. He has fought a good fight. Take my brother home." George managed a slight smile. "Knowing you, Brother Jonathan, you are already sharing stories and preaching the gospel to the kamaʻaina in heaven."

George went to the creek and splashed water onto his face and head. As he walked slowly back to his office he reflected on the life of his friend Jonathan, and their first meeting in Wailuku. E ka haole! *Oh, the white man!* George chuckled and wiped a final tear from the corner of his eye. "Thank you, Father for sending me to preach in paradise, and for preparing such an amazing man to hear the words. You are truly aware of every son and daughter. And, how blessed I feel to have such a brother through the eternities."

As President Cannon moved through the city in his shirt-sleeves, he received several sideways glances, and many wondered what worry of church or government was weighing so heavily on the leader's mind that he would forget his suit coat and hat. The speculators would have been surprised if the president's thoughts had been opened to them, for they would have seen the vision of two men, one Hawaiian, one haole, rowing an outrigger canoe in rough seas, each with his head thrown back and laughing with the joy of the adventure.

EPILOGUE

Waimea, Hawaii
November 1879

Hattie Panana Napela put down her pen and stretched her fingers. The letter to Mikanele Cannon was many pages, but there was much news to share. Panana blew on the final page to dry the ink, becoming aware of the smell of Tomi's bread coming from the kitchen, and the sound of her children's voices as they played in the nursery.

It was a cold afternoon with a dense fog wrapping everything in mystery. Panana walked to the window to look out at the large pine tree by the front fence. She could only see it because of the lighted lantern secured to the top of a tall pole that stood nearby. An hour before she had instructed one of the ranch hands to place the beacon for the expected travelers.

"He 'ohu ke aloha, 'a 'ohe kuahiwi kau 'ole." *Love is like the mist; there is no mountaintop that it does not settle upon.* She heard creeping footsteps in the hallway, and whispered children's voices at the doorway. Panana spoke without turning. "Do I hear mice creeping about again? I will need to call Tomi to bring in the cat."

There were squeals and giggles as the children ran forward. "No! No! It's us, Mommy! It's just us!"

Eva, Helen, and John surrounded their mother with pleas and protests.

Panana laughed. "All right! All right! I guess I don't need to bring in the cat, but please be quiet or you will wake Samuel." She gave the three a narrow look. "Where are Harriet and Palmer?"

Seven-year-old Eva answered immediately. "In their high chairs in the kitchen. Tomi is teaching them how to make bread."

"The dear man," Panana said.

"When will they be here, Mommy?" Helen asked, moving to the window and staring out.

"Do you think they're lost in the fog?" John followed on.

"They are not lost in the fog," Panana answered in an assured tone. She had no concern for Kamuela's ability to find his way home in the fog. He'd been navigating the track from Waimea to his mountain home all his life. What did surface with the children's questions was nervous anticipation. She had alleviated it by writing a long letter to Mikanele Cannon, but now it was back to trouble her and make her stomach hurt. Panana folded her arms across her chest and took a deep breath.

Mary was coming home.

Panana's emotions wandered through the events that brought them to this day. Two weeks after her Makua kane walked the rainbow, her mother followed. Panana knew that there would not be a long separation. Now that her heart was tied to Kamuela, she could imagine with perfect compassion the bitter loneliness. When word came of her mother's passing, Panana combined the new grief with the missing of her father.

She busied herself with her family, the running of the house, and accommodating guests. Tears were kept for her pillow.

Then, as the mantle of sorrow was lifting a letter arrived—a letter from her mother's cousin in Kauai. Two other children had come into their family, and they thought it might be a good time for Mary to join her family in Waimea. Since Kamuela and Panana had visited the child several times in the years of separation, the ties of love would easily be rewoven.

Panana felt a small hand slide into hers.

"Mommy," came Eva's voice. "Do you think she will like us?"

"I think she will."

"What does she look like?" John asked.

"Well, she's . . ."

"Mommy!" Helen yelled. "I see horses near the pine tree!"

The other three watchers were startled by the loud announcement. Panana ran to the doorway and called out. "Tomi! Bring the children! They're here!" She threw a blanket around John and shawls around her and the girls as they scrambled as a group out into the garden.

The blurred edges of horses and riders became clearer as the travelers drew closer.

Panana spoke in a whisper to the children. "Remember not to be too noisy. Mary is quite timid."

"Yes, Mommy," they chorused.

Tomi brought out the two bread makers. He'd put a coat on Harriet and a quilt around Palmer to ward off the foggy chill. He stomped his feet several times. "Oh, much warmer in kitchen."

Panana smiled at him as she took Palmer into her arms. "But much more exciting here."

"It's Daddy!" Harriet called when she recognized the rider on the big horse. She frowned at the rider on the petite horse riding next to him. "Who is that?"

"Shh," Eva said, taking her little sister's hand.

Emotion caught in Panana's throat as she stared at the young girl sitting regally on her little steed. She did not know if it was a trick of the fog, or her own longing, but she was looking at her mother in miniature. It was then she realized a truth. Her makua kane and her mother were near; they lived in Mary's face, in Eva's kindness, and in John's playful laughter.

Mahalo, my parents, she thought. *Mahalo for my life. E lei no au i ko aloha. I will wear your love as a wreath. Mahalo, Makua kane. We will pass your name from generation to generation.* A peace filled her heart. *Lele ka hoaka. The spirit has flown away, but the rainbow surrounds us.*

Panana drew her eyes away from her firstborn to smile at Kamuela as he slid from his mount. He walked calmly to the side of Mary's horse.

"Are you ready to get down and meet everyone?"

"Yes, sir."

He put his hands gently around her waist and lifted her down.

Mary stood quietly, looking from face to face. When her glance reached Panana's face, she smiled.

Panana smiled back. "Aloha, Mary. We are glad you're here." Her voice shook only slightly.

Eva stepped forward. "I like your coat. I have a coat with a fur collar too. It's warm, isn't it?"

Mary nodded.

Eva stepped closer. "I'm almost eight. How old are you?"

"Almost nine."

"We have a dollhouse in our playroom," Helen said, moving to stand next to Mary. "Would you like to see it?"

Mary looked at Kamuela and Panana. "May I?"

They both nodded and Panana found her voice. "Yes, of course."

Eva took Mary by the hand and led her off.

"And on the ranch we have sheep, and chickens, and cows . . . lots and lots of cows. I'll show them to you tomorrow," John said as he followed behind.

Tomi took the baby and headed back to take bread from the oven.

Kamuela and Panana stood in the quiet, misty garden staring at each other. Neither could find words rich enough to express their feelings. Finally laughter was their language as Kamuela hugged his sweetheart and led her into the warm house.

AUTHOR'S NOTE

Nine children would eventually come to bless the lives of Hattie and Kamuela Parker—several of whom would live to maturity and whose posterity would continue the royal line of Jonathan and Kitty Napela. Records of The Church of Jesus Christ of Latter-day Saints show that on May 4, 1897, temple ordinances were completed in the Salt Lake Temple for four of the deceased Parker children: Mary Kihalaninui, John Palmer, Harriet Kaonohilani, and Palmer Kuihelani. Their mother, Hattie Panana, was living at the time, and one can only speculate that it may have been she who requested the work done. One of Hattie and Kamuela's children, James Kekooalii Parker, joined the LDS church in 1917 at the age of thirty-one.

During the years in which Jonathan Hawaii Napela served as a missionary for the LDS church, he was instrumental in teaching and baptizing hundreds of his fellow Hawaiian brothers and sisters. It can be conjectured that thousands of righteous Hawaiian Saints are a product of this legacy.

In May of 2010, the Catholic Church presented a certificate

AUTHOR'S NOTE

to the LDS Polynesian Cultural Center at Laie, Oahu, honoring Jonathan Hawaii Napela as a friend and coworker with Father Damien de Veuster.

A statue of Jonathan Napela and George Q. Cannon stands on the grounds of the BYU–Hawaii campus. It depicts the two friends holding high the Hawaiian Book of Mormon—a joined testimony of their love for the gospel of Jesus Christ and the Hawaiian people.

ACKNOWLEDGMENTS

I give my sincere mahalo to the following individuals whose insight, help, and encouragement aided in the completion of this book: Ned Williams, Nancy and Mike Bliss, Andree Fallas, Riley Moffat's research assistants (BYU Hawaii), Tim at the Lahainaluna Museum, Nahua Guilloz, Noe Keliikipi, Tim and Donna Meyer, Michelle Tancayo and the Tancayo Family, Roy Horner, Fred Woods, Chad Orton, Amber Blair, Richard Turley, Andrea Maxfield, Candice Bellows, Michael Hetterman, Jan Lydiatt, Elder Moleni Lasitani, Elder Blake Mecham, and Nichole McMullin.

A special mahalo to my editor, Lisa Mangum, and to all the wonderful people at Deseret Book.

And finally, a tender mahalo to my dear husband, George, who somehow manages to keep me in the canoe.

BIBLIOGRAPHY

Books

Beamer, Nona. *Na Mele Hula, Volume 2, Hawaiian Hula Rituals and Chants.* Laie, HI: The Institute of Polynesian Studies, 2001.

Bitton, Davis. *George Q. Cannon, A Biography.* Salt Lake City: Deseret Book Company, 1999.

Brocker, James H. *The Lands of Father Damien—Kalaupapa, Molokaʻi, Hawaii.* Kaunakakai, Molokaʻi, HI: James H. Brocker, 1997.

Brown, Don. *Gold! Gold From the American River.* New York: Roaring Brook Press, 2011.

Britsch, R. Lanier. *Moramona—The Mormons in Hawaii.* Laie, HI: The Institute of Polynesian Studies, Brigham Young University–Hawaii, 1992.

Bunson, Margaret and Matthew. *Apostle of the Exiled—St. Damien of Molokaʻi.* Huntington, Indiana: Our Sunday Visitor Publishing Division, Our Sunday Visitor, Inc., 2009.

Bushnell, O. A. *Molokaʻi.* Honolulu: University of Hawaii Press, 1975.

Cahill, Emmett. *Yesterday at KALAUPAPA.* Honolulu: Editions Limited, 1990.

Cannon, George Q. *My First Mission.* Salt Lake City: Juvenile Instructor Office, 1879.

Cannon, George Q., Adrian W. Cannon, and Richard E. Turley, Jr., gen eds. *The Journals of George Q. Cannon, Volume 1, To California in '49.* Salt Lake City, Utah: Deseret Book, 1999.

BIBLIOGRAPHY

———. *The Journals of George Q. Cannon, Volume 2, Hawaiian Mission, 1850–1854.* Salt Lake City: Deseret Book, forthcoming.

Engledow, Jill. *Exploring Historic Upcountry, Small Town Series, Maui.* Honolulu: Watermark Publishing, 2001.

Gutmanis, June. *Na Pule Kahiko, Ancient Hawaiian Prayers.* Honolulu: Editions Limited, 1986.

Harden, M. J. *Voices of Wisdom, Hawaiian Elders Speak.* Kula, HI: Aka Press, 1999.

Hawaii Audubon Society. *Hawaii's Birds.* Honolulu: Hawaii Audubon Society, 1967.

Hawaiian Historical Society. *He Mau, Palapala Aina, A Me Na Niele E Pili Ana—Maps and Questions Regarding Them.* Honolulu: Hawaiian Historical Society, 2011.

James, Van. *Ancient Sites of Maui, Moloka'i, and Lana'i.* Honolulu: Mutual Publishing, LLC, 2001.

Kanahele, George S. *Emma—Hawaii's Remarkable Queen.* Honolulu, University of Hawaii Press, 1999.

Kepler, Angela Kay. *Maui's Floral Splendor.* Honolulu: Mutual Publishing, LLC, 1995.

Korn, Alfons L. *News from Moloka'i, Letters between Peter Kaeo & Queen Emma, 1873–1876.* Honolulu: The University Press of Hawaii, 1976.

Law, Anwei Skinsnes, and Henry G. Law. *Father Damien . . . "A Bit of Taro, A Piece of Fish, and A Glass of Water."* Seneca Falls, NY: IDEA Center for the Voices of Humanity, 2009.

Malo, David. *Hawaiian Antiquities—Mo'olelo Hawai'i.* Honolulu: Bishop Museum Press, 1951.

Meyer, Charles S. *Meyer and Moloka'i.* Alden, Iowa: Graphic-Agri Business, 1982

Mitchell, Donald D. Kilolani. *Resource Units in Hawaiian Culture.* Honolulu: The Kamehameha Schools Press, 1982.

Michener, James A. *Hawaii.* New York: Random House Trade Paperbacks, 2002.

BIBLIOGRAPHY

O'Donnell, Kerri. *The Gold Rush—A Primary Source History of the Search for Gold in California.* New York: The Rosen Publishing Group, 2003.

Peebles, Douglas, and Big Bamboo Stock Photography. *Molokaʻi, Images of the Friendly Isle.* Honolulu: Mutual Publishing, LLC, 2007.

Pratt, H. Douglas. *A Pocket Guide to Hawaii's Trees and Shrubs.* Honolulu: Mutual Publishing, LLC.

Pukui, Mary Kawena. *ʻOLELO NO ʻEAU—Hawaiian Proverbs & Poetical Sayings.* Honolulu: Bishop Museum Press, 1983.

Pukui, Mary Kawena, and Samuel H. Elbert. *Hawaiian Dictionary.* Honolulu: University of Hawaii Press, 1986.

Richards, Leonard L. *The California Gold Rush and the Coming of the Civil War.* New York: Alfred A. Knopf, 2007.

Skinsnes, Anwei V., and Richard A. Wisniewski. *Kalaupapa National Historical Park and the Legacy of Father Damien.* Honolulu: Pacific Basin Enterprises, 2007.

Spurrier, Joseph H. *Sandwich Island Saints: Early Mormon Converts in the Hawaiian Islands.* Hong Kong: self-published, 1989.

Stewart, Richard. *Leper Priest of Molokaʻi—The Father Damien Story.* Honolulu: A Latitude 20 Book, University of Hawaii Press, 2000.

Thompson, Linda. *The California Gold Rush.* Vero Beach, Fla.: Rourke Publishing LLC, 2005.

Westervelt, William D. *Myths and Legends of Hawaii.* Honolulu: Mutual Publishing, LLC, 1987.

Articles

Appeal from Napela to the Board of Health Regarding his wife. J. H. Napela, Series 334: Board of Health 1873, Letters Incoming.

Bowen, Donna J. "Love Story Hidden in Graves of Lepers," *Church News,* published by *Deseret News,* 25 June 1988.

Bruno, Frank Alan. "Faith Like the Ancients: The LDS Church in Pulehu and on Maui." Talk delivered at Kahului, Maui, Hawaii, on 29 July 1989.

BIBLIOGRAPHY

The Church of Jesus Christ of Latter-day Saints in the Hawaiian Islands from 1850–1900; An Abridgement. By William Kauaiwiulaokalani Wallace III, Laie Hawaii Stake, Sunday, January 30, 2000. In Celebration of the Sesquicentennial (150 years) Anniversary of the Church in the Hawaiian Islands.

Foley, Mike. *Catholic Church commends PCC in honor of Napela. Deseret News,* 14 May 2010.

Green, Linda W. *Exile in Paradise: The Isolation of Hawaii's Leprosy Victims and Development of Kalaupapa Settlement, 1865 to the Present.* Denver Service Center: National Park Service, 1985.

Hawaiian Mission Manuscript History, January 20, 1878. Archives Division, Historical Department, The Church of Jesus Christ of Latter-day Saints, Salt Lake City.

Kapiikauinamoku. *The Story of Maui Royalty. The Parkers of Waimea. Col. Sam Parker's Wife Descendant of Chiefess.* Article 24. Ulukat: The Hawaiian Electronic Library.

Samuel Parker (Hawaii). Wikipedia, the free encyclopedia. 2012.

Samuel K. Parker, Son of Ebenezer and Kilia Parker. Extracts from the family tree of John Palmer Parker I and Kipikane Rachael Parker, his wife. Continued from January 25, 1932 by Mary E. Low.

Woods, Fred E. *An Islanders View of a Desert Kingdom. Jonathan Napela Recounts his 1869 visit to Salt Lake City.* BYU Studies, 2006.

———. *Jonathan Napela: A Noble Hawaiian Convert.* Published in Regional Studies in Latter-day Saint Church History: The Pacific Isles, ed. Reid L. Nielsen, Stephen C. Harper, Craig K. Manscill, and Mary Jane Woodger. Provo, UT: Religious Studies Center.

———. *Most Influential Mormon Islander: Jonathan Hawaii Napela.* Hawaiian Journal of History. Hawaii Historical Society, Vol. 431, 2008.

Woods, Fred E., Riley M. Moffatt, and Jeffrey N. Walker. *Gathering to La'ie.* 2011, Jonathan Napela Center for Hawaiian and Pacific Studies, BYU–Hawaii.